Grahame Kerr lived as a c
of the Second World War and his family had an association with the Island for nearly 25 years. The author in his career worked for many years in universities before setting up a successful employment advocacy business. He was a magistrate and lay judge for some 28 years. He has contributed for many years to charities concerned with domestic abuse and protection from violence.

He wrote his first novel, *The Opportunist*, about events in the First World War. His second novel, *Don't Stand Under the Pili Nut Tree*, is part of a trilogy about the epic events of 1940–1945 in Singapore.

To all the brave people who suffered in the terrible times during the invasion of Singapore and the Malay States.

Grahame Kerr

Let's Go Sit Under the Mango Tree

Austin Macauley Publishers™
London • Cambridge • New York • Sharjah

This is a work of fiction. Names, characters, businesses, places, events, locales, and incidents are either the products of the author's imagination or used in a fictitious manner. Any resemblance to actual persons, living or dead, or actual events is purely coincidental.

A CIP catalogue record for this title is available from the British Library.

ISBN 9781528941655 (Paperback)
ISBN 9781528970822 (ePub e-book)

www.austinmacauley.com

First Published 2022
Austin Macauley Publishers Ltd®
1 Canada Square
Canary Wharf
London
E14 5AA

My thanks to the staff of the Ford Museum in Singapore for their help in collecting evidence and to those people who kindly let me see letters and records of the period. My thanks to my wife for all her help in putting the story together.

Preface

Everyone in Singapore could sense that something terrible was about to happen. At church on the Sunday morning, 7 December, the ministers were leading their congregations in prayers for the Americans and Japanese to reach a compromise. At Army Headquarters on Sime Road in Singapore, General Percival was in a quandary; he had intelligence telling him that Japanese forces were massing in Southern Thailand and although he had sent troops up to the border, he had clear instructions not to give the Japanese good cause to attack. He was forbidden from sending troops into Thailand to block any surprise attack.

In the end, everything was left too late and any advantage in crossing the border was lost. In the early hours of Monday morning, 8 December 1941, shortly before the surprise attack on Pearl Harbour, the Japanese landed at Khota Bahru in northern Malaya as well as setting off from Pattani in Thailand. The dye was cast. Hours later, the bombers came over and bombed Singapore probably seeking to destroy the RAF installations on the Island but in fact causing mayhem on a lit-up city unable to turn the lights off because the City Engineer had gone off with the keys to the electricity station.

Sixty-one civilians lost their lives and hundreds more were injured.

Throughout the months prior to the attack, the authorities had made half-hearted attempts to prepare civilians for war. A Volunteer Force was assembled made up largely of the remaining young European men stationed in the Malay States. The few British men left on Singapore Island were encouraged to join a local defence force, semi-independent of any authority, and with little or no equipment and certainly little formal training. Some men preferred to act as air raid wardens, again with little training or direction. In most cases, the local defence units were set up to protect the British and European installations, few units included Eurasian or Indo-European men and it was only later that Chinese and Indian men were asked to help.

Sir Shenton Thomas, as High Commissioner and Governor of the Malay States and Singapore saw his priority as being to protect trade and commerce; the commercial support being critical to the British war effort. He believed throughout this period, and certainly well into the campaign against the Japanese, that the Allied armed forces would pull through any temporary difficulties. He refused to encourage British and European civilians to leave Singapore preferring to argue that to encourage such an exodus would cause distress and disrupt the war effort. The official view was that the Asian communities must believe that the colonial power was confident of success.

There was also an almost overwhelming belief in the strength of the armed forces. Within the ranks of the senior colonial civil servants and the military, the belief was that the Japanese would not attack from the North as the jungle was wholly unsuited to warfare and that the Japanese equipment, namely tanks and planes, was vastly inferior to the equipment of the Allies. Many believed that the massing of Japanese forces in southern Thailand was a feint and that if they did attack, it would be by a sea landing on Singapore Island itself. There was an arrogance in the attitude of much of the long-term colonialists on the Malay Peninsula. You can almost hear the proverbial Colonel Blimp, sitting in his Club in Singapore, *stengah* in hand, telling the captive audience how we would send the Japs packing just as Corporal Jones says he dealt with the 'fuzzy wuzzies' in Dad's Army. Regrettably, the truth was vastly different.

In only 70 days, the Japanese swept through the Malay States, crossed the causeway and captured Singapore. Every possible thing that could go wrong did so because of poor leadership, and because of badly trained and non-committed troops offering little resistance at critical times. When they did put up stout resistance, it was only to find that the Japanese Army would merely infiltrate and continue their advance. The Japanese air force destroyed the RAF in a matter of days. It also quickly became evident that the Japanese Navy had sufficient naval resources to cause major problems to the Allies when they tried to bring in relief supplies and latterly in getting non-essential civilians out to safety.

For civilians living in this short war, it must have been terrifying. Eligible young men had either been spirited away to the Volunteer Force or were heavily engaged in civil defence duties. This left little time to care for their families. Few single men were around as most had been conscripted to the Armed Forces in Europe or were now fighting for their lives in the jungle. More and more dependence was placed on middle-aged men to take up air raid warden duties, and to assist in the civil defence duties. For women and children, it was a time of disruption, of fear of being bombed and strafed by Japanese planes or being told they had to leave their homes at very short notice because the Japanese were close by. Escape was often blocked by war damage or by an enemy that fought in a way wholly misunderstood by the authorities. The roads were littered by abandoned vehicles, the trains were bombed almost continually, and a sea journey risked either being bombed by Japanese aircraft or sunk by a Japanese submarine.

Added to the problem of a Japanese Army advancing towards Singapore was the fact that the Chinese Communists saw it as a wonderful opportunity to cause havoc. Without doubt, significant fifth column units also existed, made up of commando trained Japanese troops and sympathisers to the Japanese cause. There are numerous tales of the disruption that both the Communists and the fifth column created behind the Allied lines.

There are stories of people escaping from Penang, Port Swettenham and Malacca in open top cars, in weekend sailing boats, in fruit vans, even in a hearse. All too often, they only learned of the presence of the Japanese Army, as it literally cycled past. One marvellous tale was of a bank manager escaping from Penang with all the gold from his bank in an open top car with the Japanese planes harrying him, as he went south. It makes for a great story.

It was when I read about this escape with the gold and I subsequently found out about the Colonial Office giving instructions for the burning of paper money that I began to wonder how the authorities dealt with the gold held by the banks. I found out that in the Philippines, the Americans had the same problem with millions of dollars in gold having to be moved from Manila to an unknown source in Corregidor before it went missing. Tales still exist today of where this gold went, certainly the Japanese spent a great deal of time trying to find it.

Something like this happened in Singapore. No concrete evidence exists that I can find but I believe that by some means or other some of the gold from the Malay States was shipped to Singapore. I know that the Army was certainly not helpful; they had their hands full trying to stop the Japanese. There is evidence that they had insufficient vehicles to transport men and equipment to the frontline and for the transport of wounded back to Singapore. Any diversion of critical resources would have had to be by the direct order of either Duff Cooper, the Cabinet Minister, responsible for the war effort in the region, or later by Sir Shenton Thomas, the High Commissioner, or possibly by General Percival himself. I found no evidence of the Army being involved in the transport of gold bullion or that the Colonial Office was involved so I must presume it was done by the banks.

Research points to some gold being shipped out from Singapore around the end of January 1942, but there is also strong evidence that a substantial amount of gold was hidden as a means of paying for a continuing insurgency against the Japanese by non-Allied forces. The Kuomintang, the Chinese political force, were part of a guerrilla organisation later associated with Force 136, a behind the line's resistance group, and they insisted on being paid as though they were regular soldiers. Paper currency would have been worthless at the time, so gold coins is an obvious answer. The Communists having fought their own war against the Japanese agreed to join forces with Force 136 in 1943 and I would assume they were paid on the same terms as the other combatants working with Force 136.

How they were paid does not matter it just makes a good story and in this book, Robert Draper, the hero of my first book *Don't stand under the Pili Nut Tree*, ends up getting the gold out of Kuala Lumpur and then helps to get some of it out of Singapore. What happened subsequently is well-documented in how the Japanese tried to find the gold and my hero is merely one of many who the Japanese believed knew where the gold was hidden. Interestingly, Lai Teck, the leader of the Communists, and later discovered to be a double agent acting for the Japanese and the British, does not seem to have known who had access to the gold so the connection was more likely to have been through the Kuomintang or through a local source that perished before the Japanese could capture them.

This novel, therefore, is about the gold and the Japanese interest in getting their hands on it. It is also about the terrible last days before the Allies surrendered on 15th February 1942 and how European and Eurasian civilians subsequently managed to live through the period of internment. What is often difficult to comprehend is that there were many civilian internment camps dotted all over the Malay States, Singapore, Java and Sumatra. Each camp seems to have been organised a little differently; there does not seem to have been a standard model. I concentrated on one camp which may have differed from the circumstances existing in another. Even within that one camp, it's difficult to include everything that happened or could have happened. If you read *Within Changi's Walls: A record of civilian internment* you get a very good idea of one man's perspective of what happened, some of which you will recognise in this novel. But Peet's (the author) perspective was only one of many on record and others will have had a different memory of the events. In the end, what we have are hundreds of individual stories making up a rich tapestry of the period. For those who want to understand the geography of the Island, I suggest that they look at one of the maps of the period on Google. They will be amazed at how small the City of Singapore was, running essentially along the south of the Island, leaving the rest to be jungle, mangrove swamp and plantations, very different from the modern city state that is now Singapore.

Wherever possible, I have tried to include real people who made such an important contribution to life in the period 1941 to 1945.

As with my first book, *Don't Stand Under the Pili Nut Tree*, I welcome comments and questions. Please email me on pellwall@hotmail.com. My third book about the events in the years following the Japanese surrender is near completion and will cover the equally momentous years after the war.

Grahame Kerr

Principal Characters

Robert Draper – Lancastrian. A young able banker. Has failed his medical for the armed services. Goes out East in search of a better life.

Walter Trehearne – Regional Manager, Union & China Bank. He worked under Sir John Hatton who was the head of the bank in Singapore and is now the Director for Far East Banking Services. Trehearne was someone who has spent many years working in the Far East. He only gained promotion after many years of loyal service.

Gordon Fraser – Promoted by Walter Trehearne to be his second in command in Singapore and Malay States.

Peter Connaught – The most able of the bankers. Overlooked for promotion by Walter Trehearne because he, like Sir John Hatton, was keen on change in the bank. His wife, Ethel, like many women on the Island and in the Malay States, led an isolated life with a very small circle of friends.

George Barwick, Manager, Penang Branch, Union & China Bank.

Mark Forrester – Worked for Union & China Bank in Hong Kong. Recently appointed as Manager, Kuala Lumpur (KL) Branch, Union & China Bank.

Clive Sewell – Like Robert Draper, a clerk who has been promoted to the management ranks. Placed in KL and finding life difficult what with new responsibilities and a culture very different to that of England.

Frank Foley – A former Assistant Manager, Union & China Bank. Passed over for promotion, he has now gone to work for the China Bank of Malay States (China Bank for short), a bank set up to promote Chinese business in the Malay States; the bank, owned by two leading Chinese businessmen, with connections to the Kuomintang and therefore the National Bank of China.

Sir Shenton Thomas – High Commissioner and Governor for Singapore and the Malay States. A traditionalist anxious not to upset the ruling families who manage the commerce of the Malay States and Singapore. He sees his role as being to promote industry to support Britain in her time of need. He refused to accept that the Japanese were a nation capable of defeating a cornerstone of the British Empire. After the surrender, he was initially placed in Changi Internment Camp and later transferred to Japan for the remainder of the war. His wife, Lady Lucy Thomas remained in the women's camp at Changi and later Sime Road. She and Major Collinge, the leader of the men's camp at Sime Road, on 31 August 1945 raised the Union Jack over the Municipal Building in Singapore following the interim surrender of Japanese forces on Singapore Island. The Japanese surrendered formally to Lord Mountbatten on 12 September 1945 although significant Japanese forces remained at large in the Malay States for some months afterwards.

Captain John Draper – The sole surviving relative of Robert. Married to a Eurasian woman.

Harry Fisher – a fellow Lancastrian and friend who like Robert is new to life in the colony.

Jenny – A nurse who has volunteered for a tour of duty in the General Hospital, Singapore. The girlfriend of Harry.

Laura and Kay – Two nurses who come out East with Robert. Kay becomes a fellow inmate at Sime Road camp.

Fran(ces) Carstairs – From a military family. She works as a secretary in the High Commissioner's Office. Becomes the girlfriend of Robert but returns to England to join the services.

Joyce Connor – A housemate and colleague of Fran. She later becomes the girlfriend of Robert Draper.

Maurice Levy – A senior banker in the Hong Kong Bank. He recognises that the Allies are ill prepared to stop the Japanese in any attack.

Henry Preston – An Englishman who is the Deputy Station Master in Singapore. Because he married a Eurasian, his social prospects are limited, as is the case for most men who married non-European women. He has a wife, Mona, and two sons, Brian and Martin.

David Masters – In a similar position to Henry Preston. A successful businessman who is limited in his aspirations because he has married a second-generation Eurasian divorcee who brings with her two daughters and a son, Alex.

Arthur Thorsby – In a similar position to Henry Preston. However, as a small-time retailer, he had even fewer social prospects than John Draper, Henry Preston or David Masters. He has two sons, David and Jay and an Indian wife, Neecha.

Donald Shelby-Jones – The proverbial typical middle-class Englishman often sent out to manage part of the Empire before coming home to a place on the Board of a company.

Geoffrey Blackmore – A senior member of the Colonial Office involved with the civil affairs of the Island.

Hugh Besseker – A senior member of the Colonial Office.

Lawrence Muxton – An engineer who works in the City Engineers Department. Came out with Harry and Robert to work on the Island. Known affectionately as 'Laz'.

Cedric Meadows – The security officer for the KL branch of the Union & China Bank. Ex-Army.

Fred Samuels – a manager in the Malaya Tin Company. Resourceful and a hardened colonial.

General Percival – Commander in Chief of the Armed Forces in Malaya. Unable to persuade the powers in London to give him the appropriate resources to combat the Japanese.

Brigadier William Lay – Commanded the 6th Indian Infantry Brigade.

Brigadier Ivan Simson – Responsible for preparing the defence lines of Singapore at a very late stage and then hampered because General Percival believed the Japanese would attack Singapore Island from the North East whereas the main attack came from the North West. In the last days before the surrender of the Island, he was given responsibility for the coordination of civil defence and the distribution of food and water to the people trapped on the Island.

Alfred Duff Cooper – The Prime Minister appointed him to oversee the political decisions concerned with the defence of Singapore and Malay States. He left before the fall of Singapore.

Sally – Worked for Thomas Cook in Singapore as a clerk/typist.

Captain Ishiguru – A member of the dreaded Kempetai. *He was executed at the end of the War for his crimes.*

Sergeant Sato – Also a member of the dreaded Kempetai. He was hanged for crimes at the end of the War.

Colonel Sumida – The commandant of Outram Gaol that housed many of the civilians who were arrested, tortured and later executed. In many instances, the prisoners were taken to the YMCA on Orchard Road, Singapore for preliminary interrogation before being transferred to Outram Gaol or one of the other gaols used on the Island. He was the senior Kempetai officer responsible for investigating the Double Tenth incident and the missing gold. He initially only received a prison sentence but later evidence of his harsh treatment led to a retrial and his execution.

General Saito – Camp Commandant of Sime Road Civil Internment Camp towards the end of the internment period.

Mr Asahi – He was Camp Commandant for a short period but was then replaced by the military after the incident that was known as the Double Tenth i.e. it happened on 10 October 1943. (The incident was when Allied Commandos entered the Kings Docks in Singapore using kayak canoes, in a daring raid, and placed limpet mines on ships causing a good deal of damage and much loss of face to the Japanese. About the same time, although there is no evidence that the incidents were coordinated, the communists set fire to a number of godowns (commercial warehouses). The Japanese arrested many Chinese and Eurasian personnel, tortured and then executed a number although there is no evidence that any of them were involved. The Japanese military police – the Kempetai, also believed that civilians interned in the camps had a hand in the insurrection even using some of the missing gold to pay the communists to create havoc. There is no evidence that this was the case but the Kempetai took the opportunity to torture and in some cases, execute a number of European and Eurasian individuals who they suspected may know where the gold was hidden or who may have encouraged the insurrection.

Rob Scott – a barrister by training, he worked in peacetime for the Singapore Government. He fell foul of the Japanese in their quest for the gold and was tortured and then sentenced in late 1943 to five years hard labour. Col. Sumida was convinced that he was a link to where the gold was hidden but it soon became clear that he had no knowledge of the gold; it seems likely he was sentenced to hard labour because of his anti-Japanese attitude.

Chapter 1

Walter Trehearne was standing by the window in his office watching two Chinese coolies, working on ladders outside, taping up the glass. For some reason, Trehearne had insisted that the tape should be applied externally to all the windows in the bank and all morning the two men had been up and down ladders trying to get the tape to stay on the glass, much to the bemusement of the staff in the bank as they watched the men working in the heat. All the time, the poor men were wondering if an air raid was imminent, ready to slide down the ladders at a moment's notice. Robert decided when he saw Trehearne harassing the workmen that it was really all about not wanting workmen inside his lovely marble bank.

Even as he entered Trehearne's office, he could hear him remonstrating with the workmen that the tape was not being put on the windows correctly. It was 9 December 1941 and the world had changed forever. It was especially humid that day and with no electricity on, the little benefit that was normally obtained from having the ceiling fans on, was entirely lost. No electricity was just another problem to add to the seemingly endless number that the Island was now encountering, having already suffered three Japanese bombing raids in less than two days with all the disruption and terror of such raids.

The Island's electricity had been cut off that morning without warning despite assurances that the electricity station had not been hit by the bombing. On the streets, everybody was ignoring what was in front of them as they walked, just anxiously looking up to the sky. Robert even noticed Trehearne looking up at the sky, as he continued to shout at the two workmen.

What Robert had observed on his way into the office that morning were long lines of lorries, filled with troops, all with grim faces, heading towards the railway station. Very few of them were flashing smiles at the girls who waved as they went by. Other soldiers could be seen marching off to some point on the Island, he presumed to anticipate a Japanese landing on the beaches. The rickshaw driver told him as he came in that he had seen soldiers putting up sandbag barriers and digging trenches down beyond Beach Road in readiness for a sea invasion. To Robert, it all seemed like something from the Breughel paintings he remembered seeing when he used to go into one of the art galleries in London; a picture of thousands of people all hurrying about doing ten thousand tasks.

So far that morning, no more Japanese planes had been over and the strong rumour, at least from the rickshaw driver, was that they were now concentrating on attacking the Alor Star airfield up near the Thai border. He was quick to add that the British troops had been routed at Khota Bahru. If truth be told, Robert, like everybody else, knew little of the real situation and it was just as likely that the rickshaw driver did know more than anyone else. Strangely, Robert felt almost stoical about the situation but this could be because he was just dog tired with all the extra hours, he was putting in with the local defence corps. His real worry was for Harry, his flatmate, who was up country and try as he might he could not get any news of the situation at the tin mine diggings north of Kuantan. All he did know was that it was very close to where the fighting was taking place.

Robert recognised, as did everybody, that the last few days were likely to be the beginning of long months, possibly years, of a struggle to win through, although to what end he honestly could not say. Already he had heard people expressing fears of what would happen if the Japs won the conflict, but he just could not imagine how it would be.

In his personal life, he had reached a critical stage about two months ago when he and Fran, his girlfriend, had accepted that the war and all that it brought with it had forced a wedge between them. They still talked but only as friends both too afraid to accept the other's standpoint. He hadn't seen Fran for more than a week although he had had a few short phone calls with her but what with him being on duty most nights at the Drill Hall and Fran now working her last few days at the Governor's Residence, before she set off for England, any hope of saving the relationship, even if either had wanted to save it, was gone.

Robert often said to himself, after one of their arguments, '*Fran from the start was always going back home to join the WAACs*'. He knew over the past twelve months that she was not a woman to change her mind even if she seemed keen on him. Mind you, Robert had been equally determined to stay on the Island and see what came of the rising tension with the Japanese, so an impasse was inevitable.

Things had come to a head between them after their trip to Penang. Fran's brother had been sending letters, albeit it was sporadic mail, but it was very influential, in which he argued that everybody should be doing their duty. In one serious argument just after the trip to Penang, Fran had said that her brother considered anyone who did not volunteer for the armed services to be a coward. It did not satisfy her when Robert explained again and again that he had been to the recruitment office and had been told that they would send for him when they needed his reserve category, and that, unless conscripted, able-bodied men could no longer obtain a permit to leave the Island.

Finally, only a few weeks ago, Robert had been told that he was now essential to the defence of the Island although quite why had not been disclosed to him and that had finished any discussion with Fran on the subject. Joyce, Fran's housemate, and more and more, a regular tennis partner of Robert's at the tennis club, on one occasion whilst they were having a drink, put Fran's attitude down to the fact that she was an army child and to her, there could be no alternative stance.

After the Japanese had attacked Singapore early on the 8 December 1941 Robert, like the rest of his Local Defence Unit had worked tirelessly to clear the damage. He ended up working the Monday night, as further Japanese bombing brought more destruction to the City and taking command of one of the teams that were sent out to clear bomb damage. There was no respite from the effect of the bombing. He had managed to steal only a few hours rest before going into work on the Tuesday.

What he found almost unbelievable was the fact that they had been under air attack on three occasions with every likelihood of more attacks in the offing and with a possible sea invasion at any moment and yet the newspapers and indeed the High Commissioner, in a radio address that morning, was telling the population to go to work as normal. When Robert did get into work, he saw immediately that there were employees missing. He spoke briefly with some of the staff trying to reassure them about the situation, before setting off for his office downstairs. There he spent a few moments talking to Michael the young Australian clerk who had now been working with him for a few months before Mr Wuh, Head Chinese Clerk, appeared and told him that he knew Mr Trehearne was just starting a managers' meeting and nodding his thanks, Robert returned to the stairs and walked up to Trehearne's office.

Like most of his colleagues, he never savoured a meeting with Walter Trehearne and in the almost two years, he had been in Singapore, he had done his best to stay clear of him and his snide comments about head office sending out the dross. He, therefore, climbed the stairs grimacing at what was to come. He had tried to grow a thick skin to combat Trehearne's comments and done his best to take on the chin the outbursts of temper at any little foible. His time working up in KL, suffering Trehearne's constant criticism, still rankled with him.

Peter Connaught, one of the senior managers, had sought to reassure him on a number of occasions, telling him he had done an excellent job in managing the branch until Mark Forrester had arrived from Hong Kong to take up his promotion but Robert still felt he had been treated unfairly.

Apart from a short business trip to Kuching and a holiday trip with his uncle, the captain of a steamer that delivered goods and mail up the coast of the Malay States and across to Sumatra, he had been confined to working in the bank in Singapore.

Robert took a deep breath before entering Trehearne's office. Mrs Frobisher was missing from her little anteroom, so he had no guidance as to what to expect on the other side of the door. Opening the door, he paused in the entrance and it was then that he observed Trehearne supervising the poor men trying to put tape on the windows.

According to Mr Wuh, the meeting had been called at short notice, and as he stood there, he could see Mrs Frobisher fussing around the office getting water glasses from a cupboard and preparing the table but she too was watching Trehearne all the time and doing her best to stay out of his vision. Donald Shelby-Jones, Gordon Fraser and Peter Connaught were already in the room, standing in a huddle talking quietly on the other side of the table, all three smoking. A very tired Peter looked across and smiled at him.

The room was like a cauldron, much hotter than out in the corridor and for a moment as he stood there, Robert felt like he was sucking in hot air. For the ninety-ninth time that morning, he put his hand on his collar and pulled it away from his skin. He had given up unsticking his shirt from his back and his jacket felt as though it would need to be cut off him when he got home that evening. For a second, he had evil thoughts about the man at the window who insisted on managers wearing a penguin suit for work in the bank.

"Ah, you've decided to come into work, Mr Draper," Trehearne remarked sarcastically, as he turned back from the window and saw Robert standing there.

"My apologies, I was on duty most of last night and when I arrived, I had to check that Mr Lennox was not blocking the entrance with the sandbags he apparently ordered yesterday. Oh, and the generator has turned up and the security staff are getting it down into the basement." Trehearne didn't respond to this information, he just nodded at Robert agitatedly and then went over and sat down at the table giving the others the cue to sit down. Mrs Frobisher left almost at a run.

"Right, gentlemen, let's get down to business. I've not asked Lennox to join us as we need someone down in the banking hall in case there is a problem. I've managed to speak to Sir Shenton this morning and he has categorically told me that General Percival will now start to take control of the situation. He has assured me that the bombing was just a setback and in a few days, the Japs will retreat back to their holes." He paused for a few seconds, taking another suck of his cigarette before he continued, "I have tried contacting Sedgeley-Reed in Bangkok but the lines are down, so I have no news about our colleagues up there. However, Sir Shenton has reminded me that Thailand is neutral and therefore any problems up there can only be temporary."

It was clear he didn't want to talk about the possibility that Bangkok was now part of the Japanese territories and that the bank staff had probably been marched off to an internment camp. Robert wondered how he was going to report the situation to London as right up to last week, he knew that Trehearne had been insisting that there was no real crisis and everything was normal and as far as Robert was aware no precautions had been taken about getting the staff out of Bangkok or for that matter from anywhere in the Malay States.

In fact, Trehearne continued the meeting as though everything was normal. "Now, Peter, where are we up to with the East Timor project?"

Peter looked sideways to Gordon Fraser, the other senior manager, and then turned back to look at Trehearne. "Don't you think we should be discussing a contingency plan for the removal of staff and our gold from KL and Penang? By all accounts, the Japs are just over the border. George and Mark must be very concerned that they are very close to the front line."

Trehearne started to choke on his cigarette and after a bit of a coughing bout, he ground out his cigarette. "I will not have us discussing matters that are not going to happen. Talk of contingency plans; my God, if we talk of such things, it will cause panic. I spoke to them by telephone and told them that Percival has everything in hand." He was almost shouting.

"But, Walter, I know that Barclays have arranged a gold shipment to Darwin and Maurice Levy at the Hong Kong told me this morning that they are looking into ways of urgently moving gold stocks from Penang and Malacca in the next couple of days. Maurice also said that they were getting wives and children out. Frank Foley said they were doing the same at the China Bank. We are also short of staff downstairs because they are involved in the bombing of their homes up in Siglap. I think..."

Peter tailed off as Trehearne started to go red in the face. Eventually, after a moment glowering at everyone, he stood up. "Gentlemen, I will not be contradicted. I am off with

Muriel to see Pitts-Lewis tomorrow. I have decided that I should bring forward my long-planned visit to Batavia, and I will not have the bank's routines interrupted by these stupid goings on. In my absence, Gordon will be in charge and I have instructed him that there are not to be any changes. It's bad enough having sandbags outside the entrance and having to get a generator in to assist in opening the safes. The place looks like a battlefield. From what I can see, Percival has more than enough troops to sort out these damn Japs. Now for the second time, Peter, what about the East Timor account, and you, Mr Draper, pay attention, you look half-asleep."

"My apologies, sir. What with having to do my night duties, I've had precious little sleep in the last few days and the heat in here is making me drowsy. Can I say that I think Peter's right? We're likely to have more setbacks in the next few weeks and we could do with at least some guidance from you," Robert said, tailing off as he saw Trehearne getting agitated again. Peter saw what was coming and interrupted any possible further outburst from Trehearne by giving a summary of the East Timor situation.

"We should never have given them the money to develop the hardwood business," Trehearne growled, after listening to what Peter said, and still looking at Robert. He took out his cigarette case and fiddled with it before taking out a cigarette and after tapping it on the silver case, he put the cigarette in his mouth.

"I had a look at the file the other day and was surprised that we approved it. It seems far too risky," said Donald Shelby-Jones, who was sitting between Gordon and Peter, looking his usual mournful self.

"Donald, you wouldn't know a good or bad risk if you spent the next ten years studying the subject," Robert found himself saying before he knew it. He had finally had enough of Donald and his negative view on life.

Trehearne still standing, looked from one to the other, for a moment not believing what he had just heard. This time it was Gordon Fraser who interceded. "Whatever the situation, Walter, we are now involved in the project and the loan was authorised by you." Peter nodded and mumbled something to confirm what Gordon had said, all the time looking at Robert and with Robert trying to interpret Peter's facial expression and somehow at the same time, watch Trehearne for further reaction. Donald had also started to say something but when he heard what Gordon had to say, he obviously thought the better of it and only mumbled something incoherent.

"Is it true that we have a number of people withdrawing their securities from the safety deposit boxes?" Trehearne said, now focusing his attention on Gordon and changing the subject.

"Yes, quite a number in this morning, and telephone calls seeking appointments. Robert's staff have dealt with most of them in the last couple of hours."

Robert taking his cue from Gordon who was nodding at him came in with, "I've only had a few minutes discussion with Michael but it seems to be mostly families who are leaving on the *Martinique* tonight or the *Roberta* tomorrow. There's also, I understand, a Cunard ship leaving on Thursday and the *Strathmore* for South Africa, I think on Friday. There's a gaggle of clients coming in later this afternoon so we will be very busy. What with the *Straits Times* having announced all the sailings it seems to be very helpful to the Japanese Navy."

Trehearne ignored the last point and instead came out with, "Bloody cowards. Leaving at this time. I've had Forrester on the telephone this morning saying that he's coming down to see his wife and daughter off, on the *Roberta.* We may as well give in now if that's the attitude of people."

Donald coughed, not looking directly at Trehearne, preferring to look at the tabletop as though it was suddenly something of interest. Finally, he said quietly, "Well actually, Walter, I've arranged for Lucy to leave on the *Martinique* tonight; she managed to get a berth last Saturday, a suite in fact. As it's a suite, I was wondering about going with her."

Trehearne was going red again. "My god, you too."

Before he could say more, Donald continued. "I had asked to see you after this meeting and I was going to tell you that I've been called up to the Army. I must report to somewhere in India by 3 January, so I rather thought I would go now. We have most of our stuff packed." He stopped what he was saying on seeing Trehearne going a shade of purple and then mumbled further, "It's not as though the Loans Section is very busy at the moment. The past four or five months everything has rather stalled." He tailed off what he was saying, and they could all see his normal pale pallor had gone even whiter.

For once, Robert felt sorry for him. '*Poor sod. He can't have slept all night thinking about how he was going to tell Trehearne,*' he thought to himself.

Peter was the first to respond. "Excellent news about you being called up, Donald. Harry Fisher, Robert's flatmate has also been called up so you're probably in the same batch."

Trehearne was still standing, and through the cloud of smoke, Robert could see long beads of sweat running down his face. Finally, he spoke. "Why does it have to be the *Martinique*? You have three weeks. You could go later."

Donald didn't answer the question and Robert was thinking, as he watched him, about what had come first – Lucy booking to go home without Donald or Donald's call up papers. It must have been a close call. Certainly, everyone knew that the relationship wasn't good, even Mrs Lin Yuen, his landlady, had said she had heard gossip about Lucy going out with girlfriends to bars, and that she was never seen with Donald.

Peter continued to respond for Donald although Robert suspected Donald hadn't given even a hint to him of Lucy leaving or of the call up, despite him working with Peter. "Walter, there may not be other boats for some time what with the Jap submarines and the bombing. I think Donald should go. Mind you, it will be no picnic now that Sumatra is in range of Japanese bombers."

Trehearne just shook his head at what Peter had said, dabbing his face with a handkerchief he had produced from his jacket; he turned to face Gordon who had just started to say something.

"We've managed before so why not now?"

Trehearne ignored what Gordon said and turned and scowled down at Robert. "I suppose you've got an exemption because of your connections."

Robert raised his eyebrows. "I don't know of any connections, and anyway, I have been rejected."

Trehearne smirked this time. "Nothing surprises me," again using his handkerchief to wipe his face. Ignoring

Robert's quizzical look and raised eyebrows, he turned back to Gordon, "When the hell do we get the electricity on. This heat is impossible."

Gordon hated the attention being on him and immediately looked at Robert who answered for him, "Mr Gupta told me a few minutes ago that the City Works expect full power to be on around late afternoon subject to no further air raids. They're putting in some emergency system so that if the central board is hit, then there is a secondary means of power. Don't quite understand the ins and outs of it all but it seems that the City Fathers ordered it immediately this morning. We can expect power cuts for the next few mornings until the work is finished."

"Well, I want us to run this bank normally. Do I make myself clear, Gordon," Trehearne answered, once again ignoring what Robert had just said. "Now, Gordon, you met Beverley yesterday about the negotiations with the Chinese Clerical Union and the threat of strikes. What did he say?" With that, the meeting went on for another interminable half hour before Trehearne finally called it to a close.

A few minutes later, outside in the corridor, Peter collared Robert. "I know he is a pain but he's still the boss. Try and be polite."

"He's living in fantasy land, Peter. The Japs have overrun Khota Bharu and we are having a torrid time on the border. By all accounts, the Alor Star airfield is being flattened, and he still thinks Percival will stop the rot." Robert shook his head and for the hundredth time that day pulled his collar away from his neck. "Get Ethel out, Peter; maybe you should go with her. You've done your bit in the last war."

Peter shook his head. "I'm not going anywhere yet, but I do intend to talk to Ethel tonight, again, about her going to Sydney or maybe Cape Town. I can maybe persuade Celia to go with her. The trouble is they believe that fool, the High Commissioner. I suggest you speak to your uncle. We may need his ship to get us out if everything goes belly up."

Robert was agreeing with Peter and had just started to say that he had still heard nothing from Harry when Trehearne came out of his suite of offices. "Still here, gentlemen. Planning more reasons for not working. I suggest a bit of hard work all around will send the Japs back to their holes."

As he was saying it, Robert and Peter turned their heads at the sound of explosions which could be heard in the distance. "I hope you're right, Walter, because that's another air raid and the RAF weren't able to stop them the last time," Peter said. Trehearne seemed to lose what suntan he had as the noise outside intensified and for a moment dithered not knowing what to do and then he headed for the stairs leading to the banking hall with Robert following him and with Peter heading in the opposite direction towards the Loans Section.

In the banking hall, people had gathered in a group listening to the bombs going off, some already on their knees partly hiding behind a marble counter that ran down the centre of the hall. There was suddenly the very loud sound of ack ack guns starting up from somewhere behind the building, followed by gun fire which was very much closer, and the sound of planes overhead. Some of the windows looking onto Fullerton Square started to rattle. One of the older men in the hall shouted, "My God, that's machine gun fire," just as a Japanese fighter was clearly visible for a few seconds flashing across the windows. Those people not already hiding behind the marble centrepiece started shouting and running for cover, with some of the women screaming.

Seeing that neither Trehearne nor Lennox, who had just turned up, was taking hold of the situation, Robert took command and shouted for everybody to get behind the counter and get their heads down. After a few minutes when there seemed a lull in the raid, Robert shouted, “Ladies and gentlemen, I think it’s probably safer if you stand on the stairs, well away from the windows. It does sound as though the attack is quite far away from here but just in case…” and thankfully, most of the people in the banking hall moved quickly to the stairs. Out of the corner of his eye, he could see Lennox walking around agitated, shouting various instructions to the staff, with what purpose Robert could not fathom, and Trehearne was nowhere to be seen. The planes did not come over the building again, although gunfire could be heard occasionally and the ack-ack guns behind the building were still pounding away at some enemy they could see.

Robert at last saw Trehearne emerge from the stairs and quickly disappear into the cashiers’ back office but as he couldn’t see him through the open door, he presumed he must be sitting on the floor behind one of the desks. The security guards had closed the bank’s main doors at the start of the raid but when Robert heard screaming outside, he shouted across to Lennox, who was now standing with his back to the wall beside the main doors. “Open the doors and let the people in.”

“That may be a security risk. What if a bomb lands nearby?” Lennox shouted back, not moving from his spot against the wall near the doors.

"Just let them in, Mr Lennox," Robert shouted in exasperation. "There is no bombing nearby and we are not in immediate danger. The raid seems to have moved on. These people need help." Lennox still did nothing, just continued standing against the wall. Finally, it was one of the Indian security men who got up from where he had been lying on the floor (Robert had not a clue as to why he had been lying out in the open) and went over to the doors and let in around twenty or thirty people, mostly European and Eurasian women who were very distressed, all of them crying. Robert ushered them up onto the stairs and a few got down with him behind the centrepiece.

The bombing and gunfire, always in the distance, went on for perhaps another half hour, it just seemed longer, and then everything appeared to quieten down. An Indian security guard, having first poked his head outside, spoke to Robert, "Sahib, I can hear whistles. I think it is the all clear." Robert nodded at the security guard and walked out into the street. He could see police in the Square blowing their whistles and people beginning to emerge from buildings opposite. He came back in with more than fifty people having emerged from behind the centre counter and from the stairs, all looking at him expectantly, some still very distressed. For some reason, there seemed to be a cloud of dust hanging in the air and grit on the floor.

Robert spoke to the security guard. "Thank you, Mr Gupta, you are right, it is the all clear." Turning to the large number of people in the hall, he shouted above the noise the crowd was making, "The all clear has been given. Everybody who wishes to leave, it is now safe to do so." There was a veritable stampede for the door with the security men holding both sides open. Trehearne emerged from the cashiers' office and headed for the main doors, stopping for a second to say, "The Governor's office is useless. I've just telephoned them. All they could say was that Japanese bombers were overhead, with fighters, and we were putting up a stout resistance. A stout resistance; why we should be sending them off with a flea in their ear." He was almost shouting as he said it.

Robert said nothing, turning to make sure that all the customers were being looked after, when Trehearne added, "I'm having dinner with General Bennett this evening. I shall give him a piece of my mind." With that, he was off to wherever he was going, having forgotten that he had ordered a car which turned up a few minutes later.

******

Robert worked until late in the afternoon before Gordon came into his office. "I thought you said you were going down to see the *Martinique* off. You had better be going."

Robert nodded. "Mr Wuh is still balancing today's work but he shouldn't be long and I have spot checked the tills. We were two staff short today and if this continues, more will be missing."

"No news of your friend, Harry?"

Robert shook his head. "The lines are all down. They think its fifth columnists, but it could be the commies taking advantage of the situation." He had tried to get in contact with the Commercial Union offices early in the afternoon but it was just a continuous wait on the telephone to speak to someone who might have any information and in the end, he gave up, realising it must be chaos if they were trying to extract staff from Khota Bahru and Kuantan, and maybe Butterworth. “I’m hoping Jenny, his girlfriend, has some news,” he added, as he locked up his desk and followed Gordon out of the office.

Chapter 2

Arriving at the pier, Robert could see that it was chaos with hundreds of people, if not thousands, milling around. Robert quickly learned that large numbers of people were trying to buy tickets at the last moment but he knew from the morning newspaper that the ship had a full complement of passengers. Even then from what he could see, the ship seemed to be taking on many more passengers than normal. These people at least no longer believed Sir Shenton Thomas.

Try as he might, he couldn't find Fran in the crowds and he eventually decided she must have gone on board and he made his way to the main gangway. He immediately saw some people he knew from the tennis club, which he had not been to for more than a week, making their way up the gangway with the ship's officers anxiously getting them on board. "Move along, please. We may have to leave at very short notice," he constantly heard from various of the officers. One of the officers at the gangway told him that they would probably be leaving in the next few minutes because they had been told that there may be another air raid and anyway, he couldn't go on the ship unless he had a ticket.

At one point, he saw Donald Shelby-Jones on the top deck but only fleetingly before, he too was lost in the crowds looking down on the quayside. Donald had left almost immediately after the meeting in Trehearne's office and Robert was unaware of him having said goodbye to anyone at the bank.

Robert had gone up to Peter's office in the early afternoon to pass on some papers and seeing Celia McKenzie, Peter's secretary, he had taken the opportunity to speak to her about Peter's idea of her going with Ethel. "Mr Connaught tells me he's trying to persuade you to go with Ethel on the next ship to Australia, or maybe South Africa."

Celia had nodded saying she was considering it. Robert, thinking about it as he scanned the thousands of people on the decks above him, seemed to remember Celia had told him a while ago that Ethel's best friend, Jessica, had already gone back to England. There was certainly a big age gap between Ethel and Celia so maybe that was the barrier but she had been a friend of the family for many years growing up with Peter and Ethel's son.

At last, he recognised Joyce coming down the gangway and shouted over all the noise at her. Somehow, she had got on board even though she was not sailing with Fran. Joyce didn't hear him at first but then saw him waving and came across. The heat and noise and the press of people was almost unbearable and it took some moments for them to get within arm's reach.

"Has she gone on board?" Robert shouted.

Joyce looking hot and flushed was trying to hang onto her hat which had been caught by someone going past with a case on his head. She shouted something back but seeing that he couldn't hear, she came up to him and put her mouth up to his ear and said, "She's on board. She went on board about half an hour ago. She said to tell you she prefers it this way."

Robert just made a face at the news and then bent down and said, well almost shouted, "I see you didn't change your mind."

"I thought about it but decided that I can do just as much here. I don't want to go yet." At least that's what Robert thought she said. Joyce looked up to the decks above and then pointed up. "There she is." Robert followed her pointed finger and saw Fran standing at the rail looking down, not smiling in fact looking very solemn. He smiled up at her and she gave a little wave.

The noise was becoming unbearable, as people were crying, some people even screaming and the ship's hooter finally going off. Obviously, the ship was leaving early. Chinese dockers appeared from nowhere and started to pull the gangways away from the ship and if it was possible, there was even more noise with Robert recognising more of the faces peering from the ship's decks; people who were getting out while there was still a chance. Joyce had taken his arm and was holding on tightly. She was shouting something but Robert couldn't really hear her and he had to bend down to listen to what she had to say and when he next looked up to where Fran had been, she was gone. He knew already that his time with Fran was over but he had wanted it to end in a different way, not like this.

Joyce must have sensed what he was going through and pulled on his arm. "Come on," she shouted, "let's go and get a drink." As they pushed their way through the crowds, the ship had slipped its moorings and was moving away from the dockside. People were remaining on the quayside, still screaming and shouting to passengers on the ship, as Robert and Joyce jostled their way through the crowds into the customs hall, finding it to be relatively quiet.

"Come on, Robert. I'm dying for a drink. We both need one but I haven't got long as I have to be back on duty at seven o'clock."

Robert just felt himself give a huge sigh and then taking her arm, they walked the length of the hall and grabbed a taxi the short distance to the *Mata Hari*. In fact, they had two drinks with both of them suddenly finding the situation uncomfortable and it was only as Robert helped Joyce into a taxi that the tension eased. Joyce leaned across to him before she got into the taxi and kissed him on the cheek. "Please ring me with any news. I'll be in touch." Robert stayed on and had one more drink talking to some people he knew before getting a taxi home.

Chapter 3

Robert didn't make it in for nine o'clock the next morning. He had stayed at the Drill Hall throughout the night getting only a little sleep and then sometime towards dawn, he had to deal with the problem of the Army commandeering the two lorries the Unit had, despite all his protests, and then he had spent ages trying to find alternative vehicles. He handed over the problem to Captain Peters around eight o'clock suggesting that he send volunteers down to Serangoon Road to take up the offer of a builder's lorry but leaving him with the problem of finding a second vehicle.

The continual loss of sleep because of the night duties meant that Robert was very tired and when he eventually got into work, he was working more on impulse than anything else. What sleep he had got in the night on a hard camp bed had been sporadic and interrupted frequently by the mosquitos attacking him. There had been an air raid but it had been over towards the Naval Docks, well away from the City. It had been about six o'clock when the Army had arrived without warning to commandeer their lorries and from then on, he had been on the phone trying to find alternative transport for the Unit.

He had made a quick visit back home for a shower and a late breakfast before dressing in his 'penguin' uniform and setting off in a rickshaw for work. As he came into Fullerton Square, the police whistles started shrilling as another raid came over the Island.

At home, the previous evening Chunggy had given him an urgent message from Geoffrey Blackmore asking him to come to the High Commissioner's Residence as soon as possible. It seemed Geoffrey had received a letter from Bangkok, addressed to Robert, and the intelligence staff wanted to know its contents. Robert had stopped only briefly for something to eat and to change into slacks and jacket, before getting a taxi to the High Commissioner's Residence.

******

At work that morning, everything seemed quiet and orderly; an air of normality existed inside the building whereas outside everything seemed to be mayhem what with the air raids, the seemingly chaotic troop movements, large artillery guns being positioned everywhere and a growing population as refugees started to arrive from over the Johore Straits. Gordon had disappeared off to a meeting in Colonial House and Trehearne was now on his way to Batavia, presumably on the *Roberta.* Peter was around but passed a message down to Robert, who was working in the vaults, to say he was going off at lunchtime to take over at the Drill Hall.

Mr Wuh, as the senior Chinese bank clerk, was now Robert's no.2 with George Omberley long gone, having seemingly mastered Chinese in the few months he had been at the bank, passed his entrance exams for Oxford which he said were remarkably similar to the practice exam papers, and generally been a fish out of water in the eleven months he had been in Singapore. Robert had enjoyed having George around but he hadn't made any real contribution with Mr Wuh always seemingly on hand to cover for him.

Trehearne hadn't even bothered to say goodbye to George not that George would have minded. He had set off in September, on a return voyage of the *SS Narkunda*, making a last observation to both Robert and Harry that the heat did things to you that he had not experienced before. Robert and Harry couldn't get out of him what he exactly meant by that but convinced themselves later, talking about it over a beer, from what little information George had given them, that he had been visiting certain ladies up Lavender Street to assist him in learning Chinese. Laz, who had just arrived to go out with them, when he heard the story was all for them going up there and practicing his Chinese but found his two comrades not so keen.

"Come on, lads. We'll just go and have a look."

Robert and Harry however were not convinced. "Mrs Lin Yuen will find out. She knows everything. We would never live it down," Robert said looking at Harry.

"Anyway, we're supposed to be going to the tennis club. I've got a tennis match, remember," Harry added, standing up quickly and making his way to his room.

"Well, I'll go with Ash from work. He's always game to try anything."

"I don't think they would let us in the tennis club, if they find out we're trying new ways to learn Chinese," was all Robert said smiling, as he poured Laz another beer.

******

When Robert had finally got back to the Drill Hall the previous night, it had been to a Drill Hall in pitch darkness with the teenage Thorsby lads on lookout duty wandering around outside wanting something to happen. Peter had sent out patrols to make sure that the 'no lights' decree was at last being observed although from where he was standing talking to Brian and Martin Preston who had just turned up, Robert could still see splashes of light in the city and lights on the water out at sea.

"What are those lights?" he asked no one in particular, pointing out to sea, and it was Brian who answered. "We think it's fishermen. There are also some big lights over by the Battery but they've only just come on."

Inside the Hall, it was like an oven even though the doors to the outside were open. The City Engineer it seemed had reduced the power and the effect was that the fans were working at half speed.

"Peter, how the hell do you stick this? For god's sake sit outside. At least there's a little bit of a breeze."

"I'm afraid I can't. I have to sit beside the telephone." In the gloom, Robert couldn't really make out Peter's face, it was more of a mask. He did hear him chuckle as he said, "Mind you, some of the lads are trying to sleep outside but I think they are getting badly bitten."

"Have you persuaded Ethel to go?"

"Mm. I've persuaded her that if she goes back to England, she will be able to get more news about Geoffrey and which camp he's in, in Germany. Couldn't persuade her to take the *Strathmore,* as she needs to close the house down, or so she insists, so it's the next boat to India or Cape Town, whichever has a spare berth. Celia has agreed to go as well so I will nip in to see Godfrey Smythe at South Asia Shipping in the morning and see what he can suggest. The next few days, I hope."

"What about you, Peter?"

"I'll stay. I feel I've got to. Anyway, I'm not sure I would get a permit to leave. Henry's in the same boat as me. This is our home so we've got to stay and help defend it. I've nothing really back in Blighty other than memories; Ethel at least has a sister in Devon. Mind you, she hasn't seen her in years."

Robert had grown used to Peter's clipped speech, never wasting words. It always made him think of the Chinese and the way they conversed with him. For a moment, Robert mused whether Peter, like another friend, David Masters, had grown into this form of speech because of living on the Island. Robert just nodded at the news knowing it was not the time for further discussion. Brian Preston came in and said something about a large ship coming into the roads and Peter nodded, "It's could be the *Strathmore*. Go, see, will you, Robert? I've been told it would try to arrive under cover of darkness."

Outside Robert, even in the dark, could make out a large ship in the roads, escorted by a trawler, and shortly afterwards, he thought he could make out it manoeuvring into its berth in the Kings Dock. Almost on cue, the lights in the dock area came on and it was obvious that there would be a great deal of bustle with everyone working quickly just in case there was another air raid.

Borrowing the binoculars from one of the lads standing beside him, Robert could see that there was lots of activity although some of the godowns were blocking him from seeing all of what was actually going on at the dockside. Looking across the roads, Robert could see the spaces where the *Repulse* and *Prince of Wales* had been but he had said nothing when one of the lads said something about them having left earlier in the day. What Geoffrey had told him during his meeting at the HC's Residence about the capital ships going off to intercept a possible landing force off Kuantan, he kept to himself.

Robert handed the binoculars to David Thorsby who was now standing by him and asked him to keep an eye on the docks just in case of a bombing raid and he went back inside and confirmed it was probably the *Strathmore* with what looked like a great deal of activity.

Peter just grunted and started rolling tobacco for a cigarette. "Are you going to tell me what was so urgent at the Governor's Residence?" Peter asked this over the noise of someone snoring at the other side of the Hall.

Robert sat down next to him. "Geoffrey Blackmore wanted to see me because I was sent a letter in the diplomatic bag from Bangkok. It seems it was the last bag to get through so the intelligence lads wanted to know what was in my letter and Geoffrey wouldn't let them open it without me being present. It turns out it was from Marcus, a chap I met up in Butterworth."

Peter said nothing, just shifted uncomfortably. Even in short sleeves and shorts, he was hot and sticky.

"The letter was dated the 4th December so the timing was very interesting. It seems the Ambassador had got the last of the women in the embassy, along with some Americans and a few French away on the train, with the help of some Siamese

Prince who works in their Foreign Office and is sympathetic to us. There was no mention of any other Europeans though so our lot could be anywhere. The Prince was taking them down personally by train to a place on the coast called Kan Tang and had arranged for a ship to collect them on 6 December to take them up to Rangoon. The timing is very interesting, Peter. We concluded… That is Geoffrey, me and a chap called Maynard, from military intelligence, that they might have just got through before the Japs sealed off everything."

Robert continued talking, as Peter lit the cigarette he had finally managed to roll. "Marcus added that the embassy was already locked up, with the Thai's saying it was for the embassy staff's own protection and that they haven't been able to leave the compound for more than two weeks. God knows what has been happening in the city. Maybe Maurice Levy has some information as they've a branch there, haven't they?"

Peter grunted at what Robert had been saying before answering, "Maurice was onto Walter before he left for Batavia because they knew nothing and hoped we had more information. All we know is that the Thai authorities have sectioned off the business quarter so your friend Marcus would have had no information. Bill Sedgeley-Reed and his colleagues have not been able to get anything out to us for nearly five days. Whatever the case, it looks like they're there, for the duration; however, many years that might be."

Robert sighed at what Peter said and spoke again, "Marcus apparently sent a report to Maynard and it seems there was nothing new in my letter which they didn't know already, so I left the letter with him. I don't give any of them much hope if the Thais have completely capitulated to the Japs. It all sounds pretty bad."

Peter grunted once again and looked at Robert in the little bit of light there was from the hurricane lamp on the desk. Robert saw him pick a piece of tobacco from his teeth. He'd taken up smoking again, only in the last few days, and much to Robert's amusement he spent his time pulling bits of the tobacco from his teeth. Peter insisted on rolling his own saying it was something he enjoyed doing but Robert already wondered if it was a way of giving him time to think.

Robert continued talking. "Geoffrey couldn't help about Harry. Just said it was chaos up there with a lot of poor discipline, troops deserting, 5th columnists at work, and the commies taking advantage of everything. He said he would tell the military that Harry was missing and that he would be unlikely to be in India by early January."

Robert paused whilst someone came over and asked a question of Peter and then he continued after Peter had given out instructions. "What I can't understand is why I haven't been called up. Not that I really want to go, but I've had some hassle over it. A bit like Harry really."

Peter looked up from the note he had started scribbling on his pad. "Geoffrey and I may have had something to do with that. We were asked to produce a long list of people we needed for the local defence organisation and we said that you were more use in Singapore helping to prepare our civil defences than swanning off to India. Harry's a different kettle of fish. Sorry if that's not what you wanted to hear."

Robert just shook his head. "In a way, I'm glad as I don't see myself running around with a rifle, apart from the fact that the medics keep saying I'm in the reserve category. I kept telling Fran that if the Army wanted me then they would conscript me."

"Well, I'm sorry if it soured your relationship with Fran but you're more use to us than if you're in charge of stores in Shimla. You've got a handle on the languages and you get on well with the locals, so you could be indispensable compared to some of the other twerps that are around. Another thing. If anything happens to me, you have to take command."

Robert, even in the gloom was visibly shocked and Peter could see him about to argue.

"Don't argue. Henry or Captain Peters would be obvious No.2's, even Pat Reynolds or Mike Davison. I have spoken to them and they agreed with me that you are the obvious cover. We need someone with lots of energy and determination. Henry has his responsibilities at the station, Pat has a medical problem and Mike has his pharmacy to run. And Ronnie Peters is no spring chicken." Peter flashed his teeth at Robert and added, "His words, not mine. He also said something about being a captain in God's Army not the British Army. I've spoken to Geoffrey and he says he's very happy with the decision."

Robert reached out and poured himself some water from the carafe on the desk, as Peter continued talking, still taking in what he had been told.

"Robert, unless Percival gets a hold of the situation, I think we should all be worried and that goes for the bank too. Walter is living in cuckoo land and there is going to be real trouble if we get caught with all the gold in our vaults, let alone whatever Mark and George are holding." It was said with an exasperation which Robert had not heard before.

Robert looked around the Drill Hall and then said quietly to Peter, "On the QT, I understand they have sent the *Repulse* and *Prince of Wales* up to Kuantan to stop a possible landing." As they sat there in silence thinking about the consequences, Henry Preston arrived and after speaking to them briefly and Peter saying that there was nothing to report, Henry suggested Peter should disappear off home. "And you, Bob, try and get some sleep. You were on duty all last night.
I'll cover for a few hours and wake you up around 4 o'clock when I have to go to the station."

Robert merely nodded at what Henry said; he got up and said that he might sleep in one of the cars outside.

"I think you'll find they're occupied already," shouted Peter at Robert who had started to walk to the entrance. Robert without answering turned back into the dark recess of the Hall where he knew there were some cots. '*Who knows there may be one with a net,*' he moaned to himself.

Chapter 4

What became obvious was that the chaos caused by the Japanese attacks brought out the best in some and the worst in others. When he had arrived for work, dog-tired and four days into being at war with the Japanese, he found an agitated Lennox already waiting for him in his office.

"Three more staff have not turned up including one of my security staff. The electricity is finally on and we were able to open the vaults without your assistance," Lennox said the last point with some emphasis and without so much as a 'good morning' and before Robert had a chance to ask why he was sitting in Robert's office.

"Mr Lennox, I'm glad to hear you didn't need me to open the vaults but why do you need to be waiting for me in my office? Why do you need to see me?"

Lennox stood up from the chair he had been occupying, wiping his brow. Even to a very hot Robert, Lennox looked even hotter. "Mr Wuh has been most rude to me. He forgets his place in the bank. He ordered me to open the doors on time even though I have been told that I must decide when it is safe to do so."

"What the hell are you talking about? Why is it not safe?"

"Mr Trehearne gave me specific orders, before he left, not to open the bank doors if I did not consider it safe."

"There's no alarm at this moment is there, Mr Lennox?"

"I was given the responsibility to decide if we should open," Lennox said doggedly not answering the question.

"Don't be ridiculous, Mr Lennox. Mr Trehearne would have a fit if he thought we were not opening the bank, when there's no alarm. Mr Wuh was quite right in insisting that the bank opens its doors. Knowing Mr Wuh, he would not have been rude in requesting the doors be unlocked. He's been here for years and you must know him well by now." Lennox made a bit of a face at what Robert had just said. "Anyway, if you're convinced, we should not be open for business why not see Mr Fraser." Robert could see that Lennox was not pleased with that suggestion.

"He's at a meeting and Mr Connaught is with clients upstairs."

"Then Mr Wuh was the senior banking officer in the absence of a British manager and you should follow his instructions unless you know there is a raid. I wondered why the doors were closed when I arrived. Now please make sure the doors are opened immediately. Can I also suggest you get on with ensuring the security arrangements are in place for an air raid. The situation was anything but satisfactory yesterday. Oh, and more to the point what about the payroll delivery to KL? Have you got the arrangements in place for the end of next week? Michael and I have agreed the amount of money we need to send up, so we need to know the security arrangements."

Lennox didn't answer and took off in his usual manner as though there was an imminent emergency and Robert, shaking his head, got down to catching up with paperwork on his desk. Throughout the rest of the morning, he saw various clients who had come in to collect personal belongings from safety deposit boxes sometimes getting Mr Wuh and Michael Matthews, the young Australian clerk in the Treasury section, to assist when more than one client was waiting.

"Don't know whether it's safer to stay or to go," was one comment from a Lady Corden who seemed to echo what most people were saying. It had become the core part of any conversation with each client.

"I'm sure you will have a safe journey, Lady Corden. It's all just a bit chaotic at the moment but from what I know of the *Admiral Benbow* it's a splendid ship. You're quite right to take your valuables though, as it may be some time before you can come back to the Island," Robert found himself saying this to the little lady who was dressed as though she was going off to have lunch at the Ritz in the dead of winter. Looking down at her, he privately questioned whether she knew she was out of London.

"It's quite ridiculous, young man. I can't take my maid with me and they haven't time to store my furniture. I haven't got a suite and I can only take two cases. How am I supposed to manage on a voyage with just two suitcases?"

Robert made some deprecating noises about the world was all topsy turvy and hopefully it would soon all be sorted out, and then ushered her off, with another client already waiting to see him. He was so busy that he missed lunch and was just about to nip out to see if he could get a sandwich when Gordon Fraser arrived at his office door looking white. "Have you heard?" and seeing Robert looking blank, he carried on, "*The Prince of Wales* and *Repulse*; they've been sunk." Seeing Robert's look of horror, Gordon carried on, "It happened this morning, off Kuantan. I've just been told by Simon Beulieu at the Mercantile."

The news had stopped Robert in his tracks. "Wasn't that supposed to be our trump card for stopping an invasion?" Gordon just nodded unable to say anything else. Robert had never got to know Gordon well in the 22 months he had been in Singapore but on the odd occasion he had socialised with him, he had found him to be someone who valued his own space. He had little to do with anyone at the bank preferring to spend his time fishing with a few close friends, never having married although Peter said there had been a lady in his life for quite a few years who had then decided to return to Blighty. Standing there, he saw a man who just wanted life to continue as before. Peter had said something about Gordon having been at Jutland and having vowed he never wanted to see anything like it again; Robert always saw him as a man who went with the flow preferring no arguments, a man who loved a life without hassle.

"I think you need to be talking to Trehearne again about a contingency plan, Gordon. Things are not going according to the Shenton plan."

True to form, Gordon shook his head. "I don't think it's my place to contradict Walter. He's made a decision and I will follow it."

"I hope to God you're right, Gordon. It seems nobody on this Island is safe any longer."

Gordon started to get flustered as he made for the door. "You're as bad as Peter. He's been on to me this morning; so have George and Mark." With that, he was gone and Robert walked out into the banking hall towards the main doors.

He saw Lennox heading to catch him up before he could reach the doors to the street. “Have you heard? Have you heard?” Lennox was almost shouting the words.

“I have heard, Mr Lennox, but please contain yourself. We have customers in the bank,” Robert said and then on an impulse, he turned around and headed for the cashiers and seeing Mr Wuh waved him over.

Taking him over to a corner, he told Mr Wuh what he had learned. Visibly shaken Mr Wuh said, “What do we do, Mr Draper?”

“Nothing we can do, Mr Wuh. Can I suggest you speak to the cashiers quietly and give them the news? Mr Fraser has gone into the Treasury to tell them and Mr Lennox will have told the security staff by now. I think we just have to get used to hearing bad news until we start to get a grip of the situation.” Wuh just nodded and scurried away and Robert finally got out into the street where he could see groups of people talking obviously about the news. Walking through the Square, he continued down Fullerton Road towards Collyer Quay and the many cafés in the area. He could see the funnels of a liner behind some buildings at the far end and with what looked like crowds of people already congregating on the quayside.

He went down to one of the cafés on the quayside and ordered tea and a sandwich and sat quietly still taking in the news. The few other people in the café were sat quietly, some reading newspapers and he doubted that they knew of the sinkings. ‘*Harry, where the bloody hell are you?*’ he was thinking to himself, as he ate his sandwich and wondering whether he would ever see his house mate again.

There had been no bombing all day and everything was almost normal, only it couldn't be and during the afternoon more and more people, coming into the bank, knew of the sinkings. There was almost a run on the bank with customers making large withdrawals and Gordon panicking that they didn't have enough cash. Robert spent some time in the late afternoon arranging with the Government House Treasury for extra dollars to be available the next day, and for Lennox to arrange collection.

It was well into the evening before he finally finished work and made his way up to Tanglin with heavy rain reducing the likelihood of another bombing raid that evening. He sat in the lounge eating the food Chunggy had prepared insisting that Chunggy keep him company. Tonight, he had been spared duty at the Drill Hall and he later sat on the veranda when the rain had stopped with a drink and listened to the noises in the undergrowth below and only seeing occasional lights in the distance. Mrs Lin Yuen had gone off to see friends, so he planned a quiet evening.

Chunggy had found a storm lantern from somewhere and by the light, Robert did his best to read the *Strait Times* which was full of the bombings on the Island in which more than one hundred people had so far lost their lives and hundreds had been injured. '*No news of the sinkings, so it must be in tomorrow's early edition so that will be the one to read,*' he said to himself, as he heard the telephone ring and Chunggy shout from downstairs that Miss Jenny was on the phone.

Robert went through to the upstairs lounge and picked up the extension. "I left a message for you at the Nurse's Office but no matter. I spoke to Jim Pascoe late this afternoon just before I came home. He's trying to get most of his people out of Penang and the north west coast but he's failed to get people up to Kuantan to rescue colleagues over there. Apparently, the military have extricated a number of Europeans from Khota Bahru and Kuantan and they're on their way to Singapore but Harry, and his sidekick Ben Roker, are not with them. Jim said the situation was chaotic with the Indian troops being very ill disciplined and some Scots troops have now been sent up to bolster them."

Jenny seemed almost stoical in the way she asked questions of Robert, finally ending with, "It's been nearly a week since we have heard from him, Bob. I think we have to be practical about this. Harry is a bit of a daydreamer but even he wouldn't leave it this long. He was supposed to be back in Singapore on Sunday so something has gone wrong."

Robert heard her catch her breath and he said quickly, "It's early days yet, Jenny. He could just be caught up in the chaos." Then Robert heard someone else in the background speak to her.

"Robert, I'm sorry, but I have to go; the first of the wounded are arriving on a train. We're helping the girls up at the Alex." With that, she was gone, leaving Robert in the semi-darkness with Chunggy now standing beside him with the storm lamp.

Robert was suddenly restless. He had to do something even if he was tired. "I'm going up to St Paul's, Chunggy. I've just remembered that Laz said he may come to the Drill Hall. He probably thinks I'm on duty."

Chapter 5

It was late in the afternoon, the beginning of the evening really, and it was thankfully pouring with rain. The day had been long and tedious, and the humidity made him feel completely wrung out. Peter had said for him to have another night off duty, as it seemed unlikely that the bombers would come over now that the forecast was heavy rain for the rest of the day.

Robert took a taxi for the short journey down to the *Mata Hari* at *the* far end of Collyer's Quay. He had telephoned the Commercial Union offices just before he left work and discovered that Harry's boss, Jim Pascoe, was already at the *Mata Hari* so he decided to go there first before going home. In the few minutes he was in the taxi, it seemed to him that everything was very quiet with few people on the streets and for the first time, he noticed that there were a number of what seemed abandoned cars; most of the office buildings now had tape on the glass windows and doors and a good number of buildings had sandbags around their entrances.

Things had certainly changed in only a few days.

When he arrived, he saw Joe with a gaggle of office colleagues, all Chinese, as all the younger British staff had now been called up to one of the armed services or were now in the Volunteers. All of them looked very tired and there were no smiles only nods at Robert when they saw him.

After brief introductions and Robert ordering a beer, Jim brought him up to date. "I've spent the day organising our lot up in Penang. They're starting to pull the Europeans out of Butterworth and Penang as it is being bombed to bits. We managed to get some of them out by boat this morning. Hopefully, they should be with us in three or four days. But we've had to leave some of our staff there for a later boat. There's heavy fighting just over the border, apparently, and from what I can find out, the military don't see themselves being able to stop the Japs from taking the north and Penang in the next few weeks. They've sent up some extra troops and that should help but we've no air cover. The airfield at Alor Star is unusable by all accounts. Our agent, Mathew Gillespie, when I finally managed to speak to him a couple of hours ago said it was absolute mayhem getting the staff onto the ship this morning with it being strafed. He says half of Butterworth is on fire and there's lots of dead lying in the streets. He doesn't reckon Penang will hold out for long and he is just hoping that they can for long enough to get his remaining staff off."

Robert nodded at what Joe had just told him and then asked. "Any news of Harry or Ben?"

Jim just shook his head. "Not a dicky bird. The chap at Army HQ I spoke to this afternoon said that he reckoned quite a few Europeans working on the estates and up in the hills would be caught out by the speed of the Japanese advance."

Robert had another beer and then left the Commercial Union crowd drinking, preferring to make his way home and get out of his 'penguin' suit.

When he arrived at Mrs Lin Yuen's, he said little to the Chinese driver other than for him to drive safely and he gave him a bigger than normal tip. Just as he started upstairs, Chunggy emerged from the back of the house, very harassed. "Mr Drapa, many calls. Miss Jenny, she say to tell her when you come home. She ring many times, very upset."

"Okay, Chunggy. I want a quick shower before I do anything. I don't have to be at the Drill Hall tonight and I need a meal. Have you got anything I could have?" Robert saw Chunggy nod. "Excellent. I will speak to her in half an hour."

"No, Mr Drapa, she want to see you. She says she will come around." The message stopped him in his tracks. "Did she say anything else?"

"No, Mr Drapa, just that she must see you."

Robert sighed expecting the worst, feeling his stomach muscles go tense; he just nodded. "What other phone calls?"

"Mr Muxton, he telephone and say he injured yesterday but okay. He maybe try and come to Drill Hall tonight, maybe tomorrow night." Robert had walked into the lounge and headed straight for the drinks tray and was pouring himself a *stengah,* with Chunggy insistent on putting lumps of ice in it as he was telling Robert all the news.

Robert looked at Chunggy. "Mr Muxton didn't turn up last night. He's been saying for days he will come. Why the hell should I believe he will come tonight."

Chunggy put down the ice bucket before saying. "He say he injured by a bomb and will come from the hospital."

Robert looked at Chunggy. "Bloody hell. What's he been up to now."

All the time, Chunggy was moving from one foot to another, fidgeting and Robert was just about to say what's wrong when Chunggy broke down, "Lin Yuen, she dying."

Robert choked on the mouthful of whisky he had just taken. Coughing and spluttering he eventually stopped, coughed a little again and then croaking asked, "What did you say?"

"Lin Yuen, she in her bed. No move. Very cold."

"Nonsense, Chunggy. I saw her on Saturday. And the night before last. She was feeling a bit under the weather but she was okay. She went out last night, didn't she?" '*It can't get worse can it*?' he murmured to himself not waiting for any answer.

"Come see, Mr Drapa," Chunggy said and in his excitement continuing to drop the ends of words and missing his rs as he always did in times of stress. "You see, she not breathing."

Robert took a very long swig of his drink. "Right, Chunggy, let's go and see and if you're not right, I will wring your neck." Chunggy was already halfway out of the lounge and heading for the stairs.

The bedroom was in darkness and Chunggy was standing at the bottom of Mrs Lin Yuen's bed by the time Robert entered the bedroom. He fiddled for a moment looking for the light and eventually found the switch and put the overhead light on. "At least the lights are back on. I can see what I'm doing," he said out loud to no one in particular.

Mrs Lin Yuen was lying in the missionary position with just her head peeking out from the covers, so Robert observed once he had removed the netting over the bed. She did look very pale and for some reason, she had eyeshades on. '*What the hell do I do?*' thought Robert. '*Do I take her pulse? No, I can't do that her arms are under the covers and she may have nothing on.'* He leant forward a little almost touching her face. '*Was that a little breath he felt*?'

He stood up. "Chunggy, go and ring Dr Robertson and see if he can call here as soon as possible. Tell him that Mrs Li Yuen is very ill."

Robert looked around the room whilst Chunggy was on the phone in the hall. He switched the fans on to try and cool the stifling heat and then went back to sit beside Mrs Lin Yuen.

"Dr Robertson, come soon, Mr Draper," Chunggy said on his return preferring to stand at the bottom of the bed.

"Right, while we're waiting will you go and ring, Miss Jenny, Chunggy, and tell her to come over and then you wait at the front door for the doctor. There's a whole cabinet of pills and boxes of needles here, mostly with Chinese labels on them, and we better leave them out for Dr Robertson to see. And while you're doing that I must go upstairs."

Robert slipped back upstairs and went to the toilet and returning to the lounge quickly refreshed his *stengah* and drank it back too fast. He slipped off his jacket and threw it over the armchair as he set off to go back downstairs.

Just then, he heard talking downstairs and as he went down to the main hall, he saw Dr Robertson disappear into Mrs Lin Yuen's bedroom with Chunggy staying in the hall. Robert said nothing to Chunggy and instead turning back towards the front door, he went through into the downstairs lounge to check that everything was okay only to find that Mrs Li Yuen had left her jewel box open on the table. He ran his hands through the various pieces momentarily before he closed the lid and picking it up looked around to see where it would normally be stored.

"*Nowhere obvious*," he said to himself, as the doctor emerged from the bedroom and came into the lounge. "She's left her jewel box open. I've no idea where she keeps these things. There seems to be quite a bit of stuff, and some of it looks expensive," Robert said seeing the doctor looking at the box under his arm.

Doctor Robertson just nodded and said, "You know presumably that she's a diabetic and it looks as though she has had a bit of a relapse. Probably didn't take her insulin. Anyway, another half hour and she might not have been with us. Unfortunately, she may have left it too long and there may be other complications. Can't tell at this stage. I'll phone the General now and tell them to take her in." The Doctor looked exhausted and yet he said, "You need some sleep, young man, by the looks of it."

"You can talk. Can I get you a drink or anything?"

"I daren't. I wish I could have one but duty calls. I have a surgery going on so must get back."

"Do you know if she has any relatives? She's never mentioned any to me. It should really be them who should be looking after her jewels."

"Looks like you've got the job," the doctor said, as he picked up his bag to leave the room. "By the way, those two poor devils you helped to pull out of the car, on Monday morning, were the Mortimers. They lived at the top of Tanglin Road. Never knew what hit them. I saw Captain Peters this afternoon and he said he would make sure it was recorded at the Drill Hall."

Robert just nodded, then thanked the doctor for coming so quickly before going back into the bedroom and from there, he could hear Dr Robertson say something to Chunggy who must have been standing at the front door. He could hear the doctor then talking on the telephone.

He sat quietly beside Mrs Lin Yuen for a while looking at the little lady who had become his friend. Eventually, he heard more noise at the front door heralding the arrival, by the sound of the voices, of Jenny and another female.

Robert stood up and took a last peek at Mrs Lin Yuen before rearranging the netting over her bed. He quietly closed the bedroom door behind him picking up the jewellery box he had left on a chair. Jenny and her friend had already raced upstairs and seeing Chunggy, coming from the kitchen, Robert just said, "I have her jewel box, Chunggy. I'll keep it upstairs until we decide what to do with it. Can you tidy her bedroom up a bit and stay with her? The ambulance should be here in a few minutes." Chunggy just nodded and disappeared into the bedroom as Robert went upstairs dreading what Jenny might have to tell him.

"Bob, you're here," said Jenny racing across to him and hugging him which was difficult, as he still had the box under his arm. Looking at her, he saw a very strained face with dark shadows under her eyes. Harry always talked about Jenny being his rock and Robert could see why. Even with all her worries about Harry, she still managed somehow to hold herself in. Robert put down the box and turning back, gave her another big hug.

"Do you have news, Jenny? I saw Jim Pascoe about an hour ago. He had no news." Robert didn't say anything about Jim telling him that they could do no more.

Jenny shook her head, almost shuddered and said, "I've been trying too. Nothing. All they know is that Harry and one of his colleagues were north of Kuantan assessing a possible mine development for insurance purposes. They think the road was bombed and strafed by planes, at least that's what the military are saying. Apparently, the development is in the hills quite away from the coast road. The lines are down so there is no contact with the mine. They won't tell Commercial Union anything other than that the troops have evacuated Khota Bahru and are forming up new defence lines and such roads as there are down the East coast are near impassable with refugees. I had a word with Matron this afternoon and she said that she had spoken to the hospital at Khota Bahru on Monday afternoon before the line went dead. She says it's manic up there with the Japanese capturing the airfield and some of the Indian troops not being very disciplined. They were trying to get the wounded out on the last train."

Robert made a face at what Jenny said and picked up his drink. The lounge was bathed in the gloom from the one small lamp Chunggy had lit and outside heavy rain could be heard against the shutters.

"Can I get you both a drink?"

Jenny shook her head and Robert could just make out the other girl nod. Jenny suddenly realised that Robert didn't know who her friend was. "I'm sorry, Bob, this is Marion. We share a room at the Nurses Home."

Robert just smiled in acknowledgement at Marion and waved his glass at her. "What's it to be?"

"Whatever you're drinking, only a lot more soda." Chunggy appeared from nowhere with a plate of biscuits, cheese and various nibbles.

"You haven't left her, Chunggy?" Robert said perhaps more sharply than he meant.

"Nothing I can do, Mr Draper, she's sleeping and you

must eat." Seeing Marion diving into the cheeses and biscuits Robert just nodded and said a quiet 'thank you' before going over and helping himself.

As Robert was helping himself to a biscuit, he saw Marion whisper something to Jenny which he didn't catch and then she went out of the lounge. Jenny seeing Robert watch her go, said, "She's just gone to check that Mrs Lin Yuen is okay. It sounds like the ambulance has just arrived."

Robert started to go to the stairs but Jenny said, "Don't worry, Marion will have it all sorted out." Robert retraced his steps back into the lounge although he was still listening at the noise downstairs.

Jenny said something else to Robert but he was so busy listening to the sounds from downstairs that he didn't hear what Jenny said at first. He turned to face her and asked, "What did you say, Jenny?"

"What are we going to do, Bob?"

Marion arrived back in the room, as they were talking and realising from her voice that Jenny was at breaking point she went over and knelt down beside her on the settee and gave her a hug.

"I don't know, Jenny. I really don't know. Just pray that this nightmare will end soon." Robert went over to the coffee table and picking up his glass, he finished his drink in one go.

Silence existed for perhaps a minute or so and then Jenny got up and sat on the arm of the settee taking a deep breath as she did so. Again, there was a moment of silence with them all thinking of the world unfolding around them before she stood up and straightened her dress. "Come on, Marion, let's get back to the hospital," she said in a resigned voice. Turning to Robert she added, "Will you ring me, Bob, if you hear anything?" Seeing Robert nod, she said, "Try Ward 11. I may as well be at work."

Robert started to say something about Chunggy getting them a taxi but she was already at the top of the stairs and she just shouted, "Chunggy can get us a trishaw at the corner. The rain has eased off a bit." She and Marion were gone in a flash it seemed, leaving Robert standing trying to stay upright and not just collapse in a heap. He was suddenly very weary.

"A shower. That's what I need. Pull yourself together, Robert Draper. This could go on forever." He sat in the lounge for perhaps ten minutes just mulling over the events of the past four to five days and wondering what was in store for them in the next few days. Finally, picking up a lump of cheese, he went off to his room to get stuff to change into only to find Chunggy already there getting clothes out for him. "How did you…?" mumbled Robert.

"I hear what you say to Miss Jenny. I get Miss Jenny trishaw at corner. Your clean clothes are on the bed. I will make you something to eat, Mr Draper, whilst you have shower."

"I will have to go over to the Drill Hall, Chunggy, later, so after I've eaten could you get me a trishaw?"

As Chunggy nodded Robert asked, "Where have they taken Mrs Lin Yuen?" quite forgetting that Dr Robertson had said he was organising for an ambulance from the General Hospital.

"The General Hospital. The ambulance man, he say to go tomorrow morning and she may be much better."

"Will you go to the hospital tomorrow, please, and then telephone me at the bank and tell me what is happening." Chunggy didn't answer or if he did, Robert didn't hear him as

Chunggy disappeared into the bathroom and got the shower working, and Robert started to undress.

Chapter 6

By the time Robert did go up to the Drill Hall, it was again raining heavily. The heavy cloud seemed to be in layers just above the height of the trees and it made for a very dark night with no streetlights being on. Along with many other people that night Robert crossed his fingers that the poor visibility would prevent the bombers from coming over. Making his way to the Drill Hall, he was soon wet and very sticky with the humidity.

It turned out that Laz had suffered an injury. He was already in the Drill Hall sporting his arm in a sling and explaining to all and sundry that he and a number of his workforce had been caught under a bridge on the Bukit Timah Road when it had taken a hit from the bombing.

"The bombing didn't seem to be much at first. It was all over the place and then a bomb went off maybe forty or fifty yards away and we were all flung to the ground and then the bridge starts to collapse right on top of the pipes we were trying to repair. Been at it for days repairing them and all our work was gone in a flash. It took a good bit of the road away as well, so the Chief has made it a priority that we repair the road and the troops will have to go around by the West Coast Road or by Serangoon until we can get it sorted. Ash and the lads are at it now."

Laz had seen Robert arrive and when he had finished telling all who would listen, he came over. "So, what's the news? Sorry, I couldn't get here last night but I was in hospital for hours."

Robert just shook his head. "Not good, I'm afraid. Nothing has been heard of the sod since last Friday night when he telephoned Jenny and spoke to her briefly. He left a message on Saturday afternoon for me, with Chunggy, asking if I could book a passage for him to Calcutta or Madras for next week, latest 20 December. Communication is not brilliant up there but they were supposed to be on their way back, on Sunday, so he should have been at least in Kuantan but by all accounts, he hasn't got there or at least not to the Commercial Union offices."

Robert helped Laz to light the cigarette which he had got out of his top pocket whilst he was listening to Robert. "The military are stopping people going north so Jim Pascoe can't get anybody up to Kuantan. We just have to wait and see."

Robert changed the subject looking at the sling. "You okay?"

"Yeah, yeah, they said I may have broken my wrist. Only hurts when I laugh, sort of thing. Couldn't come up last night as I was at the General and then it took all night sorting out the mess," Laz said between puffs. "Jenny will be going out of her mind. You know they were talking about getting engaged. You were missing for some reason and they told me when we had a few drinks up at Rosie's."

"I was probably on duty here. I've done extra shifts as some of the older men wanted to spend more time with their families before they sent them off to Australia or South

Africa. In fact, a few go tomorrow and I gather Cunard have a ship coming in tonight on its way to Perth."

Laz was nodding at this information, looking up at the black rain laden sky. "No point in turning off the lights, not with all these clouds."

Henry Preston came out of the Hall and seeing them standing under an awning, he came over and said to Laz, "I hear it was a bit of a close call, young man. Cunningham in your office was telling me this afternoon that you lost two coolies and three badly injured."

Laz said nothing and it was Robert who said, "You didn't say it was that close," noticing for the first time that Laz had some big scratches on the side of his neck. Henry said nothing more and wandered off to check the builder's lorry parked a few yards away.

Laz just continued to look up at the sky. "Even if I was thinking of joining up, Bob, I can't anymore. The Governor told the Chief that there's to be no exceptions, all able-bodied men are to remain on the Island to help with the defence. No more permits are to be issued except to older men, even the conscripted lads are not exempt."

Robert saw that Laz had turned to look at him, as he finished saying what he had just said. It was a moment for once when Laz was being serious.

"I didn't know you were thinking that seriously about it, Laz. Anyway, you never had a chance of being released. You're far too important. You're in charge of the sewers, remember."

There was a flash of white teeth and Robert could just make out a grin. "You sod, you would have the last word."

“Come on, you poor injured sewer man. I bet there’s tea inside.”

Chapter 7

It was the next day when Robert really noticed that people had started to panic. The sinkings of the *Prince of Wales* and *Repulse* had brought it home to everybody that the task of beating the Japanese was going to be long and hard and worse still, they may not win. Sir Shenton had at last relented and allowed the newspapers to suggest that certain non-essential people could apply for permits to leave. As a result, he noticed that there were queues outside the Cunard and Thomas Cook offices and bank customers were suddenly asking if he knew of anyone to look after their pets.

Mind you for some, the problem of the war mongering Japanese was merely an inconvenience. Robert was telephoned at the bank by the Tennis Club Secretary to say that it really wasn't good enough. There had been complaints from members that Robert had failed to turn up for a doubles match. He had no choice but to report him to the Disciplinary Committee. Robert was speechless at first and then saw the funny side of it.

"There's no need to take that attitude, Mr Draper. It's not a laughing matter."

Finally, stopping laughing, he told the Club Secretary he could do what he liked and put the phone down on him. The young Australian clerk, Michael, who was standing in front of his desk when the call came through asked what was so funny.

"Michael, the world is falling apart around us and I get told I am going to be disciplined for failing to remember I had a match." Robert grinned up at Michael. "I feel quite cheered up." Waving Michael off, Robert got down to work.

Chunggy had telephoned sometime during the late morning when he was dealing with a client and left a message for him to say that Mrs Lin Yuen was still very ill and not responding as well as the doctors had hoped and they were very concerned.

All morning he dealt with customers anxious to settle their banking arrangements before they left the Island. Late in the morning he had a very difficult customer who wanted to transfer all his assets to Australia despite there being limitations imposed by the Colonial Office. Finally convincing the customer that he had to get the appropriate certificate from the Colonial Office, he sent him off to the Municipal Building some half a mile away. He had just sat down to have a sandwich that one of the Chinese clerks had obtained for him when the telephone rang and Mrs Frobisher asked if he could come up to Mr Fraser's office urgently. He made Gordon's office in double time to find Peter already there.

Gordon was clearly very agitated, pacing up and down, and he immediately said, without any welcome, "George has been wounded. Apparently, the bank's been hit; badly, if I understand the garbled message correctly." What Gordon said literally stopped Robert in his tracks but before he could ask for more information Gordon continued, "That's not all. Mark has resigned with immediate effect. The story is that he tried to board the *Roberta* with Mary and his little girl and was refused passage. Walter saw it all as he was boarding and there was one hell of a shouting match and the message I now have is that Mark resigned on the spot. He wanted to go with them to then join up in Australia." Robert sat down on the side of Gordon's desk, as he was being told all this news, trying to absorb it.

Robert looked at Peter and then Gordon. "I can't believe it. What the hell is going on?"

Peter took over. "Gordon and I have been talking. We have to get the gold out of Penang before it's too late and see if we can get George down here."

"Yes, of course. I'll go up."

"Not you, Bob. I'm going. I've worked up there so I know the layout of the town. More to the point, we need you to take over the KL show. We have all that cash being sent up on the 20th, mind you that's subject to the Army not changing their minds about us having permits. It's also obvious Clive needs help. He's been on the phone. He has some problem up there which he can't tell us about over the phone but the message we have from the police is that some of the banks have been bombed which doesn't sound good and they have had to move some of the other banks money to our vaults. Clive's sent a letter by special courier but it's not arrived yet."

Peter saw that Robert had started to protest at his decision. "We've just been onto Godfrey Smythe at Asia Shipping and they have a fast ship going up tonight to Penang. Subject to bombing, we can be up there in just over thirty-six hours."

"We. Who else?"

"I've just spoken to Kenneth Chen before you came up.

He's agreed to go up with me. Hugh Besseker at the Colonial Office has agreed to give us permits."

"Peter, the Japs may break through at any time. It's a hornet's nest. You can't go, it's not safe. The chances of getting killed are high."

"I thought you had just volunteered," Peter said smiling at Robert and getting out his little bag of tobacco. "The ship is being sent up by the Colonial Office to collect various valuables from Penang and a large number of Brits, so it will not be there for very long."

Robert said nothing; he was still taking in all the information. "We don't know how bad George is but Wei Chen, his No.2 is also injured and we understand from the police that there is at least a half dozen dead, but no information whether the dead are customers or staff."

Gordon who had still been pacing the room as Peter was talking, turned and spoke to Robert. "Godfrey says that the ship will only dock for a few hours, at most for half a day, so it will be a quick visit. In and out, and hopefully, Peter should be back on the Island before you leave on the 20th. Lennox says you can't go up to KL until the 20th because there are no civilian permits being issued for the next few days. Clive already knows and will tell the estates' managers that the Christmas pay will be a couple of days late."

"So, what do you think the problem is up in KL?" Robert asked looking at Gordon.

It was Peter who answered Robert's question. "My guess is it's to do with our gold reserves. Frank Foley has gone up to KL, I know that, so my guess is they have a similar problem. Of all things he's gone up by ship to Malacca and is then going to get transport from there to KL. Sounds like the

Colonial Office would not give him a permit to go by train so he wangled a trip up to Malacca. He was supposed to have lunch with me yesterday and didn't turn up and left a message about urgent business in KL."

"Surely, you can't go if you're trying to get Ethel off the Island."

"God, Bob. Stop creating problems. I'm going." Peter changed his tone and asked, "I presume you're okay about going to KL?" Robert just nodded at a still exasperated Peter. "I'm going home now and will see if Arthur and Neecha can take Ethel and Celia down to the *Rosemount* tomorrow night. Godfrey has got me a berth on it for them. It's coming in tomorrow afternoon, if it's on schedule, on its way to Colombo. Godfrey assures me that it will go through the Sunda Straits and then up the west coast of Sumatra. For most of the time, it will be out of reach of Japanese bombers. I'll go and see Celia on my way out and tell her to pack ready for tomorrow night."

"Right, let's get started," was all Peter said, as he stood up and stubbed out his cigarette. "Bob, you'll need to reorganise the Unit tonight." Robert just nodded, as they left the room with Gordon pacing around probably worrying about what he was going to tell Walter.

Chapter 8

Over the next few days, there were more bombing raids with most of them concentrating on the defence installations and the RAF aerodromes on the Island. More troops had come in with the *Strathmore* and the *Rosemount* and they were soon dispatched off to camps for a quick induction into jungle warfare. Robert visited Mrs Lin Yuen each day for short periods but she was rarely lucid. On one occasion, he saw Jenny for a few minutes and both said very little, their minds already telling their hearts that they were unlikely to see Harry again.

It was a few days later when Robert saw Sally. He hadn't seen her in months. He was going up to the Colonial Offices near the Padang for a meeting Gordon had asked him to go to, at very short notice, when he bumped into her. Sally had been persistent in her interest in him for a few weeks after she had slept in his bed even telephoning him at home and suggesting she would love to meet him for drinks but Robert was fully involved with Fran at the time and had managed to extricate himself from a potentially difficult situation.

"Robert," Sally trilled in her high voice, walking across to him as though everything was absolutely normal. She was wearing a lovely flowery dress with a straw hat on top of her blonde hair. She came right up to Robert and kissed him on the cheek. "I do wish you had telephoned me," she whispered, as she stood back. Robert hadn't expected the welcome and took a moment to catch up with what Sally was saying.

"How are you, Sally? I would have thought that Thomas Cook's had got you out by now."

Even as they spoke, Robert was watching a group of soldiers racing to man ack-ack guns that were positioned at this end of the Padang. Something was happening and he took Sally's arm. "I think we should get under cover. Something's about to happen." With that, he took Sally into the lower entrance of the Justice Building with other people also starting to make their way into the building and with the newly installed sirens going off.

Sally seemed to enjoy being ushered in by Robert and they stood in a corner listening to the whistles blowing and an air raid alarm sounding off. She pushed her way next to Robert and was as close as possible making Robert feel almost uncomfortable as she put her lips up to his right ear and said, "See what you've been missing." For the next few minutes, Robert almost forgot that there was a life and death scene being enacted outside, even when the ack-ack guns started up, making a tremendous noise. In a lull in the noise, he almost shouted, "You didn't answer my question; are you getting out?"

Sally looked up at him, "We're off tomorrow night on the *Fortuna,* an American ship going to Australia. So, we could meet tonight. It's my last night, Robert. I would love to spend it with you."

Robert was lost for words and then started making excuses, "Actually, I'm on duty tonight and I don't think it will be possible for me to change the roster. Anyway, you will have to get yourself organised for the trip."

"Oh, I've done that already," Sally said somehow pressing herself even closer to him.

Robert changed the subject quickly. "Have you heard from Lily?"

Sally giggled. "Robert Draper, I think you're scared." Seeing him not answer she added, "Lily has joined the WAAF's and is now somewhere in England with hundreds of young men. Well, are you going to take me out tonight, my last night on the Island?"

"I really am sorry, Sally, but I am on duty. Everything is getting serious and I can't just take time off."

"Well, it's your loss," Sally said in a little huffed voice and pulled herself apart not saying anything more for the remaining minutes until the all clear sounded. She just turned and looked at him as they emerged into the street and without a word was off down towards Victoria Street as though nothing had happened. Robert looked at her departing figure, in high heels, dress swirling and wondered if he had done the right thing. It was as good an offer as he had ever had. Walking the last few yards to the meeting, he wondered if he would ever see her again.

Inside the building, he was ushered up to a large room where it seemed the meeting was just starting. He sat down quickly in a corner, as the speaker rose from behind a table placed in front of perhaps two dozen chairs.

"Gentlemen, I have been asked to speak to all the senior managers of banks and main currency holders. My name is Rodericks and I am part of the team charged by the High Commissioner to put in place plans for the disposal of all currency should Singapore come under direct attack at some point."

Robert looked around, as he listened to the pompous introduction; he recognised many of the faces in the room of around twenty men, mostly bankers, all of them well in their forties, some much older. The Regional Manager of Barclays whom he knew by sight had turned up with two colleagues and he took centre stage by saying immediately, "I thought Shenton had a party line that everything would be fine, Percival is in control and there would be no need to worry. What the hell are you saying now?" There was a strong murmur of agreement from the audience some of whom had gasped at what Rodericks had said.

"What the Government in London is now advising is that we make contingency plans for the disposal of all currency."

Maurice Levy, from the Hong Kong Bank, whom Robert knew from occasional meetings, came in. "Are you suggesting that we start burning the paper money?"

Robert watched as Rodericks, having sat down after his introduction, stand up again, looking very hot and not enjoying the fact that he was the centre of attention. "The High Commissioner is requiring us to have in place a plan for the disposal of all currency should the instruction come out from the Colonial Office. It may never happen but we would be remiss not to take such action. The official line is that we should not cause panic but that we should make sensible plans for the disposal of currency should matters further deteriorate. I also require from you some indication of what amounts you hold and for us to agree a plan for the burning of the money at short notice."

There was a moment of almost no sound as those in the

room absorbed the information and then some of them started saying that they had no idea how much they held.

Robert at that point stood up and almost shouted his question over the noise. "Why is the paper currency of importance? Most of it will only have value in the Malay States and Singapore. The Japanese will not find it of any use on any international market. In these circumstances, its value is zero. Surely, it's our gold stocks that are of more use to the Japanese?"

"Who are you, young man?" asked Rodericks taking off his glasses and making a show of cleaning them. A few of the other men in the room were also looking at Robert and presumably wondering the same.

"Eh, Robert Draper, Union and China Bank. Mr Trehearne is in Batavia and Gordon Fraser, his No.2 has gone down with a touch of malaria. I can add that Mr Trehearne has given specific instructions that we are to operate as though everything is normal."

There was a murmur of agreement from a number in the room with a middle-aged Chinese man whom Robert later learned was one of the co-owners of the China Bank, which had been set up only a few years ago, getting quite heated.

"Mr Rodericks, it sounds to me as though the British Government does not hold out much hope for us. It's a good job my partner and I are in the process of planning the movement of some of our gold stocks in Singapore as it's quite clear everything will be left to the last moment when it'll be too late."

Maurice Levy again came in, once the noise of supporting comments had subsided, "We're moving some of our gold held here to Darwin tomorrow and if it ends up in the drink because we were not warned early enough, then it's the fault of the High Commissioner for telling us everything would be fine and dandy. My God we still have large quantities of gold in Penang not to mention what we have in Kuala Lumpur."

There was roar of agreement and Robert saw Rodericks visibly wilt under the tirade. One of the Barclays contingent shouted something similar to what Maurice Levy had just said and Rodericks finally realising that the currency figures were not to hand said over the noise that he required figures from each of them by the end of the next day.

The meeting ended in disarray with Rodericks making a bolt for it and leaving a junior civil servant to arrange for the amounts of currency held by each of the banks to be sent to the Colonial Office within twenty-four hours. Many of those at the meeting got together in groups to discuss what the contingency plan implied but Robert decided he may as well go and coming out of the building, he was shouted at and turning he saw Maurice Levy making his way to the entrance. "Are you walking back to Fullerton Square?" and seeing Robert nod Maurice said, "Mind if I walk with you?" Robert just nodded again as they set off and with Maurice telling Robert to call him by his first name.

"The bloody fools. Only last month, we had a meeting with the Governor and he assured Norman Rossiter, my senior Director, that we should not concern ourselves. Now we need contingency plans. Thank God I've persuaded Norman to move our Singapore gold out to Australia although God knows it's got a good chance of ending up at the bottom of the sea. Robert, I think you should be telling Gordon to override Walter and take action or you could end up with egg on all your faces and Walter will deny telling you to take no action."

Robert had been smiling at what Maurice was saying and it was only when he heard Maurice's last point that the smile left his face. "Gordon's not going to do that, Maurice. Walter has set the scene and Gordon will go down with the ship, obeying the instruction. Peter would do something but not Gordon. As it is, Peter has had to go up to Penang to try and rescue the gold up there and bring down George Barwick who has been wounded."

Maurice Levy seemed to know about Peter's mission and they talked about what they knew of the situation before Maurice Levy said, "Our lot are trying to get our gold down to KL today by car."

Robert raised his eyebrows at this information. "Sounds a bit risky."

Maurice Levy murmured his agreement but changed the subject back to the Union & China situation. "I bet the instructions from Walter are not in writing."

Robert looked at Maurice Levy as they started crossing over Anderson Bridge. "I'm not aware that it is in writing but I have seen a telegram sent yesterday from Batavia which clearly says that he assumes everything is still operating as normal and he will endeavour to be back as soon as possible." Maurice Levy chortled at what Robert had just said. "You'll not see Trehearne again. He'll send missives from Batavia but he won't come back. If things go wrong, he will blame Sir Shenton and then Gordon for not using his initiative."

Robert just made a bit of a face at what Maurice Levy said, as he privately agreed with him and a few yards further on they parted with Robert continuing through Fullerton Square towards the bank.

It was just as he was about to enter the bank that he was shouted at from a taxi which stopped almost beside him. It was David Masters whom he hadn't seen in weeks. "My dear boy, how are you?" David immediately got out of the taxi and stood blocking much of the pavement. Before Robert had much more of a chance to say or to do anything, David asked, "What are you doing now? Come and have a drink and let's catch up on the news."

Robert shook his head. "You wouldn't believe it but Trehearne is away in Batavia, Peter has had to go up to Penang and Gordon has now gone down with malaria so I have a Chinese senior clerk holding the fort and I've just been to an awful meeting in the Colonial Office."

David Masters laughed at Robert. "Never mind those fools up there. Come on, come and have a drink. You can spare a half an hour. Business is bloody awful with everybody leaving."

Robert stopped what he was saying and looked around. "Half an hour then and somewhere around here."

David paid off his taxi and grabbing Robert's elbow, he turned him around and they headed towards the Fullerton Building and one of the teashops Robert occasionally frequented. Taking a table in the window, now heavily taped up, Robert ordered tea for two from a harassed waitress, with some scones and jam, as he was starting to get hungry, and he knew once back in the bank that he would have little time for a break.

"I really can't stay long as my clerk and a junior from Treasury are covering for me and there are customers coming in all the time closing down their businesses before they do a bunk."

David just nodded before getting out a cigarette and after tapping it on the case, he lit it up. "First one today; I've been cutting down as I have a hacking cough. Susie has put me on a diet as well." David said it with a grimace, as he eyed the scones that had just turned up.

"How is Susie?" Robert already knew that David had brought the family down to the Island some time ago when the tension with the Japanese had made it likely the roof was going to come off, and they had taken up residence in a flat in Cathay House.

"She's fine, as are the girls. Leanne has just started her nursing course and Rebecca has got a temporary job with Asia Shipping. Alex is causing me problems though. Wants to join up but I've told him he's too young, he's only seventeen."

"Well, if he wants, he can help with the LDC. Tell him to come up to St. Paul's Drill Hall on Tanglin Road. We can do with some more help."

David shook his head as he looked around the almost empty room. "I'm getting them out tomorrow, Robert, my boy. On the *Sea Sprite* to Colombo, one of Godfrey Smythe's ships. Susie has family in Kandy and Leanne can continue her training there. Can't take a chance relying on those stupid buggars up at Sime Road. You know some of the Aussie lads have had just two weeks training and then they're being sent up north. Bloody ridiculous!" After a few more puffs of his cigarette, David added, "I've just been to the bank and got some money out for Susie and I've managed to get a wire through to Colombo transferring almost everything else."

Robert didn't ask how he had managed that. Instead saying, "Does that mean I'm paying for this spread?" Robert said it mumbling through a mouthful of scone and watching

David finally succumb and take the largest scone left and smother it with butter.

There was silence for perhaps a moment or so as both took further bites from their scones, and then David said, "When are you getting out?"

Robert looked up. The question wasn't whether he was considering getting out, but when. "I've been told I'm essential for the safety of the Island." He had grinned across at David Masters as he said it. "There's to be no swanning off for me, at least not in the near future. His Majesty had his chance. He never sent for me to hold back the hordes in Europe."

Between more mouthfuls, they both brought each other up to date with news. "Anyway, now that the Governor has decreed that all able-bodied men have to stay and do their bit you may even be conscripted into the Volunteers, David and required to hold them back at the causeway," Robert said mischievously at one point getting no reply from David, just a mock look of alarm. "In a way, I'm glad they decided to block my conscription as I couldn't see me festering away in some barracks doing stores or whatever. If I was front line material, I think they would have sent for me ages ago."

David nodded, as he picked up his cup. "I had the same problem in the last round. Said I had flat feet so when I was called up, I spent the time in some awful depot near Nottingham counting the shells coming in and then going out. Riveting! Eighteen months of that and I promised myself something better and when I saw the advert for an Assistant Manager on a rubber plantation, I was off. Mind you I had no idea where Selangor was, never mind the Malay States."

Robert grinned back. "Someone like you will always find

the right niche, David. You have the gift. I don't know what it is exactly but it oozes from you."

"I don't know about oozing. The butter in that scone has done that. Susie will know; she only has to look at me and I can't lie."

"So why aren't you going with them?"

"Same as Peter, young man. I don't think I should desert the ship just yet. Have you news of the Captain by the way?"

"The last I heard, the *Lancaster Lass* was rescuing passengers from some ship that was trying to get 'round the top of Sumatra and was torpedoed. That's about three days ago. Asia Shipping have said he's intending to drop them off in Penang but it may be he has to bring them down to Singapore, as it looks as though Penang is under attack and could be in Jap hands anytime in the near future."

Robert got up leaving some money on the table. "I think you should get out, David; go with Susie. If you need anything, let me know and I will look after it for you."

David who had also got up, wiping his moustache with his napkin, just shook his head. "I know you would, lad. I'm grateful but there's things I've got to do before I can make any journey. Too many pots to cover up, so to speak. I want there to be a future. The one good thing about this whole mess is that we might remove some of the deadwood that's on the Island."

"If you do stay, David, come up to the Drill Hall. We are desperately short of experienced men. We lost two the other day who went off the join the Volunteers and a couple are off to Australia with permits."

David walking out with him into the street nodded and said, "I'll sort out Susie and the gang and then come up."

Standing outside the building, Robert looked up at the sky. "Only one raid so far today."

"I'm told they're busy plastering Penang and Butterworth, so watch this space." David put his hand out for Robert to shake and as Robert reciprocated David said, "When this is all over, let's talk about you and me going into business together. I think we'd do well."

"What about Alex?"

"He's still young, great potential mind you but he will have to learn the dark arts whereas you seem to have been born with them."

Robert grinned at the compliment as he turned towards the bank. "Let's get this nightmare over with, David, and I'll seriously think about it. And thank you."

With that, they departed with Robert shouting over his shoulder, "My love to Susie and the family. Wish them a safe journey."

In the bank, he went immediately to his office seeing that there were only one or two customers around. For once, Lennox was not around and he was able to look at the list of notes on his desk and work out his priorities. Celia MacKenzie who had left with Ethel the night before, had scribbled a note wishing him good luck for the future. It was on the desk where he had left it and he reread it again pleased that Celia and Ethel had taken Peter's advice and got out, and even more pleased that there had been no news of the ship having been attacked or sunk. There was also a new message on his desk that a Miss Connor had been on more than once and would he ring her as soon as possible; it was a personal matter. For a moment, he was confused as to who it was and then realised it was Joyce as it was the High Commissioner's

Residence number.

He picked up the telephone and buzzed the telephonist. 'Get me the HC residence please' and as he waited to be put through, he rifled through the papers on his desk. He looked up to see Michael gesturing from the doorway just as he heard the HC telephonist ask who he wished to be put through to. "Miss Connor, please," and then put his hand over the phone. "Michael, I'll be through in five minutes. Is it a customer?" Michael just nodded, as Robert heard someone speak at the other end.

"Robert, you promised to ring me."

"I'm sorry, I really am, Joyce but I've not had a spare moment. I tell you what. Are you working tonight? You're not? Then why don't we meet for a drink or better still something to eat. It will have to be early as I'm up at the Drill Hall later. I'll get a taxi up to your place and collect you and we can go onto that seafood place near Beach Road. From memory, you like seafood. We should just have time for a decent meal." Joyce said she would love to go out for dinner and having agreed a time, he put the phone down and set off to sort out Michael's problem.

Robert later telephoned Gordon's home but his houseboy said he was very poorly and sleeping and could not be disturbed. Robert left a message for him to ring when he felt well enough and then he telephoned and asked Mr Wuh to give him the up-to-date details of the paper currency so that he could telephone the Colonial Office. Mrs Frobisher came to see him during the afternoon to say Mr Smythe had been on and told her that Mr Connaught had caught the boat back from Penang.

"And Mr Chen?"

“He didn’t mention Mr Chen or Mr Barwick.”

“Just check with Mr Smythe and let me know whether he knows if there is anyone with Mr Connaught.”

When Mr Lennox next passed the open door of his office, Robert shouted for him to come in. “Mr Connaught is on his way back, hopefully with the gold deposits from Penang. Can you liaise with South Asia Shipping about when their ship is likely to get in and take a security team down to bring the gold over here. I’ve no idea how much Mr Connaught and Mr Chen got out but we had better be prepared.” Lennox nodded for once not seeming to fuss about the situation, for which Robert was thankful.

Finally, Robert asked Mr Wuh and Mr Yin, the two senior Chinese clerks, to see him. “Sorry, gentlemen, but Mr Fraser is still ill and I don’t think Mr Connaught will be back until late tomorrow and there’s always the chance of more delays. Somehow, we’ve got to continue running the bank and its possible Mr Fraser will not be back to work for a couple more days. As you know, I have to leave on the midnight train to Kl, tomorrow night. I’m hoping that Mr Connaught is here in time for me to see him but it all depends on how active the Japanese are. Whatever happens tomorrow afternoon, we’re going to have to agree the keys handover before I leave.”

Mr Wuh nodded and smiled back, and Mr Yin stoic as always said nothing. “Mr Connaught will come, I am sure,” Mr Wuh said.

“I wish I was as confident as you are, Mr Wuh. I shan’t be happy until he is on the Island.”

Chapter 9

Peter smiled back at Robert who had been briefing him about what the Unit had been doing since he had gone to Penang. Peter was walking around with a glass in his hand, clearly very tired but exhilarated with what he had been through in the last five days. He was in shirt sleeves and wearing very dirty shorts. He had got back onto the Island in the early afternoon and had come straight to the bank.

"I will telephone Gordon later and tell him I am back and what Rodericks said about the currency. If I know Gordon, he will die of fright. Did you send a telegram to Walter?"

Robert shook his head. "The censor refused to send it as it may fall into the Jap's hands. Apparently, they are interfering with the cables from here to Batavia. In fact, he said the cable to Batavia might be cut permanently at any time. Then you will have to send messages by radio to some station in Java and from there by telegram. It may be easier to ask for Godfrey Smythe's help in sending a radio message or get one of his ship's captains to carry the message."

A very tired, grubby, Peter was now trying to roll a cigarette as they talked. "Everything organised for tonight?" Robert nodded and told Peter about the arrangements.

"Lennox on the ball?"

Again, Robert nodded. "I'm also taking up the amount Malaya Tin Mines asked for last year as there has been no indication from them of what they need. I'm taking Abilash with me and he will be my guard as I gather the commies are having a field day up there kidnapping people for ransom, and causing mayhem. Clive has had his telegrams censored and when we were talking on the telephone yesterday, the call was interrupted and he was told not to give out classified information over the line. Mrs Frobisher says that the special delivery letter has never arrived, so it must have been on the train that was bombed five days ago."

Peter took another drink of the scotch he had helped himself to from Walter's cabinet. Mrs Frobisher, still loyally coming into work every day, had given him the key to the cabinet without any protest. "You be careful up there and get whoever wants to come down here out as soon as possible. The Army is working flat out trying to fill holes in the dyke but it's only a matter of time before the Japs find a big enough hole to come through."

"Do you want me to bring the gold down?"

At this, Peter started to grin. "Walter can hardly complain. I brought some gold out on perhaps the last ship out of Penang. You may be bringing the last gold out of KL by train."

Robert started to ask what had happened up in Penang but Peter waved his cigarette at Robert and interrupted him. "Finish telling me what's been happening up at the Unit." Robert already knew that George Barwick had had to be left behind, as Peter couldn't get to the hospital to rescue him.

Robert made a face and refreshed his glass of scotch. "I'm not used to drinking in the afternoon in Walter's office."

"Can't say I've ever done it before, at least not in this office. I rather like drinking Walter's whisky though."

Robert enjoying Peter's return, briefed him on all that had been happening at the Drill Hall ending with, "We have lost seven LDC volunteers to the Volunteers or they have got permits to leave and have gone in the last two days to India. David Masters and his son, Alex, are now helping, as is Michael down the stairs. Apparently, Alex point blank refused to get on the boat with Susie and the girls. I managed to get one lorry to replace the vehicles the army took off us but we're reduced to using cars as well. There's now a coupon system for petrol which is bloody irritating and we are having to store petrol in bins."

"Sounds a bit dangerous."

"Bloody dangerous, Peter, but Simmons' on Victoria Street have been helpful and donated a half dozen metal bins with lids. If you think of anything better, then be my guest. We seem to spend more energy on getting equipment and getting organised than is necessary."

Peter was just nodding, deep in thought. "Who's on duty tonight?"

By this, Robert guessed he meant who was leading the Unit. "Captain Peters is coordinating the teams and I've asked Michael Davison and Pat Reynolds to be in charge of tonight's teams. Oh, and I've also started getting help from some of the Chinese who live around so that's helped to make up the numbers."

"Well done, Bob. It sounds like we're coping and getting the practice we need. Mark my words there's much worse to come."

"I need to disappear in a few minutes, Peter. I have to go up to the hospital to see Mrs Lin Yuen before I leave. But I want to know about Penang."

"What time do you leave for KL?"

"The train is scheduled to leave at eleven but Henry says it will not leave before midnight as there is bomb damage on the line just over the causeway."

Peter shook his head at the news. "I'm off home now to get out of these clothes. Been in them for nearly four days and they're only good for the bin." Robert had noticed when Peter had turned up that there were strange marks on Peter's clothing and over the short time in Walter's office, it became obvious it was blood but Robert held his counsel knowing that Peter would tell all in good time.

"Why don't you come up to Margaret Drive later, after you've been to the hospital. I'll see whether my house boy can rustle up a meal for say seven o'clock and I can tell you all about Penang then." Ominously, Peter added, "I suspect it's what you'll be going into."

Peter had got up as he was saying this and was off through the doorway with Robert following him out. Peter said something to Mrs Frobisher sitting in her little anteroom about how he was going to have a long sleep tonight whatever happened but that he would be at work tomorrow morning. Mrs Frobisher smiled back saying that Mr Fraser's houseboy had telephoned to say Mr Fraser was still ill but he felt well enough to speak to Peter. As Robert followed Peter downstairs, he heard him say something to Mr Wuh who had come over, when he saw Peter across the banking hall, to welcome him back. Robert continued down into the vaults to see Mr Lennox and Michael and three Chinese clerks coming out of the vaults.

"We have the gold Mr Connaught brought from Penang in the vaults but it hasn't been counted," Michael said, with dark sweat stains under the arms of his jacket.

Robert nodded and then gestured at Michael's jacket. "Michael, I'm only in charge for the rest of this afternoon and then I'm off on a holiday." Grinning, he continued, "As one of my last instructions, I have decided that managers and clerks may remove their jackets and work in shirt sleeves until otherwise instructed." Michael had started to grin as Robert said the part about removing jackets.

"Most irregular, Mr Draper," Mr Lennox said, standing next to Michael.

Robert smiled back at Mr Lennox. "Mr Lennox, please convey my decision to Mr Wuh and Mr Yin. Oh, and please tell them that Mr Connaught has told me that Mr Chen is well and safely back on the Island and will be back in work tomorrow. Mr Connaught sent him home for a rest and to be with his family."

Robert and Michael watched Mr Lennox go off to convey the decision to Mr Wuh and Mr Yin. "I bet he doesn't take his jacket off," Michael said in his lovely Australian drawl.

"All the more enjoyable to see him fry whilst we enjoy the cool breeze."

"I think that's a bit optimistic, Mr Draper," grinned a young man with dark rings under his eyes.

"You're on tonight, aren't you?" And seeing Michael nod, Robert said that he should go off home early.

Chapter 10

Robert stood by the bed looking down at Mrs Lin Yuen. She had been placed in what was normally a private ward designed to accommodate one or two beds but it now housed five. On the other side of Mrs Lin Yuen's bed, Chen Zhu Lee, her solicitor, stood looking very thoughtful. Robert had met him before and on one occasion told him about the jewels he was looking after for Mrs Lin Yuen. Chen Zhu Lee didn't seem too bothered about this merely saying that they were in safe hands.

When Robert had arrived, he had put the documents he had been using away in his small briefcase and after Robert had bent and kissed the little lady on the cheek, they had shook hands across the bed, respecting the need to merely murmur greetings. From outside the ward, Robert could hear the noise of a hospital in a state of chaotic organisation. The General Hospital had taken in a lot of extra patients in the two weeks since the Japs had starting their bombing raids. Even in corridors, there were beds with injured people and it brought it home to Robert just how many civilians were getting caught up in the fighting. Everywhere there was the smell of the very sick and dying.

Robert looking down at Mrs Lin Yuen could see a very sick woman. Each time he had come in, he could see that she looked more ill than on the previous visit and he knew that it was much more serious than Dr Robertson had first thought. She looked a tiny frail thing what with her moist, pale face and with no makeup on; her hair was now more grey than black and she was a mere shadow of the glamourous little lady he had sat with many times and talked to and played cards with, and listened with her to something from her collection of American band music.

'She must dye it,' he thought to himself as he smoothed some stray hair that was lying over her face with Chen Zhu Lee watching him. Mrs Lin Yuen was conscious but only just and Robert had to bend down almost touching her face to hear what she was saying. "Is Chunggy looking after you?"

"Mrs Lin Yuen, don't worry about that. We just want to see you get well."

Mrs Lin Yuen looked at him through almost closed eyes and whispered, "It's too late for that, Robert. The doctors can't do anything. Chen Zhu Lee came to see me, so I can get everything in order."

Robert stepped back shocked at the whispered news and then leant down again. "Mrs Lin Yuen, I'm looking after your jewel box. Should I give it to Mr Lee? I don't like hanging on to it."

Robert could see her tiny face smile a little and she said something he couldn't make out. Robert leant closer again. "I'm sorry, Mrs Lin Yuen, I didn't hear what you said."

"The jewels are no longer special. You have them, dear Robert. The house is yours as well, but look after Chunggy. He's a rogue but he means well. He's my older stepbrother although until a couple of years ago, I didn't even know he existed."

Robert stepped back even more shocked at what he had heard. Forgetting to lean forward, he said out loud, "You can't do that, Mrs Lin Yuen. You've only known me for two years." Mrs Lin Yuen started to whisper again, finding it more and more difficult to say her words this time and Robert again bent down close to her. "I have no family except Chunggy and he doesn't deserve anything, as he spent all my father left him. But he is a relation so please look after him. You, my dear boy, are the son I always wanted." The last words tailed off and Robert stood up not sure what to do. As he watched her, she seemed to go off to sleep again.

He looked across at Chen Zhu Lee who had not moved throughout the whispered conversation. "Mr Lee, what have the doctors said?"

"They have told me that Mrs Lin Yuen has kidney failure and there is little they can do."

Robert took a moment to digest what Chen Zhu Lee had said. "Is there anything we can do to make her more comfortable?"

Chen Zhu Lee shook his head and then bent down and picked up his briefcase. "I will stand out in the corridor whilst you sit with her for a while. But I must talk to you before you leave the hospital." Robert just nodded and turned back to Mrs Lin Yuen.

He stood for perhaps ten minutes or so looking down at the little lady. "*I know so little about you*," he murmured to himself. He felt her small hand creep into his as her breathing grew more regular. "I have to go up to Kuala Lumpur tonight, Mrs Lin Yuen. The bank is sending me. There is a great deal of trouble up there and I must help them," Robert said it out loud not expecting a response but immediately her hand pressed his and he saw her eyes flutter a little open.

He bent over her, as she started to speak. "Robert, you must do your duty." Robert raised his eyebrows and made a face, as she continued in a very strained voice, "Dear Robert, a man walks down many paths in his life. He comes to many crossroads and must try to choose the right way to go. You must decide, as all men must do. You have chosen a path that leads to a new life so do not take the turning that leads you back to the beginning, take the one that leads to your happiness. That should be your destiny." With that, she stopped whispering and gently pressed his hand again. This time, as Robert stood there, he felt her breathing deepen and he knew that she had gone off into a deep sleep.

For a few minutes, he sat just watching her and then he saw a doctor standing in the doorway reading a file. Making his way around the beds, he came up to the doctor. "Excuse me. Can you tell me what the situation is with Mrs Lin Yuen?" The doctor looked up from the documents he was reading.

"And you are?"

"I seem to be the son she never had," Robert said, suddenly finding it difficult to get his words out.

The doctor looked him up and down before saying, "She has kidney failure and is in and out of a coma more and more. Her body is in retreat and the poor lady is not likely to be with us for more than a few days. I'm sorry but she's beyond any help we can give."

Robert just nodded dumbly and went back to the bed but Mrs Lin Yuen was now in a deep sleep although he could hear her murmuring something in Chinese. He stood for a while looking at her and then realising that she was not likely to wake, Robert bent and kissed her pale cheek before he turned away and made his way out of the ward. In the corridor, Chen Zhu Lee was standing between two beds conversing quietly with one of the patients and seeing Robert, he excused himself and came over.

"You must come and see me soon, Mr Draper, as Mrs Lin Yuen has asked me to prepare many documents which involve you."

"I'm sorry, Mr Lee, but I'm off to KL. The bank is in trouble and I'm being sent up to help."

Chen Zhu Lee nodded at what Robert said and put his hand out and Robert shook it as Chen Zhu Lee said, "There is much danger up there, Mr Draper. Go with my good wishes and when you return come and see me." He nodded towards the ward and then looked at Robert momentarily. "Does she know?"

"Yes, I told her. I have no choice, Mr Lee. I must go."

"That is understood. You must do your duty. I will look after her and her brother will come in to see her each day. She will be much missed on the Island."

Robert found himself unable to say anything and finally, it was Chen Zhu Lee who patted him on the arm, "I must go back to work." Robert watched him thread his way down the corridor where everywhere there was beds, patients being helped to walk, and where in his brief visit this afternoon, he had seen the orderlies cover over more than one patient and then carry them out.

Sighing, Robert turned back away from where Chen Zhu Lee had gone. He could not avoid it; he had another task to perform. He was miles away still in deep thought about the momentous events of a few minutes ago and walking down past Ward Eleven when he was stopped by Jenny's roommate, Marion, coming into the corridor. "Bob, is it Jenny you're looking for?"

Robert stopped in his tracks and seeing Marion, he just nodded still lost in thought with what had just been a life changing few moments. "She's in the canteen having a quick break." Waving down to her left, she added, "Go down to the bottom, turn left and it's at the far end." With that, she was off down the corridor the way Robert had just come.

In the canteen, Robert immediately saw Jenny in the middle of a crowd of nurses all of them just sitting, not really talking, drinking their tea and far too tired to converse much. Jenny saw him approaching and got up from her chair and came over to give him a hug. Seeing his face, she didn't ask anything, as she knew he had been visiting Mrs Lin Yuen most days, and it was a moment before Robert said, "Still no news, I'm afraid. I have to go to KL tonight so maybe I can find out something there."

Jenny nodded and was about to say something when there was the sound of a bell and the scraping of chairs as dozens of nurses got up to go back to their wards. "I'm sorry, Robert, but we are stretched to breaking point and there's another hospital train due in an hour or so." She gave him another hug and this time Robert could see the black rings around her eyes.

"Don't give up hope yet, Jenny. Anything's possible."

She just nodded and with a sigh said, "I must go. You be careful up there." With that, she turned and was off, her blue uniform fading into the crowd of nurses all now vying to get to their wards. Robert turned back on himself and eventually finding an exit, he came out onto a grass verge with people sitting smoking and enjoying the relative cool of the early evening. Slowly, he made his way down onto the path and around the hospital buildings until he recognised the main road. A rickshaw was dropping off a passenger and Robert took it up to Tanglin still very deep in thought.

Before he had left to go to the hospital that day, he had signed off the arrangements for the taking up of the payroll which was much larger than normal because by tradition the workers in the mines and on the estates were paid a bonus at Christmas which was only a few days off. Robert knew that Lennox had had great difficulty in getting authority for the shipment to be sent up to KL. The military did not want another problem if the communists decided it was a prize too good to miss.

Lennox had come to see him in the afternoon just as he was leaving to go to the General Hospital and asked, "Have you handled a gun before." Robert thought he was joking at first and then Lennox produced a revolver in a holster. "It's special times and we have permission to arm you and Abilash."

"You can't be serious. I would be a danger to myself." Robert watched Lennox withdraw the revolver from the holster, "My God, it looks enormous."

"Nevertheless, you should take it. Anything can happen. The commies are just as likely to attack the train and there have been reports of 5th columnists."

Robert tried the belt on and picked the gun up; Lennox showed him how to load it and how to take the safety catch off.

"It's for your own safety, Mr Draper. We have no police escort upcountry, only from here to the station. Meadows will meet you at KL so it's more likely to be the train journey that is risky. Superintendent Davies will also do his best to have officers at KL station to assist you so there should be no funny business."

Chapter 11

Hundreds of troops marched through the station entrance at the start of their journey to fight the Japanese now well over the border and fighting ever nearer to Penang. The crunching of boots made an eerie sound in the darkness surrounding the station.

Robert stood to one side of the entrance with two policemen and Abilash; Robert wearing his revolver awkwardly around his waist, and the other men with shouldered rifles standing a few yards away close to the six boxes of currency. Lennox was off inside the station remonstrating that the porters were taking too long to provide trolleys. The station was ringed with sandbags and there was little of the usual noise you would expect from a busy rail station, rather there was just the continuous sound of men marching towards the platforms in their heavy boots with only the occasional sound of voices echoing from other parts of the entrance hall. It was pitch dark outside and the lighting in the station was minimal; for some reason, there had been no air attacks for twenty-four hours making everybody wonder what the Japanese were planning next.

Finally, Lennox turned up with two porters and with Abilash's help, they placed the boxes on the trolleys and with

Lennox leading the way, they went through ticket inspection with a cursory nod from the railway staff. Robert saw Henry Preston, on duty as Deputy Station Master, and he went over and briefly spoke to him before following the small entourage. On the train, Lennox quickly had everything arranged with the boxes placed in one of the open luggage sections and Abilash stationed at the other side of the nearest door. "I suggest you sit here, Mr Draper, so you can see everything; anybody coming down the carriage from that door will be clearly in view."

Nodding, Robert took his seat and Lennox left after a few words with Abilash. The heat in the carriage was oppressive almost to the point of being unbearable and as soon as the train set off, Robert opened one of the windows. The fans overhead were not working and before they had even reached the causeway, the emergency lights had either gone out or were invisible.

"So much for seeing anybody coming towards me," Robert murmured to himself.

It seemed that the numbers of passengers needing to travel north had greatly diminished since the commencement of fighting and he only saw a dozen or so European or Eurasian faces at the far end of the carriage before the lights went out. It was as they were crossing the causeway that the air raid alarms went off and although Robert didn't hear them at first, he saw very quickly the flashes of ack-ack guns and a moment later, over towards the Naval Base, a huge ball of fire erupted into the night sky which had the other passengers all flocking to see it from the right-hand side of the carriage.

"My God, that looks as though an ammo. dump has gone up," he heard someone exclaim, as the train completed its journey over the causeway and entered the jungle in Johore and all the action happening in Singapore was lost to the darkness.

Throughout the night, the train constantly stopped and Robert could see men repairing the tracks, working by flare lights. Time and again the train came to a standstill whilst repairs were completed or it went into a siding to let a train going south pass them. As the dawn came up, it was clear that the train would not get to KL in the next hour or so.

The conductor came in to warn everybody that they were now at risk of being strafed or even bombed and everybody spent their time watching what little sky they could see as the train moved slowly through the narrow cutting in the jungle and then worrying about exposure when they crossed small plains. Finally, around late morning, having stopped frequently for unknown reasons, Robert saw that they were entering the outskirts of KL. Opening the door and speaking to Abilash, he found him smoking a cigarette and looking at a photograph.

"Is that your family, Abilash?" asked Robert and Abilash handed over the black and white photograph of a young woman and three children all in their traditional dress.

"What is to happen to them if I die, Sahib?"

"I wish I knew Abilash. Everything's falling apart around us. It's like a nightmare and there's no indication that things will get better."

Abilash just took another suck of his cigarette and said nothing, watching the suburbs of KL, as they flashed by the window.

Meadows was waiting for them on the station platform with two security guards and two Malay policemen, all with rifles. Robert got off the train and stretched his legs and left it to Meadows to organise the removal of the boxes but even as they placed the boxes on two trolleys, the air raid alarms started up. Meadows swore and then turned to the porters. "Right, let's get out of here. Come on, everybody, follow me. We're going through the tradesman's entrance," and with that, he set off at a pace to the end of the platform and around the back of the station to where a lorry was already waiting in a small compound.

"Quick, get it on the back," he was shouting, as they could hear bombs going off only a hundred yards or so away. The noise was deafening and at one point, a Japanese fighter came over almost at roof height firing away; fortunately, the lorry was parked against a wall out of sight of any planes.

Robert waved Meadows to get in the front and with Abilash, he got up on the back, with the security staff and police, and the lorry moved off turning into the main road which was mayhem with burning cars and what looked like quite a few casualties. They could hear the planes still overhead and then the dreaded whistle of more bombs as the lorry weaved its way through the carnage, eventually moving away down the road with more bombs coming down somewhere over towards the other side of the tracks.

"They're trying to hit the train, Sahib," observed Abilash as they looked out from the back of the lorry at the flames and smoke rising around three or four hundred yards away.

At the bank, Meadows organised the unloading of the cash boxes with the bombing still going on towards the station. Robert ran into the bank and throwing down his travel case he turned to assist with the bullion boxes. Meadows came in escorting a security guard and Abilash who were carrying a box between them. He shouted, "It's all organised. Go down to the vaults."

Robert followed the first bullion box through the bank and down the stairs with two more security men close behind him with a second box. The bank other than for a few staff seemed empty.

"You check them in, Mr Draper, whilst we get the rest of the boxes. I need to get the lorry under cover as well," Meadows shouted from behind the men carrying in the second bullion box. With that, Meadows was off with Abilash and the other security man just as Clive emerged from the vaults. Robert wasn't really listening to Meadows as he took in the state of Clive.

They just shook hands saying nothing at first, then Robert asked, "Are you okay?"

Clive shook his head; he was pale and very tired. He wandered off to the table in the corridor and sat down on the chair beside it with his back to the wall. "It's been hell, Robert. Every day for the past ten days we've been bombed and strafed. All times of the day. Time and time again. I thought I knew about bombing from being in Manchester last year but it was nothing compared to this."

Robert didn't say anything, he just looked at the state of Clive before he said, "Have you seen anything of Mark?" Robert asked this as the security men between them brought in the last of the boxes. Meadows hadn't reappeared so presumably, he was making sure the lorry was parked out of sight.

"He's never come back since he took Mary and the little one down to the Island," was all Clive said, as he stood up and motioned Robert to follow him into the vaults. Robert walked in and then stopped, standing in the entrance. He couldn't believe what he was seeing. The vault was piled high with boxes and canvas bags.

He turned to Clive. "What the hell is going on?"

Clive raised his arms and shook his head. "This arrived about a week ago."

"What happened then?" Robert said, as he went over to look more closely. Some of the boxes had *China Bank* stencilled on them. For a second time he said, "What the hell is going on?"

"Superintendent Davies and Mr Chin Yu from the China Bank brought it over in police lorries. The China Bank has been bombed and Barclay's vaults are not big enough and the Hong Kong vaults are full to brimming apparently, as they have all their Penang cash as well."

"There's must be millions here, Clive. We haven't accepted responsibility, have we?" Clive shook his head. Davies said that he would see if he can arrange for it to be transported but the Army is being difficult. Apparently, Mr Chin Yu got the money out of Penang and Thailand and down to here only for the China Bank premises to be bombed. When they brought it over, I told them I couldn't accept responsibility for it. Mark had left by then for the Island so I had to make a decision.

"We guessed you had a mound of cash in the vaults but not this amount. Does nobody know?" said Robert incredulously.

They had turned as Meadows came in with forms, "You need to sign these off, sir, if you think all the boxes are here and intact."

Clive said, "I tried sending a special courier note and that never reached Fullerton Square by all accounts. I tried sending telegrams but they were censored. I tried telling Gordon and Peter over the phone just how much was here but the censors cut the line. I tried telling you but I was stopped."

Robert walked over to where the boxes had been stacked in the corridor and checked the numbers and seals against the form before he signed. "You could have got Superintendent Davies to get a message through."

Clive shook his head. "Davies has got a message through that we have a problem with a lot of gold. He said he told Gordon there was lots but not the amount. I've tried to get Davies, and the military, to move it and each time they get interested, something comes along to take precedence. Poor Davies is down to about half his normal force and having to cope with the commies, 5th columnists, deserters and now looters."

Robert could see that Clive was at the end of his tether and he put his hand on Clive's shoulder. "Easy, Clive. Three heads are better than two," he said this, as he looked at Mr Meadows. "We live in strange times, Mr Meadows. Who would ever have thought that we would have most of the gold of the Malay States in our vaults?"

"The quicker it's out the better, sir. If the Japs know that the gold has been collected in one place, they're liable to make a big push."

Robert thought he was joking at first and then looking at Meadows, he realised that he was serious. "The 5th columnists will know by now," was all Meadows added as he took the signed form off Robert. "Mrs Clemence has laid on a breakfast for us in Mr Forrester's office, sir." He turned and gave instructions to the security staff that the bank was to be kept closed and that no one on pain of death was to go down the stairs towards the vaults.

"What about these boxes, Mr Meadows?" Robert asked looking at the payroll.

"They'll have to stay out here, sir. We couldn't close the vault doors if they are placed in there," Meadows said looking across at the vaults. "Should be safe enough, as they are sealed boxes and we have armed guards in the bank as well as outside."

Robert nodded, looking again at the vaults as Meadows went over and supervised the closure of the vault doors. Going back upstairs to the banking hall, Robert could see a few cashiers working behind the grills and two others working in the hall at a temporary desk. The doors to the bank were closed and there were no customers. "Where are all the staff, Clive?"

"Some can't get to work because of the bombing and I've taken it on myself to give some of them time off to help the local LDC. They're better employed helping with the civil defence. Levowski has gone, we know not where but one of the clerks thinks he's got involved with the commies so it's just as well he's not here and sees what's downstairs."

"He'll know by now anyway," growled Meadows who seemed to have grown in stature with the world collapsing around everyone.

"Come on, let's go get something to eat and work out what to do," Robert said, turning towards the stairs up to the next level. Seeing Abilash standing there, he spoke to him, "You too, Abilash. You need a breakfast." Meadows looked at Robert and started to say something but saw that Robert meant it. "No arguments. We all need to be working together."

Upstairs, Mrs Clemence seemed pleased to see Robert and in no time had a pot of tea made and the kettle on for a second brew. Robert saw that she was using a small oil stove. Turning to Clive, Robert asked, "Is there no electricity?"

"Off and on, depends on how quickly the engineers can get repairs done. Just get it sorted and then the bombers come over and target the electricity station again. This time, we've been warned that it may be off indefinitely."

Robert just pursed his lips as Mrs Clemence brought over more sandwiches and refilled cups. Robert turned to Abilash. "When you've finished your breakfast, Abilash, you get off and get some sleep. Leave your rifle here. I presume you're staying at the hostel?"

Abilash answered, "Yes, Sahib."

Robert then continued, "I suspect, Mr Meadows, will need you on duty later as part of the security detail."

When Abilash left a little later, Robert, Clive and Meadows had a short meeting to discuss the security arrangements and then Meadows went off to speak to Superintendent Davies, at Robert's insistence, about the need for more police as there was insufficient security for the bank. "Right, Clive. I need to know the full story about Mark."

Clive waited until Mrs Clemence had refilled their cups for a third time. "You don't mind if Mrs Clemence stays, do you? She's probably knows bits I don't."

"Clive, you're in charge, not me."

Clive shook his head. "Uh, uh. You're the boss as far as I'm concerned. I can manage a bank day to day but this is way beyond me."

Robert merely made a face at what Clive said and then waved Mrs Clemence to sit down. "Where is Miss Carson? I haven't seen her."

Mrs Clemence started to cry and it was Clive who said, "She was at church the Sunday before last when the bombers first came over and there was a direct hit. Forty-seven killed and God knows how many injured. The ambulance staff and the LDC couldn't get to them because they were being strafed all the time. It was a shambles by all accounts with the church and surrounding buildings on fire. I was stuck in the basement of the Majestic with bombs all around." Mrs Clemence got up as he was saying this, and went out of the room. Clive watching her said, "She's taken it badly."

"Mark wants bollocking. He should be here to sort this mess out."

Without replying to what Robert had just said, Clive carried on, "Mark never wanted the job, you know that don't you?" Robert nodded. "He asked Trehearne if he could be transferred to Singapore in September and was given a right rollicking by all accounts."

Robert nodded again. "I know about that."

"I had dinner with him a few days later and he said that if Trehearne didn't relent he was off. Lucy was supposed to go to school in Australia but she was ill and Mary took her to hospital on the Island and they were still there when the Japs attacked. He got them off on the *Roberta*. Mark had another dust up with Trehearne just before it left; Mark was only stopped from leaving with Mary and Melanie because he didn't have a permit." Clive stopped and picked up a sandwich.

Robert shaking his head at what he had just heard, pursed his lips before he said, "I know all this," looking up as Mrs Clemence came back into the room having wiped her eyes.

Mrs Clemence interrupted Clive's flow, "There's no funeral for them just a service this Sunday."

Robert had got up, as she was telling them about the service and went across and put his hand on Mrs Clemence's arm. "You okay? There's nothing you could do. You do understand that?"

A red-eyed Mrs Clemence looked at Robert. "I'm fine, thank you, Mr Draper. I'm just pleased you're here to help Mr Sewell."

Clive had been watching them talk and then continued with what he had been saying, "I didn't see him when he returned. By all accounts, he left his keys with one of the security staff and told him he had joined the Volunteers. He probably joined the Volunteers after the Chamber meeting on 14 December; there was some sort of recruitment at the meeting. He left me a note saying he was sorry but he and Mary had been miserable up here and if he couldn't join up, then he may as well be in the Volunteers. He said he didn't care about the bank anymore. I haven't seen hide nor hair of him since the day before Davies turned up with the gold and according to Stuart, he's been sent with some Volunteers to some defence line up near Ipoh." Robert sat quietly for a moment taking it in before he said that he hadn't known that part of the story.

The heat in the office was growing all this time and finally Robert stood up and opened the door into Mrs Clemence's office. "God, this is a shambles, even worse than the last time." Turning to Mrs Clemence, he asked if the lines to the Island were still working. Mrs Clemence nodded and said they were half an hour ago, although they had to get an appointment with the post office telephonist; she got up as she was saying it.

"No, don't go yet. Let's first agree a plan before I ring Gordon or Peter although what I'm supposed to say about what we have in the vaults, God alone knows. Oh, and another thing." Robert leant across and fingered the lapel of Clive's dirty jacket. "We get rid of these stupid outfits, Clive."

Clive smiled back. "I'm all for that."

Over the next couple of days, Robert got nowhere in planning the removal of the gold and anyway a priority was to get rid of the payroll money to the various plantations in the area and the tin mines although Clive quickly dispelled this latter intention. "The mines, as far as I know, are in no man's land and I haven't heard a thing from Martin Kennedy or Fred Samuels. If we were to provide wages for Christmas, we would have heard by now."

What became very obvious to Robert was that the Japanese plan was very simple. Disrupt the movement of troops moving up to Ipoh and everything would back up for nearly a hundred miles. KL was teeming with troops trying to go north and the town seemed to be one long traffic jam. Military police check points seemed to be on all the main roads and even the Volunteers were manning one on Foch Avenue although there was no sign of Mark up there when Robert went out with Abilash to get a feel for the problems.

The station had been badly damaged and no trains had come through since Robert's train had managed to get into KL, and the lorry loads of injured troops coming from the battle further up towards Penang now had the further hazard of being part of a continuous convoy going south, trying to make their way to some junction thirty or more miles towards Gemas where they could be transferred onto a train. They made easy targets for the Japanese fighters who seemed to have a free rein and no interference from the RAF. Even when the injured had been transferred to a train, it sounded just as hazardous as the trains had to hide during the day from the Japanese planes and by all accounts, there were not a lot of sidings for them to hide in.

When Robert had finally spoken by telephone with Superintendent Davies to seek a meeting, he quickly learned that Davies had been keen to organise such a meeting for days. Judging by the weariness in Davies' voice, it sounded like the Superintendent was having to cope with many problems.

"I am trying to organise a meeting with the other bank managers but it's probably a couple of days off as Morrissey has gone to Port Dickson with staff and their families to try and get them down to Singapore. I think he will be very lucky to get them out as I am told there are thousands stranded at the dockside. Morrissey expressly said he wants to be present at any meeting, so it maybe a few days yet before we can meet. I'm glad you have arrived as Mr Sewell said he had no authority to discuss the issues and I know that Forrester is now somewhere up the Ipoh road with the Volunteers. Morrissey is also having difficulty as his Asia Director for some God forsaken reason thinks it's not as bad up here as we make out. I'm sorry I know you need more security but I don't have one spare man."

Robert remained quiet whilst the Superintendent got things off his chest and then resignedly said, "I'll fit in with your plans. I'm going to stay at the Majestic as it's nearer…"

"You'll be lucky. Half of Malaya is staying there already. If a bomb drops on it, then most of the Europeans left in north Malaya are gone. I suggest you find an alternative bed and for

God's sake make sure you have a guard with you at all times. The commies are working from China Town, and that's only down the road from you, and I haven't the resources to deal with them effectively."

With that, the Superintendent ended the call leaving Robert deciding that perhaps sleep in the bank was the only alternative although quite where with many others already sleeping there, was the problem. It was Mrs Clemence who offered a solution. "There's no point in considering staying up at the bank's residence. Mr Singh took two hours to drive down the other day and some of the checkpoints are turning people back because it's just too dangerous what with the communists and 5th columnists. If you're happy with the arrangement, you can use our spare room and I'm sure Jim won't mind. We're only just down the road. You can even walk to it if you have to."

As she was saying this Robert could hear more bombing and then without warning a plane screamed over the bank firing down the road with the windows in the bank rattling for minutes afterwards. He picked himself up from the floor where he had thrown himself and tried to dust himself down. Mrs Clemence emerged from behind the filing cabinet that seemed to be her bolthole.

"It can't go on much longer, Mr Draper. We're at breaking point," cried Mrs Clemence from where she was still partly hiding behind a filing cabinet. Robert went over and held her close, as she sobbed. "Jim says that they have to stop the Japs at Ipoh or we've had it." After a momentary gulp of air, she said, "Everything we have is here."

Robert ushered Mrs Clemence over to a chair. "Mrs Clemence, why haven't you gone already? There can't be many Brits left, surely?"

Mrs Clemence sat drying her eyes on a hankie, she had produced from somewhere. "Jim's the Manager of the Ferguson agency and the workshops are needed by the Army, so he feels honour bound to help them and I'm not going without him."

The best thing to do was change the subject so Robert asked whether there was any running water.

Mrs Clemence continued wiping her face with a handkerchief, and then she shook her head, "None since last Saturday."

"A pity. I could do with a wash and shave."

"I'll boil some water for you. Mr Ram Singh brought in some buckets this morning from the water lorry," was all she said, as she walked off with the sound of ack-ack guns still to be heard in the distance. Not for the first time, Robert noticed that there seemed a haze of dust everywhere. For the first time, he took in that some of the panes of glass in the office window were missing.

When Robert went down into the banking hall a little later, it was to see three or four Chinese clerks getting on with their work and Stuart the young Australian clerk talking through some problem with them. Going over, he shook hands with the young man who was dressed in a short-sleeved shirt and shorts and looking exhausted. "What's happening, Stuart?"

"I've been on duty with the LDC all night sorting out the mess at the hospital, Mr Draper. The bastards bombed it. Then they did the station, again."

Robert suddenly noticed that Stuart had a revolver fastened at his hip. It was something straight out of some cowboy film. He pointed at it. "How long have you had this?"

"The police issued them last week after we were attacked as we were trying to put out fires on Petarling Street."

"You ever fired one before?"

"Well, no, but I've fired a shotgun on my uncle's farm. Don't worry, if I get one of those bastards in my sights, I won't miss."

Robert grinned back at a clearly very tired clerk. "They gave me one to come up here. They must be mad. I couldn't hit a barn door so if you need help, you better not depend on me."

Stuart smiled and made a bit of a face. "Just make sure you carry it around with you, Mr Draper. We've had one or two run ins with communists and the police are unable to help. They're just stretched to the limit."

"Tell me about it, Stuart. I'm trying to get help in moving the gold and it looks bloody impossible."

Stuart looked around at the mess in the banking hall. "What can we do, Mr Draper?"

"I wish I knew, Stuart. Superintendent Davies is arranging a meeting but I don't hold out much hope if they're still talking about it." Changing the subject, Robert asked how long Stuart was in for.

"I'm sleeping in your old office, Mr Draper. Clive and I can't get to our digs; it's too dangerous. I want to check a few things over with Mr Chan over there and then I'll go and get a few hours' sleep if that's possible. I'm still on standby, if there's more bombing. Trouble is that most of the Brits and Aussies have gone and those that remain are starting to get fidgety, so we you can't rely on them to do a shift. We started with around three units of twenty to thirty men and we're down to one unit of about twenty and some of them only come in when they feel like it."

Stuart continued in full flow, "Over at the Hong Kong Bank, they haven't got anybody volunteering despite them having been bombed, they're just too scared. All we have left is a crowd of men who're too old to join the Volunteers and some clerks from Barclays, and me, and some of our Chinese clerks. Mr Meadows wanted to help us but Clive said that we were too short handed."

At this, Robert nodded. "I think he's right. We need Meadows to manage the security or we may as well give handouts. Clive and I will have to take our turn as security guards." With that, Robert moved off to talk to the cashiers working on their ledgers. At the far end of the banking hall, Clive was dealing with a customer who had been let into the bank seemingly by arrangement, with one of the security men shouldering his rifle whilst he closed and locked the doors.

Robert spoke to the clerks until Clive had finished with the customer and then walked over to him as the security let out the customer. "I'll take a couple of hours sleep and then start the payroll with some of the clerks. We can use Mark's office."

Clive nodded at that before saying, "Oh, if you want something to eat, we have an arrangement with the Chinese restaurant two doors down. Shu Yen over there has the menu to pick from. So far, there is no shortage of bucket water but I suggest you drink the beer. It's safer. Mind you, it's warm." Clive made a face and then shrugged his shoulders. "To think I could be in Manchester enjoying Christmas, rationing or no rationing."

"Christmas. God I'd forgotten about it." Robert stopped

in his stride. “It’s the day after tomorrow? No, the day after that. God, I don’t believe it.”

Clive smiled back. “I thought I was muddled but you sound worse. It’s only the 22nd today, so you’ve time to get me a present.”

Robert went off smiling, heading for Mark’s office where there was a settee he could stretch out on. Mrs Clemence was coming down the stairs, as he ascended. “If you’re going out be careful, Mrs Clemence.”

“I have to see our houseboy about the spare room and we need something to eat. The planes shouldn’t come back until late afternoon just before the light goes so it’s usually safe. Mrs Dray has managed to get in and will look after the telephones.” Robert just nodded suddenly very weary.

Chapter 12

Robert arrived at the temporary police station on Campbell Road, the main police station having suffered direct hits on several occasions and then been abandoned. Robert, with Abilash acting as his guard, had borrowed bicycles and had cycled the mile or so to the new headquarters of Superintendent Davies.

Going through the streets, he saw again the damage that KL was suffering with burnt out buildings and vehicles. Repair men were trying to get telegraph poles upright, with holes in the road being filled in by what looked like small gangs of coolies working under armed guard. On one occasion, he saw a group of soldiers stealing food from one of the few stalls selling foodstuffs; both he and Abilash moved off quickly as it looked as though it was getting out of hand with police just arriving.

At the far end of Market Street, the buildings were still on fire and the LDC with a fire tender was working hard at it trying to contain the spread of the fire and move people out of tenements that looked as though they were inevitably going to be consumed. Robert stopped for a moment watching a scene he had become familiar with in Singapore and try as he might he couldn't see Stuart whom he knew was on duty. Hopefully, he was okay as Robert already knew from Stuart that there had been two fatalities and quite a few injuries in the two weeks that the LDC had been working with the fire brigade trying to cope with the constant bombing and the consequent fires.

At the checkpoint at the bottom of Campbell Road, he was told that only half the labour force needed to repair the roads had turned up, even with the incentive of double pay; he was told forcefully by the military police guard to be careful, as there were still craters on the road. Prudently, realising that in all the smoke and dust he might not see the holes, Robert walked the last few hundred yards.

When he was ushered into the Superintendent's office, it was to discover it was in fact a holding cell for prisoners, temporarily converted into an office with a radio communications unit in the next room making a great deal of noise with reports coming in by the minute.

Superintendent Davies was already there with a group of people; a couple of whom Robert recognised.

"Merry Christmas, Ken. Merry Christmas, Frank. A bit different kind of Christmas Day."

Frank Foley shook Robert's hand and then waved him over to a large pot of tea. "Grab a cup. It's free but there's no milk!" Ken had his mouth full of currant bun with a plate of cake in one hand. He mumbled something which sounded like 'Merry Christmas'.

Robert had met Frank during his previous extended stint in KL. They had exchanged horror stories about Trehearne as Frank had worked in KL as Deputy under Fred Gilpin, for more than three years, and come into contact with Trehearne all too often. Robert guessed that Frank was around forty years old, and married, although by all accounts fond of the ladies whereas Ken Seymour, was in his late thirties and like Gordon a keen sailor and fisherman. Robert had come across him perhaps half a dozen times at bank functions on the Island and occasionally at the tennis club. Robert had found him to be a little serious; yet another who had not married although Robert had seen him with a girl a couple of times at the tennis club.

As he grabbed a cup of tea and a piece of cake, he heard the Superintendent having a serious debate with a Chinese man, probably around his early sixties, who was arguing about priority and standing beside them was Morrissey, the Barclay's Bank Regional Manager, who he knew slightly and someone else Robert didn't know. Davies seeing that Robert had arrived used it as an excuse to break off the argument and call the meeting to order.

Nodding at Robert he said, "We haven't got much time gentlemen. I am on roster and we can expect problems to start in the next hour or so. We have had six incidents of 5th columnists, in the last couple of days, attacking and attempting to blow up roads in the vicinity and I am stretched to the limit in manpower."

Nobody said anything and the Superintendent continued. "Right, I presume we all know the basics. Hong Kong and Barclays have substantial amounts of bullion and paper currency and Union have their bullion as well as that of the China Bank. I can tell you now that there are no trains and none for at least the next three days. And that's only if the Japs play ball and that's not likely. The line south of KL has been severely damaged in the bombing of the last four days and in my opinion, the line will not be repaired in the near future. We have no air cover to speak of so any repairs have to be done at night for all to see in the daylight."

"Pointless," Davies said making a wry smile as they arranged themselves around the small room. "General Heath is being difficult and will not release any lorries or provide guards. He says he's stretched to the limit what with bringing up more troops and supplies and getting the injured out. Most of them are now having to go by lorry down as far as Gemas; that's more than a hundred miles on roads that are blocked with traffic. I'm told that he has put in a requisition for a hundred or more lorries. Even if they could be supplied, it's weeks away by which time the Japanese will be having tea at the Majestic."

A stunned silence followed, as they took in what the Superintendent had just told them. It was Morrissey who came in with, "Where exactly are the Japs?"

Davies leaned over to a map on the wall near to Robert picking up a ruler from his desk as a pointer. "As at the briefing this morning, they are here, here and here. The nearest Japs are no more than sixty miles away. There are however already significant pockets of Japanese between our lines and here. Since the Penang area fell on the 17th," he said with some feeling, "we have been back peddling."

"We held them at Ipoh for a while but I don't think that was intended to be a permanent defence." Superintendent Davies used the ruler to show where the lines had been. "We have now established a new defence line along the Slim River and that is our best bet. General Heath has put in substantial numbers of troops." Again, the Superintendent used the ruler to outline where the new defence line had been established.

Robert could see immediately that the Slim River was

much closer to KL.

Davies moved to the easterly part of the large map. "Over here, towards the East, we know that they are in the process of cutting the Kuantan to KL rail link that travels through Khota Lipis, so they have a pincer move putting the easterly troops on the Slim River front at serious risk if they manage to get sufficient numbers beyond the Slim River. As you probably know, the road from Kuantan is merely a dirt track used mainly for logging and at this time of year it's not easy to get down but that doesn't seem to be stopping the Japs. It's clear they have done their homework and are working their way down it with the intention of cutting off the 11th Division. If they succeed in getting far enough across, then the Slim River defence will become untenable. We have sent reinforcements up to Khota Lipis but the fear is that the Japs have already infiltrated beyond that point."

Davies gave everybody a moment to take in the detail and then he continued. "The latest information I have from the East Coast is from the Gordons who are just west of Kuantan and they have told me that they have had no contact with the Japs for two days but they have intelligence that a significant Jap force is coming down the coast road."

Davies turned back to the group. "Now what do we do with your money, gentlemen?"

"Well, what I can tell you is that any spare lorries, and there are precious few, are starting to shift patients from the hospitals. Even then, we are severely short. Then there's the problem of getting the vehicles back to here to take more injured down south. Frankly, it's a nightmare. Two days at least for the round trip; at least that is our expectation of the convoy that set off this evening. Therefore, we are seriously short of motorised vehicles. You will no doubt have seen that many of the troops are marching up to Ipoh."

There was a murmur of agreement with all of them looking at the map closely.

"Where have the spare lorries come from?" questioned Ken.

"By lorries I mean fruit and veg vans, trucks used for building work, cars, anything we can commandeer, even a funeral hearse. Anything that is capable of carrying people. Oh, and I also have one hundred and forty plus European women and children in temporary accommodation who are awaiting evacuation, and from messages earlier this evening, perhaps another twenty or thirty making the hazardous journey down from the plantations. There's also a sizeable Eurasian contingent that I haven't even started to work out how to move. The good news is that my Inspector negotiated a deal with the commies in China Town this afternoon; shall we call it a temporary armistice. So at least we can get the rescue vehicles through China Town and down to Gemas without them attacking us."

Robert saw the flaw immediately, "Surely, the deal will never hold if they know a bullion convoy is coming through." Davies was nodding at this as he got up and shouted in Malay, through the doorway, requesting more tea, to someone in the next room.

"From what you tell me, the Hong Kong bullion is fairly easy to transport, so we may be able to move it first in small quantities on some of the lorries going south." This information was allowed to sink in before Davies added, "Clearly, you can't telegraph what we're doing by putting guards on each of the lorries. I suggest you, Mr Seymour, cadge a lift and as you're not normally up here any commies around are unlikely to recognise you. It's a chance you have to take."

"You can't be serious Superintendent. There are patients on the lorries. It's bad enough that they may be strafed by Zero's but surely we can't put them at risk of the commies attacking the lorries to get the bullion," Ken said. There was murmurs of agreement.

"I can't think of any other way, gentleman. I have only a few men available to manage the whole of KL and the situation is dire."

"How long have we got," asked the Chinese gentleman whom Robert now knew to be Mr Chin Yu, one of the joint owners of the China Bank.

"Perhaps two weeks, could be less," Davies said, watching all their faces go pale.

"Two weeks!" Ken said incredulously with Frank saying something similar in the background. "Surely not. We have thousands of men up here."

"We are barely holding our positions, gentlemen. We have hundreds of deserters, so that suggests all is not right. Half the men have never been trained. We have little or no air cover and the Asiatics are being told by the Japs that they are coming to free them," Davies said it all with a look of resignation.

"There must be some lorries around that haven't been commandeered so far?" Without anyone answering the question, Morrissey's assistant went on, "Would it not be possible to use cars? We have two cars and if we could get two more then that would be just about enough to take the bulk of the money. We could leave the coinage and burn the paper money. Our manager in Penang managed to get the gold in his branch down to us in his car." After a few seconds, he added, "Mind you, he had to leave a large amount of paper currency including American dollars."

Robert came in with. "We tried to do the same, only by ship, and we managed about half, maybe a bit more. Maybe we could get the gold down to the coast and ship it."

Davies shook his head. "Unless the Army assists, then the commies control that corridor and as I told you the other day there are thousands of refugees in Malacca and Port Dickson trying to get on a ship. By all accounts, there are two ships sunk by the quayside in Port Dickson blocking the harbour entrance." Davies finished what he was saying by just shaking his head.

Frank had been listening to the discussion between Robert, Davies and Morrissey's assistant and then said that he had moved most of the China Bank's money at the outset of fighting down from Penang but it hadn't moved down to Singapore, as they had thought that customers would need it, only then the Japs had bombed the bank.

Superintendent Davies smiled back at Frank. "Thoughtless of them." Pausing to take a drink of tea, he added, "In my opinion, they know where the gold is. We also did well to move it before the commies had time to get organised."

Frank looked at Robert and shrugged his shoulders. "Sorry, when we rang Barclay's and Hong Kong, neither could help us. So, you drew the short straw."

Ken who had been sitting quietly talking to Morrissey about the idea of cars then spoke up, "We could do something similar to what Jeremy Lasker did. He managed to bring the gold down from Penang in his car, so it must be possible for a fleet of cars to ferry it down to Gemas, even to Singapore. If we leave unexpectedly and at short notice, then the commies won't have time to organise any banditry."

Ken looked across at Robert, "Sorry, old boy, but if we can find sufficient cars to move the Barclay's and Hong Kong money, then that would solve one part of the problem."

Robert just nodded taking it all in, merely saying. "You've got to give it a try. If you get the cars tomorrow and keep them away from the banks until the last minute, then there's a possibility that no one will guess what you're planning. If you leave it too long though, the commies will find out."

The Superintendent who had been watching the way the conversation was going stood up from where he had been sitting on the side of his desk. Pointing at Morrissey and Ken Seymour, he said, "I think you gentlemen should go off and work on your idea. Just remember that any help from me is limited."

He moved around behind his desk to sit down on its top before saying, "If we don't have the reserve unit out, then it can cover you but chances are, they will be busy. If it's of help, I know the Bishop has gone down to Singapore and he's left his car beside the church. I shan't be needing my car so that can also be commandeered at the last minute. There may also be vehicles at the Majestic that have been abandoned as well or some that the planters have just arrived in. Just for God's sake, keep it low key and move soon."

The discussion between the Barclay's and Hong Kong contingents seemed to almost separate them from the problems to be solved by Robert and finally they agreed to go off and to merely send a message to Davies or his No. 2 when they had set off.

Davies waited until the Barclay's and Hong Kong bank group had departed and then he addressed Robert, Mr Chin Yu and Frank. "Of course, what we know gentlemen, is that the bulk of all the money is in the Union bank."

"So, what do you suggest we do?"

"We could offer it to the Japanese at good interest rates," Robert suggested.

Mr Chin Yu looked astonished at what Robert said and started to shout at the suggestion and then saw that the Europeans were all starting to smile. "You bloody English. You make jokes when there is no answer."

"Do you think your bullion can get on one lorry or do we need two?" Davies asked no one in particular.

Robert looked across at the Superintendent. "I'm no expert on axle strengths but in my opinion, we need three lorries and I can only supply one."

Davies smiled at Robert, "Ah, the Meadows' illusive lorry. I did ask about it and was told that Meadows had borrowed it."

"Well, it's more or less a permanent loan," Robert said smiling back. Mr Chin Yu and Frank watched this exchange and smiled at the drift of the conversation.

"So, gentlemen your task is to find at least two additional lorries. I wish you well. My No.2 has cleared out every vehicle for miles." The Superintendent turned to Mr Chin Yu. "You must have contacts Mr Chin Yu, so you may be lucky. Mind you, it would have to be very discreet enquiries or you will have Chin Peng or the local commissar, Li Bo, down on you very quickly and as I said, I can't provide much help.

Gentlemen, Lai Teck, the Chairman of their Revolutionary Committee, has agreed to suspend communist activities during the hostilities in KL but Lai Teck's hold on Chin Peng or Li Bo is tenuous at the best of times and Chin Peng and Li Bo are not prone to keeping an agreement if it benefits them in the long run."

As he was saying this, there was noise outside and Davies' Inspector put his head through the door. "We have an exchange of gun fire at the top end of Bellamy Road towards the airport. Sergeant Mekrit says around a dozen and they're not commies, too disciplined." Robert heard Davies tell the Inspector to warn Army HQ and to then go off with the reserve unit and handle the incident. Then Davies turned back to Robert and the China Bank men.

"Fine party to have on Christmas Day. Fortunately, my family is on its way to Fremantle, so at least I don't have that problem but not the Christmas I would have liked."

Robert said nothing and it was Frank who made a move. "Come on, let's make our way to the Majestic and see if we can think of a way to solve the problem. It looks as though we are on our own. I have to be back on shift with the LDC later tonight so we haven't got long. How'd you get here, Bob? Mr Chin Yu and I walked."

Robert answered, as they shook hands with Superintendent Davies and left the room, "By bicycle."

Outside in the pitch dark they were somehow quickly found by their respective guards and Robert and Abilash walked with their bikes, as they followed the two bankers to the Majestic less than a mile away. Even in the dark, Robert could see into shops and doorways with people sitting in the entrances smoking and talking quietly. It was almost eerie with no noise from the many people in the doorways and from those walking on the street and Robert felt conscious that they knew he was European and things were not the same anymore. In the distance, he could see or rather hear lorries on a main road and when they eventually got to the check point, it was to see a continuous convoy of vehicles going north.

The Majestic was lit up by storm lamps smelling heavily of paraffin and as there was no electricity, there were no fans, making it unbearably hot. The sewers smelt as though they were not working so Robert guessed that the water was off in the hotel as well. The corridor leading from the reception to the bar looked like something out of a horror movie with darkened shapes walking back and forth and shadows lacing across the wall.

Mr Chin Yu and Frank, with Robert trailing after them, headed for the far corner where it was darkest and there, they found a table and chairs. Robert had left Abilash outside in the gardens and began to think very quickly that he had the better deal with the heat in the bar stifling and the enclosed space making the smell overpowering. "Is it like this every night?"

"Worse," Frank said immediately. "This is after all Christmas Day. They've made an effort." Mr Chin Yu had somehow attracted a waiter in the dark and they ordered beers all around and they sent drinks out to the guards.

"We need at least two more lorries and double quick. I suggest we have to be out of here by New Year's Day as after that, everything will go pear shaped very quickly and we will be on borrowed time," Frank said quietly.

Robert murmured that he agreed and then looked across

at them, “Come on, you two. It’s your town; there must be somebody you know who has a lorry or a car. Presumably, you have a car, Mr Chin Yu.”

In the gloom, Robert saw him nod. “It could not carry much of what we have, though,” was all he said as an answer.

“Have you brought the problem to the attention of the HC’s office, Mr Chin Yu?”

Chin Yu looked across to Robert. “I have spoken to them and they say that we must fend for ourselves and not distract the Army at this time.”

“Do they really know how much we have in the vaults?” Robert said in a shocked whisper shaking his head in disbelief.

“They do not know how much we have only that it is safe in your vaults, Mr Draper. I hope to be able to go to Singapore soon but getting there will now be difficult as there are no trains. It will take me days and even then, I cannot guarantee that they will treat it as a priority.”

“You must realise that I can accept no responsibility for your goods Mr Chin Yu and if it comes down to the wire, I will get as much of Union’s out and leave the rest. I also have staff to extricate.”

Mr Chin Yu just shrugged and it was Frank who came back with. “We could argue that you have a responsibility because you allowed us to put our gold in your bank.”

Robert looked across at Frank, “Shush. Not so loud. You need to use different words. As to responsibility, the answer is ‘no’ and if you want to argue, then I will instruct my staff to carry your goods out onto the street. At the very least, you should be helping with security and pay us for storage.”

“Well, we know where you stand, Bob.”

Robert started to tell Frank to grow up when Mr Chin Yu came in, "Be quiet. The fact is that we have caused the Union a problem and we should help them, Frank. Mr Draper, we can get our security staff, such as we can find, to report to your bank tomorrow and your security manager can use them as he wishes. As to transport, I have a friend who runs goods up to the plantations and he owes me favours. He owes the bank money. So, let me talk to him and let us hope he can find us transport."

"Remember that he's got to be told not to talk about it. Do you even know his politics?"

Mr Chin Yu waved his arms up the air and raised his voice. "I don't know. I don't care right now. If he betrays me, he knows his business will not do well in the future, so he would be foolish to say anything."

Robert sat for a moment. He could hear a familiar voice at the far end of the bar. "Look, let's call it a day. Can I suggest that if you do find a lorry, two ideally, that you have them taken to the Ferguson Plant workshops for service and repair. It has no connection with us but I know the manager. We can then get at them at short notice." Robert shook hands with them and made his way around to the far end of the bar. "Fred Samuels. I would know that voice across an ocean."

Robert peered at someone who by his speech had had quite a few whiskies.

"Bob, how the hell… Where did you come from?"

"Came up from the Island four days ago trying to keep things going at the bank. Getting a bit worried that the mines won't be clearing their overdraft in the near future."

"Huh, you mean for years if the Japs have anything to say about it."

"Where's Martin Kennedy and Mo?" Robert asked peering at the other drinkers at the bar.

"God alone knows, Bob. They were up at some new diggings north of Kuantan and when all hell let loose, they never came back. Lines cut, everything. I finally had to abandon the Khota Lipis mine last night as the Leicesters, about seven miles up the road, took a hammering and I had to get out. Mind you, abandoning what? I didn't have many workers left and the other two Euros went on Friday to join the Volunteers. Got here today to a great Christmas lunch of cold meat, limp lettuce and warm beer. Christ man, there are better conditions down the mines."

Robert waved the bar man over, "Two large whiskies and soda. Now Fred, tell me about your journey. How did you manage to get here?"

Chapter 13

Robert sat on the floor behind the filing cabinets listening to the bombing further up the road. It sounded like a convoy was being attacked. It seemed to be happening almost constantly. The noise from the Army's ack-ack guns was deafening, preventing any discussion. Clive was sitting in a pool of dust, more grit really, with his back against the doorway. A layer of thick dust was rapidly enveloping everything in the bank. The windows in Mark's office had finally given way yesterday when a near miss took out part of the hardware shop next door.

Robert had been amused a few days before when a notice appeared in the shop window saying that the Christmas sale had commenced. That no longer mattered as the whole of the shop front had gone in the near miss and people could now step in and help themselves.

The damage from the bombs had also caused a good deal of debris in the street. Fortunately, there had been no fire and Robert along with two security guards, had cleared the worst of the debris from the road in the early evening whilst two other security guards kept an eye out for any untoward activity.

The couple who ran the shop had been in their backyard

trying to pack some of their stock of china onto a cart and had been fortunate not to have been in the shop which was now just rubble. Mrs Clemence who had known the Watsons for years told Robert afterwards that they were trying to take some stock up to their house for safety.

At Robert's suggestion, Clive had put an advertisement in the local paper to remind customers that the bank was still open for business but that customers must make an appointment to conduct business. There had been a problem with customers turning up unexpectedly and alarming the security staff particularly customers turning up with bodyguards. The two telephonists had failed to come in for the past three days with one of the few remaining Chinese clerks who were able to come in, telling Robert that one of the telephonists had been injured by the continual strafing and was in the hospital; the other one, Mrs Dray, no one had news of although Robert had been advised that she lived a few miles away and was finding it more and more difficult to get to work.

Mrs Clemence invariably came into work despite Robert telling her to stay at home but she now worked mainly down in the telephonists' room near the vaults preferring to be there when there was a bombing raid. "I have to come out. I need to try and get food, Mr Draper. We have to eat. The Central Market has no food in it so I have to go searching around. Nobody can get any vegetables or meat. If there was a meat van seen, I suspect it would be hijacked."

"All the more reason why you should be at home. It's not safe for you to be out there."

"It's just as dangerous being at home. Jim's place was strafed yesterday and it can only be a matter of time before they try bombing it."

Robert started to say something but Mrs Clemence interrupted guessing what Robert was about to say. "It's all right. Jim says he's moved the lorry to behind our garden and put covers over it. From the sky, it just looks like part of the garden." She gave a bit of a smile. "My lovely garden is now a lorry park."

"Mind you, he says the lorry Mr Samuels has given you had more bullet holes in it than there was metal so he's having his lads trying to repair it."

Robert nodded, as another burst of machine gun fire rattled out only a few hundred yards away and the scream of a fighter could be heard in the distance. When he saw Meadows later, he told him to make sure Mrs Clemence had a bodyguard with her when she went shopping. He had spoken to Jim Clemence the night before, on the small veranda of the Clemence's bungalow, about the state of Fred's lorry. By all accounts, it hadn't been able to get out of the car park of the Majestic and Jim had had to wait until dusk, two days after Christmas Day, and then take his towing vehicle up to the Majestic and drag the lorry back to the workshops.

Jim had laughed when Robert asked whether it was a possible second vehicle. "Maybe. Mind you, the Army have seen it and are interested. The engineer working on the Army lorries said he might need it but I've told him it's for hospital patients if I can get it repaired?"

"And can you?"

Jim had just smiled at the question and passed the bottle of whisky over to Robert for him to fill up his glass again.

"Out here, lad, you have to learn to mend and make do with what you can find. A pair of Mil's stockings will do as a fan belt, the lads will bang out the holes where bullets have broken open the driver's door, and I found an old radiator from a Packard that we can use; I've scavenged two tyres from a lorry that was burnt out when the bombers targeted the market last Saturday. How Mr Samuels got here in that heap is beyond me. They must have been going downhill." He was saying this as he smacked something that just landed on him. "Never get used to these bastards biting me."

"Fred's a bit like you, Jim. Resourceful."

Robert and Jim watched the moving shadows in the doorway of the machine shops about thirty yards away. "They're working on a bren carrier. It looks like one of those Swiss cheese jobs, holes all over. Can't see it's worth it myself; just how much use is it going to be stopping the Japs' tanks?"

Mrs Clemence had long gone to bed letting Jim and Robert talk. Finally, Jim had ended the conversation with a long sigh just saying, "I'll call it a day." It was the way he said the next words that Robert later remembered most vividly. "Everything we have is across the road and in this house."

Robert had on a number of times over the past few days tried persuading the Clemences to get out. "I still say that when we go you should come with us. The Japs will make you work for them, Jim. You're much too useful. You will probably both be interned."

Jim had gone over to the end of the veranda when Robert had again raised the issue, and tossed his cigarette away. "Twenty years we've been here, Mr Draper. We've never been apart except when I was in the Army and I don't reckon we would know what do if we were separated."

"Then that's settled, Jim, you need to come with us. The

Japs will probably separate you. Once you tell me the lorries are fit for the journey, then we're off, commies or no commies. The Japs may break through at any time from what I'm told, so we're on borrowed time. I should hear something tomorrow from the China Bank about them finding some transport and then we go."

Robert could see Jim shaking his head at what Robert had just said.

"Me and Mil, we've talked about it. We prefer to stay and weather it out. Our friends are staying put as well. The Japs won't bother us, I reckon. We have Japanese friends, used to be our neighbours until the police took them away three weeks ago. But thanks anyway, Mr Draper." With that, he had walked off around to the back of the bungalow.

******

Robert sat on the floor thinking about last night's discussions with Jim. The gunfire seemed to have diminished and finally it seemed safe for him to come out from behind the cabinets where he had been sitting. He stood up doing his best to dust himself down.

"Do we have any customers to see this afternoon, Clive?" Clive had been sitting in the doorway smoking a cigarette and he took his time before answering, finally saying, "We have two who want to get their stuff out of the safety deposit boxes. That leaves around thirty security boxes not opened. From what I can see, they're mostly planters and I will go around the Majestic tonight and see if any of them have come in from the hills. What I do know is a couple of them left for the Island without even getting what's in their boxes."

Robert just nodded. "Right, what I suggest is that you tell all, bar the security staff, not to report to work anymore. Give them three months wages but avoid saying that we're probably on the move. Just say it's too dangerous for them to come into work. As things stand, I think we could make a dash for it on New Year's Day or the day after, now that Frank has found a decent sized van. Jim is having a look at it tonight. Get Mr Chan to help you make up the wages."

"Won't we be giving the game away by telling them not to come in? They will guess we are off soon. There's bound to be someone who says something and then the commies will know that we are planning to go in the next few days."

"From what Mr Meadows says, they know we're planning a breakout and have people watching the bank. If it wasn't for the fact that the army are just up the road, they would have had a go already."

Clive said nothing. Standing up and stretching himself, he said, "I'll go and organise the wages with Chan. It'll help me to keep my mind off what you're planning, whatever it is." Robert came out into the corridor and followed him towards the stairs, crunching through the grit on the floor.

Meadows and Stuart were in Clive's office trying to sleep and as Robert passed the door, he saw Stuart had just got up looking very dirty and dishevelled. He came out into the corridor just as Robert started to go down the stairs. "I saw Mr Forrester last night. He says he will try and get time off in the next few days and come in to see you."

Robert said nothing and just continued down the stairs, spotting Mrs Clemence and one of the security guards and the Chinese clerk, Jai, going out into the street, presumably going off to search for food during a lull in the bombing. The floor of the banking hall was now a carpet of dust being stirred up as people moved across it. One of the Hong Kong Bank guards came in as they left and seeing Robert, he came over. "Mr Seymour has asked me to tell you that they leave in a little while." At last, they were on their way.

He hadn't heard anything from Ken Seymour at the Hong Kong bank for days until last evening when he had found him in the bar at the Majestic.

"I had no idea that it would be so difficult, Bob. When we got the cars, we discovered we had to lay the gold out in a certain way or the axles wouldn't take the weight. Then we have around a dozen of us to go as well. In the end, we needed six cars and not just any old car. Davies promised yesterday that he would do his best to supply an escort out of KL so long as there was no other emergency. It will be touch and go whether we get away with it."

Robert and Ken talked for a bit longer about the risks before Robert said, "I'll see you back on the Island then in a few days," adding, "good luck," as Ken shook his hand. Robert, as he walked with Abilash back to the bank and on to the Clemence bungalow, privately thought they had taken too long, cursing that it may be the same with the gold in the Union Bank.

He had spoken to Peter most days, for the three minutes of allowed time, and each time, Peter just couldn't understand why they were taking so long. "Get out, Bob. Take the staff in the lorry and leave everything, if you have to. Penang's gone and the Japs must be getting near to KL."

"You don't need to tell me, Peter. We know they are close but I will give it a couple of more days."

It was perhaps an hour after he had been told that Ken's

convoy was on its way when Meadows came in to where Robert was working in Mark Forrester's office, packing up files.

"Can you hear that shooting? It's in Chinatown. Sounds like a hell of a battle. I've been trying to get through to police HQ to ask what the hell's happening but the lines seem to be down."

Robert could hear some distant shooting and at Meadows' insistence, he followed him downstairs and over to the doors of the bank which Meadows unlocked and then pulled open. As soon as the doors opened, the gunfire could be heard very distinctly, no more than a mile away.

"I had a message that the Hong Kong and Barclay's lot were making a run for it, about now."

Meadows scratched the back of his neck with his left hand as Clive came out to join them on the pavement. "That doesn't sound good, Mr Draper. My guess is that the commies put up a roadblock without the police knowing about it and all hell's let loose."

Robert turned around to face Meadows. "You and I need to talk again about an alternative route, Mr Meadows. I looked at the map last night. There's a way if we go into the mountains as though we're going up to Khota Lipis, past the airport, and then turn south and find our way back onto the main road somewhere south of KL."

"There are roads mostly up to the estates in the hills but they're not metalled and what's to say that the commies don't have control of them like they control the roads to the coast?"

Robert made a face, "How do we find out then? Maybe someone has to do a dummy run and then get a message back to us. Mind you that's not going to be easy with the lines down." The noise of gunfire was more sporadic for a few minutes and then there was a cacophony of gun fire in a more disciplined manner with successive fusillades of rifle fire now apparent.

Robert looked down the road towards where the gunfire could be heard. "I would guess the police or more likely the Army has got involved as the fighting is interfering in getting the convoys moving south."

Robert turned to go back into the bank. "Come on, let's have another look at the map. You too, Clive. There has to be a way."

Chapter 14

Robert had now been in KL for ten days and still he couldn't get anywhere in moving the gold. Try as he might, he couldn't get anyone interested. Even Superintendent Davies had failed to interest senior officers of the need to prioritise the shipment: all he was told was that getting troops to the front was of the upmost importance and getting the wounded and sick away from KL was the priority for the empty trucks on their return to the south.

Sitting on the Clemence's veranda thinking about the problem Robert swatted away at the buzz of a mosquito for the umpteenth time. For some reason, mosquitos didn't seem to affect Jim as much as Robert, with only the occasional brave mosquito seeking his blood, and Mrs Clemence had remarked on more than one occasion that mosquitos didn't seem to like the taste of Johnny Walker.

Robert was partly watching the work going on over the road and at the same time coming to a decision that unless he could get help from the police or Army in the next few days, he had no choice but to abandon the gold. He knew that Gordon and Peter had made representations at the Singapore end as well as Mr Wu Tu who had now managed to get back to Singapore but they had been told that there was no need to worry because the Army would shortly sort out the situation. Robert living in KL with the daily bombing and the sound of war almost constantly around him, knew differently. The Japs were way too close to delay any longer.

There seemed to be more urgency about the work over the road with someone using a welding torch accompanied by a lot of shouting. According to Jim, the engineers were working for more than twelve hours at a stretch in the heat and humidity and were exhausted, and he couldn't see how they could keep it up. Looking across the road, Robert could just make out the men, mostly their shadows, and from seeing them earlier in the last of the remaining light, he knew that all the men, no matter what rank, were shirtless with sweat running off them as they all sought to make a vehicle roadworthy.

"The Captain is expecting to be told at any moment that they are off down south. He told me in confidence that it's at best a week we've got before the roads to the north are cut off. He said there was a two-hour standoff this morning and it took a battalion to move the infiltrators on. He's worried about me and Mil staying."

"He's not the only one. For God's sake, listen to reason. Get out. We all understand why you want to stay but it's crazy. At the very least come with us to Singapore."

Jim smiled across at Robert in the dark as the mosquito mesh door opened and Mrs Clemence came out. "You boys okay for soda and food because if you are, I'm going to bed." Neither asked for anything else and she went over to Jim and kissed him on the top of his head and whispered something to him.

"I won't be long, Mil. Just let me finish my drink."

Mrs Clemence turned and said to Robert, “I’ll see you in the morning, Mr Draper. Try and get some sleep. The next few days could be fraught.” With that, she was gone wafting a little air towards Robert, as she went through the door.

When she was out of earshot, Robert tried again, “Jim, you can’t stay. Think of Mrs Clemence. When the Japs come here, they’ll make you work for them anywhere in Malaya and who knows where Mrs Clemence will end up. The conditions for her will be awful, not worth thinking about.”

“The vicar says that if we’re no threat to the Japs, they’ll leave us be.”

“That can’t be the case, Henry. You must have heard about the killing of civilians up north. Fred Samuels, the other night was telling me that they’ve even beheaded some people. It doesn’t bear thinking about.” Robert sipped his whisky and sat back. He had said what he wanted to say, not for the first time. “Will you at least think about it?” He could just make out Jim in the dark moving around.

“Me and Mil we’ve talked it through and we’ve decided. Everything we have is here. We have a few friends who are also going to stay and when we know the Japs are here, we will go and stay in the church.” Robert knew he was getting nowhere and he changed the subject.

“You ever been over towards the airport?”

“Yeah, loads of times. When they were building the aerodrome, I would take over equipment for clearing the ground.”

“The map says there’s a road from there down south, comes out about sixty miles south on the main Gemas road.”

Jim shifted and sat up with a jerk. “You’re not thinking of taking that road, are you? You’d be crazy. It’s dirt all the way and the last time I used it; it was full of potholes."

"But you did use it, Jim?"

"Well, yeah. Had to go all the way down and then back up the Gemas road cause the road into KL had been swept away in a flood and was being reconstructed." After a moment, Jim said, "If you're going over to the aerodrome, why don't you get them to fly in a plane to collect the gold?"

"I tried that ploy but apparently the runway is smashed up and the coolies have all deserted. They need a large labour unit to repair the runway and they just seemed to have vanished."

Robert finished off his drink. "Superintendent Davies is still clearing up the mess in Chinatown. By all accounts, three cars got through, another one was riddled with bullets, both the driver and security guard dead but at least the bullion was recovered. The last two cars had their tyres blown out and then the drivers killed. The security guard and Morrissey, the manager, it seems they managed to get out of the cars but were killed in the gun fight. By the time the police got there, the gold was long gone. Apparently, one of the cars broke down about fifteen miles down the road and was then strafed by a Jap fighter. Ken Seymour from the Hong Kong Bank was shot up and its touch and go for him. A bloody mess."

"The Army's got to help, Mr Draper." Robert was sick of asking the Clemences to call him by his first name and he said nothing when Jim again addressed him formally.

Robert shook his head and put his glass on the tray beside him and stood up. "The Superintendent said again that the army is up to their eyes in trying to hold onto the situation and can't spare men or vehicles. They're having a job to evacuate all the patients and staff from the main hospital. I don't think they're very hopeful of getting all the wounded away from the temporary hospital up beside the racecourse. Thankfully, Chin Yu says they have found a vehicle although Frank says it's probably never done more than 20 miles in one go, so with the two we have, barely enough. Frank will bring it over tomorrow and I'm hoping you can make something of it. Fred and Frank can drive so they're lined up and hopefully, Stuart will be around as he has driven farm vehicles. The gold is all upstairs in the banking hall now but it will take some time to load it."

"Is that safe, Mr Draper?"

"If you mean the gold, it's as safe as in the vaults. We have security around the clock on the outside of the building and we have guards inside. So, it's like Fort Knox. At least for now. I don't know how long we would last if we are attacked."

Robert could see Jim's face in the light from the storm lamp he had brought over. He was smiling. "So, when are you going?"

"I wish I knew, Jim. I still need help. I think I can get the staff out but not the gold. We won't get five miles without an escort and nobody seems to be listening. It's just taking so long to get organised: I try and see someone in charge and just get passed on. The Superintendent says it's chaotic up at Army HQ. I came up on the wages run thinking I would be back on the Island for Christmas Day and I'm still stuck here. I've tried a dozen ideas and all founder on getting sufficient transport to carry the gold. If it was just the staff, we would be long gone."

There was a noise from over the road and some shouting and they both turned to watch. It was something and nothing.

“Come on, let’s call it a night.” He left Jim going into the bungalow and walked over to the small gate which was the entrance to the front yard. Abilash was sitting quietly on a stool on the other side of the gate with his rifle across his knees.

“We’re going in, Abilash, so come and sit on the veranda. Mrs Clemence has left some water and sandwiches for you. Remember, any funny business, just start shooting. Those lads over the road will be here like a shot.”

Chapter 15

Robert ran into the entrance of the Majestic through the crowds of military and remaining Europeans all trying to avoid the rain which had just started, the first for days, with a thunderclap to announce the deluge. Everyone seemed to be congregating in the hotel on New Year's Day and in the light from the storm lamps, it looked like a football crowd trying to get under cover with little regard for the people on either side of them.

The day had been frustrating to the nth degree culminating in Jim, when he came up to the bank, expressing an opinion, as he surveyed the amount of bullion on the floor of the bank, that two lorries would be insufficient and that a third would be needed and he had grave doubts that the vehicle that Chin Yu had found was roadworthy enough to go on any dirt roads for at least 60 miles and if necessary, the whole way to Gemas. Hours were being wasted every day, going from one idea to another, with no running water, food running out and electricity something of a distant memory.

Any idea about moving some or all the gold, when he tested the options, came down to the basic problems of sufficient transport and accompanying security. Already, the security guards had reported to Meadows that some Chinese had been chased off at the back of the bank and Robert when he thought about it had little doubt that they were checking on the level of security. Meadows was convinced that if and when the Army declared KL to be an 'open town' the commies would surround the bank very quickly.

He had spent some time in the afternoon speaking with Mulhandra Singh and the Mukarjees who had come into KL as it was no longer safe out at the bank's bungalow. "We have families in the town, Mr Draper, and it is better that we stay with them." Robert raised his eyebrows at the suggestion from Mulhandra Singh that it was safer in the town especially as only that morning, on the way to the bank, he had seen a large number of bodies lying outside a tenement block that had been hit by the bombers.

"The Army has been using the bungalow as a rest home for some of the officers but they are moving out today so we thought it better if we also came into town as we would have no protection out there," Mr Mukarjee went on to explain apologetically. Mulhandra Singh said that the army had commandeered the car and he handed over a receipt which an officer had issued to him.

Clive was quite amused at the contents, *One car, black, soft top, made by Singers.* "How are we going to claim on that, Bob?"

Taking the note off him, Robert smiled at its contents. "Clive, we shall say it was brand new and the Japanese destroyed all the records. We will get at least one and four pence in compensation." They were both smiling as Robert handed the note back to Clive.

******

Walking through the hotel, Robert noticed right away that there was an atmosphere of quiet resignation with the few remaining Europeans in huddles presumably planning how they would get out when the word came that the troops were moving to the new defence lines being prepared south of KL. Stuart coming into the bank an hour ago to try and get some sleep in his makeshift bed had said that large quantities of soldiers and equipment was now being shipped south and no more troops seemed to be going north.

Robert had come looking for Fred who had been on duty with the local LDC and from what Stuart had told him he should be resting in one of the guest rooms in the Majestic, as he would be on duty later. The bombers had been over KL as usual about four in the afternoon, this time targeting the roads in KL and just south of the town, and it was obvious that the Japs were now trying to stop the Army escaping south. From what Stuart had told him, the hospital was full to bursting with injured people and many would not be able to be moved before KL became an open town.

The night before he had heard heavy gunfire coming from just north of the racecourse and when Robert had seen Davies' No. 2 that afternoon, he had been told that the Volunteers had been engaged in fighting with what looked like a regular unit of Japanese troops and they had to get Army HQ to send in reserves to disperse the insurgents.

After repeated enquiries of the various Europeans walking around the Majestic, as the reception staff seem to have deserted the hotel, Robert found out that Fred was sleeping upstairs in one of the guest rooms at the end of the first-floor corridor. Exasperated and tired by the continual fight to achieve even the simplest of tasks, Robert set off for the stairs when he saw Brigadier Lay coming down the corridor from the ballroom with an entourage of military staff trailing behind him. He had never been introduced but he had seen him on a few of the occasions he had been to see Fran or Geoffrey Blackmore at the Governor's Residence. Taking the plunge, he stepped out in front of the Brigadier.

"My apologies for blocking your way, General, but I need to speak to you on a matter of national importance." Two of Lay's staff came up immediately and started to push Robert aside but he held his ground and added, "I have ten million in gold and if I don't get immediate help, it will probably fall into Japanese hands." Lay stopped trying to get past Robert and looked at him incredulously; to be fair the two staff officers had also stopped in their tracks at what Robert had just said.

Brigadier Lay continued to look astonished, finally saying, "You are?"

"My name is Robert Draper and I'm acting Manager for the Union and China Bank. We have a branch on Market Street. We currently hold all the gold and currency left in the north Malay States. I've been trying to get it out for more than ten days but I keep being told that there is no help from the Army or the police or anybody. You're all too busy and I keep being told it's my responsibility to get the money out."

The Brigadier Lay started to look around and then said, "Ronnie, see if you can clear them out of that lounge over there, now." He said something to the entourage which Robert didn't catch and then turning to Robert he said, "Follow me," and with that, he went into the lounge where a half dozen or so people had been sitting and were now being asked to leave.

When the room was clear, Brigadier Lay turned to Robert. "This had better not be a joke."

From somewhere towards the doorway, a voice said, "I can vouch he's a banker, sir." Robert turned and saw Major Docherty whom he had last seen in Penang nearly six months ago.

"I have all the gold and currency from our bank and also from the China Bank which was moved to us three weeks ago after their bank was bombed. Two days ago, Barclays and Hong Kong banks tried to make their way to Gemas in a convoy with all their bullion and it was intercepted and the commies made off with two carloads of money. The police managed to retrieve one carload of money and that is also now in our bank. We have security staff patrolling outside the bank but what use is that if we can't get out of KL. I have tried the RAF but they can't get a plane into the airport as there is insufficient labour to repair the runway. We considered going down the coast road to Port Dickson but as you will know, it is controlled by the communists and anyway there is no guarantee that we could get the bullion on a ship; I am told there are thousands on the dockside waiting for a ship. I have two lorries to carry some of the gold and a battered old fruit and vegetable van to carry the remainder but the advice I'm getting is that it won't make it to Gemas. We need better transport and more importantly military protection. We have to break out soon or we're not going to make it."

The Brigadier had been patient as Robert talked. From his side one of the staff officers whispered that Superintendent Davies had already put the argument to General Bennett and General Heath and been told that the priority was Army personnel. Lay was nodding and then said, "General Heath probably doesn't know exactly how much gold is involved." Turning back to Robert, he asked, "How do you know it's ten million?"

"My colleague and I have weighed some of the bags of gold coins and then multiplied it accordingly and there is certainly close to ten million."

"Where the hell did you get ten million in gold?"

"As I said it's not all our money. The China Bank owner tells me that the Chinese prefer as far as possible to deal in gold; it's a form of international currency. In addition to the gold coins the China Bank has, my bank has around three million in gold and by the looks of it, the Hong Kong Bank has around half a million, possibly more. Then there's the paper currency which is well over two million dollars in small currency."

Brigadier Lay was looking at his watch as he was listening. Ronnie, standing slightly behind him said something quietly which Robert thought was to the effect that they were getting late for a meeting. Lay turned and nodded and then turned back to Robert and asked, "Can you burn the paper money."

Robert nodded. "But it will take days and when I have managed to get through to the Colonial Office, they said they couldn't give me an immediate answer about burning the money as it would have to be approved by the Cabinet Minister, Duff Cooper. In any case, it's only paper money. It's the gold that's the problem. If the Japs or commies get a hold of it, then they could finance a war against us for months if not years."

Lay was nodding at what Robert was saying and then he turned to Major Docherty. "We've got to move. Larry, go and see for yourself the problem and then get a hold of Colonel Morrison at the aerodrome. The British Battalion are acting as a reserve for the next few days. See if you can come up with a plan with them for the evacuation of this bullion. From memory, we have them scheduled to be the rear guard on the East Road in any pull back."

He looked momentarily at one of the other officers who nodded as he spoke. "God, we can't have that money falling into the hands of the Japs." With that, Lay nodded at Robert and was gone with his entourage following almost at a run.

Major Docherty came over and was smiling as he shook Robert's hand. "Nothing like causing a stir, old boy. The Brigadier was quite shocked at what you said."

"Major, I have tried everything up to now bar asking the commies to help me ship it out. Superintendent Davies is unable to help; he has only a few dozen men left. They're not even holding down the deserters that seem to be everywhere. Add to that the fact that the commies seem to know every move we make. I'll lay you odds they know we have moved the cash up to the banking hall ready to load onto lorries. My security staff are at the end of their tether; two of the China Bank security staff have now gone missing and if things continue, others will desert." Robert had started to cough as he was speaking.

"Seems to me you're not firing on all cylinders, old boy."

Robert looked up from coughing, "Just get the gold to Gemas and that will be a start."

"Right, let's go and see the problem." Robert followed him out having completely forgotten about seeing Fred. Outside the hotel, the rain was still beating down but the Major seemed oblivious to it and disappeared around the back of the hotel, materialising moments later sitting in an Army car with an Army sergeant driving the vehicle. The driver got out and opened the back door for Robert.

"One moment, I need to find my guard," Robert said and finally finding the guard, he told him to sit in the front with the driver and direct the army driver. "It's not far but we have to go a bit of a detour to avoid the damage to the roads near the station."

The bank was in pitch darkness when the car stopped outside its entrance and the street seemed empty. The rain had eased to just a heavy drizzle but the humidity had gone up leaving all of them with clothes that stuck to their backs. From behind the sandbags at the entrance, two faces emerged with rifles pointing towards Robert and the Major but they were immediately lowered when they recognised Robert.

"Sahib, you left walking," was all one of them said, as Robert banged on the door and when asked who it was, he shouted his name. It was Meadows who opened the door, looking dishevelled and certainly no longer, the spruce security manager Robert had first met eighteen months ago. He had a storm lamp held high and ushered them in quickly, and then locked the door. Turning and seeing that Robert had a senior Army officer with him, he came to attention, "Good evening, sir," and Robert was amused to see he was addressing the Major and not him.

"This is Major Docherty, Mr Meadows. He's going to help us, I hope. Can you show him our problem?"

Meadows swung the lamp around and said, "Follow me, sir." With that, he took the Major and Robert, squelching in his wet boots, to where the bags and wooden cases had been stored beside the central marble dais.

There was an immediate response from Major Docherty. “My God, I see what you mean, Mr Draper. There must be enough here to fund the whole Japanese war.”

“It’s all the stupid policy of Sir Shenton in believing that the Army would send the Japs packing from day one and we should carry on as normal.”

The Major chose to ignore the comment and bent down and tried to lift one of the bags of coins. “Careful sir,” murmured Meadows. “It’s takes two lads to carry one.”

“My god, I can’t believe it. I had no idea what you really meant when you said ten million.”

“There’s also the paper money. It’s in bags against the wall. I kept it separate in case the Colonial Office authorised us to burn it but as the lines are down half the time, it’s almost impossible to get a proper discussion and get anyone with any sense to make a decision. We got Superintendent Davies to send a message but there has been no reply from the Cabinet Office.”

Major Docherty lent against the marble dais and said, “Bring over that lamp please.” He had got out a notebook and gold pen. He started to scribble down details. “You say it needs more than two lorries to carry it?”

“I have been advised that the axles won’t take the weight if we try and get it all onto two lorries. I have two lorries hidden away ready for the move. I need two more to make it a safe distribution plus an escort.”

“That’s the rub, old bean. We have no spare troops. Even the Volunteers are fully occupied.” In the distance, shooting could be heard and the Major cocked his head to one side.

Robert seeing the Major frown at the shooting, said, “That’s probably deserters. There is more and more every day. Mostly young Indian lads. They're getting more and more aggressive every night, looting and stealing food. We've had one or two run ins with them. The police are at their wits' end trying to move them on."

Docherty merely nodded. What could he say? He put his notebook and pen back in his pocket and then turned to have another look at the bags and boxes on the floor. "If we get you to Gemas, what then?"

"You tell me, Major. The obvious point is that we need to get safe passage to Singapore but Gemas is at least a start."

"Right. I need to get back to HQ and also talk to the new commanding officer of the British Battalion. I'll be in touch." With that, the Major headed for the door with Meadows racing after him.

Robert shouted after him, "How long, major?"

"Don't know yet, old boy, but it will have to be very soon as there's a meeting at HQ about maybe moving to new defence lines in a few days. The Slim River is not proving to be much of an obstacle. General Percival's here at this moment discussing it."

Chapter 16

Clive, Stuart, Meadows, Frank and Fred were sitting on a range of chairs in Mark's office. The windows looking out into the small courtyard at the back of the bank were broken with panes missing and the tape that had been stuck to the panes was flapping slightly in the hot wind that they could feel blowing into the room. The Union bank officials were dressed in various types of shorts and long trousers, procured army boots and wearing short-sleeved shirts. Frank was dressed in shorts, a shirt that had come from Hawaii by the looks of it and trousers, by the width and shape, that were clearly not his. Only Fred in some way looked a little more coordinated in his dress with a matching khaki outfit throughout. All six men now wore holsters or shoulder belts with small arms.

At first glance, it was like a scene out of one of the films that Robert had occasionally enjoyed in London on a wet winter's evening. As for Robert, he had just had a meeting with Mark Forrester which had been difficult and Mark had left about an hour ago to get some sleep before going back on duty with the Volunteers.

Robert was producing bottles from Mark's drinks cabinet with Mrs Clemence endeavouring to clean some glasses that had been standing on the top of the cabinet. Everything was covered in dust and for the umpteenth time Robert coughed.

Mrs Clemence looked across at him. "Are you all right, Mr Draper?" Robert just nodded, as he pulled out a full bottle of malt whisky and passed it over to Frank for him to fill the glasses.

Robert's meeting with Mark had been tense and Clive who had been there at the start of the meeting had walked out halfway through it. Robert had let vent with his anger once the three of them were in Mark's office.

"Where the hell have you been, Mark? This is your bank. You deserted your staff when they most needed you."

Mark had taken Robert's angry comments for a few minutes before finally interrupting and saying, "I told Walter that unless he transferred me from this hellhole that I would resign and I did just that. I never wanted the appointment and Mary more or less said that she was leaving me, she hated it so much. I sent him a letter on 11 December confirming that I had resigned with immediate effect."

Robert just shook his head and walked around the room. Clive said nothing. "It seems to me that whether you intended to resign or not, it was all overtaken when the Japs attacked us. You surely had a responsibility for your staff, and to get the bullion out."

"Walter wouldn't listen. He said to carry on as normal and stop being a namby-pamby. I told him my marriage was in ruins living up here. He wouldn't listen so I said I resigned and I would prefer to join up. Anything was better than here."

"Christ almighty, you still don't get it. You had a responsibility for your staff. You left Clive, only a few months into the job to manage it. Have you seen the problem we have downstairs? While you're playing soldiers, we have a major problem which if not solved shortly will mean that the Japs get their hands on enough bullion to fund their war for years."

Mark started to shout. "Who the hell do you think you are?" "You are at best an Acting Manager."

At that point, Clive walked out of the meeting saying he had had enough.

Mark walked away and then sat on his old desk and eventually in a calmer voice said, "Look, I told Walter before the war started that I was leaving; Mary and Lucy went off to Australia as soon as Lucy was well enough. I would have gone as well but I was refused a permit and the Colonial Office said I had to do my bit here. So, when the girls left on the *Roberta,* I joined the Volunteers."

"That doesn't make sense, Mark. You could have carried on at the bank and joined the LDC. Stuart and some of the clerks have done that."

"It makes sense to me. I told Walter I was not coming back. He knew that before the Japs attacked and I tried to leave with Mary and Lucy on the *Roberta.* I saw him just before he went off to Batavia and I again told him. I only came back up to clear out the house."

"So why did you need to send a letter on 11 December?"

"Because Gordon got a message to me through Clive asking where the hell I was. I had told Clive but Gordon wouldn't accept my decision third hand. I was in KL on 11 December before I went off to the Volunteers so I took the opportunity to send a letter to Walter confirming that I had resigned. I told Walter I hadn't wanted to leave Hong Kong. Mary and I were happy there."

"You wouldn't be enjoying it now. They surrendered on

Christmas Day."

Mark said nothing in reply. It was clear that Mark had no conscience about leaving Clive and his staff in jeopardy and had washed his hands of any commitment to Union and China Bank. Robert just sighed. "Let's leave it, Mark. You need some sleep, so you better get off."

Mark just nodded, accepting the role reversal, and left without another word, leaving Robert standing beside Mark's old desk running his finger through some of the dust and writing something in it before wiping his hand across it. Robert never saw him again, only learning years later that he had fought bravely with other Volunteers trying to delay the Japanese entering KL and thus enabling thousands of civilians to flee south.

******

Robert raised his glass and looked around. "You haven't got a drink, Mrs Clemence."

"I don't drink, Mr Draper. Thank you."

Robert just nodded and raised his glass, "Gentlemen, and Lady, here's to a good year ahead. May we all survive this war. Who knows what lies in front of us?"

There was a murmur of agreement and then Robert said, "Right to business. First, Clive, tell the security staff the bank will close on the night of the 4th and thank them for all their hard work. Tell them that when we reopen that there will be a job for them."

There were a few smiles at what Robert said with Stuart murmuring, "When we reopen."

"Second, Mr Meadows, will you and Clive pay the guards double pay for the past three weeks and three months' pay as we have done for the rest of the staff. Can you also pay the Hong Kong staff double pay for the past three weeks? It goes without saying that you should thank them for all their hard work."

Frank interrupted and said, "I'd appreciate it if you could pay them the three months you're paying your lads. We can settle up when we get down to the Island."

Meadows looked at Robert who just nodded. "Make sure they all believe we're closing on the 4th and that we're going on that evening, please." Robert looked at both Clive and Meadows as he said it. "You have got Abilash on duty tomorrow night, Mr Meadows?"

Meadows finished his drink and nodded. "All arranged. As you instructed; he's on duty because he's guarding you at Mrs Clemence's bungalow."

"How are we going to get the money on the trucks, Bob? We haven't got sufficient staff. It will take hours if we have to do it ourselves," Frank asked, as he accepted the bottle being passed to him.

"It's all arranged, Fred. You and Frank have to walk down to the Ferguson workshops, separately mind you; be there for tomorrow night at 10 pm. Jim Clemence will have both lorries ready for driving away with a full tank of petrol. Get in, no messing about, and drive straight up here. We won't be using the fruit and veg van; Jim doesn't think it will make it. Fred, you bring the first lorry, and you, Frank, give him a few minutes head start.

Everything being equal you Fred should be here no later than ten past. The army will have sealed off the roads around here from 10 pm and you will both get through because they have given me recognition stickers to put on the front of each lorry which is a good as a password. When you get here, park up at the main entrance. There may be a lorry there already. Just park behind it. The army is supplying a lorry and will bring troops for loading the gold. Mr Meadows, you will be organising the loading of the lorries. When you have the right amount on each lorry, it will set off with an escort of soldiers."

"Where to?"

"That bit the Army is keeping secret. Clive, you must go with the first lorry. It's your responsibility for the gold on that truck." Clive nodded looking amazed as the plan unfolded.

"Right, then it's our first lorry. Once loaded, it will set off to wherever. Fred, you will have an army sergeant who will know your rendezvous. Stuart, I suggest you go in that lorry. My guess is that the Army plan is for us all to end up at Campbell Road and then I know not what."

"Who is responsible for the bullion?" asked Fred.

"As you're driving, then it's Stuart who will be with you." Robert looked across at a twenty-year-old Aussie who just nodded at what Robert was saying. "It's your responsibility, Stuart. You'll have half a dozen soldiers with you in the back."

Robert turned to Frank, "Finally, we do the same with the last lorry and it will take Mr Meadows who will be responsible for the gold. Is that all clear? Oh, and make sure you take Abilash with you. I have talked to the remaining clerks and security staff and none of them want to risk a trip to Gemas so it is only us and Abilash."

"What happens to you once we've loaded up and gone?"

"I get to go in the smart army car that follows you a few

minutes later. I will lock the bank doors, tell the security staff to go home, and that's that."

It was Fred who said, "It all sounds simple but it will take us ages to get all that gold piled up on the lorries."

"I am assured by Major Docherty that there will be sufficient troops on hand to manhandle the gold onto the lorries and shift it in moments. If there is a risk, it is to the last lorry. We think we can be out of here by no later than ten thirty which gives the commies little time to get themselves organised, especially as they don't know which way the Army is taking us."

"Surely, you know where the lorries are going?"

"I've told you I don't know. It was part of the explicit orders I had to agree to that I put the gold and ourselves in the hands of the Army who will get it to Gemas by hook or by crook and then we have the next stage to worry about. Those of you responsible for your lorry will have to adapt these arrangements if we get separated and the Army starts getting twitchy feet." Turning to Stuart, Robert said, "Stuart, when I catch up with you, I will take over responsibility for your lorry. Is that clear?" Stuart just nodded.

It was Stuart who turned to Mrs Clemence. "Come with us, Mrs Clemence. You and Mr Clemence will have a bad time when the Japs come."

Mrs Clemence shook her head. "Don't you fuss about us, Stuart. You just get the gold to Singapore. Me and Jim, we'll be fine. We've thought about it and we can't leave everything we have. Where would we go?"

Robert realising that further talk was only going to upset Mrs Clemence turned to Clive, "Make sure that Mrs

Clemence has three months wages like the rest and also make sure she has money for me lodging with her."

Mrs Clemence started to protest but Robert interrupted, "I won't take no for an answer. You'll need every penny and when all this is over, I'll come and find you."

Mrs Clemence started to bubble up and it was Stuart who came over and gave her a hug. "I think you're bloody brave, Mrs C." She just nodded and pulled her hankie out and wiped her eyes.

"Right, everybody, you know your part. Try and make everything look as normal as possible for the next thirty hours. I've only told you now just in case in the bombing I get injured; Frank in the event things go pear shaped and I'm not here, I'm looking to you to take charge." Frank just nodded, raising an eyebrow and then moved over to refill his glass.

Robert looked around the meeting. "God knows what we do if the British Battalion get pulled into something else. At the moment, they are having forty-eight hours r&r and are being used as the reserve. Try and get some sleep between now and tomorrow night. And for God's sake, keep your mouths shut."

It was Fred who said, "Have you noticed that they haven't bombed KL today?"

And Frank who answered, "What's the point if they know it's theirs in a few days. Let's just hope it's not sooner."

Robert refilled the glasses and stood up, "Good luck, everyone."

After Fred and Frank had gone and Abilash had taken Mrs Clemence down to her bungalow, Robert continued sitting with Clive and Mr Meadows and he took the opportunity to update them on the outcome of his discussion with Mark and on his earlier telephone call to Singapore. He had managed to speak to Peter who was covering for Gordon who was at a meeting in Colonial House. Again, Peter had asked why they were taking so long to get out of KL.

"It's total chaos here, Peter. It's not safe to go outside anymore. The roads are blocked with debris and the dead. I sent you a telegram with some details of our problems. There's just no transport out. If you go outside, you're liable to be strafed and if not strafed then shot at by God alone knows who, commies, deserters or looters. Meadows is running a 24-hour security regime with staff who sleep on the premises. Davies is down to a handful of police so there's little law up here and the military are just too busy to help. If nothing is obvious by the 4th, then I think we have no choice but to abandon the bank and make our way down as best we can; after that KL is at risk of being an open town."

"Not before the 4th. It can't be that difficult surely. What's the problem?"

"I'll can't tell you over the telephone. Suffice to say it's bloody complicated. Mark is finally coming in to see me; in about an hour. He wanted us to meet at the Majestic but I told him that it must be here as we're so shorthanded on the security roster."

Peter merely grunted and said that Robert's first priority was to get out, nothing else, and then the telephonist interrupted them. "I'm sorry, gentlemen, but the three minutes are up." They just wished each other 'good luck' and then the line went dead.

When Robert asked a few moments later if he could make another call, he was told that there was only one-line functioning to Singapore and the army had priority. "Well, what about a telegram?"

"You can leave the message at the Post Office, sir, and it will be processed when the Army messages are not marked urgent; no more than ten words mind."

He thanked the telephonist and then decided it was too risky trying to get to the post office.

Chapter 17

Robert slowly cycled up to Campbell Road in the late morning heat. He was tired by the sheer effort of just trying to survive. The past twenty-five days, since the Japanese had first attacked Singapore, had been a constant battle dealing with attack after attack and trying to just stay alive. In KL, the constant hiding under desks in the bank as the bombs reigned down and the skulking in doorways as fighter planes came over strafing the streets had brought nerves to a raw state. Dust was everywhere, getting on his chest and he spent a good deal of time coughing. As he cycled to his meeting, he could feel grit inside his shirt irritating his skin.

The weather was hot although the humidity was at least absent. Finding food was a constant struggle; the bank now relied upon an Army unit a few hundred yards away for the supply of water, and there had been no electricity for nearly two weeks.

Abilash cycled behind him with his rifle slung over his back and they kept to the main roads where an Army presence was apparent. When they had ventured out yesterday to go to the Majestic Hotel, they had been shot at by deserters and today the Army was patrolling the streets up to Campbell Road.

At the check point, Robert explained they were going to see Superintendent Davies and the Military Police let them through. Robert stopped for a moment to watch a convoy of lorries going south. There were also a large number of trucks parked by the wayside with drivers and men taking full advantage of there being no enemy planes around, sitting smoking and having a bite to eat.

"Good to see the Japs have stopped bombing, Sergeant." Robert addressed the MP who was like him watching the soldiers, mostly Indian by the looks of it, who were sitting at the roadside enjoying a few minutes of quiet.

"They must know something we don't know, sir."

By that, Robert took it to mean that all the lorries seemed to be going south. Robert looked at the Sergeant who still looked remarkably smart. "I think we'll all learn soon, Sergeant." The MP moved off realising that Robert probably knew no more than he did.

Robert got back on his bicycle and worked his way up to the police HQ a few hundred yards away. He noticed right away that there were more police than he had seen on his previous visits, most of them sitting on temporary benches eating and smoking; there was a quiet hum only with little snatches of conversation from the exhausted looking men. Robert mused that the Superintendent was pulling his men in. Abilash took Robert's bicycle and with his, he wheeled them over to the corner of the building and squatted. Robert went in to see Superintendent Davies for the last time.

"Well, young man, you certainly caused a stir. I tried God knows how many times and got nowhere and in one go you get the works. Mind you, I didn't say you had ten million stored in the vaults." There was no malice in what Davies said, more it was ruefulness.

"My apologies if I stepped on toes but it seemed too good an opportunity when Lay appeared in front of me."

Davies merely nodded and sat down at his desk. "We've been told the whole shebang is moving south to a new line being formed at Gemas. The Japanese breached our defences at the Slim River two days ago and we have been desperately holding them in order to get as many away as possible but I think we will be lucky to hold them for more than twenty-four hours. KL will be an open town in two to three days by which time hopefully, the 11th Division is safely south of KL. They are leaving a small force about fifteen miles up the road to delay the Japs as long as possible"

"What will you do, Superintendent?"

"I will stay and offer to keep the peace in KL. My No. 2 will stay as well. I've spoken to a number of the Japanese internees and they seem to think the Japanese military authorities will accept that for a while."

"I'm sorry," and then as an afterthought, Robert questioned what the Superintendent had just said. "Japanese internees? I didn't realise we had any."

"We have nearly two thousand up at the racecourse. There's no doubt some of them were planted on us before the war to observe our military installations but quite a few are just businessmen or rubber planters. By and large, they've been no trouble." Davies looked across at Robert and said ruefully, "Probably because they knew that the Japanese military would get here eventually."

Davies pushed over a plate of Rich Tea biscuits to go with the black tea he had already given Robert. "So, do you have everything in place, Mr Draper. I don't know exactly when you're going, other than at the briefing this morning, I was told it was all arranged."

"We go soon, very soon, Superintendent, and yes everything is in place. All being well, Li Bo has no inkling of the plan and there seems to be plenty of men involved just in case he does try to interfere. It's gone from one extreme to the other."

Davies smiled back at Robert. "When you've been doing the job as long as I have, you'll realise that it's easier to go with the flow especially when you have no cards in your hand capable of winning a trick. Heath and Bennett wanted no distractions until Lay told them that there was ten million lying in a vault and the C-in-C Far East would likely take a dim view of the Japs getting their hands on it."

"Is there ten million by the way?"

Robert smiled back, sipping the hot black tea with sugar he had just added. "It's at least that much, Superintendent. What I will say is that there's a hell of a lot of money lying on the floor of the bank and it would be embarrassing if the Japs did get their hands on it or for that matter Chin Peng."

Davies pursed his lips. "After this war ends, Chin Peng is going to cause us great problems, Mr Draper. If he gets hold of the money, you can say bye-bye to paradise. He will use it to make this a communist state."

Robert left shortly afterwards, shaking hands with the Superintendent and thanking him for all he had done. Davies just shook his head. "I wish I could have done more, but I just didn't have the manpower."

As Robert was going through the door, he turned, "If it's possible, can you keep an eye on the Clemences at the Ferguson workshops? They still refuse to come with us believing their faith will hold them in good stead."

"There are quite a few like that I'm afraid. There's nothing to go back home for; this is their home. They just don't accept that the Japanese will be so cruel as to not allow them to continue living in the community." There was a momentary pause. "You remember the Gilpins, of course?"

Robert nodded. He had tried to contact the Gilpins a couple of times since he had come up to KL, without success. Mrs Clemence had said that she had only seen Mr Gilpin once in the past six months and it seemed that they had become virtual recluses up in the hills northeast of KL.

The Superintendent pursed his lips before saying, "One of the Volunteer patrols went up into the hills yesterday and found them in their house. They'd been executed. Well, he had. They just shot her and her nurse in her bedroom. The place was ransacked. Can't tell you whether it was the Japs or the commies."

Robert said nothing, what could he say. He just turned away and kept walking through the building and out into the sunshine. Abilash saw him as he came out and brought the bicycles over. Robert took a moment to look up at the sky and let out a sigh. "Come on, Abilash; let's see if we can find some food on our way back."

In the afternoon, Robert tried to get some sleep. Mrs Clemence had gone or rather Robert had sent her off telling her to go and try to do something entirely normal at home. He gave her a big hug as she left but said nothing else and then Clive did the same but whispering, "Look after yourself, Mrs C. I'll miss you."

Robert got Abilash to escort her down to the bungalow and then he went into his old office and finding Stuart missing, he went over and lay down on the bed he knew he usually occupied. It looked as though Stuart and Meadows had already packed their personal stuff; Robert had everything on him, nothing else was worth taking. As he lay down, he coughed again in the dusty atmosphere hoping that he would spit up no more blood.

Chapter 18

The lorries were in a long queue under the shelter of trees. Robert was standing a few yards away under some palm trees gazing out over the water separating them from Singapore and in the haze in the distance he could just make out the outline of buildings and plumes of smoke coming from further inland. He could hear Fred shouting that there was a brew and he turned to go back.

All along the road down to the causeway, some hundreds of yards away, there were lorries with men sitting at the side of the road. As he walked across the road, he could see some female nurses tending men on stretchers which had been taken off the lorries and put under the shade of the trees. The Japanese planes had been over earlier in the morning but had directed their attention to the convoy coming over the causeway from Singapore and there had been a terrifying half hour or so of strafing, with the ack-ack guns placed near the causeway firing at targets that seemed to emerge almost at tree height, giving the gunners little chance to focus on targets.

Robert and his band of men had been in a ditch literally cowering from the shooting and the noise, before emerging to see a number of lorries burning but fortunately none of the British Battalion lorries.

Fred handed him a mug of tea from the pot he had brewed over the little fire.

"The MP said we would be going over after dusk," Robert just said, as he sat down with his back against the trunk of a tree. Stuart was trying to sleep on the other side of the tree with Abilash drinking his tea, a few yards away.

Fred walked over to the back of the nearest truck. "Frank, wake up, you sod, I've made you tea."

From the truck, there was groan, "Just let me sleep for a week," and then a shuffle as Frank appeared on his knees. "Those bags are sodding hard to lie on," he said to no one in particular as he turned around and holding onto the side of the truck, he clambered down. Coming over beside Robert, he sat down and took the mug of tea from Fred. One thing Robert had learned since they had left KL was that Fred was a great person to have around. He produced tea and water from seemingly nowhere and always appeared to know where to get food.

Robert groaned and scratched himself. "I hope to God there's running water. Do you think they can smell us coming?"

Fred was smiling down at him. "I reckon you could do with a good shave first, or the weight of the beard will take you to the bottom of the bath."

Robert looked up and grinned. "You should have seen that Colonel I saw a few minutes ago. I swear he stood behind the MP just so as not to get too near to me."

"So why do we have to wait?" Frank asked.

"There's an Australian Division coming across at the moment and then we go across around dusk. Did you see the train that just went over? It had holes all over it. The last one out of Seramban I think."

Frank sat up with a jerk. "Seramban, didn't we go through that yesterday or was it the day before?"

"Yes, two days ago, very early in the morning. Remember before we got under the trees in that plantation where the MPs were arresting those deserters."

As they were talking, Robert could see an officer coming up the road and watched as he turned more or less opposite them and approached.

"You lads, all okay?" There was a general murmur from those awake as Fred offered him a mug and he nodded. "Could do with one."

Frank looked up at him. "We're fine, thanks Captain. Your lads have done us proud. It's been everything from one of those thrillers my wife reads. We've been strafed, bombed, and then soaked to the skin. We've had to repair burst tyres in the dark and we've had people shoot at us in the middle of the night. The only thing missing is we haven't got Ava Gardner to fight over."

The Captain was smiling at Frank's description of the past week and then his face grew more serious, "I suspect it's nothing to what is going to happen in the next few weeks. The Japs took Seramban two days ago and the train that's just gone over, that was the last. It's been stuck in a siding up the track whilst they repaired the line." The Captain paused for a moment before adding, "A good number of our troops were caught in the encirclement."

He finished his tea and then turned to Robert. "Hopefully, we go over in a couple of hours. My CO has asked me to say that our responsibility for you effectively ends now. He apologises for not seeing you but he's been sent over to the island for some conference or other." Robert got up and shook his extended hand and the Captain then shook hands with the others.

"I can't thank you enough, Captain. You and your lads have looked after us royally."

The Captain started to move off with the parting remark, "If I ever have children, I will tell them about the gold I helped to rescue from the Japs."

When he had gone, Robert said to Frank, "Getting here is only half the job. The next task is to get the bloody gold off the Island." Frank was heading back to the truck and as he climbed up, he said, "We had better start planning now, Robert my boy, because the Japs are still coming."

Stuart groaned from the other side of the tree, "You lot talk too much."

Robert hunkered down and closed his eyes and thought about all the things that had happened since they had moved the gold out of the bank at the dead of night nearly seven days ago. Thinking back, it had all worked like clockwork. Meadows had the men, who had appeared at the bank doors, working in pairs and carrying the bags out to the waiting lorry without any words being needed. The Union Bank boxes had been heavier and sometimes needed three men but in only a few minutes the first lorry was loaded and away even before Fred had turned up with the first of the trucks from the Ferguson workshops. The soldiers had been piling the gold at the door in the meantime and in no time, they had it on the back of the lorry and off it set, with Frank having just arrived in the third lorry.

Meadows had made sure that all the gold was on the last truck before going off and then Robert, after a quick thank you and good luck to the remaining security staff, had locked the bank doors saying a little prayer as he did so and then he was off with the Captain who had charge of the exercise.

The trucks had been taken up to Campbell Road, as Robert had suspected, and corralled for a short time before joining onto a long line of trucks, of all shapes and sizes, all going south, not by the main road but by a dirt road closer to the hills. It was impossible to tell which truck was which, at least not until daylight by which time they had covered a dozen miles and were southeast of Kl. Shortly afterwards, the British Battalion and a contingent of engineers had split off again taking an even more easterly route before eventually again heading south, all on dirt tracks.

It was then that they had hit trouble as they were continually strafed and bombed for two days, barely moving at times, with a number of lorries being set on fire and Robert and his crowd taking what shelter they could whilst the troops, largely with rifles and bren guns, attempted to send the fighters packing.

Robert, like all of them, felt absolutely vulnerable and he marvelled days later that none of them had been killed. On two occasions, they had to transfer the gold to serviceable lorries as the bullion ones had been damaged by gunfire from attacking Japanese planes. On another occasion, they had had to hide on a rubber plantation with the planes literally seeking them out but fortunately, the trees were sufficiently close to each other to give them good cover.

Throughout those hot days the men worked at repairing the damaged lorries with Fred and Stuart turning out to have real skills at repairing vehicles and Robert turning his hand to helping the cooks with making tea and meals for the very hot soldiers. It was during this time that the Colonel and his fellow officers were most anxious, as they were convinced that the Japanese could not be far behind but luck was with them and they managed to keep one-step ahead for most of the time. Over to the west, they would occasionally hear loud explosions which Robert was told one evening was probably the engineers blowing bridges to delay the Japs on the main road.

Fred, on one occasion as they were hiding in a rubber plantation, from somewhere produced water, tea and biscuits and cheese which they later learned was from the abandoned kitchen of the plantation house they could see in the distance. Meadows was also a star having scrounged some tins of bully beef from a quartermaster.

What was quickly apparent was that patience was the name of the game. You snoozed as much as possible, stayed in the shade and away from the vehicles just in case the Japanese planes going overhead happened to guess where they were, and then moved off as soon as it seemed safe. Somehow most of the lorries were coaxed into working although towards the end, as they reached Gemas, the lorries seemed to be seriously overloaded with men, equipment and gold.

Corralled up on the fourth day, still short of Gemas, Robert could see in the distance, on the metalled road they had just joined, cars and lorries burning having been strafed by Japanese planes. "They took a chance," murmured a Major who happened to be standing near Robert. "It'll take us a while to move that lot before we can get on the road. Luckily, KL is an open town now so hopefully, that slows the Japs down."

Robert asked what he meant.

"The Jap troops will want to get a few mementos so it may be difficult for their officers to chivvy them on. We can only hope. It would be nice to have a few days respite although the bombers and fighters are not letting up."

Speaking later to Meadows, Robert learned that the British Battalion had come down the dirt road to Khota Lipis which for a large part was also the single-track railway line, fighting a rear-guard action all the way. "They held them up for five days at Jitra, Mr Draper, getting as many people down to KL as possible. Some of their lads got split off from the rest of the Regiment and they're hoping that they managed to cut through and have headed south. They're not a complete battalion, more a composite of two battalions that have been badly mauled so that's why they have been allocated to look after us," Meadows said it all knowledgeably.

"Are we the last out of KL then, Cedric?"

"Maybe not down the main road but there's nothing behind us on this road." Mr Meadows said looking back up the road. "I think the Colonel may have a few lads bringing up the rear but that's it." It had been on the second day of the escape from KL when Robert and Meadows had been stuck in a monsoon drain for more than an hour being strafed that Robert had asked Meadows for his first name on the pretence it would be nice to know the full name of the man he could die alongside and Meadows had taken this as a great compliment although Robert noticed that he still called him Mr Draper or sir when in the company of others even though Robert had told Meadows to call him by his first name.

As they worked their way down to Gemas, there had been fewer and fewer troops in front of them, and on one occasion, they only got across a bridge minutes before the engineers blew it up. They all stood and looked back to where the bridge had been before being shouted to load up and move off before the Jap planes came investigating the plume of smoke. As they sat back in the trucks, Robert shouted, over the noise of a very tired engine, across at Meadows, "I thought you said there were a few soldiers in the rear."

Meadows just shrugged his shoulders, "That was yesterday," and then he closed his eyes trying to get some rest. Robert sat with one of the officer's one night sharing a bottle of whisky Meadows had produced, looking remarkably like one of the bottles he had last seen in Mark's office. He learned that the Captain had been in the Volunteers before being seconded to the Leicester's and then to the composite battalion, as an interpreter.

"I've lived out here since I was a boy and I speak Malay and some Chinese, so I was an obvious candidate for the job of Liaison Officer with the locals. I lived on a rubber estate in Johore not far from where we're heading in fact." Looking across at some of the soldiers sitting quietly in groups doing their chores, he said in a soft voice, "They're a fine set of lads, Mr Draper, brave and as obstinate as hell as the Japs have found to their cost. It's an honour to be with them but most of them have never even had to march in this heat let alone fight. We're wasting a lot of good men."

"I gather we're the last troops coming down this road," Robert said just as quietly. Robert had seen some of the troops, digging tank ditches on the roads, a few times during the day and a great deal of activity with troops trying to find ways of delaying the Japs. There had been a scare on the third day when cyclists had been seen in the distance with the first thought being that it was Japanese troops only for moments later a group of Catholic priests to come cycling up to them, escaping from a seminary further up the road.

The Captain had nodded at what Robert had said, "We're surprised the Japs haven't reached us yet but it maybe they are being cautious as we've set a number of booby traps and the engineers have laid some mines. Maybe they're just regrouping before they come again, who knows? We do know that they have pushed their tanks down the main road so the Colonel's concern is that we get to the main road just north of Gemas and the Japs are already there." Robert, as he had sat with the officer, remembered hearing lorries coming into the camp the night before; it must have been the engineers who had arrived after laying more mines a mile or so up the road. Later that night, there was shooting further back up the road and a platoon of men was deployed to act as a rear guard as the rest of the battalion set off at a very slow pace on the mud road.

When they did eventually reach Gemas, it was to find it in complete disarray with the Japanese bombing the area almost continually in daylight hours. They were sent to a position a mile or so away from where most of the action seemed to be happening whilst the Colonel in charge of the makeshift battalion tried to find out where the rest of his men were and what to do about the gold. When the Colonel eventually saw Robert, it was to tell him, "Mr Draper, we'll be here at least twelve hours and then I think your lot will still be with us. It seems some of the East Surreys and Leicester's have fought their way down to here and have been sent on to Singapore to regroup, so I suspect that's where we will all end up."

“Colonel, we’re entirely in your hands. I would think we need a change of lorries though in order to go all that way as these are barely able to move. Oh, and if we have to use these lorries then we need petrol.”

The Colonel made a face at Robert. “By God, you chaps want more. We get you out of a pickle in KL and now you want petrol and another lift,” smiling as he said it.

Robert just grinned back at the Colonel. “Well, we could do with some food as well.” The Colonel just left shaking his head. About an hour or so later, an Army lorry turned up with a large urn of army curry, at least that’s what the cook said it was and Meadows just added, “Don’t ask what’s in it, just eat,” which they did.

In the end, they were stuck in Gemas for nearly two days before a Major turned up with three newish looking lorries, “Right shift everything onto these lorries and there’s spare petrol tanks in the back as well.” He had shouted at some of his men who appeared from out of the lorries and they moved the bullion to the new trucks, although they were much slower in the task than the lads had been on the last night in KL. “We’re off now, gentlemen, so get your stuff. Leave your lorries. The engineers will take care of them.”

Chapter 19

They finally got the order to cross the causeway closer to eight o'clock in the evening by which time Robert had been down to see the MPs at the crossroads on two further occasions to find out what was causing the hold up only to be told that the priority was to get the last of the Australian Division over, then some lorries with wounded soldiers, followed by some civilians, and only then would it be the odds and sods such as the British Battalion. Telling the guards that they had a very valuable cargo did not get very far with the sergeant MP controlling the traffic who used a few very choice words about there being a war on and what Robert could do with his cargo. Explaining to the lads where they were on the priority list merely got a groan from them but Robert noticed the soldiers still with them were all taking the opportunity to get some sleep; they knew their priority.

Once over the causeway, a mere half mile wide, they were stopped by the Military Police and warned of serious road delays through Bukit Timah and redirected to take the Western coast road past Tengah aerodrome. The MP Robert spoke to was despairing as he said that all the roads seemed constantly choked and were not geared up to cope with the volume of traffic and would not be cleared by the time the Jap bombers arrived next morning.

They had just started off, having taken nearly an hour to transfer the gold to Australian army lorries because the British Battalion were being assigned to another part of the Island, when Robert saw a telephone box. Stopping the small convoy, Robert shouted that he needed to make a call.

"What's wrong now?" yelled Frank from the last lorry.

"I need to tell Peter we're on our way, so he can open up the bank or we could be sitting outside all night. Imagine Chin Yu's face if we get this far and then we are robbed."

There was a flash of teeth from twenty yards away and Robert could just see Frank's head and shoulders leaning out of his lorry window laughing. "Tell him to have a strong drink ready and that he will know when we are getting near; he'll smell us."

Getting into Fullerton Square, after a horrendously slow journey past all the bomb damage around Tengah air base and what seemed like thousands of people on the move towards Singapore City, it almost seemed like Robert had been away forever.

Suddenly, he felt enormously tired. He just wanted to sleep. He hadn't coughed for the last two days so maybe his chest was getting over the humidity and clouds of dust of KL. Stopping outside the bank's side doors, they were met by Lennox and a group of security men who were expecting them. They had first to move crowds of people sleeping on the pavement and then work in the dark although inside the bank Lennox had produced a number of storm lamps. It took them much longer to unload the gold because there was less of them to manage the boxes of bullion but it was done eventually and Robert went and thanked the Army drivers who set off to try and find their motor pool somewhere up towards the Naval docks.

Robert sat on a bag of gold as Peter came around with Michael serving them tea with a shot of whisky for those who wanted it, which was all of them.

"Bob, I had no idea," was all Peter kept saying as he looked around at the bags and crates on the floor. "We knew it was gold but this is a fortune. I'll ring Gordon in a minute. He'll have a fit."

"It's not all ours, Peter. The canvas bags are mostly Frank's lot," said Robert waving his arm across at Frank who had put his arm out for a second cup of tea and snifter. "We also have some of Hong Kong Bank's bullion which I'm not sure Maurice Levy knows about."

Peter nodded, "I spoke to him about four days ago. Two cars of gold turned up on the Island, one for Barclays and one of theirs. The others had to be abandoned so God knows what happened to that money. I gather Ken Seymour didn't make it."

Robert looked up and frowned. Getting up wearily, he said, "Morrissey was killed in the shootout as well." Nothing was said between them for perhaps a moment and then Robert asked, "You got any instructions for us?"

Peter shook his head. "It's your game."

Robert merely nodded and turned to the rest of them sitting around the banking hall, "Right," and pitched in to everybody. "Mr Lennox, you have the responsibility of taking all the gold down to the vaults as soon as you can find sufficient manpower. Unless Mr Fraser says otherwise, the bank doesn't open until you shift it." Robert looked at Peter, as he said it and saw him nod.

"Frank, you need to see Mr Chin Yu as soon as you've had a rest and arrange with Gordon, or Peter here, what you intend doing about this money. Hopefully, the Colonial Office when they learn how much is now hanging around on the Island, can arrange a shipment for all the banks. Stuart, you said you would bunk up with Michael. Is that still on?" Michael and Stuart confirmed the arrangement with nods and mutterings which Robert could just make out under the light of the storm lamps. "Cedric, you said you had your own arrangements. You still okay for that?" Mr Meadows said he was happy to head off and stay with an old army pal.

"Fred, you said you would stay with a pal over at Beach Road." Fred nodded as well.

"Well, if there's any problem. That goes for all of you then let me know and I know of a very nice lady on Lavender Street who can provide very cheap accommodation." There was a loud hoot of laughter. It was one of the Aussie lads, it must have been Stuart, who said, "I'm too tired, Bob."

Robert walked over to where Abilash had been drinking his tea quietly. "You get home Abilash to your family. Here take these dollars and get a taxi. No, don't say 'No'. And don't come back for two days. Speak to Mr Lennox and tell him I said two days."

Abilash got up, "Thank you, Sahib." He went off to find Lennox who had disappeared into his office.

"Oh, and leave your rifle here, Abilash," shouted Robert at the departing back.

Peter came over. "I think we can leave it to Lennox to lock up. I'll just have a quick word with him and then I'll take you up to Tanglin. You won't recognise it. I've come down in the car so it will be a bit quicker."

Robert acknowledged what Peter said, before adding, "Clive is staying with me."

Clive sat in the back of the old Sedan car as Peter drove them to Tanglin. For the first time, Robert saw large numbers of people sleeping on the streets and there was a smell of burning and lots of dust which had been less apparent, as they had come down the coast road earlier. Orchard Road and where it joined on to Tanglin Road was more or less bombed out with a fire tender still at work on one of the buildings.

"Has this been happening every day, Peter?"

"Too much to tell you now. I'll bring you up to date tomorrow. You and Clive get some shuteye and come in when you're ready. I will sort things out with Gordon." Peter worked his way through some bomb damage and then turned to look at Robert briefly. "I presume you know that Mrs Lin Yuen died on New Year's Day," Peter said the last point quietly and Robert just grunted an acknowledgement as he watched an LDC unit helping to clear a building at the start of Tanglin Road.

"Our mob is up helping with some fires towards Farrer Road tonight and I got Henry to take over with Captain Peters although Henry must be exhausted as he's been on duty for days at the station." Peter nodded towards the LDC unit they were passing. "That looks like the Orchard Road lot."

"What about Arthur?"

"Poor chap's down with a dose of malaria. Not doing too well when I spoke to Neecha, so I suspect he'll not be fit for a while." In the back of the car, they could hear gentle snoring.

"I'll tell you all about KL over a beer," Robert murmured as Peter drove up to Mrs Lin Yuen's front porch. They woke up Clive from his deep sleep and clambered out into the hot sticky early morning darkness. The house was in total darkness. Robert borrowed Peter's torch and went up onto the front veranda and tried the front door which was locked.

"Hang on a minute, I'll go around the side and shout Chunggy." Peter and Clive, who was still half-asleep, stood silently as they heard Robert go around and then start shouting and a moment later, they could hear Chunggy shouting back with sheer excitement. Even from twenty yards away, they could make out Chunggy getting all his words mixed up. Seconds later, Chunggy was with Robert at the front with a key.

Peter got back in the car and started the engine. "Right, I'm off then. I'll see you sometime later today hopefully. Try and get a decent sleep although the Japs are likely to be over in a few hours. They seem to like routine. Nine in the morning and late afternoon."

Robert and Clive barely said anything, too tired to function. They watched Peter drive off before turning and following Chunggy into the house which seemed cluttered with stuff but Robert decided he was too tired to question what it was all about. Chunggy had lit a storm lamp and he led them upstairs.

"Is Mr Fisher's room made up, Chunggy? I was thinking Clive could use it."

Chunggy turned, as he led them up the stairs. "It may be not very tidy, Mr Drapa."

Robert said nothing about that and just said to Clive "It's yours to use, Clive. The bathroom's there if you want a wash before you go to bed. Drinks are over there." Robert waved his arm over in the direction of the bathroom and then at the drink's cabinet. "I suggest we get our heads down and have baths in the morning."

"Chunggy, tell me the water is running."

Even in the semi-darkness, Robert could make out Chunggy's broad smile.

"Water very good, Mr Drapa. I have food, also. You want some."

Robert just shook his head, watching Clive disappear off to Harry's room with his little suitcase. "I'm sorry I wasn't here for the funeral, Chunggy."

Chunggy shrugged his shoulders. "You could not help it, Mr Drapa. Many people come. She was buried in Bidadari cemetery next to her mother. We had to have service in darkness and very quickly as bombers came over. Chen Zhu Lee speak very good of her. He must see you soon." Robert nodded again, as he started towards the bathroom.

"You know what Mrs Lin Yuen has decided."

It was Chunggy, still excited at Robert having come home, who this time nodded. "I very happy here, Mr Drapa. I happy to look after you."

Robert stopped and turned around. "Don't worry, Chunggy, we'll look after each other. Now lock up again and let's see if we can get some sleep before the damn Japs come over."

Sleep took over and even the bombing of the docks area just after nine o'clock scarcely registered with Robert and Clive and it must have been the noise of people talking loudly and coming up the stairs that first woke Robert. For a moment, he couldn't remember where he was. Then the moment was shattered by the door being flung open and a bundle of swirling dress entered and someone threw herself on the bed.

"You're home. I never thought I would see you again."

Somehow, Robert extricated himself from Joyce's stranglehold and the mosquito net that seemed to have collapsed after she had flung herself on his bed. "I think you should show a little decorum, you know," Robert tried to say in between trying to extricate himself. "Anyway, how did you know we were back?"

"Chunggy told me."

Robert swung his legs out of the bed. "Hang on a minute I've only got my briefs on," he yelled, as Joyce again advanced on him.

She stopped suddenly. "My god, look at you."

Robert who had been trying to cover himself up said, "What do you mean?"

"You look like one of those mountain men in the films."

"What do expect? We've been on the road for seven days with hardly any washing facilities."

"Oh, I wondered what that smell was."

"Right, that's it. Out you go or I will stand up and that will really scare you."

"I'll wait in the lounge. Chunggy is making me some delicious coffee with lovely little cakes he says are your favourite. You can have a bath and let us hope that smell is not permanent, you mean man." With that, Joyce left laughing and with Robert grabbing for a towel and heading for the bathroom.

Emerging sometime later, a new man, apart from a display of bites on his neck, he met a grumpy Clive seeking to go to the bathroom. "What a bloody noise. A man can't get an honest day's sleep. You should tell your women to come here at reasonable times."

"I heard that," Joyce shouted from where she was sitting

on the veranda.

Robert raised his eyebrows at Clive and made a bit of face, "My women have got sharp ears so be careful what you say." Robert, once dressed, came out to the veranda as Chunggy arrived with a fresh pot of coffee and a bowl of fruit.

Robert could only sigh contentedly as Joyce came over and sat beside him. "I began to wonder if I would ever see this again," was all he said, as he closed his eyes for a moment and again sighed.

Chapter 20

Over two pots of coffee, wonderful slices of mango and an endless supply of little caraway cakes, just the way Robert always liked them, he caught up on some of the news. Some way through the second pot of coffee, Clive joined them and after introductions, Robert continued to ask Joyce questions.

"So why are you not on your way to Australia or India?"

"I didn't want to go until I knew you were okay. Anyway, we had a draw at work for who should remain until further notice and I lost. Claire and half a dozen of the girls have gone; they went last Tuesday and I think they're okay." Robert had made a face at what Joyce had said and she picked up on it.

"Don't tell me off. I was worried about you and I did lose in the draw. Five of us have had to stay."

As they were talking, they could hear the air raid sirens going off in the distance. "They're bombing every day now. Up Siglap Road there's lots of damage as though they're trying to isolate Kallang aerodrome because the RAF have got some Hurricanes based there. And you should see the state of Beach Road." Even as Joyce was telling them this news, Robert and Clive could see planes away in the distance circling each other in the sky over Kallang and there was also the drone of heavier aircraft coming from the north.

"Was it very bad up there, Bob?" Joyce asked moving her seat a little closer as Chunggy fussed around behind them wanting to know if they wanted any more caraway cakes.

Robert shook his head at Chunggy but Clive nodded and Chunggy produced another plate of little goodies. "God, you people live well. This is wonderful," they could just about make out Clive saying with his mouth full.

All the while, they watched the sky with the interlacing of men and machines dicing with death. Finally, Robert answered Joyce, as they heard the first bombs dropping on the other side of town. "I think if we get into the state KL is in, then we are in for a dreadful time."

Clive murmured something in support. Robert turned to face Joyce. "I don't really care what draw you were in. You need to get out now, Joyce, before we are cut off. The Army are not likely to stop the Japs unless they get real help from the Yanks, and maybe more Hurricanes." The latter comment coming as they all watched a plane, clearly Japanese, fall out of the sky and as they didn't see an explosion, Robert presumed it had fallen into the sea. Over towards Kallang, the sky was now a plume of black smoke with the sound of ack-ack guns being heard even though the aerodrome was four or five miles away.

Robert turned to speak to Clive. "I think we should go into work and see what's going on. We can't just sit here all day. Joyce says she has got to go back to work in a little while so I suggest we go in at the same time and see what's happening at the bank. We can always come back later and have a snooze."

Clive merely nodded and got up. Turning to Joyce, he said, "Nice to meet you Joyce. Hopefully, we'll get a chance to have a drink sometime." With that, he was off and Robert heard him go into the bathroom.

"Who're you staying with? You're not on your own at Flower Road, are you?" Joyce shook her head and moved closer to Robert.

"I moved out last Tuesday. The local LDC advised it was no longer safe. Next door was flattened and the two houses opposite no longer exist; you remember the one that looked like a castle? Well, that and the black and white bungalow next to it were burnt to the ground. Mrs Snetterton who apparently was a manager at Robinsons was killed as well as her houseboy. The people in the castle had already gone to India."

They heard Clive come out of the bathroom and go off to Harry's room.

Joyce got up and came around the back of Robert and put her hands on Robert's shoulders. Robert could feel her warmth as she stood behind him and her deliciously fresh perfume. "Was it very bad, Bob?"

"There was no order really, Joyce. The planes were literally just strafing anything that moved. You couldn't get anything organised. Everything had just broken down. I left some friends up there and I suspect I won't see them again." Robert had replied in a quiet voice as he put his hand up and touched Joyce's hand on his shoulder. They both watched, as the last of the planes moved out of sight and there was another explosion, this time further north up towards the Naval Yards.

"So where are you staying?"

"I've found temporary accommodation with some friends.

It was a bit of an emergency and a very kind Chinese man said he didn't think the owner of the house would mind."

Chunggy appeared and after looking at Joyce, he started clearing up the breakfast.

Robert turned to him, "Did you say Chen Zhu Lee wanted to see me?" Chunggy nodded and disappeared back into the lounge, reappearing seconds later with a sheet of paper which in his spindly writing had names and telephone numbers written on it.

"Many people want to see you, Mr Draper."

Robert stood up. "Right, I'll go and get ready and I'll take you to your digs," he said to Joyce. Joyce giggled and looked at Chunggy who continued clearing the breakfast plates.

"Make Joyce another coffee Chunggy, if you will, while I try and find something to wear for work."

"I'm okay, Chunggy. I'll just sit here quietly," Joyce said smiling at Chunggy. With that, Robert squeezed Joyce's hand, as he got up and then set off to his bedroom.

It was only a moment later that Robert came back. "Chunggy, what's going on?" Robert was looking at Joyce though, who was trying to look innocent. Chunggy went and stood by Joyce. "I've only just noticed my room has ladies clothing in it." Joyce giggled for a second time.

Chunggy started to get agitated. "Mr Drapa, she had nowhere to stay. The ladies were bombed out of their homes. Miss Jones and Miss Cooper are sleeping in the rooms downstairs and Miss Connor has used your room."

Robert was looking horrified and Joyce was now less sure of herself. "You've only just buried Mrs Lin Yuen. Are you using her room?" Chunggy was also looking less sure of himself.

Getting very excited he said, “Mr Drapa, Lin Yuen would have told me to use her room. The ladies have nothing. They are good ladies.”

“That’s as maybe, Chunggy…” Robert had started to say when Joyce intervened.

“If you want us to move out, we will Bob, but it was an emergency. Sally and Morag lost everything. It’s just as well they were at work. It’s my fault. I didn’t think you would mind, so I came and asked Chunggy if we could use the house until you got back. I’ll tell them we have to move out when I see them later.” Joyce finished in a small voice and it was Robert who went over and put his arms around her.

“I’m perfectly happy with the arrangement. If Chunggy said *yes,* then it’s fine by me. I’m just a little concerned about the sleeping arrangements in my room.”

Joyce was blushing as they separated and Chunggy was smiling away. “There’s also a problem in the room where Clive’s sleeping,” Joyce added.

Robert looked around at the door of Harry’s old room. “You don’t mean Clive has a girl in the bed now.”

Joyce was smiling back as she said, “I’m not sure he would notice if there was.”

“Who and when?”

“Her name’s Monica and she’s an administrator at the hospital. Jenny brought her up about ten days ago.” Joyce looked at Chunggy as she said it and Chunggy shifted a little uncomfortably.

“Clive probably won’t have noticed because Monica keeps all her stuff in a suitcase, as she has a berth to go to South Africa in the next few days. Anyway, she’s working night shifts.”

"How is Jenny?" Robert asked them both changing the subject and it was Chunggy who said, "Miss Jenny she okay. Very unhappy. I tell her today, you home."

"So, where do Clive and I sleep in this boarding house, Chunggy?"

It was Joyce who answered. "You can have your bed and I will use the couch in the lounge downstairs and Clive can use the couch up here. Chunggy can move it over into the corner away from the middle of the room."

Robert was suddenly too tired to argue. "Come on; let's get away from this madhouse. Chunggy, you better organise the upstairs couch for Clive and get him to move before Monica arrives back. He might just see the arrival of Monica as some sort of wonderful dream. And don't take in any more lost souls please. As far as I can see, you're as soft as Mrs Lin Yuen. No wonder she was worried about you." Robert was smiling at Chunggy as he said it and Chunggy had a grin like a Cheshire cat.

"Are there still taxis at the corner of Margaret Drive?" to which Chunggy nodded and then smiling at Joyce, he said, "Lin Yuen would have loved all the young people here in the house," shouting it, as he went off to finish clearing up.

Chapter 21

Clive and Robert came into the bank by the side entrance wearing the overalls and steel helmets they had now been issued with for their work with the LDC.

Lennox was waiting for them in the banking hall. "The meeting is in the Board Room."

Robert just nodded and set off up the stairs with Clive trailing after him. Mrs Frobisher's desk was vacant and already there was a film of dust on the top. Robert ran his hand along it, as he walked past.

"She went last week but we haven't heard if the ship is okay," was all Robert said, as he entered the inner office heading for the meeting room.

Gordon was sitting at the table looking very hot and from what Robert could make out, he had not fully recovered from the bout of malaria he had gone down with weeks ago. The bombing and all the smoke and dust over the City was getting to him as it was to Robert who at Joyce's insistence now wore a cotton scarf over his mouth and nostrils when he was walking around. Running his hand across his face, Robert could feel grit on it from the work they had been doing clearing debris from the roads in Chinatown in the early morning. The customary early bombing raid today had been mainly over towards Changi so that at least was a bonus.

Sitting beside Gordon was a Director of the Mercantile Bank whom Robert had last seen at the meeting he had attended in the Colonial Office, also Maurice Levy. Robert had not seen him since his return but he knew Maurice had been into the bank to see the amount of gold being stored in the vaults. He looked absolutely exhausted; Peter had told Robert that Maurice was doing voluntary work at the General Hospital.

Peter Connaught followed closely in behind them also wearing LDC overalls although he had been with a different group of the Tanglin crowd helping the fire service with rescuing people from tenement blocks over towards River Valley Road. He arrived with a number of other bankers from Barclays and other banks based in Singapore. Everybody had just greeted each other and the Mercantile Bank Director was being introduced to Robert when Chin Yu and Frank Foley arrived with Meadows and Lennox bringing up the rear.

Patrick Gillespie-Jones, the Mercantile Bank Director, presumably knowing that all who should be there, had appeared, took the lead. “Right, gentlemen, let’s get on with it. The First Secretary has asked me to hold a meeting today about what we do with the gold held in this bank and in the other main trading banks on the Island. I met…” Patrick Gillespie-Jones stopped momentarily and waved his right arm, “with other banks’ directors yesterday and with the First Secretary and Herbert Rodericks of the Colonial Office and we invited Mr Chin Yu of the China Bank to be in attendance. We did in fact have a preliminary meeting about two weeks ago, and as a result, some of the excess stocks of gold in a number of banks has been shipped to Australia. That essentially leaves the large amount in the vaults below, and some bullion still held in the China Bank."

Maurice Levy interrupted at this point. "We have some gold reserves in our vaults aside from the gold we have stored downstairs."

Two other bank managers took up Maurice Levy's comment by adding that they still had stocks of gold, with one adding that no one had asked them to ship any gold out. "The Colonial Office told us to carry on as normal even though one of our Directors did ask about the transfer of gold to Sydney. Nor am I aware of any meeting two weeks ago."

Gillespie-Jones looked exasperated at the interruption. He waved a hand at Maurice Levy and shouted for quiet. "I should add that the First Secretary was most critical of Union & China and the China Bank for taking so long in getting the gold down to Singapore and I must agree with him. It has created a possible major problem."

There was a stunned silence at this observation and then an outburst of protest. Chin Yu waved his arm in the air for quiet. "I protested, yesterday, most strongly about those comments. In my opinion but for the efforts of Mr Draper and his colleagues, the gold would have fallen into the hands of the Japanese. I made it known to Mr Rodericks on 28 December as to the amount of bullion being held and that it was highly irresponsible of the Colonial Office and the Army to ignore our daily requests for help. If not for Mr Draper, personally confronting General Lay with the problem, all would be lost."

There were murmurings from most in the room with Frank openly saying, "If Bob hadn't done something, we would be in Queer Street."

Peter looked at Gordon. "Why weren't you there yesterday?"

Gordon looking extremely uncomfortable merely said, "I wasn't invited. I'm not a Director."

Peter shook his head. "You didn't know about any of this?" Gordon just shook his head. Peter looked across at Robert, "I give up."

Gillespie-Jones, ignoring Peter's comment and seeing a gap in the outburst as people took in what the First Secretary had said, carried on. "Frankly, if the bank sends a junior manager up to KL to manage the situation, then the consequence must be that the senior officers on the ground are less likely to listen to him about the seriousness of the situation."

From Robert's side, a Clive not known for speaking out, spoke with some anger, "Morrissey was there and he couldn't get you prats to take the problem seriously. Superintendent Davies tried and tried and still you wouldn't do anything."

"Oh, it's not me. I'm a Director of the Mercantile Bank. I merely tell you the view of the Colonial Office although I do agree with them." Gillespie-Jones had turned to Gordon as he spoke. "Gordon, I resent the way I'm being spoken to." Clive just waved his arm in a gesture of disgust and Gordon said nothing, choosing to sit quietly.

Maurice Levy came in this time speaking very softly. "Whatever the problem of sending up a senior or junior manager and I am aware that the Union Bank like all of us have severe shortages in the management ranks, it is the case that the Colonial Office knew of the problem from Mr Chin Yu on 28 December and they chose to ignore it. I lost a good colleague trying to get our gold out so I for one congratulate Bob and his colleagues in having sufficient determination, indeed courage, from what I've heard of some of the problems of their trip from KL, to have got the gold down here."

Robert watched as Chin Yu, Frank and Peter Connaught all said *hear, hear,* and with Clive clapping him on the back. Somewhere in the background, he could hear Cedric Meadows also adding his support.

Patrick Gillespie-Jones looked around the room as though he hadn't heard the comment from Maurice Levy and then carried on. "Whatever your opinion, gentlemen, it is now up to the Colonial Office to try and rescue the situation and find a means of getting the bullion out to Australia or India. Rodericks has told me to say that they require the gold to be packaged in wooden boxes that can be carried by two men and the boxes must be clearly marked on the outside with identification as to who owns what. The boxes must also be sealed."

Pointing at Maurice Levy, who was sitting two down from him, he added, "The Colonial Office have agreed that Mr Levy should supervise the project. Oh, and after much discussion Rodericks has said that each bank can send three representatives with the bullion when we do ship it out. Permits will be issued. We don't know what kind of ship yet but we are presuming it will be a destroyer."

There was a pause whilst everybody took in what had been said. "I need not tell you that it is imperative that nothing gets out about this exercise until the shipment has been sent."

There was a hollow laugh from Frank, and Peter snorted before shaking his head, "How do you think we are going to keep it a secret if half of Singapore can hear us sawing and hammering boxes together."

Gillespie-Jones turned to Maurice Levy and then to Gordon, "I don't really care how you do it. Only you should deal with it as a priority. The Colonial Office will gauge the urgency and then arrange the shipment at very short notice." With that, Gillespie-Jones got up clearly believing that he had done his duty and departed with Lennox escorting him out.

There was a pause for a moment or so as people got over the shock at what had been said and then Maurice Levy took over. "Look, I didn't ask for the task. My Regional Director saw me a couple of hours ago and told me what had been decided. It's a disgrace but there's not much we can do about it." He turned to Gordon, "Unless you have another idea, I'm happy to work with whoever you suggest to get the bullion boxed and checked off." Gordon merely shook his head and murmured that Maurice should continue.

Maurice turned to the managers of the other banks. "Are you happy to fit in with any arrangements I make." They nodded murmuring that they were in agreement.

"What it looks like is that those who know the First Secretary have got their gold out and Robert and the KL crowd turning up with their bullion has seriously embarrassed them. It looks like what is downstairs is ninety percent of what is left on the Island." Everybody was nodding at Maurice's comment, as Gordon said that Walter had sent a radio message yesterday to say that he expected the bank to carry on as normal. There was a hoot of derision at Gordon's comment.

Peter turned to Chin Yu. "It sounds like you had a difficult time yesterday Mr Chin Yu but presumably you agree with the arrangements." Chin Yu just nodded stubbing out the cigarette he had been smoking.

Maurice Levy turned back to Gordon. "How are we going to do it then?"

Gordon sat there not saying anything for a moment and then Frank Foley spoke up. "Don't think I'm interfering but it seems to me that Robert, Cedric Meadows and myself are the best qualified. We know how much there is downstairs, and that's the bulk, and we can quickly get things started."

"What if we could get hold of old ammunition boxes? They would be partly made up. We just have to bang the tops on," Cedric Meadows came in with, only for Maurice Levy to say, "That's already been raised with Rodericks and checked out but the Army are saying they are up to their eyes in managing what is going on in Johore and haven't time to go around collecting empty boxes. The other problem is that we need them now as it will take us days to box everything up." Maurice paused momentarily and then added, "To be fair, the Navy are being more helpful and only this afternoon, they have told Rodericks that they have empty ammunition boxes on the quayside. That does mean of course that Rodericks has told other people about the gold and the need for boxes."

Robert, up to now a very quiet Robert, finally spoke. "Let's not mess around. We need timber cut to size so that a group of people can bang boxes together. We have to do it ourselves or get labour to do it and that will advertise what we're doing. It so happens Mr Hussain, one of our customers, has a timber yard up near Bukit Timah village. He could cut the timber for us. If we order today, he could start to get some of it to us by tomorrow, day after at the latest. We should be able to finish the job in a week well before Rodericks is likely to give the signal. Mind you I suspect Rodericks has no more idea than us when the gold can be shipped out."

Maurice Levy looked around the room. "It seems to me that what Frank suggests is the best solution and Robert has a contact, so let's go for it."

"What if Hussain has urgent work for the military? They'll be needing timber," said Gordon.

"That's where you and Mr Levy come in," Robert said. "You need to get Rodericks to pull his finger out."

Gordon and Maurice Levy grimaced at the style of language being used by Robert but the KL crowd were smiling.

"It's just like the old days," Frank said lighting another of the cigarettes he had filched from the box on the table.

Peter Connaught who had been quietly listening to what Robert said then added, "We will need saws, nails, all that sort of stuff. I'll take Michael or Stuart with me to the hardware shop on Bras Basah Road and buy what I think we will need. I'll tell them that the LDC is making coffins for the dead on the streets. If nothing else that may confuse the commies."

Maurice Levy stood up and said to Robert, "Right, let's get on with it. The quicker we start, the better I'll feel about this."

Gordon put his arm across to stop Maurice Levy setting off. "We have to decide who goes with the gold and how we identify it. Patrick said the First Secretary was insistent that he knows so that permits can be prepared."

Chin Yu spoke first, "I nominate my partner, Jai Lee Kwan, and his son, Wai Mung, to go with the gold, and Mr Foley." Frank started to protest but Chin Yu put up his hand. "No, Frank, your wife is in Australia and you have told me that you wish to volunteer for the Army."

Chin Yu smiled at him. "If the Army do not want you, then you can work with Jai Lee Kwan to make the gold into even more gold." Robert and the others were watching this interchange realising that Chin Yu had thought a great deal about it since the meeting the day before. "When all this is over, I will need you fresh and ready to make our bank even bigger and stronger." Finally, Chin Yu turned to Robert and Clive. "We will also need half as many boxes again as you think we will need for the gold of ours downstairs. We have more gold at our bank on Bras Basah Road."

"What!" said Robert, Clive and Meadows, almost simultaneously. Robert said, "Are you minting your own coins?"

Chin Yu smiled back, "The Chinese like gold."

Maurice Levy who had been listening to the discussion came in with, "I have suggested to my Regional Director that as he's not young and not able to contribute much to the defence of the Island he should go, as well as our security man, Roberts, and we have a young clerk who has said he wants to join up."

The other managers said they would give Maurice names by the end of the day.

"I'm counting myself out as my wife is in hospital and not likely to be out in the near future." Some of them made sympathetic noises at what Maurice Levy had just said.

Maurice Levy after a momentary pause continued, "So, that leaves you, Gordon. What are you going to do?"

Gordon looked around not wanting to face any of the Union bank crowd. "I need to think about it. I think I should send a telegram to Walter."

"Come on, Gordon. What's there to think about," Robert said getting exasperated. "You have your arrangements with your fishing pals so you're sorted out, so it has to be Peter. He is the obvious one. He must go." Peter started to protest but Robert put his hand up and came in again, "We've been told that we need a senior manager in case there's a problem so you're the obvious one. I suggest you take Mr Lennox with you and either Michael or Stuart; both of them want to join up."

Peter was still muttering something about staying but Robert interrupted again, "Christ, Peter, you're the obvious nominee, as is Mr Lennox, and on reflection, I suggest Michael. Stuart says he's going to join the volunteers, with Cedric, in the next few days."

"How do we identify who owns the gold in the boxes?" Clive queried, as Maurice Levy pushed back his chair to get up for a second time.

"Can I suggest we leave that to Cedric and Bob to settle when they report to Maurice in a couple of hours," Frank added quietly, still looking at Chin Yu.

There was a murmuring of agreement and Robert looked across at Cedric Meadows. "You on for this?" Meadows nodded and as they followed Maurice Levy out of the meeting, he said quietly, "We would have been there all day if you hadn't put your oar in."

Maurice Levy spoke with Robert and Cedric for a few minutes and then left. Chin Yu came across to Robert, "Mr Draper, whatever those fools say I and my partner are eternally grateful for what you did in KL. We will not forget it." He shook hands with both Robert and Cedric and left with Frank, in deep discussion about some problem they had up at

Bras Basah Road.

That night, Robert sat having a drink with Clive, Stuart and Michael in the *Mata Hari*. Robert had been working with Cedric Meadows for most of the afternoon getting the making of the boxes arranged and he had come into the *Mata Hari* for a drink and there met Clive and the two clerks who had been working with the LDC since lunch time.

"So, is everything organised?" Clive asked looking around as if expecting someone else might be listening, who shouldn't be.

Robert looked up from where he was reading a *Straits Times* that had been left on a table. "Hussain will start delivering the cut timber to us tomorrow morning. Peter got all the tools and nails this afternoon. Apparently, they gave him a discount because he said we were making coffins. Hussain will deliver in the quantities Cedric and I have calculated and he will invoice us later. Mind you, Peter is trying to worry me. He reckons that many of our clients are hoarding their money and if they brought this money in, we would be swamped even more than we are now."

Robert continued to look at the pictures of the troops in action as he went on, "There's hardly anybody coming into the banking hall and Gordon has finally agreed with Peter that the European staff and any volunteer Chinese staff should be released more or less from duties and he's told Kenneth Chen, Mr Yin and Mr Wuh to run the bank when it is open." After a short pause, Robert added, "Mr Wuh has been in discussion with some of the clerks and they are coming in to help us tomorrow make up our boxes."

"What does Gordon actually do?" asked Clive.

"Not in front of the lads, Clive. We shouldn't make the

natives restless," Robert answered watching the lads returning from the bar where they had been talking to Brian Preston who had just walked in. Brian came over with them and shook Robert's hand.

"I haven't seen you for ages, Bob. I've been up in Johore helping with the repair of tracks. When did you get back?" Brian didn't wait for Robert to answer and carried on. "You've been missing all the fun, Bob. It's been manic. Martin tells me that the hospital's been bombed, half of Tanglin Road has been burnt down and Robinson's got hit a second time. Even bombed the café so no more Victoria sponge. Mind you, how they keep missing the station is beyond me. Dad is as calm as a cucumber when the bombs are dropping all around us just telling the porters to assist passengers who have injured themselves and getting me to arrange ambulances. He's nearly dropping, he's been on duty that long. He's only gone home tonight because mum said she was leaving if he didn't come home and get some sleep." Finally, Brian took a breath. With Robert still not answering, he added, "I'm on at the station in an hour with Carmichael in charge. You watch he'll be the first under the desk when the bombs drop."

Robert just sat smiling back as Brian had wittered on. Finally, he said, "I'm sorry I haven't been much help. I've been on a holiday whilst you have all been suffering down here, Brian. I feel terrible I've only been able to do a few stints these last few days."

Brian looked suspiciously at Robert. "I thought you had gone up country. Are you telling me you went on holiday whilst we're getting bombed?"

"Well, the trip had been booked." Robert dropped his

voice. "Girls, Brian, like you've never seen them. I think they call them hula hula girls. Every night dancing with those dusky maidens, I don't need to tell you how exhausting it was. We came back early because we just couldn't stand the pace."

"You bastard, Robert Draper." Brian stopped suddenly realising that his outburst was being heard all around. He looked suspiciously again at Robert, still not sure. "You're not trying to send me up, Bob Draper, are you? You've done this to me before. Uncle Peter would never have sent his right-hand man on holiday whilst he does a shift every night and we're getting bombed to bits."

Robert continued to look straight-faced at Brian. "Brian, all I can say is, I had one hell of a time. You may never know the likes of it. Anyway, Peter asked me not to talk about it too much as it would upset the younger men so I'd appreciate it if you didn't say anything."

Brian left a few minutes later looking back at Robert not sure if he was being fooled or not. It was only once he had left the *Mata Hari* that Clive, Stuart and Michael burst into uncontrollable laughter. "He will kill you when he finds out where you've really been."

"Don't worry, Stuart. Brian will see the funny side of it. His brother, Martin, and his dad, will never let him forget it." Robert and Clive got back to the house around eight in the evening having walked the last part down Tanglin Road, stopping to speak to some of the LDC volunteers who were passing in the lorry. "We've been up Farrer Road and Nassim Road all day helping the Fire Brigade. We will need to go back tomorrow. Sir Shenton came out to see the mess so Dad had to look after him whilst we got on with it," Jay Thorsby told Robert.

"What have you done to your arm, Jay?" Robert asked seeing the arm all bandaged up.

"Mr Masters and I got burnt pulling a little Chinese girl out of a burning house. Mr Masters has gone with her and her mother, to the General, in one of the cars."

"You should have gone with him, Jay, and had it seen to. You should know better."

"My mum used to be a nurse so she will sort me out." Jay was all of sixteen and suddenly, it made Robert feel very old. Robert just said *well done to* the lad and left it at that.

Robert and Clive cadged a lift for the few hundred yards to the house which now had three burnt out or bomb-damaged houses within a hundred yards of it. Somehow, Mrs Lin Yuen's house had been spared. Entering the driveway, he walked past the flowering Frangapani trees leaving Clive still talking to the lads. For a moment, he forgot where he was. There was no noise of the war, only the smell of the blossom and the sound of birds settling down for the night.

Looking up at the veranda, he saw in the gloom Monica coming down the steps from the house and getting ready to mount a bike, presumably to go to the hospital. He'd only met her a couple of times in the five days he had been back but he already knew that she was a woman who seemed to like her own company; mind you he had noticed that Clive and her seemed to get on well.

Monica smiled at him over the few yards of darkness made partially light by the clear sky and moon. "Good evening, Bob. I'm just off to work."

"I'm glad to see you. Joyce tells me this is your last shift and you're off tomorrow."

"Mmm. I'll come back in the morning and try and get

some sleep for a few hours and then make my way down. They've told me I must be down at the docks by no later than five o'clock as the ship may leave early. I left you a note, Robert, thanking you for putting me up."

Robert stood beside her as she got on her bike. "Well, I hope you have a safe journey. Do you know where you're going?"

There was a flash of teeth, as she answered. "From the rumours, Darwin via Batavia where the ship is to collect a large number of Dutch civilians wounded in the bombing over there. The troop ship is coming in early tomorrow morning with urgent supplies and more troops and then it's a quick turnaround before the Jap planes can get at it."

"Do you want one of us to take you down?"

"Oh, you're very kind. Clive has in fact offered to see me off and carry my case. All my other friends have already gone so Clive kindly volunteered."

Robert grinned back at her. "Then you're in safe hands. Hopefully, we'll meet again." As an afterthought, Robert, as he shook her hand, said, "Just make sure you get there early as it is chaos down at the docks." With that, Robert watched her cycle off and turned right at the end of the drive and then he heard her stop at the lorry and start to talk to someone, presumably Clive.

Inside, Chunggy had made a meal somehow, as the electricity was again off, and as he came in, he could smell the cooking, making him suddenly very hungry. Robert went up to his bedroom which Joyce had insisted he take back as the couch in the downstairs lounge was more than adequate and she could share the bathroom downstairs with the two girls. He found the note from Monica and read it in the dim light from the storm light he had carried through from the upstairs lounge.

The gong sounded downstairs and Robert quickly changed and went through to the bathroom and washed his face. He hadn't coughed as much since he had been wearing the cotton scarf and when he'd seen Dr Robertson, although he was concerned, he had told Robert that it was the dust essentially that was aggravating the lung, and he advised, "Keep the scarf over your mouth as much as possible and listen to your girlfriend. She seems to be speaking plenty of sense. There's nothing I can do for you."

"She's not really my girlfriend. More just a friend," Robert told Dr Robertson, as he put his shirt back on.

"Whatever she is, lad, she has your best interests at heart." Downstairs, the two girls whom Joyce had brought with her, and Clive, who had gone immediately to the dining room, were already seated and diving into what Chunggy assured them was a chicken casserole although quite where he had found the chicken from Robert was just about to question when the front door banged and they all knew who it was. "We're in here," shouted Robert, as Joyce could be heard heading for the downstairs toilet. Two minutes later, a hot looking Joyce descended on them.

"Have you left me anything? I'm starving." There was a shuffle of seats to find room for her and then there was a moments silence whilst Joyce piled her plate and then she looked up. "What?"

Robert answered for them. "Come on. Last night you said that the bigwigs were having a really important meeting today. You just came in here like a rocket. Not a 'how's your day been'? You just take most of the food and now Chunggy has nothing, and we're all waiting. What happened?"

Joyce was looking around at her friends and then at Robert. "I can't say," she almost wailed and then tucked in, breaking a piece of bread and dipping it in the gravy. "Anyway, I know Chunggy. He will have reserves somewhere."

"Clive, I know you will say I lost my mind when the police arrest me for throttling a woman, namely Joyce Connor," Robert said this, as he part stood up with the other girls giggling.

"No really, I'm sworn to secrecy. All I can tell you is the new front hasn't stopped the Japanese and they're thinking up another plan. They're getting really desperate."

Joyce's two work mates looked at each other. They obviously knew more than they were saying and it was now the turn of Robert and Clive to look at each other questioningly. The meal finished with Joyce's workmates discussing how they were to get to the Residence. "I'm not on duty tonight and I have an invitation for a drink with Cedric Meadows later, it's maybe his last night, before he goes off to the Volunteers. It's over your way so I'm happy to escort you," Clive said, as he got up from the table.

Robert and Joyce left them to it and taking the last of the bread they went onto the veranda where they knew Chunggy would appear in a moment with fresh coffee having made it over the little stove in his shed at the bottom of the garden. Robert had already tried to get him to move into the house but Chunggy was adamant that he had his little house and he was very happy. The few times Robert had been in it, he had seen a little room, spick and span, with a small vegetable garden at the back. There was a wash house at the side and Chunggy did much of the laundry for the house in the hot tub although Robert had persuaded him to get the laundry man on Orchard Road to do the sheets whilst everybody was using the house. They sat there for perhaps ten minutes not really talking just letting the worries of the day evaporate and listening to the sounds of the undergrowth. Finally, Joyce said, "They're really worried Bob. They have more troops and hurricanes arriving tomorrow and maybe some in a couple of weeks but they're no longer convinced it will be enough. The High Commissioner has at last agreed that the newspapers can say that all non-needed civilians can leave without permits. The papers over the next few days will say that as the Island is getting overcrowded that the non-essential Europeans should leave but the young men are still needed."

Robert turned and looked at her as Chunggy arrived with the coffee. "What do you mean the Europeans? We have thousands of Eurasians and other nationalities. They're equally important."

Joyce pursed her lips and said quietly. "That's not what they've decided."

"It's a disgrace, Joyce. They're in as much danger as us. My friends are mainly Eurasian. And what about the Asian women and children?" He stopped for a moment and then asked, "What does Geoffrey say?"

"He wasn't there, Bob. It was Percival, Wavell, the High Commissioner and the First Secretary."

"If they want all our neighbours and work colleagues to continue helping, even fighting with us, then they have to treat them as equal."

"The First Secretary said that they hadn't the resources to get them all off the Island."

"It's a bloody disgrace. How am I supposed to look Henry Preston and Arthur Thorsby in the eye if they haven't even got the right to get their wives out." Robert got up. "I knew you were holding something back at the table." He stood up and walked back into the house, shouting, "When does it go in the paper?"

"Tomorrow."

"Right, we'll see about that." Robert went over to the telephone and got the exchange. He gave a number to the telephonist.

Joyce had followed him in. "Don't say it was me."

Robert shook his head. "You have not said a word." "Geoffrey, good evening. It's Bob Draper. Look, I've just learned some news about getting Europeans out. What's that? You know about it already." There was a silence for a couple of moments whilst Robert just said 'mmm' a few times and listened to what Geoffrey said. Finally, he said, "I leave it in your hands, Geoffrey. If you want any support, let me know please. I'm quite willing to get a protest going." He put down the phone and turned to Joyce. "He's on the case. Other people have also telephoned him. He has told that fool, the First Secretary that if he wants the railway service, the electricity service, the City Works department, the Docks and Uncle Tom Cobbly and all, to go on strike tomorrow, then he's doing a good job of it."

Joyce came over and kissed Robert full on the mouth. "I thought you were wonderful."

"I didn't do anything."

"No, but you were going to. You were just like my dad. He would have stood up to the First Secretary."

Robert put his arms around Joyce's waist. "I rather liked

the way you thanked me. Could I have another?"

"Ahem." The girls and Clive were standing there behind them watching and grinning. One of the girls said, "I think we will need to leave a chaperone here tonight."

"I think you can be assured that I will be safe," Robert replied smiling at them, still holding onto Joyce, "I have Chunggy to protect me."

At that, Joyce batted him playfully and they both shouted, "Have a good evening," at the departing crowd, as they went out to their coffee. Later, they even put on some of Mrs Lin Yuen's records and tried to forget what was happening.

Chapter 22

Gordon was sitting at Walter Trehearne's desk when Robert found him. There were piles of paper on it and it looked as though Gordon had been sending out handwritten correspondence.

"There you are. Peter asked me to find you. The boxes are all filled and he wonders if you would like to inspect our work."

Robert stopped what he was saying and looked at the desk and Gordon seeing Robert's quizzical look, said, "Well, one of us has to continue doing the bank's business. Walter sends me a radio message almost every day demanding to know what is happening."

"You won't see him again, Gordon." Robert tried to say it with some softness. "He's left us in the mire." Looking down at what Gordon was doing, he continued, "I can't for the life of me see what banking there's left to do."

Gordon picked up a letter from one of the piles. "Mr Roberts of Roberts and Roberts wants to know what is left in the business account of the Mortimers who ran the drapery business on Scott Road. We also need to get our marketing ready for next season."

Robert merely raised his eyebrows and shook his head in disbelief. “Do you want to see what we’ve done or not?”

Since he had been back on the Island, he had seen Gordon become more and more indecisive. While the Island burned around him, he preferred to have a routine as though the myriad of commercial customers and the relatively few remaining personal accounts still required constant monitoring. Peter, only the day before had said to Robert that if the bank closed completely, nobody would notice, other than possibly some of the retail shops such as Robinsons who might want to bank what little takings they were still deriving. “Even that I doubt, Bob, in view of the fact that Robinsons has been largely bombed out of business.”

Robert left Gordon to go down to the vaults, and he wandered off to see Kenneth Chen who he had seen in the corridor momentarily. Going through the doors of the Loans Hall, he saw Kenneth talking with Mr Yin. Two or three clerks were also in the room supposedly bundling up files but he could see that they were talking quite concernedly about something.

“How are you, gentlemen?” Robert said, as he came up to them noticing that they looked very worried.

It was Kenneth who turned to Robert. “Today’s *Tribune,* it says that those people who are non-essential in the fight with the Japanese should get out but it has not said where our families should go or how we will be able to afford the cost.”

Robert stopped what he had been about to say and changed tack, “I know about this. The High Commissioner has decided that all non-essential people should be allowed to go if they want to.” Pausing for only a second, Robert said, “I tell you what, Kenneth, let’s go and see Mr Fraser and Mr

Connaught. We need to sort out how we can help staff who want to get their families off the Island." Kenneth nodded at Mr Yin and then followed Robert who had set off and then stopped at the doorway waiting for Kenneth to catch up with him.

"I've not really had a chance to talk to you since I got back, Kenneth. Was it very bad in Penang?" Kenneth and Robert talked, as they descended the stairs to the banking hall and Kenneth told Robert how the Japanese could be seen in Butterworth just across the water, as they set off to rescue the gold and find George Barwick. Kenneth explained how when he got to the bank, he organised the burning of the currency and he had to then race off to the ferry to meet Mr Connaught who had taken a cart of gold down to the docks with a security man who had remained loyally at the bank to protect the gold. "No one gave me permission, Mr Draper, to burn the money."

"I wouldn't worry yourself, Kenneth. They don't know the half of what is going on. Anyway, why did you have to get a boat out to the mail ship?"

"It would not come any closer because the Japanese artillery was in range of the island."

"Mr Connaught said that he tried to get up to the hospital."

"It was not possible, Mr Draper. There was too much bombing and people injured. He only had time to find a cart and bring it to the bank."

With that, they heard Gordon and Peter's voices coming up the stairs from the vaults and they went to meet them without Robert getting a chance to find out more about Kenneth's short time in Penang.

Gordon stood there horrified at the suggestion that the Bank should in some way assist employees to escape the

Island. "My God, Robert, what are you suggesting? We have nearly seventy staff. It would bankrupt us if we had to pay passage for all the staff and their families. Anyway, Walter would never countenance the suggestion."

"Not everyone will want to go. I think we should make the offer. Anyway, I don't think it can cost that much as I've heard that Cunard and South Asia are barely charging for berths now."

Gordon started to walk off with Peter, Robert and Kenneth left standing there.

"I'll pay the cost," Robert shouted after him, more than exasperated at Gordon's attitude. "These staff have been loyal to us and it's the least we can do."

Gordon stopped in his tracks and turned around, looking amazed at what Robert had said.

"Come on, Gordon. It can't be that much."

Peter who had been standing there listening to the argument then came in. "I think Robert's right. We should do something, Gordon. When the Japs do get to the Island, we shall need the support of all these men and if they think we're not going to help their families, then God help us."

Kenneth started to say something but Robert stopped him. "I mean it, I will pay. I will not have it on my conscience."

"You won't pay all of it," Peter interjected. "I'll pay half. You're a disgrace, Gordon. For once in your life, stand up to Walter."

With that, Peter walked off and Robert turning to Kenneth, said, "Come on, Kenneth; let's agree the arrangements and you can pass the information around your colleagues."

"Mr Draper, we can't accept your and Mr Connaught's

offer. It's not right."

"Yes, it is and that's the last word on it. Come on, let's go find Mr Yin and meet in his office. I'm sick to death of the attitude in this place."

Robert stopped momentarily and then said, "I tell you what. Go and ask Mr Wuh to join us, there's a good fellow. He ought to be involved."

It was later on that afternoon when Robert took the phone call from Frank Foley. "Well, we were right, Bob. I've just heard that the troops are to withdraw to the Island over the next couple of days. Now we are really in the soup." After briefly talking to Frank about other things, he cut the call and wandered off to find Gordon and Peter whom he found in Gordon's office reading a radio message presumably from Trehearne.

Peter waved the piece of paper at Robert. "Walter says 'dismiss Draper. He's a communist'." Robert said nothing and remained extremely unperturbed about what Peter had just said. It was Gordon who was very agitated. "What the hell do I do?"

"Why has Trehearne suddenly decided to sack me, Gordon?" Robert asked looking at the piece of paper Peter had given him.

Gordon looked sheepish. He really wasn't managing the situation Robert decided for the umpteenth time. "I sent him a radio message advising him of your offer to the Chinese clerks."

Peter came in with, "It should have said '*our offer*'."

Peter could see that Robert was smiling and that he didn't seemed upset at the contents of the telegram. He looked at

Robert guessing that he had come to see them for a reason. "What do you know that we don't?"

"I've just been told the Japanese have reached the Johore Straits."

"What! They can't have done," Gordon almost shouted.

"The troops are being withdrawn to the Island over the next two days and then the causeway is to be blown up. From now on, they're within shelling distance. The quicker we get you and the gold out, Peter, the better."

Peter said nothing. He just stood up and picked up the radio message from Trehearne. First folding it in two, he then tore it up into many small parts and threw it up in the air. "That's your solution, Gordon. You never got it because the Japanese arrived at the Johore Straits. I suggest you see your fishing friends tonight and get yourself off for Australia. You could pick up Walter on the way if he hasn't already scarpered. Come on, Robert, we have work to do."

Robert later found Clive in his little office in the Treasury, sitting with Cedric Meadows. "You've heard the news, Bob?"

Robert nodded.

"The quicker we get rid of the gold downstairs, the better for all of us. There can be no further delay by the Colonial Office."

Robert nodded again. He collected his scarf from the hanger behind the door. "I'm off. I'll see you later at the Drill Hall. I've got to see Mrs Lin Yuen's solicitor and then I want to go up to the hospital and see Jenny."

Cedric Meadows interrupted, quietly, "Stuart and I report to the Volunteers in a few hours."

Robert stopped in the doorway and turned around and looked at him. "Good luck, Cedric. Here's hoping we see each other again." He walked back into the office and they shook hands with Cedric murmuring something about it being a privilege to have worked with Robert and Robert too full to say anything. He preferred to just nod and turn around and walk out.

Walking out into Fullerton Square, he found the street full of people. Over the past few days, more and more Chinese had been moving into the Square, some he suspected having just arrived from the mainland but others moving out of Chinatown where there were now whole streets of ruined buildings. Hundreds seemed to be preparing to use the pavements as areas to sleep on. Finding a trishaw at last, he sat back and watched as the driver tried to get through the crowds and the slow-moving motor traffic.

At Chen Zhu Lee's office, he found that it had been bombed a few days before with Chen Zhu Lee now operating effectively from a corridor and a small landing going down to the back stairs. "Welcome to my new offices, Mr Draper. Be careful how you place your chair or you may slip backwards down the stairs." Robert was too weary to think up any cynical comment and just sat down gingerly. The heat in the narrow corridor was oppressive despite the air from a glassless window a few feet away and the corridor entirely open to the elements at one end; the noise from the street below made it also difficult to hear Chen Zhu Lee who spoke in a soft voice.

"I'm sorry I didn't catch everything you said."

In a louder voice, Chen Zhu Lee repeated himself. "Mrs Lin Yuen was relatively speaking a rich woman. She has left you the house, some property in Siglap, shares in Standard Oil, her jewellery, some American dollars and a safety deposit box with contents I have not seen yet."

Robert sat there stunned. "But I hardly knew her. We got on very well but I never expected this."

Chen Zhu Lee took out a cigarette pack and offered one to Robert who declined before selecting one himself and lighting it. "What do you wish me to do?"

Robert sat for a few moments mulling over what had been said and trying to think over the noise coming from outside. "How do you concentrate with all that noise?"

Chen Zhu Lee shrugged, "We live in strange times."

"I want a trust to safeguard Chunggy's position. A pension so that if anything happens to me, he is secure for life."

Chen Zhu Lee was smiling at Robert's suggestion. "In my last meeting with Mrs Lin Yuen, she said to me you would suggest that."

"I also need a will, Chen Zhu Lee, leaving everything to my uncle and his family should I not survive this war; he's my only relative."

"Captain Draper is well known throughout the Straits, Mr Draper, as a good man. That is a wise choice. I will draft something and send it up to Si Chung for your signature."

Robert merely nodded at this suggestion before going on, "I will keep the jewellery and the dollars. I may have need of them in these difficult times. Can you keep the shares in a safe place?" Chen Zhu Lee nodded at this as he got up and went over to a cabinet part covering a doorway, the other side of which seemed to be the street below. He pulled out an envelope and withdrew from it the American dollars. Robert counted with him, as he flicked through them.

"I make it $800. Do you agree?"

Robert nodded and took the money and the deposit key

that Chen Zhu Lee fished out of the large envelope.

Chen Zhu Lee went to a bundle of papers on his desk and picking one sheet up, he handed Robert a letter of authority he had already prepared. "Take this with the deposit key to the Hong Kong Bank and they should be able to let you have access to Mrs Lin Yuen's deposit box. If there are things in there, you want me to look after then bring them here and if I am not here, then leave them with Mrs Helen Yang downstairs. They will be safe with her." Robert nodded at these instructions and got up still not sure if everything was real.

"What about your bill, Chen Zhu Lee?"

"I have been paid already, Mr Draper. Mrs Lin Yuen was always most anxious to pay her bills up front. I also have some money she has given for the upkeep of the houses she owns on the Island. If you or Si Chung have maintenance bills, please pass them to me."

For a little while, Robert questioned Chen Zhu Lee on Mrs Lin Yuen's background just trying to learn more about her. "She enjoyed life, Mr Draper but she also had time to marry well, and in later life to support many charities. She was part of the old Singapore. Many people will remember her with great affection."

Robert left in a partial dream. If David Masters wanted him to be a partner after the war, then he now had the means. Eventually finding a rickshaw, he got the runner to take him up to the hospital which he hadn't seen since before going up to KL. It had not been spared by the Japanese and had been hit by a number of bombs and there was still a great deal of rubble around. He could see that temporary awnings had been put up in part of the grounds and underneath some, he could see beds and people milling around.

"Where the hell do I find the needle in this haystack?" Robert murmured to himself. He eventually found an Indian security guard who directed him to the Nurses Administration Office and giving Jenny's name, he discovered she was in Ward Twenty, one of the wards now placed outside. Wending his way through the corridors jammed with beds, in some cases merely mattresses, and with hundreds of patients all apparently with injuries sustained in the bombing, Robert at last managed to find his way out to where Ward Twenty should be.

Asking around, he got to the far end of one of the awnings and there she was with a badly discoloured apron. She saw Robert standing at the end of the beds and quickly walked down the length of the ward.

"I can't see you now, Robert, but I have a break in about twenty minutes."

"Okay, I can wait. I'll sit over there out of the way."

When Jenny came over a little later, it was with Laura whom Robert had only seen a few times since they had come from England two years ago.

"Laura's off tomorrow with her fiancé." Laura looked absolutely shattered and when Robert asked who the lucky man was, she didn't answer and it was Jenny who spoke for her. "Dr Van Sheer. He's South African. They both came out in the draw to go and help set up the new hospital facilities in Port Moresby, which was fortunate." Seeing Robert look a bit blank at '*Port Moresby*' Jenny came in with, "It's in New Guinea."

Robert looked around him. "I would have thought there was more than enough work here."

This time, it was Laura who spoke. “They’re starting to cut back on the staff. We have quite a few more medical staff from Penang and Kuala Lumpur so it has helped.”

Robert nodded not saying anything about the fact that the hospital was releasing staff just as the battle for Singapore was about to start. He mused to himself that they knew something he didn’t, and then he spoke directly to Jenny. “How are you?” He had spoken to her two or three times on the telephone since he got back, but Jenny had decided that they didn’t need to meet. It was obvious that she just wanted to work.

“Oh, I’m all right. Not got any time to think really. I just don’t want to think about it.”

“Get out of here, Jenny. If Harry’s in the bag, then we will hear one day but, in the meantime, he would want you to get on with your life.”

They spoke for maybe another ten minutes, Robert telling them a little about what it had been like up in KL, and then there was a bell sounding and the girls said they had to get back to the patients.

Robert wished Laura well for the future and said again to Jenny that she should get out and then they parted. Robert didn’t know it then but that was the last time he ever saw either of them.

Chapter 23

Robert was on Thomson Road with the Tanglin LDC volunteers helping out their colleagues from that area with clearing the roads and buildings following extensive bombing by the Japanese, and trying to help the fire brigade contain a fire that had swept down a large part of the east side of the road. The heat from the fire was intense and two of the volunteers had already been badly injured by falling masonry and had been dragged out to safety and taken to a temporary first aid shelter in a nearby convent.

They had been working on Thomson Road for hours and Robert eventually had to split the unit into two trying to give a group at a time some rest but even then, he knew that some of them were on their last legs. Robert at one point as he entered a burning building saw David Masters leaning against a wall on the opposite side of the road drinking water that Alex had brought to him before he again went into a burning building.

The noise from the fire was horrendous, like a giant explosion and added to this was the noise of hundreds of screaming people and a smell that he later realised was burning flesh. The hair on his head and arms had frizzled in the heat and his skin felt like parchment. At one stage, Alex had put the hosepipe he was manning with Captain Peters, partly onto Robert, as he came out of a building and they watched him steam.

The volunteers worked in a daze, numb with the knowledge that two of their unit, friends to some of them, along with three volunteers from the Thomson Road LDC had been caught in one of the blazing buildings when the roof had collapsed and all had been badly injured. Some passing soldiers had also stopped and had pitched in to rescue people from the burning shops and the flats above.

It was as Robert and David Thorsby emerged from one of the burning buildings, helping the last of the families to get out, that they heard David Masters shouting, even above all the noise of the fire, to take cover. Momentarily, the two stood questioning what he was shouting about and then realising what he was saying they flung themselves behind a little wall with the two little girls they were carrying, as overhead they heard the scream of a plane and gunfire being raked down the road towards them. The fireman who had been leading them out, and the elderly woman he had been helping, were both hit and went down in a heap.

Death of friends, volunteers and of people they sought to help was now firmly a part of the work of the LDC; it was just a relentless orgy with the Japanese planes having free rein on bombing and strafing the Island with the too few Hurricanes unable to stop the number of enemy planes that came over from their bases in Johore and the neighbouring Malay States. Only the day before the Royal Navy had closed down the naval yards in the north of the Island as it was now within artillery range. Talking to an officer who was on his way through to the north of the Island Robert had been told that you could even see Japanese troops on the Johore shoreline.

It had been on the previous afternoon that Rodericks had finally sent a message to Maurice Levy that the gold must be ready for immediate collection and a couple of hours later, lorries with Marines had arrived to load the bullion up. Robert had managed to get down to the bank and had gone from there down to the King's Dock; a King's Dock that was a bomb site, and watched as the gold was loaded onto a launch that took it out to a destroyer, the *HMS Tenedos* he thought, although the smoke and clouds of dust made it difficult to see anything clearly.

The launch in the end had to make half a dozen trips, with the Naval officer at the quayside getting more and more agitated at the length of time it was taking to load the gold and passengers; Peter opted to go on the last shuttle delaying his departure as long as possible. Robert had said a brief goodbye to Frank who had gone across with the first shuttle and had shook hands with a very old looking Gillespie-Jones, who had had to be helped down into the launch.

Maurice Levy standing beside Robert shook hands with Peter Connaught, with little said between them other than each saying, 'good luck,' to the other.

Finally, Robert put out his hand to Peter and said, "Thanks for putting up with me."

"It's been an honour, Bob. The LDC is yours now. I've told Geoffrey that you're the best man at organising the Tanglin crowd."

Robert didn't argue just squeezed Peter's hand a little harder. "You look after yourself and get that gold to Darwin."

It was only then that Maurice Levy said, "There's a spare place, Bob. One of the banks has only sent two employees for transit."

Robert looked at him and at Peter Connaught for a moment and then turned to where Clive was standing a few yards away saying goodbye to Michael. "Clive, get your skates on. Peter needs you to go with him."

Clive didn't really argue. Shock at the last-minute decision and the urgency all made for the moment.

"I haven't got a permit."

"As far as I can see, the Navy hasn't asked to see any permits. If you're a stowaway, they'll give you duties in the kitchens so that's no hardship. Come on, get on with Peter and good luck, mate. If you get back to Manchester, have a pint of Boddies for me."

Clive and Peter were helped onto the launch, with Michael, and Robert and Maurice Levy watched for as long as possible in the smoke and gloom of an early evening.

"You could have gone you know, Bob," Maurice Levy said still watching the launch, as it went out to the waiting destroyer.

"I'm having too much fun here, Maurice. Anyway, they'll need to count the gold when they get there and Clive has more patience than me," Robert said whimsically. "Mind you, I don't know whether they're safer or we are," he added, as they watched the *Tenedos* start to get underway.

Robert turned to face Maurice. "We brought four lorry loads of money from KL and when Cedric and I went around the other banks, there was enough gold for at least four more lorries. I didn't see eight lots of gold being transferred to the ship."

Maurice just smiled back at Robert. "It must be your imagination, Bob."

******

Both of them lay still for a moment hearing the crackle of the fire only a few yards from them. The little girl Robert was holding was trying to cry but it was beyond her in her distress. David Thorsby was talking in Chinese to the little girl he had in his arms.

Only moments later, David Masters shouted from over the road, "All clear." They realised just how near they had been to being killed when they looked over on the other side of the two-foot parapet at the dead Malay fireman and dead Chinese grandma.

For a moment, they looked at each other taking in the nearness of death and then Robert said, "Come on let's get these little ones over to the nuns." Only then did Robert find he was having difficulty in getting up and that he was in pain. David Masters came across the road and helped Robert up with his left arm covered in blood; the pain had started to come in waves. The little girl went to David Masters when he said something in Chinese to her and he took the children to the waiting nuns who all afternoon had been ministering first aid, and Robert sat back on the little wall with his feet almost touching the dead fireman. In the heat and the wooziness, he was now suffering he failed to notice as other firemen came up to help move their dead comrade.

He heard David Masters shouting to someone to help Robert and seconds later, he realised someone was speaking to him. He couldn't make out exactly what was being said, only that someone was now gently touching his left arm and then pressing something on the wound making him yell, but in the heat, he was having difficulty in focusing.

“It looks like a flesh wound. Fortunately, it just grazed you. You’re damn lucky. A fraction more and it would have hit bone.” Robert had no idea in the haze of heat and pain who was talking to him only that he recognised the voice. He next remembered being helped to a shady area away from the burning buildings and he heard the noise of other injured people around him. He did not know how long he was there, only that he was going in and out of dizziness. Slowly, he could make out the nuns walking around giving out water and a priest talking quietly to someone leaning against a wall some yards away. He moved himself trying to get up.

“Whoa. Where do you think you’re going, Robert Draper?” He finally recognised the voice. It was Dr Robertson.

“I’ve got to make sure the lads are okay, doc. Help me up please.”

“The men are fine, Robert. Captain Peters and David Masters have taken over and the fire is at last under control. I don’t think there are any other people we can get out. The little girls you rescued were the last by the looks of it. You did a magnificent job getting those kids out.”

“How bad is it, doc?” Robert asked watching the doctor finish strapping the arm and watching the bandage start to turn red.

“Nothing a few stitches can’t solve but you mustn’t use it for a week or so or you will split it open again. You really were very lucky. A couple more inches and you might not be with us. You need to go up to the temporary hospital we have at the convent and they can dress it properly and give you more painkillers. Those I’ve given you will last you a couple of hours.” Dr Robertson smiled down at him. “For some reason, young David has volunteered to go with you and get you back home." The doctor was shaking his head. "Talk about sticking together."

When he emerged onto the road a few minutes later, it was to see a number of bodies piled up at the side of a crater and the remnants of the LDC sitting on the other side of the road a few yards from the smoking buildings. David Masters came over to see him as he was being helped onto a lorry. "I'll speak to Henry later and tell him the form. I'm sorry, Bob, but Sam Sowerby and Philip Swann didn't make it. The Fire Officer says he will deal with them and Captain Peters has given the officer all the details. He will go around and tell Sowerby's staff; he's not married, no family as you know and Philip was single as well, although he has a daughter in Vancouver."

Robert stopped getting onto the lorry and turned not able to say anything to David. Sam Sowerby had been one of the first volunteers. Well in his sixties, always willing to help, a widower who had no family to mourn him. From the conversations Robert had had with him, he remembered that he said he was a bit of an expert on the dialects of the nomadic people of North Borneo and had retired to Singapore a few years before in order to be near his research. Philip Swann he had only known for a couple of weeks. A Canadian, who preferred to be known just as '*Swannee*'. He worked up at the Goodwood Hotel as head of the estate grounds. On the two occasions, Robert had talked to him, albeit briefly, he found that he was a man that preferred his own space. Robert knew absolutely nothing about him.

At last, Robert mumbled, "David…where is this help we've been promised?"

David Masters didn't answer the question and instead

handed Robert a cup of water; he knew what Robert was referring to but there was no answer. "Here lad. You were brilliant. What you and young David did was very brave. If you were in the army, they would give you a medal."

"I don't want a medal, David. I want a Hurricane to take out those bastards," Robert was almost shouting, as he finished.

"Go on, off you go and get that arm sorted. We can manage without you. Captain Peters will make sure we get back to the Drill Hall and Arthur will take over later." Robert just nodded, too tired to say anything, just looking around to where the bodies lay at the side of the road not even fully covered by blankets.

"I'm glad Alex persuaded you to let him stay."

David looked up at Robert. "Don't you ever tell Susie what we were doing today? I promised her we would just help a bit and there was no risk."

Robert grimaced with pain and then tried to smile. "I thought you said you're not very good at lying. You haven't a hope in hell."

David just grinned. "I can always blame you." With that, he turned and started shouting, getting people to stand up and start again on clearing the road. Robert had been watching Martin, just sixteen two weeks before, smoking a cigarette as they had been talking. Martin seeing he was being watched threw down the cigarette he had cadged off one of the Chinese volunteers and shrugged at Robert.

"If your mother catches you smoking, Martin Preston, you will be for it." A very old looking sixteen-year-old grinned back at Robert.

Robert had not been a priority at the makeshift emergency

centre and it was some hours before they were done with him. He had been on duty since eight that morning and now more than twelve hours later, he was tired to the point of exhaustion and he felt quite woozy with the painkillers. The stitching, if anything had been nothing, it had been the cleaning of the wound that had been more than painful. Somehow, the bullet had grazed him across the back of his arm. He could only surmise that the arm covering the little girl had been showing above the little wall of bricks.

Robert, David Thorsby and Martin, who at the last moment had also stayed with Robert, somehow found a taxi that was still operating and eventually, the three of them arrived at a Tanglin Road that looked more and more war ravaged, with Robert saying very little during the journey.

Martin began to find the funny side of the whole day. "Wait till I tell Brian."

"What do you mean; tell him what?" Robert mumbled.

"I can tell him I have been on one of your holidays."

"You sound a bit high to me, Martin. Just go and have a good shower and then get some sleep."

It was David Thorsby, not quite eighteen years of age, who was more morose. "Those little girls, Bob. What will happen to them? Everybody in the building was killed except them."

"I don't know the answer, David. The way the Japs are strafing and bombing the place it can't be long before they attack the Island."

The Chinese driver who had been listening to them talking agreed saying it would be very soon; all the time, the noise of heavy guns at the north of the Island could be heard.

Getting out at Mrs Lin Yuen's, Robert scarcely had the strength to climb the steps up to the veranda. Chunggy and Joyce had come running out having heard the noise of the taxi at the front of the house and even in the dark, they must have seen Robert struggling.

"What happened?" Joyce asked letting Robert use her shoulder as a makeshift crutch.

"I got a flesh wound in the strafing on Thomson Road. Nothing serious. I just need a good sleep." He almost collapsed, stumbling and Joyce held him up against the wall. "You should be in hospital," she screamed seeing the bandage on his arm was discoloured.

"They have thousands to look after, much worse than me. They looked after me at the emergency centre and gave me some pills."

"My God, you're filthy, and your hair's half burnt off," she said and with Chunggy's help, she somehow managed to get Robert through to the downstairs lounge and into a chair.

"I don't think I can get up the stairs tonight, Joyce. Even getting up those steps to the veranda was a struggle. I will have to sleep and wash downstairs." Even as he said it, there was the sound of the sirens going off for another bombing.

As they had helped Robert into the house, the noise of heavy guns pounding away could be heard from the north of the Island.

With an enormous sigh, Robert said, "Get me a drink, please, Chunggy."

"Don't you dare, Chunggy. He's on painkillers. Water or juice for him." Chunggy and Robert were looking at each other. "Don't even think about it, Chunggy, if you want to remain my friend," Joyce said almost in a growl.

Chunggy left yelling that he wasn't getting involved.

"Just a little one, please."

"No, I will get you a large orange juice and then I will give you a wash."

At that, Robert started getting up grimacing as he moved his arm. "You can't do that. I hardly know you."

"Well, while I get to know you better, I will give you all my news." While they were talking all the time, the Japanese guns over the Straits could be heard in the distance pounding the north of the Island.

"When did that lot start?" Robert said, as though noticing it for the first time, and Joyce knowing what he was referring to, said, "It really started about an hour ago. I was trying to get some sleep when it started. I thought I was going to be on duty tonight but I'm not now."

Robert looked across to where she was pouring a bottle of orange juice and mixing it with soda water into a long pint pot. "Why not?"

"I had a telephone message. They are going to try and get us out tomorrow. The High Commissioner has at last released all the secretaries. He and the remaining staff are moving into the Singapore Club tonight as the Governor's Residence has been bombed to bits."

"We think we will be going on the *City of Canterbury* which is hoping to come in tonight but nobody's very sure. We just have to be ready to go at a moment's notice," she answered as she brought the drink over. Robert took the pint of juice off her and drank a good half of it before looking up at her worried face.

"It's the best of two evils. You're better trying to get out. This could go on for months. I suppose you know Clive went yesterday whilst you were at work."

Joyce just nodded at that. "I know, Chunggy told me." "Come with me, Bob. Now that you're injured, they can't refuse you a permit."

Robert just shook his head. "It's only a flesh wound. Anyway, I'm needed more than ever, Joyce. I can't desert them now."

Joyce had begun to cry, as she sat beside him. "I knew you would say that." Robert told her more about what had happened at Thomson Road and Joyce said nothing, just taking the pint pot from him and going over to the table and refilling it.

Fortunately, Chunggy arrived with food and further discussions on Thomson Road were diverted; Robert was too tired to do more than just nibble at what Chunggy had produced. Joyce disappeared whilst Robert fiddled with the food and sat quietly, feeling his arm thump away, and then she reappeared wearing an apron and carrying two towels and a bowl smelling of Dettol. "Right, let's get your shirt off. Chunggy, have you got scissors?"

"I'm not sure about this, Joyce."

"I seem to have lost one argument. I've no intention of losing any more," was all she said, as she stood beside Robert and taking the scissors from Chunggy, she cut up the back of his shirt.

"Oh, and I will need your trousers off as well. If you can call them trousers, they're half ripped and burned." Robert made a face and realising the futility of any further argument, with Chunggy's help, he shimmied out of his trousers, showing lacerations on his legs. Joyce was trying to wash his good arm and back, and seeing the state of his legs, merely said in a quiet voice, “I thought as much.” Chunggy had said nothing throughout this, just removing the ripped clothing and finally discreetly making an exit.

Chapter 24

Taking more painkillers, Robert lay on the couch trying to get some sleep although the crescendo of the guns, with the Japanese now only seven or eight miles away, made the prospect unlikely. Joyce had made Robert take the couch after she had cleaned him up and Chunggy had helped him into a clean shirt and shorts. She had then disappeared for a short time and eventually returned wearing cotton pyjamas and without a word, she put a netting over Robert and moved the armchair next to him. She then unfolded a cotton sheet and put it around her; somehow, she pulled the netting over her as well. Chunggy was still around doing whatever he thought needed doing and in the mist of his pain and tiredness, Robert heard voices and suddenly, Joyce was hiding under her bed sheet.

It was Laz. "Bob, it's Laz. Chunggy just said you've been wounded. Are you okay, mate?" Even in his pain, Robert was tempted to lay it on. Clearly, Laz hadn't seen Joyce hiding under her sheet.

"You know how it is Laz. When the going…"

Laz said, "Yeah, yeah. So, you're okay. Do you want me to do anything?"

"You could drink a very large whisky for me."

At that, Joyce giggled.

"Have you got a woman in there with you?"

"Only one tonight, Laz."

Before Laz could answer, Joyce sat up clutching her sheet to her chest. "Bob, what did you say?"

Laz lifted the netting. "Now this is a very cosy little set up. Get yourself wounded and you get the best-looking woman left on the Island to look after your needs. I tell you what, Joyce, you don't know the half of what I could tell you."

Joyce said she preferred not to know. So, the three of them sat in a huddle under the mosquito netting for a few minutes, catching up on the news. Laz hadn't been around for more than a week and it took some time for them to exchange all the news. He still sported plaster of Paris on his wrist but he said it was no longer painful, only when he banged it.

In a way, it was almost as though the war was happening somewhere else. While they were talking over the noise of the guns, Chunggy had brought in a beer for Laz and a bowl of what looked like curried chicken. Robert again wondered where the chicken had come from.

"Been up on the north of the Island for the last two weeks working my socks off trying to get the water pipes all working again. They moved us out a few hours ago as it was getting too dangerous," Laz said and then groaned. "This bloody barrage will mean all our work was for nothing."

Finishing his beer, Laz tried to untangle himself from the netting.

"Look can I use a bed upstairs? My place doesn't exist anymore."

"Use Harry's old room. Clive has gone with Peter to Darwin."

Laz didn't ask any more questions, just finished untangling himself and said, "Good night."

The next morning was the 8th February. When Joyce put on the radio, it was to hear that the Japanese had managed to fight their way onto the Island. "The Australian troops are putting up a stout resistance," Robert heard the clipped English voice of the radio announcer tell him; he was feeling bloody awful with his arm on fire. He had taken more painkillers, as he listened to the news but they were taking a while to kick in.

From somewhere, Chunggy had found something worth eating and good coffee; Joyce and Robert sat in the lounge just eating, not talking and listening to the rumble of guns. When Joyce opened the doors onto the veranda, the noise of the constant gunfire seemed to be almost on top of them, with the smoke and grit in the air making it even more unbearable in the hot, airless lounge.

"When will you be told when you go, Joyce?"

"I don't want to go, Bob. I can stay and look after you."

Robert just shook his head. "If we get rid of those who are not involved in the fighting, then we can get down to business. Even I can work that out." He tried to say it as nicely as possible but it still came out stark and unforgiving.

Joyce didn't say anything at first. After a little while, she said in a very quiet voice, "Just when we were getting to know each other. I always knew Fran wasn't that interested in you." Robert didn't reply to what Joyce had said instead saying, "Joyce, you get out of here because it's going to be even more unsafe than getting to Australia or wherever. Just get on with it. I've got to stay. My friends are putting their lives on the line to try and save this place. I can't desert them."

Joyce didn't look at him, "I know. My dad would have done the same."

"Well then, that's an endorsement." Nothing more was said and finally, with Joyce's help, Robert got up and went to the bathroom and managed with one arm to have a wash and almost dry himself; Chunggy came in and helped him dress. When he went back into the lounge, Laz had joined Joyce at the table sitting in the semi-gloom.

"The Japs have made big inroads, Bob. The radio's saying people have to move out of Tengah and Bukit Timah village." Laz had shaved and dressed in clean clothes including trousers that looked a shade too short. Laz saw Robert looking at the trousers. "They're Harry's. The sod wouldn't object and I prefer them to shorts." Robert merely nodded.

The scream of low flying planes somewhere over the reservoirs to the north-east could be heard as they sat wondering when the hell they were living in would end. Laz finally said he had to go and for some reason they both knew it was a pivotal moment by standing up and shaking hands. Robert didn't see him again for nearly four years.

Robert sat there for a while after Laz had gone. Finally, he said, "I've got to go to the bank. Chunggy, can you see if you can get a taxi or a trishaw, or something?"

Joyce started to protest and then said, "I'll come with you. I can go to the Fullerton Building and see what's happening, rather than wait for a phone call."

Robert looked at her questioningly.

"I told you the HC has moved the staff down to the Singapore Club."

Chunggy went off to try and get a taxi and Joyce came over and sat with Robert.

"You should take your stuff with you, just in case, Joyce. It maybe you have to go without any notice." Joyce just nodded at what Robert said and went off into Mrs Lin Yuen's old bedroom and came back shortly afterwards with a small hand case which she said was all she needed.

"When you get wherever you're going, Joyce, get on with your life. This war could take years." Joyce was crying again, quietly, and just shook her head. "It's not fair."

It took some time for Chunggy to find a rickshaw because it seemed most people were trying to stay off the roads unless it was essential. Robert had a word with Chunggy before they left. "I may not be able to get back, Chunggy. The LDC could get cut off from getting back to Tanglin. I just don't know what will happen next. You'll be okay?"

Chunggy came over and gave Robert a bit of a hug. "I be okay, Mr Draper. You come back one day. I live in my house. I have plenty to eat."

Robert just shook his head and got into the rickshaw, waving his good arm at Chunggy standing on the veranda. "God knows what's going to happen to him."

The rickshaw driver took them down towards Alexandra Road and Robert got him to stop for a few moments at the Drill Hall. Arthur Thorsby was on duty beside the telephone but no one else was around. "Good morning, Arthur. Where is everybody?"

"Captain Peters took them up to Thomson Road whilst there's a break in the bombing to clear up yesterday's mess. I gather it was pretty bad. I heard you got injured." Arthur said nothing about Sam Sowerby or Philip Swann.

Robert just nodded, as he looked at the sheet on the desk telling him who had come in. "We're a bit shorthanded by the looks of it."

"Lewis and Cromarty have gone in the night on the *Monarch*. Also, Dennis Phelan has been called up to the Volunteers."

Robert raised an eyebrow. "He did tell me yesterday that he was likely to be called up. I asked him to give my regards to Stuart Marsden and Cedric Meadows. I suspect they're already in the thick of it judging by the noise up there." Robert vaguely waved his good arm towards the north of the Island. "I've got to go, Arthur, but I'll be on duty tonight."

"David said we wouldn't see you for days."

Robert grinned back, well more of a grimace. "You're not getting rid of me that easily." As he walked out to the rickshaw, Robert shouted over the noise of the guns, "Keep your head down, Arthur."

Getting to Fullerton Square was no mean feat. It took them well over an hour to travel the short journey into Fullerton Square with the Alexandra Road LDC still clearing the area from bomb damage that had happened that morning on the route into town. The road was filled with ambulances and lorries taking wounded soldiers and civilians down towards the City Centre.

"Where are they taking them?" Robert asked the rickshaw driver to be told that they were now using the Cathedral and the adjoining Padang as an emergency hospital. All the while, Joyce had been sitting quietly, holding onto Robert's good arm. Robert turned to her. "I presume that Sally and Morag are also on their way."

"They were on duty last night and will have slept beside their desks," was all Joyce said.

Finally, they got to Fullerton Square by a roundabout way

through the back of Chinatown and Robert paid off the rickshaw driver giving him a good tip and telling him in Cantonese to be careful. The Chinese man shook his head. "Bad times, *Xian Sheng*, bad times."

Joyce stood there on the pavement until Robert turned back to her. "Let's not say goodbye, Joyce. Let's just say we'll see each other sometime." Joyce lowered her head a little and Robert could see she was crying. He brought his right hand up and gently wiped away some of the tears. "Come on, Joyce Connor, stiff upper lip and all that or I will end up crying."

Joyce took a deep breath and leant forward and kissed him. "You take care and look after that arm." With that, she picked up her little case and turning around she went into the Fullerton Building, not looking back, leaving Robert suddenly feeling very lonely even though the Square was packed with people. Half of Chinatown seemed to be there.

The bank was closed with a notice on the door saying that customers could arrange an appointment by telephoning the bank. Robert banged on the door and after a few moments, it was Abilash who opened it, looking pleased to see Robert. "Sahib, good morning," and seeing his bandaged arm he said the obvious, "You are wounded, Sahib."

Robert grinned back at Abilash. "I didn't have you protecting me, Abilash."
"Is there anybody in?"

"Mr Fraser is upstairs. Mr Wuh and Mr Yin are in the Treasury, and Mr Lee is upstairs packing." With that information, Robert set off to find Gordon.

"Still here then," Robert said when he found Gordon in his old office. Gordon spun around from where he had been looking at a map.

"Christian has finally been allowed to leave the Island so we go in a few hours. We should have been off days ago but the First Secretary wouldn't release him."

"Yeah, I gather the HC has finally acknowledged that we are in trouble and we should move as many people off the Island as possible."

"What the hell have you done to your arm?" Gordon asked suddenly taking in the fact that Robert's left arm was bandaged and in a sling.

"Got in the way of a Japanese fighter."

Gordon looked appalled. "That close."

"That close. Poor fireman didn't make it."

"The line with Batavia is down again and the Post Office say it may be permanent. And we can no longer get radio messages through. The Japanese Navy is now close enough to block the signals. The Colonial Office think the Japs have taken Borneo and may be about to invade Java."

Robert guessed that Gordon had got his information from his fishing pal, Christian, who worked for the First Secretary at the Colonial Office. "You mean you can't get any more missives from Walter," he said smiling at an embarrassed Gordon.

"Look. I'm sorry. I didn't ask for the job. In fact, I don't want it. Anyway, effectively the bank is closed from now on. I'm glad you came in as I was going to get Mr Wuh to go up to your place and tell you that we had closed."

Robert walked around the room feeling the dry heat move in swirls. He had taken the scarf away from his mouth and he could taste the grit in the air. All the time, they could hear the thump of heavy guns and somewhere over towards the docks there was suddenly an enormous explosion which made the few glass panes left in Gordon's office window shake.

"That sounds very near. God, they're not bombing the Hospital, are they?" Gordon said almost shaking. Robert didn't answer the question, just shook his head as he thought the explosion was in the wrong direction.

"Do you think the Japs or communists killed Fred Gilpin?"

Robert wasn't quite sure why Gordon suddenly asked the question. He had informed Gordon and Peter when he got back to the Island of what Superintendent Davies had told him but there had been no real discussion. From what they had said neither Gordon nor Peter had been close to Gilpin so there had been little discussion at the time about the circumstances of Gilpin's death merely a resigned acceptance that something terrible had happened.

"I think it was the Japs, Gordon. They beheaded him; as far as I know that's not the communist's way. I also think Chin Peng would have got Li Bo to use Fred as a hostage for the gold."

Changing the subject, Robert asked, "What are you doing about the paper currency?"

Gordon had been putting some papers into a box and stopped what he was doing. "Rodericks says it's too early to destroy it so I've told him that we cannot guarantee to have sufficient time to burn it if we leave it much longer. He has agreed that we can take it over to the Treasury and they will burn it later. I've asked Mr Wuh to take the money over." Gordon had clearly wiped his hands of any responsibility.

"I presume that Duff Cooper or someone in the Cabinet Office is offering compensation for any destroyed currency?" Gordon didn't say anything and it suddenly occurred to

Robert that Gordon hadn't considered that possibility, he just wasn't interested. Gordon continued his packing without answering the question. Robert realised that Gordon was already halfway to getting off the Island. "I'll make sure it gets there, Gordon." Seeing Gordon nod, Robert went out to look for Wuh.

Wuh was with Yin in the vaults bundling a great deal of currency into gunny sacks ready for carrying upstairs. "Do you know how much we have here, Mr Wuh?"

"It is all in the cash ledgers, Mr Draper. We are making entries." Robert looked around. There must have been forty or so gunny sacks filled with money already. On the shelves facing him was perhaps enough money for another twenty or so gunny sacks.

"Presumably, your priority is the larger denominations?" Wuh agreed and said he had labelled the bags accordingly. "It doesn't seem right, Mr Draper, that we spend all our life worrying about balancing the books and now we are going to burn the money."

Robert grinned back at Wuh. "It goes against the grain, Mr Wuh. All our training says otherwise but we mustn't let the Japs get the money. At least they can't get the gold now." Wuh nodded as another bag was filled and Yin sealed the top.

"When are you planning to take the money across to the Treasury?"

Wuh stopped what he was doing. "We will have to take it over by three o'clock or we are told it will be too dangerous to be on the streets. The security staff have said we can take it any time." Pointing at Yin who was over by the shelves, he added, "Mr Yin has found us a van." Robert stood there feeling his arm starting to throb.

"Have you arranged security?"

Wuh said that Mr Fraser had said to just take the money over and had not mentioned security.

Robert shook his head at Wuh. "I don't think that is good enough Mr Wuh. Too many things could go wrong. Even in the short distance to the Treasury, it would be worth the communists to make an attempt on the money. We need to make sure you are safe." Even as he was saying it, they could hear more tremendous explosions somewhere nearby and regular popping sounds.

"I suggest you stop what you're doing and take the larger denomination bags to the Treasury now, whilst there's no air raids. You must take Abilash with you for protection. Get them to count the money with you and make sure you get a receipt." Wuh started to say something and then changed his mind.

"Mr Wuh, if you think about it the main bags have bundles of hundreds, fifties and tens. That's the currency that amounts to something. If the rest is lost or never burnt, what would be the consequence. Very little. So, I suggest you get the bags with large denominations over to the Treasury and we worry about the small change later. Mr Yin, is your van available now?"

Seeing Yin nod, Robert added, "Right I'll go and ring the security office over at the Treasury and tell them to expect you; say in an hour. It's less than a mile so we should be able to get there even with all the trouble outside. I will come as well and go on from there to a meeting I have." As he started for the stairs, he asked Yin, "Where is Kenneth by the way?"

There was a momentary pause and then Yin replied, "He has gone, Mr Draper. He went with his wife last night."

Robert stopped and then smiled. "You mean the Kuomintang got him out."

Both Wuh and Yin looked amazed and it was Wuh who said, "How did you know, Mr Draper?"

Robert was grinning broadly as he said, "It was more a guess really. But I kept wondering at some of the things he said. I am glad he has gone as he certainly wouldn't be safe if the Japs captured him."

Back up in Gordon's office he found Gordon, having finished packing his files away, having a moment's private contemplation. "I've told them to take over the larger denominations in a few minutes time with Abilash as guard. I'll just give the Treasury a ring and tell them we're on our way. I'll go with them, Gordon, and make sure they agree the amount so we get compensation." Gordon said nothing whilst Robert made the call.

When Robert had finished, Gordon said, "Walter in his last message said he had no alternative but to go to Australia because Monica was terrified of the bombing of Batavia and needed his support."

Robert standing on the other side of the desk from Gordon just raised his eyebrows at the information. "Maurice Levy said he would never come back. I'm glad I didn't take out a wager."

Gordon finished his cigarette and stubbing it out, stood up. "By the way, what was that explosion?"

Robert answered, noticing that the last of the panes in the window were now missing. "Looks like the oil tanks that are over at Collyer's Quay have gone up. Thank God, the wind is blowing the stuff out to sea. Abilash has been out in the Square and says a couple of the godowns have been set on fire. Fortunately, it's mostly booze in them which is now exploding."

Gordon put out his hand as Robert finished speaking, and Robert with his good hand shook it. "I don't envy you staying, Robert. It's going to get very tough stopping them."

Robert made a face at Gordon, "You don't really believe we're going to stop them. Do you?"

Gordon shook his head. "They say help is on its way but can Percival hang on for a few weeks? The *Empress of Asia* going down was the last straw as far as I'm concerned. Christian doesn't think we have an earthly. The trouble is most of us have been ready for weeks but it was Christian's launch." Gordon said it with an air of resignation. As Robert watched him, Gordon picked up the small bag on the spare chair and then sighed, as he looked around. "I shan't miss this place. Never really liked the work."

Robert walked out with him into the corridor and down the stairs with Gordon saying, "The hardest bit will be getting to the launch. I need to go now or I may not get there before it's dark. Who knows the Japs may already be there."

Robert had put his scarf back over his mouth ready to go outside but then removed it so Gordon could hear him. "I think the smoke and grit over the city makes it like dusk already, Gordon. Anyway, best of luck in getting to Darwin." At the front entrance, Gordon opened up the doors and turning around handed his keys to Robert, "I shan't be needing these anymore." With that, he turned and walked away through the crowds. Robert never saw him again.

Robert locked the front doors and turning walked over to the back stairs. The noise of him walking, rather crunching his way, across the banking hall was all the more strident because there were no other people in the hall. He was alone. Robert looked around and remembered his first day coming into the hall just two years ago.

After a few minutes, Wuh and Yin appeared from the vaults bringing up the last of the bags and Robert followed them through to the side entrance where Abilash was standing with his rifle. Abilash acknowledged him and when Wuh and Yin had put the bags in the van, he got in the back and closed the doors.

"Those are all the big denominations, sir," Wuh said looking very hot.

"Thank you, Mr Wuh. Now you and Mr Yin get in the front with the driver. I will get in the back with Abilash." Wuh started to protest but Robert waved it aside. "I'm younger than both of you, Mr Wuh, and you have the paperwork." With that, Robert locked the side doors of the bank with the keys he had just acquired and knocking on the rear van doors was let in to the hot house. Levering himself into the back of the van he muttered to Abilash, "Just like old times, Abilash," and saw a flash of teeth.

When they had finished transferring the currency, they took the van back to Fullerton Square where Robert stood beside the van for a few moments with Abilash, Wuh and Yin. "Look, Mr Wuh, use the small denominations that are left and pay everybody three months wages. They will need the cash. Take the money and do your best to contact everybody. You can only try. If there's any cash left, leave it behind my desk in the Treasury. Here, have my keys to get in; you can leave them with Mr Smythe's assistant at South Asia Shipping." Wuh looked astonished at the last suggestion but Robert smiled at him.

"I don't think it matters now, Mr Wuh. What matters is that the staff have some money to live on; I suspect even that will not be enough." Robert put his good hand out and somewhat embarrassingly, Wuh and Yin shook it in turns, Abilash preferring to come to attention. Robert just smiled at him and said, "Thank you for looking after me."

Wuh put the key in the lock and opened the doors and the three of them went in and closed the doors, leaving Robert outside. Robert never saw Wuh and Yin again.

Robert turned around and made his way through the crowds and walked out of the Square and back over Anderson Bridge conscious all the time of people scurrying along the pavement constantly watching the sky, before he turned left up towards North Bridge where the Hong Kong bank was located. The bank, like the Union and China, was closed but he knocked and eventually, the door opened.

"I have arranged to see Mr Levy," was all he said to the security guard before being let in. He took out of his pocket the security box key he had been given by Chen Zhu Lee.

Chapter 25

Singapore should have had another bright, sunny day. In fact, the city was covered in dark clouds of smoke caused by the shelling and with the bombers now coming over every two hours or so, like clockwork. As the sun rose in the sky, so did the intensity in the fighting; the danger seemingly growing as the heat of the day worsened. The dust and the smoke from the burning buildings and blown-up oil storage tankers, making life for the million or so civilians caught in the fighting absolutely dire.

Those living in the city now knew that the shelling from the Japanese artillery was much closer. Even more worryingly, it seemed to be not just in the north but also from the west of the Island. It was the fourth day that the Japanese had been on the Island and more and more refugees were coming into the City streets and sleeping rough. Bombed out buildings were makeshift camp sites; burst water mains now provided the only means for most people to get access to some water albeit often little more than pools of dirty liquid. Everywhere there was a haze of oily soot hanging in the air and coupled with the overbearing heat and humidity, it made life almost unbearable in the streets as the space in the city receded.

From all around, people could be heard coughing and children crying. There was a new smell as well; the stink of death with more and more bodies being left where they had fallen. Amazingly, the electricity supply seemed to work albeit with interruptions and Robert had been told that a team of engineers were working non-stop to keep the supply functioning as it was seen as a priority for the hospitals.

Robert had worked almost continuously for the past three days since he had last seen Joyce, with an ever-diminishing volunteer force, trying to help the fire brigade clear burning buildings. Time and again, just as they solved one crisis, another came along to confront them. The volunteer force was now increasingly made up of middle-class Chinese and Eurasians who had volunteered once they had been encouraged by their community leaders to help, together with a few retired, mostly military personnel, and a few youths too young to volunteer for the armed services. Robert had even been told by Geoffrey Blackmore when he had turned up to see how the Unit was managing that some other units had folded through lack of available volunteers or through sheer exhaustion.

As his volunteers dealt with the bomb damage, he spent more and more of his time trying to find equipment such as ropes and buckets; petrol was practically non-existent, as were blankets and gloves for handling the fires and removal of rubble.

Robert was now requisitioning any sort of vehicle he could find, more often than nought hand pulled carts to carry equipment. Nuns and retired nurses emerged from the convents and their homes to provide first aid and increasingly this was aid for the Tanglin LDC volunteers who between them sported burns, scratches, ripped hands and a list of injuries too long to note. Fire equipment became increasingly difficult to find as it was destroyed in the fighting or captured by the enemy.

Trying to find food and water for thirty plus men, nurses and nuns, in a city supposedly abundant with inestimable stocks of all manner of luxuries and essentials, was never-ending due to the chaos of the bombing, and now shelling; stocks of the basic essentials appeared to have evaporated. The government's supply chain had broken down completely leaving it for LDC leaders to do their best for the volunteers in their team.

Geffrey Blackmore got a message through to Robert in the early evening of the fourth day for Robert to attend a meeting around ten the following morning in the Singapore Club. Robert hardly had time to think of the significance of any meeting as he and his Unit had been assisting the fire brigade in trying to quell a firestorm in the houses that lined the roads near to Orchard Road and with those houses now in range of the Japanese artillery.

Henry Preston who had been largely absent from the LDC for the past four days as he was now in charge of the railway station had come, on his way home for a few hours' sleep, to see if he could help. Robert had just finished a discussion with the fire officer and agreeing with him that there was nothing much more they could do that evening; most of the fires were containable and no more people could be rescued. Seeing Henry's car arrive, he went over as Henry got out.

He shook Henry's proffered hand. "Thank Mona again when you get home, Henry. She and Mrs Clumbie somehow managed to get food and drink over to us. What we would do without them, I can't imagine." Robert swatted away a mosquito. "They seem to be getting worse."

Henry leaned against his car, acknowledging what Robert said, as his two sons, Martin and Brian appeared beside him. He clapped them on the shoulders, smiling and greeting them, before saying, "I've been told to destroy everything in the station and yards but there's hardly any engineers left who know what they're doing, so I'm left with two men and a few coolies trying to disable rolling stock. I ask you, Robert, what has it come to?" Robert just shook his head in despair.

Henry took out a cigarette and lit it. "Who's on later?"

"Arthur should be on as well as David Masters plus half a dozen of the new volunteers. They're having a few hours rest and it may be their last chance for days. We're starting to get really short-handed in the mornings so I'm trying to switch things around and put more of them onto distribution of food; the night crowd can concentrate on keeping roads clear as the Japs seem to be doing less night bombing. I've left Captain Peters manning the telephone although what good that will do, I don't know as there are only three volunteers in the reserve team."

Henry was half listening and nodding, as he said to his older son, "Brian, you'll have to be on shift from four in the morning. I'm sorry but Roger was injured in the bombing today and I need some cover from then until I can get in. I'll do my best to be in for nine."

He turned to Robert, "The Alexandra Road lot came down to help clear up the fire at the side of the station. They could only muster five volunteers; no Chinese or Eurasian volunteers for some reason."

Robert was too tired to follow the point up, just raising his eyebrows a little, then turning to the Preston boys, he shouted over the noise of shells falling a few hundred yards away. “You two may as well go back with your dad whilst I finish off here.” Robert watched the two youngsters get in the car and then he turned to finish what he was doing.

When he did manage to get home later, for a short rest, he had gone onto the upstairs veranda, and stood there watching shells land over towards where he thought Bukit Timah village would be. The noise of the British guns, some now based in the Botanic Gardens and from the gunfire of the front line just beyond the Tanglin Barracks a half mile or so from where he was standing, was so loud it was as though they were firing from the garden.

Every so often, there would be a flash in the distance as something blew up and there was the smell of something in the air which he had not noticed before. Chunggy who had come to stand beside him said he thought that the fighting was getting very near.

“What’s that smell, Chunggy? It’s not wood burning or oil. I think it must be the smell from the guns firing.”

Chunggy shrugged his shoulders, “I not know, Mr Draper.”

Robert had talked more than once to Chunggy about whether he should go to somewhere safer and as they stood there watching the flashes in the night indicating the unfolding battle, Robert again said or rather shouted over the noise.

“Look, Chunggy, I know I’ve said it before but it may not be possible for me to get back here tomorrow. I’m surprised I’ve been able to get here these past two nights. Are you really sure you want to stay here?”

"I stay in my little home, Mr Draper. I have buried the jewels and money you give me under the vegetable garden. I am safer here." Robert couldn't argue with Chunggy's logic. What was the point? There was nowhere left to hide. The house next door was now a ruin as was half a dozen on Tanglin Road. He dreaded to think what the streets nearer to the barracks were like. The artillery seemed to be installing guns in the garden on his left and he could hear the yells of the men as they raced against time to set them up. On Tanglin Road, he had noticed for the first-time bodies lying at the side of the road. The priority was no longer the removal of the dead.

Robert ate the piece of fruit Chunggy had found for him and finished off a bottle of warm beer. He then put his hand in his pocket and pulled out a wadge of money he had taken from one of the bags hidden behind his desk when he had gone into the bank for a short time at the start of the day. "You'd better have this, Chunggy. But keep it hidden. The Japanese may search you when they come."

Robert sat for a short period trying to rest but it was impossible. He was practically on the frontline. Hearing the strength of the gunfire increase as the guns in the next garden started firing, he knew it was time to go back to the Drill Hall. Wearily, he went out into the road working his way between abandoned army vehicles and with a large section of Indian troops just arriving. He just kept going without stopping, not looking back. He didn't see his home again for nearly four years.

As he had left for the last time to go to the Drill Hall, he saw Chunggy rearranging dustsheets over furniture and then switching off the electricity much to Robert's amusement. "I don't think we'll be getting a bill for a while, Chunggy." Chunggy just shrugged.

At the Drill Hall, other volunteers, not just those who were scheduled to be on duty, had also started to come in perhaps like Robert realising that tonight may be the end. They stood in the hall, a group of exhausted, mostly middle-aged men, with the sound of the guns overlaying any conversation. Everyone seemed to be in a dazed state, saying very little as they waited for Robert to give out instructions. The heat with no fans working was oppressive and the noise of the gunfire made conversation difficult.

Robert had dispensed with his sling the previous day despite the pain but kept the scarf across his mouth as much as possible because the dust and oily specks floating around made it difficult to speak without swallowing bits.

Robert, having taken a telephone call, eventually came to the front of the group of perhaps thirty men and a few hangers-on and started shouting. "We've just been asked to go down to Alexandra Road and assist with the bomb damage there. The volunteers down there are very short handed. There's also still the problem up near Orchard Road and the fire brigade has asked that we try and help as the fires have started up again and it's hampering some military task. From what I've been told that situation is not as critical compared to Alexandra Road, so I suggest that we send the lorry up to Orchard Road with just half a dozen volunteers and when they've finished, they can come down to Alexandra Road and help us. Captain Peters, can you take responsibility for that exercise? I'm told you can still get up Tanglin Road but I suggest you return down Orchard Road and back through the centre as there are large troop movements expected on

Tanglin Road later. I don't know where we will be based when we get to Alexandra Road but if you come around from the City, you are more likely to come across us. David..." Robert turned and looked around for David Thorsby, "...has managed to filch some petrol from cars in the area so there should be enough to get you there and back." David Thorsby just nodded at what Robert had said.

"We've also managed to find some cars that can transport most of us down to the Military Police point on Alexandra Road but there is little or no petrol in them so be prepared to dump them once you're on Alexandra Road. It might be a good idea if you, Martin, and Alex, go now and see if you can rustle up some trishaws to carry any equipment we need to take. Just be careful. The shells are so far falling up towards the top of the road near the Botanic Gardens but that won't last."

Robert paused for a few seconds before he continued. "Now the Military Police point we've been told to report to is near the hospital which I gather is very close to the front line, so that's a real hazard. Does everyone understand?"

Robert couldn't really hear any assent but could see in the dim light some semblance of nodding. The volunteers started to move off but Robert put his hand up. "Just a minute. The Japs are at best three or four miles away. I'm told their tanks have caused havoc in Bukit Timah village and were only stopped by some major rear-guard action. On the west side of the hospital, as I said, they're even closer. I will understand if any of you want to drop out and go home and look after families. We are volunteers after all and those of you with families must think of them first. From what I know, the Japs have reached Tanglin Barracks and there is fighting on the north side of the Botanic Gardens, so that's very close. Any of you that live towards those areas should think seriously about tonight, as it may be impossible to get back home tomorrow morning. We have a few volunteers who are catching some sleep and I have left messages that if they can join us in the morning, they should make their own way down to where we are on Alexandra Road."

"I have a meeting with Geoffrey Blackmore in the morning so if there is urgent news from that meeting, I will do my best to get the information to you. Lastly, for God's sake, be careful. Try and always work in pairs and help each other. We lost two colleagues a few days ago and they were not careless in any way. Some of us are carrying injuries because we're so tired, so we must be careful. The Revd. Cole…" Robert looked around for him. "Ah, there you are, Reverend. I believe you wish to say a few words."

The Revd. Cole came forward and asked everybody to stand for a moment in silence in remembrance of the two colleagues who had died and a short prayer was said; all this to a cacophony of shellfire from over by Tanglin Barracks. When the Revd. Cole had finished, Robert said, "Thank you, gentlemen."

Robert turned to David Masters. "If I'm missing, will you take charge, David?" A very tired friend, who had slept on a bunk bed in the Drill Hall, just smiled back at Robert, too overcome by the situation to say anything.

Robert walked over to Arthur, as that was easier than shouting. Robert looked at Arthur before speaking, frowning as he tried to talk over the noise of the guns. "I have my doubts we will be here tomorrow night judging by the fighting on the other side of the Botanic Gardens. I think you should go home and stay with Neecha."

Arthur shook his head and shouted back. "I got Michael Davison to cover the telephone this afternoon and I took Mona and Neecha down to the convent on Hill Street. I arranged it with Henry." There was a pause and then Arthur shouted again, "The Japs took Bukit Timah Village today and Henry said they have taken one of the reservoirs this afternoon. Macquarie and Peirce are under attack now, so once they've gone, there's no water."

It wasn't '*if they go*' but '*when they go*'. They stood there for a moment digesting this news before Robert said, "Come on. Let's go see what poor devils need our help."

Robert worked with his team helping to put out the fires on Alexandra Road. The Japanese bombers had destroyed a large part of Alexandra Road and across to the nearby Singapore River. He had now been working the better part of fifty hours like some of the younger ones such as Jay and Martin, with only short breaks. He had split the twenty or so remaining volunteers into three teams trying to give one team a rest period every so often although that was not always easy as crisis after crisis unfolded with Japanese artillery fire now well within range and a second surprise bombing raid occurring just after midnight.

The fire service had too few machines available and not enough men so Robert pulled some of the younger men out from road clearance and put them under the charge of the fire officer helping with the hoses where there was still sufficient water pressure. Burst water mains beyond the intersection with Tanglin Road was however making the water pressure very low, and half the time the volunteers and the Chinese locals, whom Robert had coerced into helping, were trying to find sufficient buckets to fill from the river to put out the fires but with little real effect. Watching the volunteers on one occasion it was like watching the living dead; his friends and neighbours no longer moved with speed, everything was at a slow ponderous pace.

The Alexandra Road LDC were also there but seemed to be leaderless and in the end, Robert, seeing them not working as a team, spoke to them and got them working under David Masters' direction concentrating on working with the fire brigade in putting out fires in a block of flats a few hundred yards from the hospital. Sometime, perhaps a couple of hours after the first raid, the bombers came over again and dropped bombs indiscriminately. The volunteers had sought shelter where they could in ditches, against rubble and in one case, Robert learned later, in the stinking river; a river that in parts was a blanket of flames.

When the all clear was sounded, it was to find that much of their work in clearing the road was undone and that new fires had been started all down the road towards Chinatown. One of the Tanglin volunteers had been wounded and Robert had to send him off in a rickshaw to the General Hospital. The next time he saw him was in an internment camp.

All the time that they had been working on the roads leading to the City Centre and helping with the clearance of burning buildings, the Army had been literally carrying munitions forward on the backs of men, occasionally on horse or mule, and once Robert saw Chinese women carrying boxes of ammunition. The sound of machine gunfire could now be clearly heard in the distance.

Around seven in the morning, after nearly nine hours of constant work, with no more than a few minutes of respite,

Robert was told by the MPs to get his volunteers back from where they had been working on some buildings ablaze just north of the hospital grounds.

"It is no longer safe, sir. The Japanese are within firing range of the buildings." Robert too tired to even discuss the issue, just nodded, and then set off, with David Thorsby in tow, to find his volunteers. Finding the half dozen volunteers who were clearing the buildings and helping dozens of people to move out of buildings that were on fire, he quickly told them to get back. The volunteers, mostly Chinese, had rescued a number of families who had been trapped and it took a few minutes to organise them, with small arms fire clearly to be heard above the immediate noise of the screaming and shouting of the residents.

As they worked their way back, hearing small arms fire only a few hundred yards away, it was David who said, "That's a machine gun, Bob."

Robert looked back and, in the gloom, he could see Indian soldiers taking cover behind makeshift defences and bren guns working their music of death. Through his scarf, he shouted, "Come on, David. I think it's time we really got out of here."

Back at the MP station, after a brief conversation with Arthur Thorsby and David Masters, he withdrew both LDC units towards the City Centre and arranged with a local shopkeeper for the men to have some drinks, and chocolate bars which for some reason was all the shopkeeper seemed to have in stock. Everyone just lay at the side of the road, impervious to the dirt that lay around them. The few remaining firemen that had been working with them sat a few yards away. Nobody was capable of conversation. The firemen now without a tender which lay on its side a hundred yards up the road having been hit by shelling.

The numbers of troops and amount of munitions going forward had lessened; from time to time, an ambulance struggled past taking the lightly wounded towards the Padang with more and more medical staff sitting at the back of the open ambulances. The sound of small arms fire could be heard in the hospital grounds.

"Are you still planning on getting out with Godfrey Smthye, David?"

David looked across to where the blackened faced Robert, with his hair still frizzled from it getting singed four or so days ago, was leaning against a wall drinking water and taking another painkiller. "I think if we do go now, it may be too late, Bob. I don't think we ever envisaged this unholy mess."

Robert slowly stood up and let out a sigh. "I have a meeting in a little while. It doesn't sound like good news to me."

David just nodded as he sat, too tired to speak with Alex already asleep beside him.

"Are you up for taking over?"

David slowly nodded his head, as he looked around. "I don't know that they're going to be much use, mind you. They're exhausted. Some of them have done more than twenty-four hours solid."

"Pull them further back down the road. Take them towards Coleman Bridge. Don't try and get back towards Tanglin Road. I should think it is even more manic there. If we have any volunteers coming down from Tanglin, they should be able to find you as I told them to make their way towards the City. Captain Peters should be around soon with his team. See if you can find a hall or something where this lot can put their heads down for a few hours. One of the Alexandra Road crowd might know of somewhere we can use. I understand that the troops are going to make a counterattack in a little while, so it could get a bit hairy around here." David just nodded at what Robert said.

David used the short sleeve of his shirt to rub his face and neck. "Are there still patients in the hospital?"

"As far as I know. I think they managed to get the slightly wounded out during the night but the more serious cases are still in there with hospital staff. You might have the Police ask you to help with some of that but up to now, the nurses and orderlies have been bringing them out a few at a time."

"If you do get asked to help, just send half the cohort and just those that are up to it. No point in all going up and then you end up having to carry some of them back." Again, David just nodded.

Robert got up slowly and looked around. "I'll see you later. When I'm down there, I'll see if I can rustle up some food for us."

Robert set off walking towards the city; he could distinctly hear a new sound – of mortars firing only a short distance away much closer than he had heard them the night before. Occasionally, there was the whizz of a shell as it flew over his head but the intensity seemed to have died down a little. Judging from the direction the sound of fighting was coming from, it looked as though the front line was very close to Tanglin Road as well as fighting in and around the hospital grounds.

The Fullerton Building was remarkably quiet when he eventually got there. It was almost as though everybody was trying to sleep even though shells were landing on Clark's Quay searching for the guns on the other side of the river. Outside in the Square, it was full of people walking around in a daze, with children sitting quietly and families huddled together. There was a smell that was certainly not of spices, and when Robert looked across at where he had worked for the last two years, it was to see a pavement covered with people trying to rest but all the time watching the sky for the dreaded bombers.

Inside the Fullerton Building, Robert found that the café he had often used was now an office with male Army typists, and a few Eurasian women, working away. The windows were heavily taped letting only a little light in. He followed a few other people who had just arrived and who sported Local Defence armbands; two senior policemen were just in front and had started to climb the stairs up to the third floor where an MP on duty had told them the meeting was to take place.

As he climbed the stairs, he heard his name being shouted out and turning around he saw Henry Preston, in his station uniform, climbing the stairs to catch him up. "I got into work only to find that Brigadier Simson wanted me at this meeting," Henry said looking Robert over. "Bad night?" Robert shrugged and half smiled.

The meeting took place in the main lounge of the Singapore Club and most of those attending the meeting spent a few seconds looking at the splendour.

"So, this is how the other half live. Carmichael told me it was quite something but I had no idea," Henry Preston said, as he and Robert found chairs towards the front. He knew many of the persons in the room and shook hands with a few and acknowledged others whereas Robert just sat surveying who was there.

Maurice Levy came up behind him and clapped him gently on his shoulder. "So, what have you been doing, Bob?" Robert smiled a very tired smile. "Much the same. We clear up in one street only to find the Japs have bombed the next street. The lads are absolutely done for."

"I hear that Thomson Road is no longer in our hands. No more news from the BBC," Maurice said looking around at Robert.

"Well, in some ways, it's better not to know," Robert said, remembering that the BBC studios had been on Thomson Road.

Maurice briefly said he had been doing voluntary work at the hospital but didn't mention his wife and then someone Robert recognised by sight came over to Maurice and Robert was introduced to a Charles De Lacey, who it turned out had been put in charge of food stores on the Island.

"Don't suppose you know how to get some food up to my LDC unit on Alexandra Road."

De Lacey looked a bit shocked at what Robert said. "I don't. I've taken responsibility for the food stores in the godowns, and the warehouses down at the docks."

With that, he was off and Maurice grinned at Robert. "Typical civil servant. He will have it being measured in cupfuls, as the Japs enter his office. Getting it out of the godown is however someone else's job."

Robert could see that the meeting was coming to order and sat down. From nowhere, a waiter appeared distributing tea and biscuits much to the amusement of the majority of those present, and with more than one person remarking that standards had to be maintained. Brigadier Simson came straight to the point and told them in very clear language that the situation was dire and that they hadn't much time.

"Mr Besseker and Mr Blackmore have prepared a list which is going around you now. The individuals on the list, we need them to stay and assist with civil defence and maintenance of civil order. All other persons who are not on the list we are now advising to get out today. The Navy is arranging for a convoy of ships to leave tonight and I have been given permits for allocation. Those required to stay will have priority for members of their family to go. I have asked Mr Besseker to go with the convoy and he will be organising the departures along with Mr Smythe." Brigadier Simson looked around and finding Godfrey sitting at the end of a row, he pointed him out.

"There will be permits for LDC members no longer required as well." He paused for a moment and then continued. "I am sorry if you are on the list but we see you as essential for the operation of civil order and the continuation of services. Some of you in LDCs will be very important in providing back up services and for the continued clearance of bomb damage."

There was no reaction to the news merely an acceptance of the situation. A few stood up and started to leave the room. "Just a minute, gentlemen. I ask that you speak to Mr Besseker or Mr Blackmore before you leave as there may be a need for a handover or for the destruction of essential equipment. You will also need permits."

The list finally landed on Robert's lap and he looked down. His name was as he expected, on it. At the bottom of the sheet, it asked those on the list to report to Mr Besseker for further instructions.

Robert got up and went over to one of the waiters who guessed that he was coming for more tea. “Tuan, sit down please. I will bring you more tea.”

“You couldn’t get me a sandwich, could you? I need more than biscuits.” The waiter smiled back. “I will find you something, Tuan.”

Sitting down again, he found Godfrey Smythe taking the seat next to him. “I thought I saw you. You’re on the list I see.”

“I don’t know why I’ve been singled out,” Robert said wryly, adding as an afterthought, “I’m just hoping they’re putting me in charge of the sleeping arrangements.”

“That’s the spirit. Glad to see you haven’t lost your sense of humour. I’ve got the task of getting people on ships. You can imagine what that will be like.”

“Where’s the Captain, Godfrey. I haven’t heard of him for more than a week.”

Godfrey took a moment to reply. “We don’t know for sure. He managed to get some repairs to the ship.” Robert was about to say what repairs when Godfrey added, “The ship was hit and was listing but the old devil managed to get it into the dock and they got it repaired enough to go out again. He took the *Lass* out to the Banka Straits to help with rescuing some of the poor sods off the *Empress of Asia* and by all accounts, the *Lass* was hit again by bombs and the last anyone saw of her, she was listing and was trying to make her way to Sumatra. That’s not good news though as we know the Japs are over there in force.”

Robert just made a face, “It’s what he would have wanted, Godfrey. Being in the thick of it.” Godfrey saw Robert’s arm and asked what had happened.

"I got nicked by a plane. Not too bad really. Just bloody painful."

Before Godfrey could say anything, there was noise from the front and both turned to face Brigadier Simson as he again began to speak, "Gentlemen, those of you who are still here have been selected to work with the police and fire service in ensuring that as far as possible the City continues to work in the next few weeks. A few of you are also involved in the evacuation arrangements. As I see it, we have three critical areas – fire, water and food. We have I understand a population of around 400,000 normally and it is guesswork at the number of refugees we also have but we should assume we are dealing with the better part of a million civilians. Each of the critical areas will create a civil problem which we have to try as best we can, to solve." Godfrey got up as the Brigadier was speaking and whispered, 'good luck' and left, Robert presumed for Clarke's Quay. Robert didn't see him again for nearly six years.

The Brigadier was a quiet spoken, serious man and Robert had to listen intently in order to hear him over the sound of artillery guns that had again started up. "The Police Commissioner has allocated a senior officer to each area of the City still under our control and they will be in overall command of the law and order for that district. As civil defence workers, I ask that you work with your designated commander in keeping local order, in clearing roads and assisting the fire service, as well as getting food to the populace. The fire service will operate somewhat differently and try and concentrate its remaining resources in dealing with major problems, particularly where the damage is preventing the military from their essential tasks. We will have to leave other fires and damage to take its course. The City Works have three emergency teams dealing with burst water mains and trying to maintain a water supply but it sounds an almost impossible task. As at three hours ago, we still have two reservoirs under our control but there is heavy fighting around both of them. General Percival is treating the reservoirs as a priority."

The meeting broke up shortly afterwards and Robert went over to the group of volunteers standing around the Police Commissioner and his deputy and obtained the information he needed. He also got a handful of permits and Geoffrey who handed them to him told him to fill the names in.

As he was giving Robert the permits, Geoffrey said, "I'm glad you've agreed to stay."

"I didn't know I had a choice, Geoffrey. My name was on the list," Robert said, scratching one of the bites he now had on his face.

"Oh, you could have objected but we need some good people for the next few weeks."

"That rather sounds as though we haven't long."

This time, it was Geoffrey who made a face. "We rather depended on the *Empress of Asia*, it had tanks on it and more troops, and now that's gone…" Geoffrey tailed off.

It was Robert who said finally, "Look, I need to be going. I need to find my crowd and tell those who want to go, to get down to the docks as quickly as possible, with these. He waved the permits he was holding."

He shook hands with Geoffrey Blackmore and walked off towards the stairs. The waiter who had gone to find a sandwich for Robert arrived at that moment with a plate of sandwiches and Robert, thanking him, grabbed a handful and set off down the stairs leaving others in his wake reaching for the remaining sandwiches.

It took Robert more than an hour to walk the short distance to Alexandra Road through Chinatown and a further half hour before he located his units. He found them resting in a local market where they had managed to commandeer a corner with some shade.

Robert called them together and told them what he had learned and immediately some of the Chinese volunteers said they must try and get back home, in some cases to try and get up towards the far end of Tanglin. Arthur Thorsby and David Masters were standing together in deep conversation and after Robert had talked to some of the volunteers who were anxious to depart, Robert went across to them.

"Arthur, Henry was at the meeting and he has gone up to Hill Street to collect Mona and Neecha. He asked me to say that he will bring them down if you will bring the lads over. David, you and Alex need to go as well. I have sufficient permits for all of you."

Robert looked around. "Michael's not here but I have permits for him and his girls."

It was Arthur who said, "He didn't come with the last of the volunteers this morning. He said something yesterday about taking Mary and his girls down to the convent on Hill Street, so maybe he's got caught up there."

David had been untying the scarf he now sported around his neck, as he listened to Arthur. "We've been talking about going. We think you must come as well."

Robert shook his head. "They've asked me to remain and help with the civil problems that are likely to continue."

David started to get exasperated. "For God's sake, Bob.

We've maybe only got a few days. What difference are you going to make?"

Arthur was nodding, "I agree. We should all stick together."

Robert repeated what Simson had said. "If you're not essential, then you get on one of the boats and make a run for it." He added, "Think of your wives, and the lads. I haven't got any family. It's as simple as that."

From behind him, Brian, and Martin, both of whom had come up behind him both said, "If you're not going, we're not going." Robert turned and addressed Brian, "Look if you want me to lead you, then listen to me. If you get to Australia, then you can join up; surely that's more important than ending up in a camp on the Island." Brian said nothing more. "Come on, Arthur, David, help me for God's sake. Get your lads down to the docks and get them out of here."

There was a murmuring and shaking of heads and then Robert seeing them beginning to weaken said, "Off you go and get down there. It bound to be chaos, so it's best if you go now. I need to see who is left and talk to them about what we must do. I also have to go to the police station to meet a Chinese Society representative who is going to find me a team of Chinese volunteers. Geoffrey Blackmore has done a deal with the Chinese community to get them working with us."

Brian, who had wandered off to talk with the Thorsby lads and Alex, came back over to Robert and put out his hand. "Good luck, Bob. I'll be back to get you, I promise."

Robert grinned a very tired smile. "You're not teasing me, are you?"

Brian grinned back. "You sod."

David Masters followed Robert, as he went around and

found out who was staying. "How long do you think, Bob?"

Robert turned around to face David. "Maybe a week, more likely a few days. Geoffrey Blackmore gave strong hints that the reservoirs are under threat and not likely to stay in our hands. Once that happens, we have no water."

"Anything I can do for you?"

"Just make sure they all get on a ship and stick together. I suspect it's not going to be a picnic for you out there. Arthur doesn't know yet but Henry will be staying."

"I guessed he would be on this list you spoke about." As they were speaking, there was a constant racket of machine gunfire from towards the hospital.

Robert nodded his head towards the new shooting. "They've sent up some Indian troops in some form of counter-attack. There are still some patients and nursing staff stuck in the hospital. So, we can expect the Japs to start shelling the road and this area again."

David murmured something about the Japs were damn close to the General Hospital as well to which Robert nodded. Robert turned to the small band of people who were gathered at the corner of the market. "Right, friends, I suggest you stay here and try and get some rest. Captain Peters, I would appreciate it if you will take charge in my absence."

Turning back to David, Robert put out his good hand. "Good luck, you old reprobate. I shall miss you. Just make sure you look after yourself." David said nothing, just squeezed his hand and turned away.

Chapter 26

Friday, 13th February 1942 was a black Friday. Robert had worked his way back towards the hospital with literally thousands of, mostly Chinese, refugees streaming down the road in the opposite direction. More and more he saw young troops running towards the City with no officers controlling them.

The smoke from the various fires was acrid and the noise was increasingly of crying people in great distress. The river on his right side for some of the way, was on fire. The devastation was immense. The oil tanks situated north of the docks that had been blown up an hour or so before had produced large smuts of warm oil that stuck to everything even burning exposed skin.

He had been told to report to the police inspector but that was not easy with the crowds of refugees streaming away from the fighting, the heat from the fires and the shells coming from Japanese mortars that must be based, Robert guessed, somewhere just north of the hospital.

The last hundred yards to the police station was something he hoped never to experience again; he had literally crawled for most of the way up to the building hugging the wall on his left and cowering in doorways as bullets flew past. Shellfire hit buildings across the road bringing them down in clouds of smoke and dust; with soldiers behind a sandbag nest firing at targets unseen in the hospital grounds only yards away. At the police station, he was dragged in, and over the crackle of small arms fire, he was told to report to the inspector who was in a back office. Even as he crawled on his knees down the corridor, soldiers from an English Regiment were firing from windows that opened out towards the hospital grounds.

The inspector, a Scot judging by his accent, was shouting apologies down the telephone at somebody seeking more help from what Robert could make out. The inspector put the phone down and shouted something in Malay to a policeman standing just in the corridor and then turned to Robert. Robert briefly explained who he was and the inspector nodded as he also waved at Robert's right arm that had started to bleed again.

"You have the enviable task of trying to keep the roads clear so that the army can get up here and we can get casualties out. Fat chance with the Japs using their mortars and pinpointing the road. We have another counterattack planned to start about now so there may be some respite. Fredericks down at Rochor Canal has also been on to say that they're sending up some food for distribution but where the hell can that be done. Tell me."

Robert wasn't sure whether he expected an answer or not. Still a bit unsure of himself, he said, "We could use the market on Havelock Road, the one that's beyond the intersection with River Valley Road. It's sufficiently far down the road to be out of range of the fighting for people to come and collect food."

The inspector didn't argue so Robert continued, "As for

the roads, that's more difficult as we have no heavy lifting equipment so it's a hand job. I need more volunteers." At that, the inspector perked up. "Ah, there's a Chin Zhi, sitting somewhere around. He's supposed to be your liaison. Been here about an hour." The inspector turned and yelled at somebody who must have been in the corridor and this time Robert did understand what he said.

In came a very tired and harassed medic who took Robert to one side of the inspector's desk and redressed his wound. "You must take care of it, sir."

"That's easier said than done," Robert said but thanked the medic who disappeared off back along the corridor. The inspector again shouted and Robert heard someone in the corridor take up the call. The man from the Chinese Society obviously did not seem to want to be in the front line.

Chin Zhi finally arrived looking anything but comfortable at standing up, preferring to be on his knees and looking ready to make a run for it. Robert moved over to him and explained that they had to clear the road back down towards the City Centre and distribute food that the Inspector would arrange to be sent to the market on Havelock Road. Robert questioned him about how many Chinese volunteers there would be and Chin Zhi answered over the noise that perhaps a dozen would come. Robert shook his head and shouted that they needed more. Chin Zhi said he understood and he would try and get more. Finally, with a nod at the inspector, Robert said that he and Chin Zhi would make their way back down the road.

The Inspector shouted that he had sent a runner earlier to the LDC asking for help with people who were being rescued from the hospital. Robert nodded and shouted back that he had expected the task and he would send Chin Zhi off to get more help.

At the front of the building, the shooting was now more sporadic and there was by the sounds of it heavy fighting in and around the hospital buildings; Robert could see people, patients and staff, some running, others being helped, making their way past them. As these people came past the police station, Robert turned to Chin Zhi. “Come on. Let’s give them a hand and when we get down to where my crowd are, then you can go and find your volunteers.”

Robert ran perhaps twenty yards to where a nurse had fallen, clearly injured and with difficulty helped her up in a very distressed state. A doctor came by carrying a nurse in his arms still wearing his surgical gear. Robert got the nurse who kept falling to stand upright and somehow with one good arm, he got her a hundred yards or so past the police station just saying all the time to her, ‘just a bit further, just a bit further,’ gasping with the effort in the heat. Eventually, two Chinese men turned up and recognising them as part of his LDC team, he let them take the weight off him.

All around him, he could hear yelling and screaming, and at one point, he saw an orderly and a nurse put down a patient who had died in the struggle to get to safety. The orderly, a Scouser by the sound of his voice, was shouting and swearing what he would do to the Japs when he got a hold of them and this tirade continued until he and a group of other hospital staff were piled onto a lorry that had somehow got through. Eventually, having managed to turn around the lorry moved off back towards the City.

Robert saw that it was a cohort of the LDC that was clearing the ground and helping the lorry turn around. “The inspector sent a runner about thirty minutes ago asking for volunteers to help with people rescued from the hospital, so I brought half of us up here and I left the others having a rest for a couple of hours. We saw the lorries were blocked from getting through, so we cleared a space to get one through at a time," Captain Peters explained this to Robert when he finally managed to get a moment to talk to him. Chin Zhi who had been with Robert at the start was nowhere to be seen. One minute Chin Zhi had been with Robert and the next he had gone.

Robert just nodded at what the Captain had said; it was clear that they were not going to get much rest in the next few hours. Robert briefed Captain Peters in a few words before saying, "Captain, I'll take over here. Can you go back down to the market? There should be some lorries arriving with food for distribution. Will you take charge of the distribution? It's not going to be easy. You'll just have to trust to some form of honesty about whether people need food or not. You should be used to doing that sort of thing in your former life."

Captain Peters smiled back at Robert. "Too often, young man."

"Any males that seem fit and healthy send them up to me to do road clearance and tell them they get no food for their families until they have helped."

Captain Peters, all of seventy years of age, just nodded. "Consider it done."

With that, Peters went off with Robert momentarily thinking that thc old duffer was thoroughly enjoying the challenge. He went back to clearing the road. With the dozen or so volunteers and with some local labour that Robert had quickly commandeered, they made inroads into the bomb damage scattered across the road before the mortars started again; any burning buildings had to be left to their fate. Robert noticed after half an hour or so that fewer staff and patients were coming past and only a few fleeing civilians. It was only about then that Robert realised that he had blood all over his front where he had helped the nurse to get to the lorry.

For hours, the road clearance team worked at their task working progressively further away from the hospital, interspersed on two occasions by further bombing raids, both times quick raids only intended to terrify people and cause chaos. The shelling was becoming intermittent with the small arms fire now constant.

Fortunately, no more bombs hit the road but buildings in some of the side streets were set on fire and Robert had to take his volunteers to these buildings as there was no fire service in the vicinity and it was clear from the screams that people were needing help; threatening the gang of coolies he had commandeered with dire consequences if they left their task of road clearing.

Later in the afternoon when Robert brought his volunteers back to the main road, the coolies had gone but fortunately, most of the road was clear. He called a halt and he led the volunteers down to the market where Captain Peters and the remaining members of the LDC were finishing the distribution of food. He no longer walked normally; he felt as though his mind had separated from his body, he was so tired.

Leaving the volunteers trying to rest, he stumbled his way to meet Inspector Forsyth in a shop only a hundred yards or so away where a temporary police station had now been set up.

“The Army has moved south of the hospital but I can’t see them staying there for long because the Japs can fire on them from the upper floors of the hospital. There are also Japanese infiltrating through some of the side streets. I have had to move down here and I'm proposing to move all residents out, to say, at least four hundred yards beyond the market. My men have started telling residents to move out or risk being killed in the fighting."

Robert nodded as he tried removing sweat and grime from his face.

"You look as though you need a doctor," the inspector said looking at the caked blood on Robert.

Robert shook his head. "I helped a wounded nurse to get out and some of her blood got on me."

The inspector looked at Robert grimly before saying, "They raped God knows how many women. You could hear the girls screaming. Then they bayoneted the patients. Some of the Indian troops when they went back in said they found doctors who had been beheaded."

Robert accepted the drink of water the inspector had offered him and sighed out loud. He just stood, slightly swaying, not sure what to say. The grit in his eyes made them feel that they were on fire; he could no longer think straight.

"Mr Draper, take your men down to the Coleman Bridge. You can't stay in the market as that will be too near the frontline. Try and get some rest. God knows you will be back on duty soon enough." As he finished saying it, a Japanese fighter came over almost at roof top height firing all the way down the road towards the City Centre. Robert who had helped himself to a packet of biscuits got up to go as the Inspector said, "The water mains have been blown again so there's no fresh water." Robert put his scarf back over his mouth and nodded goodbye to the inspector.

******

Robert and his band of volunteers made their way over Coleman Bridge. It was now dark with smoke and fires everywhere. Captain Peters had collapsed an hour or so ago and was being helped, almost carried. Other members of the LDC were also being assisted and a nurse who had attached herself to the group was doing her best to treat minor injuries with some basic first aid kit the LDC carried with them. There was no conversation. Indeed, the noise around them had greatly diminished and all Robert could really hear was the crackle from a fire in a tenement about a hundred yards away. Robert, leading the group, saw a policeman just ahead wave them to stop at a checkpoint beside the Bridge. The police sergeant, a large Malay, told him that they should continue up to the central fire station on Hill Street or go on to the Padang.

"I don't think my crowd are good to do anything for at least twelve hours, Sergeant. They are completely spent." The police sergeant said nothing; he had probably heard it all already. Not thinking straight, Robert asked a question he knew the answer to. "How far to the Padang?"

"Less than a mile, sir."

Robert nodded at what he was told. The Fire Station was only a hundred yards or so from the bridge and he turned and waved his men on. They followed him blindly until he turned into the Fire Station telling them to find a space and rest. Robert could just make out other souls lying on the ground exhausted. One of the younger Chinese volunteers went with him to look for water. A policeman, leaning against a wall, directed them to a water tanker at the back of the yard and eventually, they found a bucket and filled it.

Everything seemed to be in slow motion with the heat of the evening draining what energy was left. Out to sea, he could hear planes bombing what he presumed to be the last ships to leave Singapore; there was no shelling thankfully. At last lying down beside the group, who had moved under a balcony Robert drank his water and then put his head back and even in that most awkward of sleeping positions, he fell asleep.

It was some hours later when Robert awoke and he guessed it was around eight in the morning. The sun was probably well up but there seemed to be only minimal light as the smoke and grit in the air made it impossible to see a clear sun. Robert looked guiltily around and saw that most people were on the move and seemed to have been so for a while.

Three of the Chinese volunteers saw him awake and came across, clearly wanting to speak to him. "What's the problem?" Robert asked trying to get up with his good arm. One of the Chinese helped him to stand up as one of the others spoke. "Bob, we think we must try and see if we can get back to our families. Now the Japanese are very close our families will need us. We should be with them."

Robert did his best to smile back at the three men who were all in their thirties, one of whom he knew well because he worked in the Commercial Union with Harry, or at least he had. "I agree. You must go. I cannot thank you enough for all your help. Who knows in better times we can maybe have a drink together and try and forget this nightmare?" Robert put out his good arm and clapped the man who had helped him up, on the shoulder. "Good luck." With that, the three men scurried off and Robert turned to see what was left of his unit. After wandering around for a few minutes, he realised that they, like him, knew it was near the end. Few of them said much, more just acknowledging him. As they talked, Robert saw another LDC coming into the yard. Recognising the leader, he went over to him.

"Mr Russell." Russell looked across at him not recognising Robert through all the dirt on his face. "Robert Draper, Tanglin outfit."

"Ah, yes." Russell looked around tiredly at the remains of his unit. "We've been told to rest here. You been here long?"

Robert said he had been at the fire station for a few hours, as he watched the Hill Street contingent come in quietly, a couple of them being helped by some of the other volunteers.

Russell seeing Robert looking at the injured shook his head. "They had been working all night on trying to put out fires over on Bras Basah Road and one of the buildings collapsed around us. We ended up with two volunteers being shipped off to hospital and four others injured. How someone wasn't killed is a miracle."

Robert nodded watching Captain Peters, somehow recovered, and one of the few remaining Chinese volunteers, getting some water for those who had just arrived.

As they stood speaking, a Fire Officer came out of the offices on the far side of the yard and came over. "Just been told that the last two reservoirs are no longer in our hands." He added that the Salvation Army was on its way with food, then just turned and walked back into the offices. Neither Robert nor Russell had the energy to discuss what they had just been told. They both knew what it meant.

Just making a bit of a face at Russell and saying nothing, Robert left him standing there contemplating the situation. He went over to Captain Peters. "You sure you're okay?"

Captain Peters smiled across at him. "You look in a worse state than I do."

"Well, that doesn't say much," Robert said smiling back at a very tired and hot old man.

"We are not needed by all accounts or the Inspector would have sent a runner by now. I've just been told that the Salvation Army are coming down shortly with some food for us. So, in the meantime, I will try and find some means of us cleaning ourselves up before we go on duty again."

Captain Peters just nodded at that and then said, "I did say to the lads who delivered the food rations yesterday afternoon that we would make ourselves available to help again."

Robert looked at Captain Peters, shaking his head at the Captain's enthusiasm, before saying in a resigned voice, "I will see if I can get a hold of the Inspector, eh, Forsyth, and see if it's safe to go back up Havelock Road."

Captain Peters went off still doling out water and organising two volunteers to get more water from the tanker. Robert had decided not to say anything about the Japanese having captured the reservoirs, that would soon become obvious. Instead, he set off across the yard to the Fire Brigade offices to see if he could contact Inspector Forsyth.

When the lorry arrived with food, about an hour later, it also brought incongruously two nuns from the convent up the hill who immediately set about tending the scrapes and burns that most of the men had accumulated. The friendly nurse had somehow disappeared whilst Robert was asleep and in fact, he began to wonder if it had been a dream.

When they got to Robert, one of the nuns took off the bandage on his left arm. It had stopped bleeding in the night and had dried to a red cake around the edge of the bandages.

Cleaning it first with a little hot water, the nun eased off the bandage and smiling a little timidly, she then told Robert, "This might hurt a little."

Taking some cotton wool, she dabbed the edge of the wound with Gentian Violet, bringing him to life immediately, yelling his head off. "I am sorry but this is all we have. Mother Superior says that it cures everything," the nun said looking very upset at Robert's reaction. Robert wanted to say what he thought of Mother Superior but through his watering eyes, he could just make out the slightly unsure but smiling nun's face. "Come on, cry baby. The children don't cry when I put it on their scratches." Robert didn't say anything, just bit his lip and then jerked his head up hearing the whizzing of a shell coming over and landing perhaps fifty yards away. Suddenly, there was yelling all over the place as people raced to see what damage there had been and taking cover in the expectation of more shells.

"It's a range finder," someone shouted. Robert thanked the nun who finished putting a bandage on his arm. As another shell came over, Robert went to find John Russell who was getting up from the ground over at the far side of the yard.

"We'll deal with this situation; my lads have had a few hours rest. We'll call you over if we can't manage the damage. Let's see how that works." Russell nodded and went off to tell his unit to stay put as Robert and his volunteers set off to deal with the damage as more shells came over, landing a bit further up the road.

The shelling continued sporadically for a little over an hour without it being obvious what the Japanese artillery was trying to hit. Then for some reason, the shelling stopped as though they too had run out of steam. Fortunately, the shells landed mainly in buildings that did not seem to be occupied or had already suffered shelling. From one of the burning buildings, several Indian troops emerged and it was immediately obvious that they were deserters. Robert could see Captain Peters already in an argument with them, as they seemed unwilling to help with checking that the damaged buildings were empty and with clearing the damage off the roads.

The troops ran off as Robert approached and he could hear Captain Peters shouting at them, "Well if you won't help, then buggar off. No wonder we're in such a mess with troops like you." Captain Peters was remonstrating and yelling at the departing dozen or so Indians.

"I wouldn't waste your breath, Captain. It looks as though they have been hiding there for a while."

Captain Peters turned to Robert, "I have never sworn in my life but these beggars reduced me to it. They said that when the Japs come, they are going to join them, as they will get their independence. What hope have we with scoundrels like that around?"

Robert looked at a small plump man, very old and tired, wearing a large leather belt to hold up a pair of shorts that seemed much too big for him, and a shirt that was covered with dirt.

He just shook his head. By all accounts, Captain Peters had served his faith all his life, probably never sworn and certainly never contemplated using a gun and here he was defending the Empire. *You bring hope, sir, where there is little*, Robert thought for a moment, as he turned to deal with another problem.

Chapter 27

What was left of the Tanglin and Alexandra units worked slowly until mid-morning finding a few occupants needing help with the fire service using the last of the water in their tanks to douse some of the fires. No water pressure was available, so it was not possible to use the hoses that were available and, in the heat, Robert found that the task of putting out even small fires by using blankets and brushes was slow and very tiring. Finally, he called a halt and told everyone to take a break. No bombers had come over in the final part of the morning and already someone had remarked, 'what was the point as the City would be theirs shortly'.

It was as they sat down, with mugs of tea supplied from somewhere in the fire station, that there was the most almighty explosion that went on for ten minutes or so, with repeated eruptions and it was one of the fire officers who told them it was the oil terminals on Bukom Island. Even though the oil terminals were the better part of ten miles away, the sound of the explosions was ear splitting making conversation impossible and the plume of smoke could be seen for miles, and for days afterwards. Everybody just found a resting place and sat with their own thoughts.

It was later in the afternoon with the sky growing darker

and darker from the cloud of smoke and flying oil specks from the terminals which the wind was now blowing over the City that John Russell, Robert, the Chief Fire Officer, and Inspector Forsyth and one of his Sergeants got together in the fire offices.

"We have a new front line about a mile from here," the Inspector told everybody. "A second line of troops is situated around 400 yards up Havelock Road and it goes all the way through to Orchard Road in the East and across to Keppel Road in the West." He then addressed Robert and John Russell, "I think we have to leave the fire service to look after what buildings are damaged between here and the reserve line. What we need to do is distribute food, so can I suggest that you two agree between you a number of distribution points and let the Sergeant here know what you have decided and he will arrange for the food to be sent down by lorry from the food stores." Forsyth had been looking at Robert and John Russell, as he suggested the organisation of food. "We can expect a new attack around late evening so we have a few hours in which to distribute the food. I think we should assume it may be our last distribution for a while."

John Russell and Robert said nothing at first, taking in the enormity of what the inspector had just said although if truth be told they were resigned already to the situation. John Russell made a number of suggestions for distribution centres for his unit with Robert coming in, "We're rather cut off from Tanglin, so can I suggest we assist by distributing from the Union & China Bank in Fullerton Square. There are large numbers of people sleeping on the streets there, clearly refugees." With that, the meeting broke up and Robert went over to his volunteers to tell them that they had a walk of about a mile to Fullerton Square to assist in food distribution. Without any dissent, Robert led his volunteers off towards Anderson Bridge and across to Fullerton Square walking in an increasingly hot late afternoon with the smell of the oil getting onto Robert's throat even through a scarf, and looking around, he noticed about half his contingent now copied him and had covered their mouths. Troops were in large numbers, many just sitting at the side of the roads looking exhausted, some wounded men were being attended to under the shade of some trees and a group of officers were huddled together by the side of the road, in deep discussion.

In the distance as they were making their way to Fullerton Square, they could hear shells exploding over towards Keppel Road, the main west road that led down to the docks, and on one occasion, there was the sound of heavy machine gun fire. The sounds seemed to suggest that they were walking nearer to the fighting although no one stopped them. For the first time, as they crossed the bridge, they saw the bodies of soldiers piled at the side of the road. Army lorries were parked end to end as they started walking into Fullerton Road, with some burnt out.

Coming into the square, they saw on the side where the Union and China Bank was located that large numbers of people had made temporary homes whereas the side where the Fullerton Building was situated was relatively clear. Outside the Fullerton Building, there was a small military presence but there was no indication that the High Commissioner was in residence in the Singapore Club. Robert recognised no one as he crossed the road and using the keys he had first gone over and found in Godfrey Smythe's office, he opened the side entrance of the bank and let the volunteers in. He quickly arranged for volunteers to stay on duty and watch for the distribution lorries and told the others to find somewhere to settle down and wait, before going off to his old office.

He found two bags of the small denomination money he had asked Wuh to hide behind his desk and brought them out. Opening one bag, he saw that Wuh had split the money and put it in envelopes as he had requested. Robert went upstairs and walked around and saw that the ledgers had all been boxed; hopefully, the Japanese soldiers would not be interested in paper files. Going down the backstairs to the vaults, he found them open, with the trays of small coinage that he had told Mr Wuh to leave in the vaults as the total amount was of small value. In the room where the safety deposit boxes were, they were nearly all open with perhaps thirty or so unopened and he briefly thought about just how long it would be before the Japanese brought in cutting equipment to open them up.

As he came back up the stairs, he could hear the drum of bombers overhead and the screams of people trying to hide as fighter planes came screaming past almost at building height although he couldn't hear any gunfire. One of the volunteers had found the water barrel normally kept in the staff rest room and was doling out water to everyone and Robert gratefully took a glass.

Pat Reynolds, who had been in charge of the City Works until he retired in 1934, came over. "So, is this where you work?"

Robert nodded and merely said 'yes'. Adding after a little hesitation, as he looked around at the mess in the banking hall, "I don't think I will be back here again, at least not for quite a while."

Captain Peters, looking anything but well, came across from the side door and joined them extending out his hand with the keys for the bank.

"I don't think we will be needing those, Captain Peters. I suggest you leave them in the door. It's not as though there's anything left to steal. Actually, there is. If some of the men feel like doing something, there are eight or nine trays of coinage in the vaults. Can I suggest they bring them up and when we distribute the food, we can give out the coinage? Better the poor sods out there get it than the Japanese."

It was Reynolds who answered. "Leave that with me. I shall enjoy giving out the money. Trehearne would have a fit if he knew what we were doing."

Robert grinned at Reynolds. "So, you knew him?"

"Pain in the arse, Bob. How anybody worked for him is beyond me. Spent his life trying to climb from one ladder to the next. He couldn't hold a candle to Peter Connaught." At that, Robert smiled and Reynolds finished off, "Smarmy sod. What happened to him, anyway?"

"Last I heard, he was sending missives from Batavia telling us that the Japanese were nothing to worry about and he was going to Australia with Muriel because she didn't like the bombing. Who does! Even had the cheek to say that we should be made to stay and fight them."

Reynolds nodded. "That sounds just like him. He's the kind that survives mind you, while all about—"

"Let's get off the subject. It's even more depressing than the pickle we're in."

With that, Robert went off to the side door to see what was happening and to make sure the volunteers out there had had some water. Going outside for a moment, it was to see people emerging from under the walkways onto the road now that the enemy planes were no longer flying over. There was a great deal of wailing and crying but Robert found he no longer heard it; it had become almost part of the struggle to stay alive.

He spoke to the two volunteers he found stationed outside the door and said he would arrange for them to be relieved soon and went back in to get volunteers to assist outside. It was now late afternoon and any gunfire was sporadic with only the occasional enemy shell to be heard although the Allied artillery from the Battery was more regular. Everything he did was at half pace.

It was perhaps six in the evening when two lorries turned up and brought water and food and Robert immediately had two teams working on distribution of rice and water. "We don't know how many that need help so I suggest a cup of rice for each person and a cup of water. If we have some left over at the end, we can give a second dole out to the children."

One of the drivers came over to Robert as he helped with the distribution. He was wearing a very dirty Royal Navy uniform. "Don't suppose you've heard but Percival has gone to talk to the Japs. We reckon we're surrendering."

Robert just puckered his brow at the news and it was one of the other volunteers, who had heard what was being said, who asked, "When did you hear?"

"One of the lads from Fort Canning came down with instructions that we were to get on with destroying all the booze in the warehouses immediately. He told us that the General has gone up to Bukit Timah to parley."

Robert turned to the volunteer. "I suggest you go around

and tell the rest."

It took them about two hours to distribute the food and water to a remarkably well behaved, docile crowd of mainly Chinese people, with only a few Malays seeking food. When they had finished, Robert called the volunteers together.

"You're welcome to stay here but if the naval rating was correct, then any minute now, we should expect to see Japanese soldiers. I don't know how they will behave but some of the stories I have been told doesn't give me a lot of optimism. The rating said that there are many civilians congregating on the Padang so maybe we should make our way up there and wait with them." There was a little discussion and then Captain Peters said the consensus was that they should go up to the Padang.

"Right Captain, if you would lead them up there, I will catch you up. I have a task to do on Victoria Street and then I will follow on and see you at the Padang."

Robert went through to the Treasury and collected the two bags of money he had left there, first taking half a dozen envelopes out and stuffing them inside his shirt. The bags were much heavier than he first imagined and eventually, he used a broom handle he found in a cleaner's cupboard and placing the bags at either end, he put the handle over his good shoulder and left the bank leaving the side door open.

It was dark by the time he found what he was looking for on a road off Victoria Street and he knocked on the door to the side of the building. He repeated the knock after a few minutes and eventually, a Jewish man opened it slightly.

"Eh. Good evening. I'm looking for Maurice Levy. My name's Robert Draper."

The Jewish gentlemen said nothing, just opened the door

and let Robert in. “Wait here, please.” Robert seemed to be standing in a small courtyard with what looked like a garden off to the left. Maurice arrived a few moments later.

“I’m sorry to disturb you, Maurice.” Maurice waved aside the apology. “You said I could leave my stuff with you in the synagogue and I wonder if you can also keep this for me.”

Maurice could see it was moneybags and just nodded.

“I can’t see why we should burn it all if we might need some of it.”

Again, Maurice nodded, “I’ve done the same. We don’t know what we will need.”

“You know that Percival has surrendered,” Robert said.

Maurice nodded and said, “I understand that he has gone off to negotiate a cease fire. We’re just having a meeting inside about the situation.”

Robert said, “Ah,” and then added, “I’ll leave you to it then.” He put out his hand, “Good luck.”

Maurice shook Robert’s good hand and smiled back, “I think you should go and get some rest. You will need it in the coming days. Oh, if you need any of this money and I am not here, then ask for Rashid. He is our caretaker and I will tell him that you may call. Your belongings will be well hidden, I promise.” With that, Robert turned and opened the gate and let himself out. Robert never spoke to Maurice Levy again.

Making his way to the Padang, he heard church bells begin to ring and he noticed that lights had come on in some of the buildings.

Chapter 28

When Robert woke, it was already well into the morning. His mouth tasted like a midden but thankfully the pain in his arm was more of a dull ache. He saw that most of the men were up around him. It had taken him some time the evening before to find his group as the crowds of civilians camping out were far more numerous than he had expected; as were the crowds in the streets much larger than he had expected with most of the military men getting drunk before they surrendered to the Japanese in the morning. It seemed that everybody just wanted to come out and celebrate that the nightmare of bombing and shelling had stopped.

As Robert looked around from where he was sitting on the grass not far from the Cathedral, he could see over on the far side of the cricket ground that there was a sizeable military presence. There had been a great deal of shouting in the night from over that way and the soldiers had clearly got a hold of liquor but over towards where he was the noise in the night had been more of despair with men crying, mostly it seemed men, possibly in pain or maybe it was just despair, and as always children crying. As he sat there taking things in, a very tired and ill looking Captain Peters came over with a mug of black tea which he had managed to get hold of from an unknown source.

"Here you are, lad."

"You had some?"

"Yeah, I had mine a few minutes ago and then refilled the mug for you."

"I'm grateful, Captain. Are all of them okay?"

"Yeah, they're fine; got as good a sleep as can be expected."

"Have the Japs come yet?"

"We're expecting them any minute now. We've organised a reception party ready to meet them. Hopefully, there's no trouble. The squaddies have already piled up their guns over by the road."

Robert got up and finished the tea. "Tell our lot to take off the armbands and those that are wearing LDC boiler suits to remove them. I have a feeling that any sort of uniform might freak the Japs out." Captain Peters nodded and a few minutes later, Robert saw various people removing anything that looked like a uniform.

As he was standing there, he looked across to the entrance of the cathedral which he could see was now a temporary hospital. He recognised one of the nurses and shouted across, "Kay," and went towards her. Kay looked across and seeing Robert hurried over to him.

"What the hell are you doing here?" Robert asked.

"I could say the same to you."

"I asked first."

"I drew the short straw to stay and help as we are very short of surgical nurses. The general nursing staff nearly all went."

"Christ, Kay. They should have sent you off; the Japs are

bloody unpredictable."

Kay didn't acknowledge what Robert had just said. "I'm sorry, Bob. I have to go. We're starting some more ops in a few minutes."

"What happened to Jenny?"

Kay shouted over her shoulder as she hurried back to the cathedral entrance, "She was sent off with matron two days ago and about fifty nurses." Looking around, Robert noticed for the first time that all the nurses within eyesight were Eurasian.

"*Christ, what makes them think it will be easier for them*," he murmured, as he turned back.

Perhaps an hour later, there was a general raising of voices and people standing up. Pat Reynolds growled over to where Robert was lying in the shade, "They're here."

Robert got up and with the hundreds of other civilians on the Padang stood mostly in silence as Japanese soldiers, with fixed bayonets, approached. The first soldiers went past Robert and stopped, perhaps fifty yards beyond. They had said nothing. The second squad of soldiers stopped almost opposite where Robert was standing and immediately one of them shouted at one of the Alexandra Road contingent and started grabbing his left arm.

"He wants your watch," someone shouted and the volunteer quickly took it off and handed it to the soldier. Similar actions seemed to be going on now as far as Robert could see and with difficulty, he took his watch off and handed it to the soldier in front of him.

There were screams and shouts, from perhaps fifty yards away to Robert's left where he knew the civilian representatives had congregated. Pat Reynolds, who was to

Robert's left, turned to Robert and those around him. "The bastards have just bayoneted someone."

There was more shouting and then a young Japanese Officer arrived in an open car and stood up and shouted in English, "Everybody must bow to Nipponese officers. Senior Officer will come soon. Men in uniforms and with weapons must go beside the soldiers over there." He waved to where the Allied soldiers were standing to attention a few hundred yards or so away. "Go now." Perhaps a hundred or so men moved away from the civilians and towards the military units. The senior Japanese officer arrived in another open car and addressed the delegation who had come forward and Robert could see that they bowed to him. Geoffrey Blackmore was one of the group. Robert couldn't hear what was being said and was more intent on keeping his eye on the Japanese soldiers closest to him who were starting to move among the civilians. Finally, Robert heard the car engine start up and some Japanese orders being shouted out and the soldiers ran back to the road and formed up. The car drove off and the Japanese soldiers relaxed and went over the road and settled down as a group not seemingly very interested in the thousands of civilians resting on the Padang.

"I think we got off lightly, old boy," Captain Peters said almost in a whisper.

"Mm. Question is whether those beggars over the road remain under control. We shall have to see. Until Geoffrey asks us to do something, I suggest we continue to rest. Bugger all else we can do," Robert said. Robert and around forty or so men, all LDC volunteers, went back to where they had been sitting.

Robert could see some medics and two orderlies dealing

with someone over where the delegation had been and Geoffrey talking to another person whom he recognised as a retired military officer. "That's old McRae, been retired for years. Was a general in the Indian Army; he's heading the delegation," Captain Peters said seeing where Robert was looking. Robert said he knew McRae and then sat down and closed his eyes. His arm was starting to thump a bit and he had no more pills.

It was perhaps an hour later that Geoffrey came over. "I know you are injured, Robert, but are you up for helping with getting us water and food? The count is just over two thousand Europeans including a hundred and twenty children. The Japanese Officer, Major Kato, who addressed us is issuing permits for us to go and get essential supplies. We can use the army lorries over there. Apparently, they are still operational. They have engineers trying to sort out the water situation now but it may be a couple of days before they get it working again."

Seeing Robert nod, Geoffrey Blackmore added pursing his lips, "Your Chinese volunteers are to report to the Cricket Club pavilion by six o'clock and Eurasians are free to go home." As Geoffrey was saying this, both watched as the Japanese set up a machine gun on the roof of the Cricket Club pavilion.

Robert walked over to the crowd of men lying on the ground and had a quiet word with the various Chinese and Eurasian men under his command and told them what the Japanese officer had said. Some of the Eurasian's got up and shaking hands with friends and colleagues quietly made their way to the road; the Chinese men got up and went into huddles and one came across to Robert to ask why they were being separated.

"I honestly don't know. As far as I can see, it wasn't a negotiable point. It was an instruction and the officer gave a threat if we didn't obey the orders, it would be worse for all of us. They have only agreed to us being allowed to fetch food and water if we obey their orders."

The Chinse man nodded and sighed. "It is not good, Bob. We should all stay together." Geoffrey was still going around talking to people and the Chinese man went off to speak to him.

Robert set off to where the delegation was stationed and joined a group of perhaps twenty men who were congregating, some of whom he now recognised as LDC volunteers. Geoffrey arrived back from walking around the Padang and addressed the men. "Mr Kennick at the table over there has passes for all of you. You must always have the pass with you. The Japanese military police, the *Kempetai,* are not a forgiving bunch by all accounts. You will be in teams of at least three, a driver, someone on the back of the lorry, sometimes two men and an organiser. Each lorry will have at least one Japanese soldier. Do not under any circumstances get into a conversation with them; they will be no help if you get in to trouble with the *Kempetai.* They're scared to death of them as well; so, I'm told. Each of you will have different priorities as we expect to be here for a few days. While I remember, we are all required to register tomorrow over at the Municipal Building or at the Raffles Hotel and that is being organised at the moment. Please make sure you tell everyone. Do not under any circumstances depart from your itinerary as lateness may place you in trouble with the *Kempetai."*

"How do we pay for the goods?" someone asked.

"We have some money which Mr Kennick will hand out to the organisers and if you are short, then you will have to persuade the shops you are going to, to give us tick. We are still in the process of working out how we will fund things now that the Japanese have said we must buy what we need for the near future." Smiling a wry smile, Geoffrey went on, "Some of you worked in retail, so you should know how to deal with the problem of getting 'tick'." There was a general laugh at the comment and a few tired smiles.

Robert waited in turn to talk to Kennick and discovered he was listed as a fatigues organiser with a driver who was a salesman for an Australian car company and a clerk who normally worked for Cunard. It turned out that it wasn't food but bedding they were being asked to find, for the women and children, with half a dozen suggested venues on Hill Street, Orchard Road and Bras Basah Road. Mr Kennick handed him a handwritten note of standard Japanese words that might be needed.

Crossing the road, they found the allocated lorry with a Japanese soldier already standing beside the cab. They didn't speak to him, Robert just bowing slightly. The Aussie, Jess Martins, started up the engine and Robert clambered on with difficulty; the Japanese soldier got up onto the passenger step with his arm through the open window holding on as Jess got the lorry into gear and set off.

"It's just up from my office, so I know where Miller's is," Jess shouted, as they worked their way around to the bottom of Hill Street, to the first port of call. All of a sudden, they had to halt as one of the lorries in front of them had stopped. Jess looked out. "Shit it's a checkpoint."

It wasn't obvious what was happening ahead until the

lorry in front moved forward and stopped, revealing the lorry two ahead. Three *Kempetai* soldiers were shouting at the driver who was getting out and when he did so they hit him to the ground. Finally, they yelled at him to get up which he did limping over to his lorry and with a screech of gears setting off.

"Christ, they were playing footsie with him," Jess said and Robert turned at the same time to see their guard alight and move off, looking very scared.

The lorry in front then moved forward to the checkpoint. The *Kempetai* soldiers yelled at the driver, literally pulled him out and kicked him to the ground and then turned away laughing. The driver dragged himself to the steps of the lorry and managed to clamber up into the cab. Seconds later, he started up the lorry and moved off jerkily with the *Kempetai* soldiers still laughing and shouting abuse after him. Jess gingerly moved them forward but the *Kempetai* soldiers waved them through. Their guard leapt back on the moving truck grinning at Robert.

Jess let out a sigh. "This is my lucky day, mate. With that arm, I don't suppose you can drive?" Robert shook his head. When Robert said he didn't drive anyway, Jess grinned back, "Pity, because I was thinking maybe you should take over."

Robert just smiled back and then said, "Is this Miller's?" as Jess pulled up outside a bedding and furniture store.

"Everyone knows it as Miller's but actually it's owned by a Chinese family. Had it for five or six years. Cracking looking daughters which the old man keeps a good eye on, you know what I mean," Jess said in his broad accent having already remarked that Robert had a strange accent.

"I'm a Lancastrian."

“Is that part of England, mate?” Robert had to smile at Jess. Even in times of adversity, the Aussie had time for a bit of a crack.

Robert beckoned to the Japanese soldier that they were there and with Jess and the Cunard clerk, Kenny James, he went over to the doors and banged on them loudly with his good hand. The Japanese soldier had pulled out a cigarette and leaned against the lorry, losing interest in what they were doing.

It was late afternoon before Robert’s contingent finally drew up beside the grass verge close to the Cathedral. The back of the lorry was filled with cheap mattresses, buckets and mosquito netting. Robert bowed to the soldier who had accompanied them and walked across the road with Jess to a desk where Kennick was standing slightly to the side of a Japanese officer.

Robert knew enough by now to bow almost down to his waist before coming to attention in front of the Japanese officer. The officer said nothing only looked at him questioningly. “I have a lorry full of mattresses and other utensils for the women. I am sorry if we are late but we were stopped twice at roadblocks and had to get the stuff out each time.” The officer, who clearly understood English, barely nodded before waving his arm at Kennick, getting up and moving off to a car a few yards away.

Waiting for the officer to get in the car, and for him to be out of earshot, Kennick then rounded on Robert. “Where the hell have you been? You’re more than an hour late. You were told to be back by three.”

“I told you, we were stopped twice and had to get everything out each time. The bastards even walked over some of mattresses and urinated on a couple. Thought it was a huge joke."

Jess started to go back over the road and Kennick stopped him. "Not now. We'll have to get permission from Captain Neguchi when he returns. Can't ask him now. He's been chomping at the bit to be off." They had watched the car move off with Captain Neguchi sitting in the back smoking a cigarette.

"What about Kenny? He's in the back of the lorry."

"Good God, they're liable to have a fit. Shout over to him not to move until he's told." Jess looked at Robert who nodded and Jess went to opposite the lorry and shouted to Kenny to stay in the back and not to move around until told.

Robert gave the paperwork to Kennick and went off looking for his contingent merely saying he would see Jess again.

"You missed the food distribution," Pat Reynolds said when Robert eventually found them.

"It's okay. We managed to get some food at a Chinese restaurant on Bras Basah Road."

Looking around at the long faces and worried looks, he asked, "What's been happening here?" Everything was quiet around them other than in the distance the usual sound of people crying, and the wailing of hungry children. Pat didn't say anything nor did any of the others around him. Robert realised that something had happened. "Well, go on, what has happened?" Robert said, looking around and raising his voice slightly.

It was Captain Peters, from where he was lying on the ground, who answered. "Crosby-Rees, one of the delegation got into an argument with Major Kato about the behaviour of the troops with the womenfolk. Kato slapped him over the face with his stick and then the Nips dragged him off to the cricket pavilion and executed him." The Captain's voice caught, as he finished saying it. Robert looked at the old man and bending down, put a hand on the old man's shoulder.

"What do you mean executed him?"

"They beheaded him, Robert. Everybody saw it. The women, the children, everybody. They won't let us collect his body. It's over there." Captain Peters waved his left arm towards the pavilion, perhaps a hundred yards away.

"Christ, what have we got ourselves into," was all Robert said, as he stood up and took a pouch of tobacco out of his trouser pocket handing it to Pat. "I managed to scrounge some tobacco for you and the lads." With that, he went over to a corner and sat down against a tree. He no longer noticed the heat.

In the night, it rained heavily and as many as possible of the children were moved into the Cathedral although it was still being used as an emergency hospital and it was an unpleasant experience for the children. Eventually, the rain subsided and the air was noticeably clearer with less grit and smoke around. Everyone had been bitten to death in the night and Robert could feel bites all down his neck and on his face. "*They love me*," Robert mused to himself, as he went to see where the latrines had been set up. As he looked around, he saw in the distance at the Cathedral entrance, Kay, who seemed to be dabbing stuff on children's bodies.

Kennick turned up as Robert was trying to take off his shirt. The packets of money were lying on the ground, the envelopes wet and partly revealing what was inside. "The Committee may have need of that money."

"Maybe, maybe, but not yet," was all Robert said trying to wring out his shirt with his good hand.

"You can empty your lorry now," Kennick said and turned around.

"One of the happier lot," Reynolds said, as Kennick moved off.

Robert just shook his head and then said to Reynolds, "Look after that lot for me, will you, Pat? We may have need of it. I'll be back once we've sorted out the lorry."

At the roadside, Kennick and a Japanese NCO and two Japanese soldiers were already there with Kennick getting agitated. "God you took your time, Draper."

Robert immediately headed across the road with the soldiers and Kennick trailing behind him. "Why the hell did you wait for me?" He didn't get an answer and as he reached the lorry, he turned to Kennick. "I presume they know Kenny is in the lorry?"

"Of course, they don't."

Robert threw back the tarpaulin, at the same time shouting, "Kenny, sit up and make it look as though you're guarding the stuff." The soldiers had come around the back of the lorry and started shouting when they saw Kenny emerge from between some of the mattresses.

"For Christ's sake, tell them we were told to leave someone to guard the lorry," Robert said to Kennick who for once reacted quickly and shouted in pidgin Japanese what Robert suggested.

"Kenny, start unloading the stuff. Ignore them. Make it look natural." More helpers arrived and Kenny started throwing stuff off the back as Robert clambered into the lorry and with his good arm started passing down, to more helpers, the buckets. The Japanese soldiers had started to check stuff before it was taken over the road but stopped when Kenny passed out the soiled mattresses and after that just stood a few yards away shouting at the helpers to get a move on. Finally, Robert shouted, "Okay, Kenny, off you go," and taking the last bucket, he lowered himself down leaving Kennick to show the NCO that the back had been emptied.

Back on the Padang, all the stuff was being distributed by various people under the eye of one of the delegation team. Robert took his bucket over. "I have some stuff for the medics so I'll take it over to them." Without waiting for a reply, he set off for the Cathedral entrance.

Inside the Cathedral, the sickly-sweet smell of death hit him immediately. He grimaced and found he was almost choking. "What are you looking for?" a voice behind him said and turning around Robert saw someone who looked as though a week's sleep would be insufficient.

Taking a moment to answer, he finally said, still half-choking, "That smell. How do you stand it?"

"Gangrene, I'm afraid. Not much we can do in most cases. Set's in so quickly."

Robert just raised his eyebrows at the information and then said, "Look, I've got some drugs in the bucket. Got it past the Japs." Robert lifted the shirt covering the bucket and showed what he had.

"My dear chap, you have a treasure trove."

Others had gathered around by this time and somebody took the bucket off him. "Hey, hang on a minute. You can have the medicines but the new shirt is mine. It's worth more than gold."

"Where did you find this little lot, old boy?" somebody

asked.

"The pharmacy on Hill Street had been smashed up so I took full advantage. I just hope it's of some use. Mind you, it nearly didn't get here as the *Kempetai* searched the lorry but fortunately they didn't finish the job, too busy peeing on mattresses." Before he left, he got one of the medics to dress his arm and he took the two precious painkillers offered to him.

Back with his contingent, he was told that they had been told to queue for a piece of bread and some water and then go across to register at the Municipal Building. Pat Reynolds gave him his half-dried money back. "It's needs a bit more drying, I'm afraid."

"Can you keep the packets for this now? I suspect I will be on fatigues again, so it's best if I don't carry the money around. They're less likely to search you. Oh, on a different matter, I think we should give a hand with burials; God knows how many bodies there are over there." Robert waved his good arm towards the Cathedral. "There are far more people here than I expected, and probably far more than the Japs expected," was all Robert said he moved again in the queue. As they were talking, they could hear shooting.

"I've been told that they will punish anyone heard calling them Japs."

Robert looked across at Captain Peters who had just made the remark. "What do we call them, then?"

"Nips in their hearing." Robert took the piece of bread offered him and drank the mug of water, making a bit of a face at the taste.

"Come on, let's go see what is going on over the road. You okay, Captain? You look very hot."

“Spot of malaria coming on, I think. Been a bit dicky since yesterday afternoon.”

As they crossed the road, further down, they could see the Nips, a word Robert told himself he must remember, clearing the road and stopping other civilians from crossing. Allied soldiers were marching up the road and as they stood on the steps of the Municipal Building, the soldiers came to a halt below them and a British sergeant major was bellowing out orders. The soldiers quickly formed up in a continuous line on either side of the road. More troops came past as Robert stood there watching and formed up further up the road towards Raffles.

‘What the hell is going on?’ he mused and then turned and followed his contingent who had largely disappeared into the building.

Chapter 29

Inside the building, the temperature was stifling with Nipponese soldiers dotted all over the place, including some officers sitting listening to what was being said at the tables. Robert saw at once that the women and children had been segregated and were being registered at different tables in the far corner of the room.

Somewhere in front of him, he heard a familiar voice and then he saw Henry, having registered, talking briefly to some of the other volunteers. "I've been told to remain in my home and to work at the station until further notice," Henry told Robert and Pat Reynolds as he came past them.

"Any news of the others getting away?" Robert asked but Henry shrugged.

"I've heard nothing. All I know from Ken Pace over there..." Henry pointed at a person standing further down in the adjoining queue, "is that in the chaos quite a few families got separated."

"Have you seen Godfrey Smythe around? He would know surely."

Henry shook his head. "Ken says that Godfrey was told to go with the last ship. Ken was supposed to go as well but, in the confusion, he missed the ship. The last I saw of my lot was

Brian getting Mona and Martin on one of Godfrey's ships with him at the gangway directing things. God knows where Arthur and his lot were. I did see David and Alex get on the *Vyner Brooke.* David was yelling something at me but I couldn't hear with all the noise."

"Mona and Martin will be fine if Brian is with them."

A worried looking Henry nodded. "I hope to God you're right, Bob."

The queue moved forward and Henry nodding at Robert moved off.

A few minutes later, Robert found himself at the front. "Name." Robert gave it to the Eurasian clerk who was copying everything into a ledger. "Your address." Robert gave that. "Profession."

Robert, without hesitation, said, "Banker." The Officer sitting a few feet away sat up as Robert gave his details and snapped his fingers at a soldier and shouted something to him. The next Robert knew about it the soldier was standing in front of him gesturing with his rifle for him to move away from the desk.

The clerk said quickly, "Go to the room over there. They have you on a list to be questioned."

Robert turned right and went through into what looked like a courtroom where a few men were already sitting. The soldier had been pushing him with the butt of his rifle to hurry along and literally jabbed him in the back when he got to a spare seat. The soldier left at the trot and Robert looked around.

He vaguely recognised one person and said, "Is that you, Ash?" He didn't see the rifle butt coming towards him; the next he knew he was on the floor.

“No talk, no talk,” screamed a soldier he hadn’t seen in the room who was now standing over him. The butt had hit him on his left shoulder and his arm was yelling with the pain. Robert had put his arms up to protect his face but the soldier had moved off and somehow, he scrambled up and righted his chair before sitting down.

He must have been there for two hours before two soldiers, *Kempetai,* came for him. In that time, he had seen perhaps half a dozen men being taken into an adjoining room, none had returned to the courtroom. The man next to him, before he went into the other room, had wet himself. No more men had been brought in from the registration hall since Robert had come in.

The *Kempetai* soldiers didn’t say anything to him. They just grabbed him by the arms and dragged him through to the next room with him screaming from the pain as his wound opened up. An officer was sitting on a chair with a stick which he was flicking and tapping against the boot on his left leg. He had a sheaf of papers on a small desk to one side of him. He pointed with the stick at a chair perhaps six feet in front of him and the two soldiers dragged Robert around and dumped him on the chair. Robert saw that there was blood on the floor in front of him and over behind a large table, he could hear whimpering and someone saying something he couldn’t make out.

The officer spoke. “Look at me. Do not look around. It will do you no good. Answer my questions and maybe you will live.” Robert turned his eyes to the front and looked at the officer.

“You are a banker. You work for Union and China. That is right.” Robert nodded.

"You moved a great amount of money from Kuala Lumpur." Robert wasn't sure whether it was a question or a statement of fact and started to say that it had all been transported to Australia. "Be quiet," screamed the officer making Robert jump back in his seat. "My name is Captain Ishiguru and I will not be interrupted. Do you understand?"

Robert didn't move or say anything and Captain Ishiguru continued, assuming that Robert did understand. "I have information that you moved twenty million dollars out of Kuala Lumpur. That is correct, is it not?" Robert this time did nod. "Where have you hidden it?" Robert didn't answer immediately. "Well, where is it?"

"On the *HMS Tenedos*."

"You lie."

"No, I helped to put the money on the ship. I know it went on."

"You lie," Ishiguru yelled, losing his temper and this time, Robert heard the movement behind him before he was sent sprawling on the floor.

He lay there for a moment looking at the feet of the officer and he felt the stick hit him on his back. He wanted to scream with the pain in his arm. He didn't see him do it but the officer gestured to the two soldiers and they came around the chair, picked him up by the arms and dumped him back on it.

"You are a fool, Mr Draper. You are wasting my time. I have information that the money is still on the Island. Where is it?"

Robert moved slowly on the chair trying to reduce the pain in his back and his arm. He groaned and looked across at Captain Ishiguru.

"I only had responsibility for the gold I brought back from Kuala Lumpur and for boxing the gold in the Union's vaults."

Robert saw Captain Ishiguru tap his stick against his foot repeatedly before he again spoke, "I can kill you now. You know that."

Captain Ishiguru said it so quietly that Robert strained to hear what he was saying. Robert just sat on his chair saying nothing, screaming inwardly with the pain in his arm and groaning softly.

Captain Ishiguru continued to ask questions ignoring Robert's pain. "Who was involved in making the boxes; if the gold had been shipped out who had gone with it to Australia; who did he know from the other banks that had stayed behind?"

The questioning went on like this for what seemed like an eternity with Robert landing on the floor once more. At a command from Captain Ishiguru, one of the soldiers hit Robert across the face with the rifle butt knocking him sideways nearly off the chair; somehow, Robert managed to stay on the seat. Still Robert gave the answer, that the gold he knew about had been put on the *Tenedos*. He did not say anything about some gold not being sent to Australia. Each answer brought another question as though Captain Ishiguru was not listening. He could taste blood in his mouth.

The officer finally said something to the two soldiers and they came around and picked him up by the arms and dragged him over to a door, with one of them opening it; they threw him out. Momentarily, he saw a body move beside the table as he was thrown out.

"We know where you are, Mr Draper. I will check what you say," was all he heard before the door closed.

He was lying in a long corridor, there was blood on the wall beside him and on the carpet incongruously there was a cuff link. He sat for a moment or so leaning against the wall and then picked himself up very slowly, staggering as he attempted to move away from the door he had just come through. He could scarcely see such was the pain he was in. He wanted to scream but he knew he must get away. But which way to go? Something told him to go the long way and when he finally opened the door at the end of the corridor, it was to find himself back in the registration area.

People were still queuing in the hall and there were some startled faces when they saw him emerge. Soldiers immediately came over yelling and telling him to get out, at least that's what he thought they said, as they shoved him with rifle butts towards the main entrance. Outside, he fell down onto the steps and it was perhaps only seconds later that Doctor Robertson appeared.

"Good God, Robert, you're not in trouble again." He knelt down beside him and looked at his bloody face and the blood on his left arm. "Just sit quietly for a few minutes and the next men that come out will give you a hand across the road." Robert said nothing, moaning every so often. Doctor Robertson gave him a water bottle and he drank a long swig using his relatively good arm to lift the bottle to his lips.

"Here's two now who can help you," and he heard the doctor talking to them but not sure really what was happening. They helped him up and took him across the road to where Pat Reynolds and one other of his contingent had seen him being helped across and had come to take over. Crossing the road, he vaguely remembered being half-dragged between large numbers of Allied soldiers as they marched past.

That night, he had a lousy time, with the pain from the beating and from his arm nagging away although a doctor had come over from the Cathedral and rebandaged his arm and from somewhere produced a painkiller. Robert vaguely heard the doctor say that it was one of the painkillers he had salvaged from the pharmacy.

Robert lay there in the early morning sun. He was feeling ghastly. Somehow, someone had cleaned up the blood from his face and one or two passers-by said the bruises were coming up wonderfully. Reynolds had brought him a mug of water and some cooked rice. "I've told them they will have to do without you for a few days."

Robert tried to smile. "I'm surprised Geoffrey accepted that."

"We're on the move later. Somewhere up towards Changi. Ronnie is not good so I'm trying to get him taken on the lorries with the sick but apparently they've only allocated about a dozen lorries for everything." Robert knew that by Ronnie, Pat Reynolds meant Captain Peters. Momentarily letting his mind wander, he wondered what had happened to the other Captain in his life.

"Will you be okay to walk?"

"Got no choice, Pat. Just don't ask me to run though. I might not manage it." As they were talking, they could see the women and children being sent off, with the very young and their mothers in lorries, and all the others setting off towards Raffles and from there presumably up Beach Road, some of them trying to pull suitcases and others carrying bags over their shoulders.

"Do we know how far?"

Reynolds shook his head at the question. "I've not been

told but in this heat, I hope to God not far. They marched all the troops off towards the north presumably up to Changi or the Naval yards. Made the poor sods stand all the way down the road for General Yamashita to review them before they marched off." Robert nodded at last understanding what he had briefly observed the day before.

Later in the afternoon, Japanese soldiers started appearing and eventually, a staff car with two senior officers arrived, one of them the dreaded Major Kato, although Robert knew nothing of this because he was starting with a fever so was lying in the shade of the Cathedral along with a couple of dozen other people who had gone down with fevers and exhaustion. There was a general shuffle of people on the Padang, but little noise, with the delegation trying to get more than two thousand men and their belongings organised for the march on the road towards Changi.

Pat Reynolds and some of the Tanglin volunteers from somewhere had found two poles and some hessian and cobbled together a stretcher to transport Captain Peters who had been delirious since early morning. Robert knew little of what was going on and only vaguely remembered some of the volunteers, some of whom were not in much better shape than him, helping him up and walking with him. Somehow, he walked up onto the road and set off. The sun was still very strong and every step he took was purgatory. Days later, he was told that it took them nearly four hours to walk the six miles or so with the Japanese insisting they go a longer way around which some people thought had been deliberate.

"Why we had to walk up Serangoon Road and around that way is beyond me," the Revd. Cole said one evening a few weeks later. "It was just to show the Indians that we were no longer in charge."

It was more than a week before Robert came around from the fever and the beating, he had taken. The one good thing was that his arm had started to heal as he had managed not to put pressure on it for days. Food was almost non-existent with only a few ounces of rice each day, and water strictly rationed to two large mugs a day. Two men and a child had apparently died since the Japanese had first appeared on the 16th February and Doctor Robertson who was looking after Robert said it was probably the heat and the lack of enough water. Robert could see that Captain Peters who was lying a few yards from him was very ill and asked the Doctor when he felt able to, what the prognosis was.

The doctor just shook his head. "You can't expect a seventy-seven-year-old man to be able to cope with what he's done in the past month, day after day, and survive. Mind you, he's had a lifetime of hard toil so that's probably helped him to last this long."

Robert looked across to where the Captain was lying on a stretcher, delirious and clearly very ill. "I've never had a chance to find out where he served other than he was in the Salvation Army."

Doctor Robertson, sitting on the ground beside Robert, smiled back. "He was stationed in a rural area near Shanghai for years and when he retired, I understand he only had a small pension and came to Singapore rather than back to Blighty. Like a lot of us. Been here about ten years. A great one with the children; does the magic shows for the kids' parties. He will be greatly missed."

Robert looked a bit shocked, "You mean…"

"He might be with us for a couple of days, Robert, but

probably no longer. He's a tough old bird but there's nothing I can do for him. Even in hospital, he would not be with us for long."

"You know I think he actually enjoyed all what we've done the last four weeks."

Doctor Robertson nodded at what Robert had just said, as he struggled to get up. "I wouldn't be surprised, Robert. Now you get some more rest."

It was the nights that were the worst. There was no cover from the mosquitos that seemed to invade the temporary camp they were living in; the smells were beyond anything you could imagine and there was the constant noise of groans from the men, even sometimes the sound of men crying, and then there was the constant scuffle as someone got up and raced for the latrines at the back of the building.

Lying there one night with his spare shirt over his face, he felt the Revd. Cole, who was sleeping on one side, move and he knew he was awake. Partly lifting his shirt off his face, he said to the minister, "Where are we Revd.?"

The Revd. shifted and took a handkerchief away from his face. "According to Pat we're in Joo Chia gaol. We got the short straw apparently. Quite a few are housed in the grounds of an old plantation house, *Karikal,* just up the road. The rumour is that we're on the move again quite soon and the sooner the better as we keep getting more people every day. And there's no room for them here."

He didn't say anything more for a few minutes and then said, "I wish I knew what was happening with Elizabeth and the girls. The Nips won't let us near them."

"I'm sorry, Revd." They sat in silence with the waft of the latrines overwhelming them.

“How are you feeling, Bob?”

“I’m much better, thank you, Revd. I hope to do a bit of walking around tomorrow and in a couple of days, I should be able to contribute towards the chores.”

There was rustle of activity a few yards away and Pat came over quietly and spoke to the Revd. who got up and departed towards where Robert could see Doctor Robertson leaning over somebody? Pat saw Robert looking across to the group and said quietly, “The Captain won’t last long. Doctor Robertson thought the Revd. should be with him these last few moments.” Robert just sighed and nodded as Pat went back to where Captain Peters was lying. Robert put his shirt back over his face and lay there in the heat of the night.

About a week later, by which time Robert was finding it possible to wander around the small camp, the rumour of another move turned into reality and they were told to expect a march to Changi gaol the next day. In the days since he had started to move around, Robert had been given little day jobs such as cleaning the rice and cutting up some of the few vegetables they managed to purchase. He found that more than one hour working in the heat was too exhausting so everything was at a slow pace. What he did observe was that by and large, the Nips left them to manage themselves in the temporary camp and Robert could see that new Indian guards with *lathi’s*, a long stick like a spear, had taken over some of the duties of guarding the civilian camp.

Robert and Pat had talked on some of the evenings about how to organise themselves and how to keep the Tanglin group together although it looked as though the Alexandra Road contingent was now inextricably linked. In all, there were nearly thirty men, mostly well into middle age, in the two contingents who wanted to stay together and Robert had said he was happy for Pat to take responsibility to lead the group with the Revd. Cole as well as Michael Davison, one of the original volunteers, a quietly spoken pharmacist in civilian life, both agreeing to take a leading role as necessary.

"Once you're back on your feet you can take over," Pat said.

Robert shook his head. "As far as I'm concerned, you're more than able, Pat. You're certainly used to it. I was only in charge of the LDC before you came along." Pat grunted and mumbled something like 'we'll see' and it was left at that.

Geoffrey Blackmore came to see Robert a few times and they talked about the situation and Robert learned that a camp committee had been formed and was organising various essential tasks as though they had a mini-city to manage.

"We've had a large contingent arrive from Beach Road as well as our lot from the Padang so the numbers are swelling."

"I suppose it is like a small city," said Robert lying in the shade peeling fruit and putting the peeled fruit into a bucket ready for boiling to a mush. He hadn't really thought about it, all his energy just devoted to getting better and in surviving the day.

"Once you're up for it, we will need you to help with organising the camp. You're good at it."

"My mother used to tell me I was good at telling other people what to do," Robert answered, smiling back at Geoffrey.

Geoffrey was looking at the mound of mixed fruit Robert had peeled. "I wonder what delicacy they're going to make that into?"

Robert added more peeled fruit to the growing pile. "Who

knows? You may be in luck tonight and get two spoonful on your rice. It will certainly keep you heading for the latrines." It was on the last visit to see Robert that Geoffrey had asked why the *Kempetai* had wanted to interrogate him. "I said I was a banker. Couldn't see the point in lying; that could only make things worse when they found out. Maurice Levy and I, when we talked about the situation, we reckoned that we would be on a special list. We agreed that we should not tell each other what we were doing just in case we were interrogated."

Geoffrey nodded saying he understood and then told Robert that about a dozen men had been taken out for interrogation. "I did see someone on the floor, behind a table. It looked as though he had crawled there. He was in a hell of a state," Robert said.

"Don't suppose you know who it was?"

Robert shook his head, "I'm sorry. I couldn't see his face. I have a vague recollection he was bald but nothing else. Not really thinking about him at the time."

Geoffrey said, "No. No. Of course. I fully understand. We have seven who didn't come back from registration. We are fairly sure five were shoved off to Outram Road Gaol but we don't know what happened to George Casey or Lawrence Charters."

Robert again shook his head. "Sorry I know the names but never met either of them."

"George is the Chief Accountant and in charge of the Treasury and Lawrence was the Head of the Mint in the same office."

Robert nodded, as he knew of them. "Sorry, I can't help."

"I think you were lucky they let you go."

Robert looked across to where Geoffrey was sitting on a

concrete slab, swatting something away with a straw whisk he had made with some of the long grass at his feet. “I told the Jap officer I watched all the gold go off on the *Tenedos*. He said he was going to check my story.”

Geoffrey pursed his lips and swatted away again. “His name’s Captain Ishiguru. By all accounts, a nasty piece of work.” Robert said nothing just carried on with the task he had been allocated by the kitchen staff and Geoffrey got up and wandered off.

Chapter 30

They came for him two months later. Robert had begun to hope that Captain Ishiguru had forgotten about him. He had settled into life within the confines of Changi gaol and like the now nearly three thousand internees, he had got into a routine. In his case two days a week, he worked in the camp Fatigues Office organising the roster of duties for everybody. As Geoffrey had said, it was like running a mini city and fortunately, they had all the skills and talents needed to cover most contingencies.

The reduced diet, the effect of the heat and the general lack of fitness of many of the internees meant that most days there was a need for a large number of alterations to the work rosters and Robert and the team he worked alongside found they were kept very busy with rearranging work routines. The Nips were adamant that everybody must work on fatigues in some way or other and they paid workers a few cents daily which internees needed in order to buy tobacco or extra food from the shop that had been set up by the camp committee. Those that couldn't work or refused to work and there were a few quickly found that they were on basic rations.

Robert on the days he didn't work in the Fatigues Office did some work in the kitchen garden and one day a week, he went on outside fatigue duties usually to a local coconut plantation where the camp committee had reached an agreement with the Chinese owner to harvest coconuts. With what spare time he had, he had started attending a Japanese language class although the heat and the general atmosphere of despondency often made it difficult to concentrate.

The march to Changi gaol had been like the first one from the Padang, long and hard even though not as many miles and it had taken him, and many others, some days to recover. Geoffrey had suggested that Robert was not up to heavy physical fatigue duties like many of the other younger men and instead, he used his talents in assisting in organising the range of tasks needed to help the internees survive. Robert and most of the Tanglin and Alexandra Road contingent had been housed in cells on the first floor of the main block of the gaol but he saw little of them other than at the brief mealtimes when they all tried to find a space in one of the yards where they could congregate together, something not always possible when space was at a premium. They quickly learned that it was better to bed down early to save energy and to get up in the early morning with the cooler air.

In the first few weeks until the newly formed camp committee had managed to get things organised the supply of food was woefully inadequate with the Nips having little sympathy and offering no help other than allowing the camp committee to buy supplies outside, by arrangement through the Camp Commandant. Discipline in the gaol was also strict and the least misdemeanour by one of the male internees and the Camp Commandant would call all the men out for a roll call that lasted for hours with many men with stomach complaints and fever being unable to go to the latrines or sit down.

Fortunately, the Camp Commandant accepted very soon after they moved into the gaol that the camp could administer discipline through its own police force, judiciary and the camp committee, with the Nips only involved if it was something serious such as attempted escapes or use of radios. In the former case, it was quickly realised by most of the internees that there was nowhere to escape to so what was the point and in the second case, Robert never quite knew when he heard 'the latest news' whether it was kosher or not. Rumour was the thing that kept the camp going all day and indeed every day for the 1292 days, Robert was incarcerated.

It was Michael, a thirteen-year-old boy, who was acting as runner for the camp administration office who came hurriedly looking for him one day two months after they had surrendered; Robert was working in the new kitchen garden.

"Mr Draper, the Nips want to see you now. The Commandant's office. You've to come immediately."

Robert stopped what he was doing and made a face and then nodded at Michael, before handing his hoe over to a fellow gardener on another row of fledgling onions. As he walked towards the office, he passed to Michael the four small envelopes of money he carried with him at all times.

"Take these to Mr Reynolds this evening, Michael. He'll be in Cell 21 on B Floor. You understand what I'm asking."

Michael said, "Yes, Mr Draper."

"Nobody else must get the bags. You sure you're up to it."

"I can do it, Mr Draper."

"Right, well, tell Mr Reynolds that you've to be paid one dollar." With that, Robert passed the envelopes over just before they reached the administration block.

"You stay out here, Michael. It may be safer."

Michael had gone white and less sure of himself. "Yes, Mr Draper," then he whispered 'good luck' as Robert entered the building.

Inside the block, there seemed to be no one else about except the two *Kempetai* soldiers who were waiting for him and as soon as they saw him, they marched across the few yards of the hall and without warning, one of them hit him across the face, knocking him to the ground. The other soldier yelled something in Japanese and Robert understood enough to understand that they were hitting him for taking so long to come to the building. His once-a-week lesson in Japanese had already proved useful.

They literally picked him up and one of them bent his right arm behind his back and they marched him out the building to a waiting truck. Letting him go, Robert clambered up to see two other internees already there, one bleeding badly from a cut eye with the other trying to stop the bleeding. At the checkpoint, one of the *Kempetai* soldiers leaned out of the cab on the passenger side and when the Sikh guard saw who they were he waved them through immediately much to the amusement of the soldiers.

Robert still very dazed sat on the floor of the truck for a moment or two and then tried to assist the other internee to stem the bleeding from the eye of the third internee whom he recognised as the General Manager of the Shell Oil Refinery who had banked with Union and China. In the end, Robert took his shirt off and used it to help stem the bleeding.

Looking at the floor, as he staunched the bleeding, he could see that it wasn't just the blood of the General Manager that was there.

The lorry set off back to the City and eventually turned into Orchard Road and stopped outside the YMCA building. Robert could feel his legs trembling as they were shouted at to get down and then shoved and pushed into the building, with the two of them trying to help the General Manager who had collapsed just inside the entrance.

One of the *Kempetai* started kicking the General Manager repeatedly, shouting in Japanese *'move, move'* and eventually, the two of them managed to get hold of one of his arms and drag him along the floor to a desk where a sergeant, a giant of a man, was sitting.

He said something to one of the *Kempetai* soldiers who answered and before Robert could translate what had just been said he felt his arm twisted behind his back. He was marched, stumbling and yelling with the pain of the arm twist, and taken down a corridor. The smell coming from the cells and corridor was numbing and, in the cells he passed, he could see men crouching on rope netting, most of them wearing little or nothing. The *Kempetai soldier* stopped halfway down the corridor and shoved Robert into a cell.

The blast of heat and smell of faeces was overpowering making him want to gag. His legs seemed to be divorced from him and he collapsed onto his knees only for an Indian *lathi* to be used on his back. An Indian cell guard shouted instructions at him first in broken English and then in Hindi and Robert pulled himself up and worked his way to the end of the cell that was perhaps twelve feet in length. He put his hand on something on the cell floor as he stumbled trying to get up onto the rope netting and realised it wasn't just blood and tried to wipe it off on the concrete as he moved forward. There were already four people in the cell, three on his left and one on the right. He clambered up onto the rope netting and took his boots off as instructed. The Indian guard took them and Robert never saw them again.

He sat on the netting and the guard again shouted at him. He must sit cross-legged. He did so. He tried to look around and immediately he was hit across the arms. "Only look to the front," yelled the Indian guard. Looking straight in front of him, he looked into the face of a woman. He blinked and looked again and realised that she was stripped down to her pants. Her face was a mass of purple bruising and it looked as though someone had used a belt on her chest and upper arms. He could see her eyes but there was sign of acknowledgement. He had been there about an hour when a bell rang and the Indian guard scurried out and this gave Robert a momentary opportunity to look at his other cellmates. Next to the woman was a man who looked remarkably unscathed but who seemed to rock all the time and talk to himself; clearly, he was not well. Furthest along was a man hunched over, covered in blood and with an arm at a peculiar angle. It took what seemed an age for Robert to realise he was looking at Maurice Levy.

The guard brought in a metal bucket and passed it along the three people on the other side. Maurice took nothing. The next man and the woman dipped their hands in and brought out a handful of rice and stuck it in their mouths. The Indian turned to Robert and yelled, "Eat." Robert dipped his hand in and took some of the oozing rice and put it to his mouth, gagging at the taste and smell. The Indian moved to the man on Robert's left side and he took a handful. The Indian left and brought in another bucket and the process was repeated. Only this time, there was a mug attached to the bucket. Maurice again took nothing. The next man took the mug filled it from the bucket and drank it back. He took a second mugful and then the Indian guard moved down to the woman who drank the first mugful and then washed the hand she had used for eating before finishing the mug of water. Robert realised that he was getting a message and did the same, taking the opportunity to clean the hand he had put on the ground.

The light stayed on all night and each time one of them fell over on the netting the guard who sat on a stool under the window, would get up, extend his arm and whack the culprit with his *lathi.* All night, Robert heard people being taken down the corridor and screams from men, and occasionally a higher pitched scream that could have been either a man or a woman. Only occasionally, he heard prisoners being dragged back. It was well into the night when the man on his left side was dragged out and Robert was fairly sure the new smell was of him defecating in fear of what was to come.

The morning brought no relief. Maurice had collapsed completely and two Indian guards dragged him off somewhere. One guard then came in with a hose and shoved the end in front of the woman who somehow crawled off the netting and started cleaning out the cell spraying it down and using a hard broom that had been produced to brush out the cell with the water and dirt going through a hole that had been made in the wall and into a drain on the other side. The smell of the cells down the corridor being washed out was overpowering. The woman clambered back onto the netting making eye contact with Robert for a fraction of a second and lifting her chin. Sometime later, a new Indian guard came in with a bucket of water and the same water drinking routine was followed.

Robert was not interrogated for more than thirty-six hours

and then they came for him in the middle of the second night. Maurice had never returned and a new cellmate had arrived and was now in the position next to him. The man opposite was rocking more and more and talking to himself all the time, quite loudly, and the Indian guards who had hit him at the beginning no longer bothered. The woman had been out twice for periods of a few hours but Robert could not see any difference in how she looked when she returned. He could not decide how old she was other than that she had grey hair.

Chapter 31

For years afterwards, Robert was unable to go into a gymnasium. He only remembered being dragged the last few yards, his legs progressively shaking as they refused to cooperate and the two soldiers effectively dragging him down a short set of stairs and then along a corridor before taking him through double doors into a small gymnasium. It was much like what he remembered his school gym in Lancaster had looked like. He had never been much use on the wall bars or the pummel horse and here he could see the same equipment only it wasn't being used in the same way. He could tell that immediately.

The guards took him to the far end of the small hall to where there was an overhead bar with chains hanging down and they fastened him up by attaching his arms to handcuffs that hung down from the overhead bars. His feet could barely touch the ground and one of the guards raised the bar, somehow by two or three inches making it even more difficult for his feet to touch the ground. Stretching with all his might, his toes could just reach the ground and take some of the pain off his wrists but he couldn't help yelling with the pain. He could feel the sweat rolling down his back and between his legs. How long he was doing this he didn't remember, perhaps only a moment or so but it felt much longer.

He heard a door open at some point and a chair being scraped on the floor to a position perhaps ten feet to his left. Try as he might, he could not turn sufficiently to see who it was to his left and when he did so, he lost his balance and the pain in getting back on his toes left him yelling and swearing. "We meet again, Mr Draper," the voice said in very precise English. It was Captain Ishiguru. "I hope you have fully recovered from our earlier meeting." Robert said nothing, just kept groaning with the effort of trying to stand on his toes. "When we last met, Mr Draper, you told me that you had sent all the gold to Australia on the *HMS Tenedos*. You told me a lie. All the gold did not go. Your friend, Mr Levy, has admitted that it did not all go. You have had time to think about what you said and to realise that to tell the truth is better. You can save yourself a lot of pain if you cooperate."

"I only helped to take the gold from my bank to the *Tenedos*. I do not know of any other gold."

He did not see Ishiguru make a gesture at the soldier behind him but a second later a heavy stick crashed against his thighs and he screamed with the pain.

"You are a foolish man, Mr Draper. Your friend, Mr Levy, died admitting that not all the gold was put on the *Tenedos* and we know from one of his clerks that some gold was held back by the Colonial Office to pay the Chinese to fight us. You were Mr Levy's assistant in boxing all the gold."

"I was not involved in any deal with the Chinese. I do not know of any involvement by one of the Hong Kong bank's clerks. I only helped to box…" This time, the stick came across Robert's back.

"I am in no hurry, Mr Draper. I know it is somewhere here

on the Island. I can wait for you to change your mind and tell me where it is or who knows where it is."

Robert hardly heard what Captain Ishiguru said he was so busy crying with the pain. Each time he was asked a question, he told Captain Ishiguru the same story; that the gold was put on the ship on the 5th February and he knew nothing about any other gold. Each time he answered a question, there was a momentary pause and then the guard behind him hit him with the stick, each time going a little higher until finally he hit him across the wrists above his head.

By the time he was hit across the wrists, Robert was barely conscious; eventually, he felt the guards lifting him a few inches up off the floor and roughly undoing the handcuffs they had used to fix him to the chains. He fell to the floor and from the smell, he knew that he had defecated. He was whimpering with the pain, lying with his mouth open and in his blurred vision, he could see he was lying on a concrete floor with black pools over it.

The bucket of water thrown over him at that point did no more than make him realise that he was wet. The guards took an arm each and dragged him out and up the stairs with him crying out with the pain on his wrists. All the time, the guards were talking to each other and laughing.

The cell seemed almost like a haven. The woman opposite waited until he was cross-legged on the netting and the Indian guard had turned his back and she managed a smile and lifted her chin. Hours later, the Indian guard brought in water for the cell inmates. Robert could barely lift his right hand across to the bucket and collect water, dropping some of it onto the floor much to the amusement of the Indian guard. The bucket of hot wet rice was brought in and Robert somehow realised that he had missed the morning food and this was the evening meal.

Robert was not interrogated again for days. His arms came out in bruises, yellow and purple and red. The agony in his legs was excruciating with cramp, and he found himself crying with the pain. His wrists were cut and red raw where the cuffs had chafed into the skin. Sometime in all this, he learned by two whispered words when the guard was out of the room that the woman opposite was called Rachel Knowles. On another occasion, he learned that she was the wife of a Chinese chemist, and on another that she had been in for perhaps two weeks before Robert was brought in.

They came for him a second time in the middle of the night and again took him to the gym and strung him up. This time though, Captain Ishiguru had given over the task to the sergeant Robert remembered from the entrance to the YMCA. He was a bull of a man and Robert immediately knew he loved his job. This time, the torture was slower; the questions almost as though the sergeant was repeating a script and Robert again could say nothing to stop the hours of painful interrogation.

The sergeant finally yelled in very poor English that he wanted to know the name of the man who was hiding the gold or Robert would regret it. Robert crying with the punishment already endured told him again that he did not know of any hidden gold. Almost at the same time, the two soldiers in response to a yell from the sergeant grabbed Robert's left foot and one of them stuck a wedge of wood between his big toe and second toe. He felt rather than saw the sergeant take the foot and then there was the most excruciating agony as he felt the big toe being wrenched and the toenail being torn out.

He screamed and screamed and screamed, and all the time

the guards were laughing. He fainted with the pain and when he woke, he was lying on the concrete floor perhaps five or six feet from the overhead beam. The guards were sitting on a bench smoking, sharing a cigarette and talking in low murmurs; the sergeant was not in his view.

The pain from his toe was shooting up his leg and he yelled repeatedly when the guards, taking an arm each dragged him back to his cell. By the time they got him there, he had fainted again with the pain and when he woke, he was lying in the entrance to the cell, face down. The Indian guard had got out the hose and he started to hose down Robert, whose shorts for some reason were ripped to shreds; the guard was spraying water on his legs and as soon as it touched his left foot, he screamed and tried to move it away from the spray only for the guard to follow the foot with the spray.

The guard started shouting at him and at first, Robert could not take in what he was saying and then realised that the guard wanted him to stand. Somehow, Robert dragged himself up at which point the guard handed him the hose and told him to clean out the cell. From somewhere, he got the inner strength to stand on one foot, holding onto the edge of the netting and hosing down the cell. Finally, the guard handed him a broom and he brushed the foul-smelling floor contents into a heap and through the drain hole. He started crying when he scraped his foot against the rough concrete floor as he finished the task and collapsed against the netting looking into the face of a new cellmate, sitting cross-legged, where Rachel should have been.

Rachel was gone and without thinking, he murmured, "Rachel, Rachel." The guard hit him on his side with his *lathi*, shouting at him to shut up, and told him to get up on the netting and he was given a new place nearer the doorway. Crossing his legs was an effort, almost beyond him, and he was crying uncontrollably as he did it until sometime later, he found he had stopped and was sitting hunched forward, in a daze. The rocking man who had been on the opposite side had gone.

They came for him for a third time a day later, this time in the late afternoon although Robert did not know what time of day it was. The pain in his foot was now bearable if he did not move it and the pain from other parts of his body no longer meant anything so long as his foot was protected.

This time, they tied him with his back to the pummel horse with his legs splayed apart and fastened to the back legs of the horse. His left foot had started bleeding, he knew that, because he could feel the blood on his toes and the pain from his foot was shooting up his leg. From somewhere, he felt an inner strength come over him and he determined that he would survive to get the bastards. That thought lasted momentarily. Out of the corner of his eye, he saw Captain Ishiguru come in with the sergeant and his heart sank. All his resolve had gone in one second.

Captain Ishiguru came up beside Robert and smiled as he tapped his stick on Robert's chest. "You seem disappointed that Sergeant Sato has come today, Mr Draper. He tells me he much enjoyed your last meeting. He told me that he was convinced you knew something and you would tell me today." Sato had from somewhere produced a large pair of pliers and Robert could see them in the giant's hand.

"Now I want you to tell me the names of the men who handled the gold, Mr Draper." Robert, all the time watching Sergeant Sato, for the umpteenth time, told Captain Ishiguru the events of the 5 February. "Who was in charge, Mr Draper?"

Robert told Captain Ishiguru what he knew already, he had told him many times before but nevertheless, he said again, "Mr Gillespie-Jones and Mr Maurice Levy." Almost pleasantly, certainly quietly, Captain Ishiguru said, "You lie, Mr Draper. Mr Levy was not responsible alone, and we know Mr Gillespie-Jones left the Island. Your friend, Mr Levy, was most unhelpful. But I know you will tell me the truth. We know that the banks had millions in gold and you did not send it all to Australia on the 5th."

Robert didn't answer for a few seconds and then said, "When I was in Kuala Lumpur, the banks in Singapore sent gold they didn't need to Australia. I only became involved with the transport of gold from Kuala Lumpur and then the boxing of the gold once I was back in Singapore." He saw Sergeant Sato moving towards him.

"Please, I don't know any more. I was not privy to any decisions by my bosses." Sato had taken hold of his right foot and Robert was trying to squirm it away despite the pain in moving his body on the pommel horse. He could smell smoke so guessed Captain Ishiguru must be smoking a cigarette. "Please, I beg you. I know nothing else." Nothing happened for perhaps a moment and then he heard Captain Ishiguru grunt and then shout an order and Sato stepped back.

Captain Ishiguru left the room and Sato turned and hit Robert across the face with the pliers yelling at him at the same time. Robert screamed at the pain and felt the warm blood from the cut the pliers had made, coursing down his cheek. He heard Sergeant Sato shout orders at the guards and then he too left although Robert could only see a little of what was happening as his head was fixed to the top of the pommel. The guards untied him and he literally fell to the floor. For a moment, he lay there wondering what was to come next and then the guards grabbed his arms and dragged him out of the gym and took him down a corridor and threw him into a cell where two men already lay, not moving just groaning.

Perhaps an hour later, it may have been much later, the guards came again and they dragged the three men out, one at a time, taking them through double doors to an outside yard where a lorry was stationed. Indian guards took over and threw them on to the back of the lorry as though they were meat, before getting on beside them.

Robert, in the time he had been in the cell, had crawled across the room and pulled himself up to a sink in one corner and found the water working. He put his head under the tap and let the water cool him. A small towel lay on the floor and picking it up he rinsed it two or three times and then placed it on his face. From what he could feel, the pliers had ripped some of his flesh and he put the flap of skin back after he washed it a number of times and tried by pressing the piece of towel on his face to stop the bleeding.

The journey in the back of the lorry was short, no more than fifteen minutes, and he recognised where they had come as they were let in through the gates. He had passed Outram Road Gaol on numerous occasions and today he was to see the inside. Inside the gaol, he found the corridors of the administration block were incongruously clean, almost like an austere hospital. The guards had pulled him out of the lorry and made him shuffle down to the administration office where he had to give his name and other details, the same as at the time of registration on the 16 February; the other two prisoners he had come with had been dragged by the guards to the administration office and he failed to hear their answers as he was too much in pain.

The Eurasian prisoner who recorded the details showed no interest in him and the Japanese sergeant sitting in the corner with his feet resting on his desk, smoking a cigarette, seemed to take little notice. A large overhead fan was working and Robert had briefly felt the draft on his torso. When the details of all three had been recorded, the Eurasian took the ledger to the sergeant who wrote something against each name.

Robert learnt over the months he spent at Outram Road Gaol that the sergeant allocated a cell according to whether the prisoner was to live or die. He learnt later that those prisoners destined for long periods of imprisonment were on the upper floor of the prison and those for execution were on the ground floor. He did not see the two other prisoners again and only learnt after the war that one was a ship's captain who had deliberately rammed his merchant ship against a launch full of Japanese soldiers in Port Swettenham to prevent the soldiers from massacring civilians who were trapped on the dockside; the other prisoner had refused to bow to the Camp Commandant at Changi by all accounts. Both were executed. He stood outside the administration office door; the other two prisoners having been dragged off to ground floor cells. Eventually, one of the Indian guards shouted at him to follow and he shuffled as fast as possible on one foot down two corridors into what was the hospital wing where the guard motioned him to a chair. He fell into it and waited, closing his eyes and trying not to move and to give the pain from various parts of his body a chance to subside.

The Eurasian doctor didn't introduce himself. He came up to Robert, put his hand under Robert's chin and lifted it with Robert yelling with the pain. "This needs stitches and to be cleaned. Follow me." Robert groaned and tried to get up and fell back. "Come on, I haven't got all day." The doctor put his arm out and helped Robert up. "Come on."

Robert followed the doctor into a room at the end of a ward. The smell in the ward was bad but not as bad as he had already endured. In the room, he was told to sit and the doctor proceeded to clean the wound. "I've no painkillers so this will hurt," was all the doctor said and Robert did his best to stay still as the doctor stitched. "There. Not my best but it's the best I can do with what I've got."

"My toe, doctor," Robert groaned and the doctor looked down.

"Ah, now that's a real mess." He put some newspaper on the floor. "Put your foot on that. How that hasn't gone gangrenous is beyond me. You're a lucky man." He cleaned it and then said, "This will hurt," and poured something on it. Robert shot out of his seat yelling.

"For God's sake, sit still. I'm trying to clean it."

"What did you use?" whimpered Robert, as the pain from his toe ran up his leg.

"A little of the last of the surgical spirit I have. Rather precious stuff so don't complain." He felt the doctor put something over the toe, and then a sock over the foot. "There, that's all I have. The sock was one from a patient who died yesterday. So, it's come in handy. You need a shower. You have sores all over, so I will tell the guard you are to report to me tomorrow for treatment. Try for God's sake to keep from banging your toe. It looks as though they broke it and I can do nothing to sort it now."

Robert wasn't used to such kindness and he started to well up. What he said came out all jumbled, "Thanks, doc. I don't know what to say."

"Keep a low profile, Draper. You might just survive. It's no picnic in here; life is very cheap. Here, take these shorts." The doctor went across to a small table on which some clothes were spread out. He picked up the shorts and threw them onto Robert's lap.

"The patient who they adorned can't use them anymore and what you have on doesn't cover you." Robert took the shorts and started to get up. The doctor moved away towards the door. "Change here. Leave the rags in that bin over there. I can give you maybe five minutes and then the guards will come for you."

In all, Robert was in Outram Road Gaol for more than nine months.

Chapter 32

The lorry took them up to Changi gaol in the early evening. Robert had been standing as he had done on dozens of occasions being checked off in the evening parade when unexpectedly there was a commotion as a few dozen new prisoners arrived. The cells had been full for weeks and it was almost impossible for prisoners to lie down in the cells; in some cells, Robert knew they were taking it in turns to sleep on the floor.

The new prisoners were harried and beaten in front of those parading in the yard waiting to be counted and from Robert's quick observation, they looked like they were merchant seamen. The yard was filled to almost bursting and in the heat of the dying day tempers rose very quickly. Without warning, there was screaming and shouting by Colonel Sumida, the gaol commandant, who was standing in the shade on a small dais at one end of the yard, and the Indian guards started collecting prisoners and ushering them out. Robert found himself suddenly being shouted at and hit by a heavy stick. "Out, out, out," the Indian guards screamed.

What Robert never learned was whether there was any logic to the prisoners at one end of the parade being pushed out of the yard, through the corridor of the administration block where they briefly gave their names to a clerk before being loaded onto a lorry. He had been working in the hospital and had stood with other defaulters at the end of the parade hoping he was not going to be punished for arriving late for *tenko.* So it was sheer luck he was out of his normal spot for roll call.

As the lorry moved off, his first thought was, as was probably the thoughts of the dozen or so other defaulters, that this was it. Robert had seen enough executions in the past months to not expect any mercy and for most of the journey, he thought that he was being taken to a place of execution. Instead, the lorry went through the City, up Hill Street, along Serangoon Road and turned up towards Changi Road eventually arriving at Changi gaol.

"Out, out, out," was again and again screamed at the men in the back of the lorry and as quickly as possible the dozen or so men alighted, and without more ado, the lorry drove off. The guards at the gate stood looking astonished, not sure what to do with the assortment of men, until a Japanese officer, still buttoning his tunic up, came out. The defaulters immediately sorted themselves out and bowed. The Japanese officer shouted at them asking why they had come and Robert stepped forward and spoke in halting Japanese. He had no idea why they had ended up at Changi gaol but said, "We were ordered onto the truck to be sent to live here, sir."

The officer strutted up the line and then walked back towards Robert. "You sleep in yard tonight. You register tomorrow." With that, he walked off back into the gaol and the Indian guards started yelling at the Outram Road contingent to get into Changi prison. Robert had no idea whether they had been sent back to Changi on purpose but he was congratulated by some of the other prisoners for his quick thinking.

"Chances are they won't miss us, they're having so much fun down there," was the type of black humour expressed by some of the prisoners over the next few days as they tried to disappear into the routine of Changi gaol.

That night, they slept out in the open with the noises of the prison all around them. A guard came out every so often to check that they were there but generally left them alone. Three or four of them knew where the latrines were and this proved to be providential as some of the defaulters were suffering badly. By the early morning, the whole gaol knew that a dozen men from Outram Road had turned up unexpectedly and soon there were internees shouting from windows and doorways across the yard and by the time the sun rose high enough to put light into the yard, most knew who the dozen were.

A mug of black tea and a piece of fruit was brought to each of them by the kitchen staff at breakfast and they stood or lay on the ground as internees went past to go to their work. All the time, there were people as they went past, asking, "Have they seen so and so? How long you been in Outram Road gaol? What's happening down there? Do you know how the war's getting on?" A few came across and shook hands with old friends and welcomed them back. Robert had seen two or three old colleagues he knew but none had recognised him at first and it was only when he spoke to them, as they went past, that they stopped and looking shocked, had a brief conversation. They were being shuffled into the administration wing after breakfast when Pat turned up.

"My dear boy, we all thought you were dead. We've heard nothing of you for nearly ten months." Robert was having difficulty in speaking, nodding and enjoying the warmth of the welcome. One of the other Outram Road contingent had broken down and started crying when he had seen an old friend and Robert could understand how he felt. He had dreamt of this moment, ludicrous as it may be, for nearly ten months. Compared to the YMCA and Outram Road, this was a haven of safety, of friends sticking together.

As Pat was talking, another ghost from the past arrived. "My God, is that really you?" It was Henry Preston. Robert had to lean against the wall. Too much was happening at once. He started to slide down the wall and it was Pat who caught a hold of him. "Easy, young man. You're with us now. Take your time. We'll see you later and we can talk then. For now, just get your breath back." Robert just nodded, too choked to be able to say anything.

In the administration wing the dozen or so men, of different ages and condition, all sat on little stools that had been constructed in the workshops and were left there by their owners while they did their fatigues. It was Geoffrey Blackmore who addressed them. A very different looking Geoffrey from the dapper civil servant of old; now Robert saw a man who had lost a lot of weight making his shorts look voluminous. He wore open toed sandals that looked as if they had been made from tyres. With him was Paul Kennick, also looking much slimmer, who had recognised a few of the contingent and welcomed each of them in turn.

Someone brought in mugs of water and distributed them as they talked. One of the contingent had to go to the latrines and didn't return. Finally, some medics turned up and each of them was given a quick medical whilst Geoffrey talked to the rest of the group. After about half an hour, just as most of them were starting to flag, other internees turned up and Geoffrey announced. "Gentlemen, meet the floor representatives. They will take you to your quarters. Those of you who have been here before will remember that it is pretty cramped but we have found some space for each of you. Not quite the Ritz but it's the best we can do at this time. By the look of it, three of you are to go with the medics and spend some time in the hospital. The floor representative will explain all you need to know about mealtimes, and when to report to the Fatigues Office although we will give you a day to get your bearings. The rules we must obey will be explained by the floor representative but if you don't understand anything, then please see Mr Kennick. I shouldn't think any of you have any money. You will need some to buy extras from the camp shop, so I have here a few dollars for each of you to tide you over." Geoffrey finished at that point and the floor representatives mingled and took the new internees away with them.

Robert followed his floor representative outside and across to the old prison dining room where he was taken to a corner at the far side of the room. "This is the best we can offer, I'm afraid, Bob. As space becomes available, you can move to a better spot. George Lomas will be next to you. Not the best of companions, I'm afraid, as he is finding life in here very trying. Aren't we all? But George is very unsettled, so he was moved here a couple of months ago."

Robert was looking around. "Looks as though it gets busy in here at night."

"The problem is when someone wants to go to the loo; they have to climb over everybody. No way of solving the problem; just too many people. Now I suggest you get in early this evening, or you will find George spreading out into your space."

With that, the floor representative, Donald Murray, took Robert back to the dining room door and left Robert to it as he set off to carry out his own fatigue duties. Robert found a space outside and let the sun warm his face. Slowly, he went to sleep, for the first time in months not being on tenterhooks. He somehow guessed somebody had come up and stood over him and he looked up.

"You'll need a mattress. Go over to the hospital and they may have a spare cover and get it filled with grass from what the gardeners have cut down."

Robert nodded at what Geoffrey had just said. "I have a lot of information. Some of it may be risky for those who know but I need to get it on record in case something happens to me."

Geoffrey looked around as he said, "Some of the other men have said the same." He crouched down with his back to the wall beside Robert. "Have you any news of outside?"

"The only news I got was from a poor sod who was caught with a radio up at the barracks. They executed him in front of us about two weeks ago. They said it would be a lesson to all of us. I saw him the night before he died and he said that the Yanks are starting to give the Nips a bad time. One of the men in Outram Road also said the Nips are withdrawing all spare troops, as they're getting short of frontline men."

"What was his name?"

"Corporal Harrison, Royal Engineers. He was quite resolved about what was happening. I promised to write to his wife when this is all over. They had given him a fair old beating but he didn't tell them who else was involved."

Geoffrey got up slowly. "I'm glad to think you believe it will one day be over."

Robert half smiled back at Geoffrey. "I have no intention of giving in. I have things I want to settle with the bastards."

"Don't forget to get a mattress." With that, Geoffrey disappeared off into the administration block. In the distance over the prison wall, Robert could hear women and children yelling at something. In a strange way, it was a lovely sound. Pat came and sat beside Robert after a lunch of soup in which Robert had found a few cabbage leaves, and a piece of bread with two spoonfuls of a green jam that had turned out to be a kind of spinach. Pat brought him a new shirt. "I have a spare. We need to get you some shorts and some shoes."

"Some underwear is needed, more than shorts, Pat."

Robert took off his shirt to change into the clean one and Pat saw the scars on his back.

"My God, young man. What did they do to you?"

Robert was quiet, not answering as other LDC friends came up and told him they were pleased to see him. Eventually, he said, "It's best you don't know too much just in case they decide to come back for me."

It became a routine over the months that followed that they sat together after lunch, having a period of quiet solace with as many of the LDC volunteers as could be there sitting around them. In being together, there was a bond that in some way helped them in coping with the day-to-day drudge and the unspoken fear that they could be there for the rest of their lives. Robert looking around on those occasions noticed that in many other parts of the yard, other internees took this short period to sit with friends in quiet contemplation.

Chapter 33

The sun was particularly hot. It was late in the afternoon and Robert had had a morning on garden fatigues outside the walls of Changi gaol. He sat on a small stool which he was looking after for Michael Davison, who was in the hospital suffering from tropical boils.

Sitting opposite him was someone Geoffrey had asked him to speak to. "So, you have things you want to record about your time with the *Kempetai?"* Robert nodded, looking across at Rob Scott, a barrister in normal life. He had already learnt that Rob had been in the YMCA for a time. Rob had some sheets of toilet paper and a pencil. They sat well away from other people, at least as far away as possible, in B yard. No guards were around at this time in the afternoon, slumbering in the shade of the guardhouse, their routine being well known by now; if they did turn up, then there would an early warning from A yard.

"Keep your voice down. Don't assume you can trust anyone in here. Life is too cheap."

Robert nodded at what Rob said. "Tell me about it. You could trust no one in Outram Road." Robert moved to a more comfortable position on the stool; he squinted his eyes at Rob and said quietly, "What will you do with what I say?"

“I have someone I trust who will hide the statement.”

“What happens if the *Kempetai* comes back for you or me? One of us may be forced to say something.”

Rob shrugged a little. “We have to take that chance, Robert. We’ve little choice. Be reassured that the statement, along with others we’re collecting will be buried deep.” There was a pause as both watched some internees come into the yard and sit down a few yards away. “Are you happy to start?” Robert nodded. “Then let’s get on with it.”

In all, Robert met Rob Scott perhaps five or six times to give his statement. To provide a cover for what they were doing, they had enrolled for classes in Japanese and if anybody came within earshot, either one would break into Japanese and the other would get the hint. People passing by would hopefully presume that they were helping each other with their Japanese language practice. Rob wrote onto toilet paper much to the initial amusement of Robert and as far as possible, Rob hid what he was writing in the Japanese textbook he brought with him.

After the first meeting, Rob brought with him a friend, another barrister, who kept an eye out for any trouble. When Robert had finished giving his statement, he forgot about it but for a few weeks afterwards, he continued to meet Rob to make what they had been doing look authentic. Geoffrey when he saw Robert working in the Fatigues Office one day, where he had got some work again, never referred to the task but just asked if he was satisfied and Robert nodded.

More civilians were being admitted to Changi as the Japanese brought in more and more Europeans from the Malay States as people holding down essential jobs no longer seemed indispensable. From what he could learn, on the rumour mill, which was always rife in the gaol, there were still teams of skilled civilians, working on the repair of facilities in the City such as the water and sewage systems and repair of the docks so he presumed that Laz and maybe his colleague, Ash, were out there somewhere.

More and more Eurasians were also being brought in as life in the City became more austere and the Nipponese became more and more antagonistic towards the contribution being made by the Eurasian community. The Jewish community, who had at the beginning been exempted from any restrictions, were now out of favour and gradually they were being interned in Changi gaol. They were largely Asiatic Jews, mostly shopkeepers who had had little contact with Europeans in peacetime and from the outset, kept to themselves although it quickly became evident that they had money and means of contact with the outside world.

One thing that the new arrivals did provide was information on what was happening outside and Robert found that meeting the new arrivals brought with it the opportunity to learn of news of not just what was happening in Singapore, bad as that was, but also of the war in the Pacific. Robert already knew that one or two radios existed in Changi, although he did not know who controlled them. The new internees had had in some instances access to radios before they were interned and were able to tell him that the Americans were now making big inroads in fighting the Nips and even that the Russians had stopped the advances of the Germans. The news that Montgomery had won the great battle at El Alamein when the news went around the gaol caused a great lift in spirits with the guards rushing around trying first to find out what was happening and then lashing out at internees who were going around singing '*There'll always be an England.*'

The weeks rolled into months with routine being the order of the day. Sitting one evening with Pat and a few other LDC friends, Robert was asked how he had ended up in Outram Road Gaol. "I was in the YMCA for about three weeks, maybe a bit longer. I lost track of the time. Then I was sent to Outram Road. I had some sort of a trial in front of a senior Nip; a Lieutenant Colonel, I think. I was only there a few minutes but when I went back to Outram Road, I was told I had been sentenced for not being cooperative with the military and wasting their time." Robert stopped what he was saying and then added, "They didn't say for how long I was sentenced, mind you. I still think I only got out because they ran out of space."

It was on one of these evenings that Pat said that the money Robert had brought in was nearly finished and the group would have to think of alternative ways of raising money for the extras they all enjoyed or for procuring drugs for one of them if they became ill.

"I have more, Pat. Leave it with me and I'll see what I can do." When Robert had come back to Changi, he had told Pat to keep control of the money, as he didn't believe that Captain Ishiguru was finished with him.

Chapter 34

"Jess, I have a job for you." It was early morning and Robert was standing beside one of the lorries ready to go out to collect wood and food for the internees. Jess was sitting in the cab waiting for two internees to clamber up in the back and the guard who was yet to turn up. Jess looked down at Robert suspiciously.

"What are you up to?"

"You know the synagogue at the back of Hill Street. Well, I want you to stop there and get me a package."

"Just how am I supposed to do that?"

"Stop the lorry just about outside the main gate. Tell your guard that the radiator needs more water. Go to the gate and shout the caretaker that you need a bucket of water. The guard can see what you're doing so he won't be suspicious. A Malay gardener, his name's Rashid, will come to the gate when you bang on it. Just say Mr Draper sent you and would like his parcel. He will fetch you a bucket of water. Lift up your bonnet and put some water in the radiator. There will be a package inside the bucket that Rashid gives to you. Fasten the package to the inside of the radiator. Take the bucket back. Close the bonnet and drive off. It's all arranged."

"What's in it for me?"

"I'll see if I can get you some smokes."

"Real ones, Bob. None of this stuff they're growing in the gardens. It smells like shit."

"Jess, please, language like that will frighten the guard," Robert said and grinned back, as the Sikh guard turned up and shouted at Jess to get moving.

It was a few days later as Robert came out of the prison library where he had had his Japanese lesson that he met Geoffrey Blackmore. "Ah, just who I'm looking for. Get your food and bring it with you to the camp committee meeting. We're holding it in Broadmoor; the guards won't go in there because the old lads are half demented and scare them."

Geoffrey went off without another word and Robert headed for the dining room where his contingent was due to be first to get the evening meal. He stuck his textbook in the corner, under his mattress, noting that George Lomas had again filled his space as though he didn't exist. Poor George was getting worse wandering around half the time talking to himself and not able to do any fatigues.

As Robert stood in the queue waiting for his meal, he wondered why the committee wanted to see him and then seeing Donald, he went over once he had collected his food. "We're going to have to do something about George. He's getting worse, Donald."

Donald who was setting off to sit with some friends, half turned. "I've had a talk with the medics and if it continues, then they will put him in Broadmoor." Robert said nothing more and carried his plate and mug out into the yard and across to where Broadmoor was located.

The committee of five had been supplemented with Rob Scott, and an elderly man who was introduced to Robert as

Herbert Carson, a judge, and by Edward Beverley, a businessman, whom he knew had connections with Patrick Gillespie-Jones. Robert had never ever seen either the judge in his time in Singapore nor could he remember seeing him in Changi. It was the judge who started the proceedings although Robert knew the camp committee chair reasonably well as he was often on garden duty with him.

"We have learned, Robert, that you obtained a package from the synagogue on Waterloo Street the other day." Robert like some of the others was eating what little food was on his plate. He looked nonplussed and didn't answer. "Well, did you?" Robert just nodded beginning to realise that nobody was smiling. He knew Jess wouldn't have said anything so it had to be one of the fatigue workers who had gone with them. Robert paused momentarily and then explained. "I arranged with the new Jewish internees to get a message out to the synagogue where I had a package I needed. It was no great deal."

It was the chair who interrupted before Judge Carson could continue. "That's for us to decide, Robert. You put at risk an arrangement we had at the post office. The driver, Jess…"

"Thank you, Stephen. If I may continue." The judge who had no food with him took a drink from his mug and then asked, "What was in the package?"

"I can't tell you that. Knowledge in this place is dangerous. Anyway, it's no longer with me. It has been distributed."

Edward Beverley came in, losing his temper. "It was money, of course, and it wasn't yours. You're a banker working for Union & China and you were told to hand over all the currency to the Treasury."

"Actually, I wasn't told to hand it all over. The Treasury wasn't sure what to do and I had the Head Clerk take over the large denominations."

"Don't you try that one with me, young man," yelled a man who Robert could see was well used to getting his own way.

The judge held his hand up to stop Edward Beverley from going on. "Was it Treasury money?"

"I can categorically say it was not, judge."

The judge asked a second question. "Were you told to bring over the small denominations?"

Robert replied, "No, sir."

It was one of the other camp committee members, who then said. "What we're concerned about Robert is that what you did may cause the Nips to start searching the place. The rumour going around is that you brought in thousands of dollars. We have the possibility of a Red Cross delivery in the next few days and if the guards think they've missed something they'll take it out on us."

"I'm sorry if what I did has caused a problem. The amount I collected was certainly not thousands and I gave it to my LDC friends to help them get some extras; we also needed some drugs for Michael Davison, and old Tom Garvie who have both gone down with malaria again. I did nothing more than what quite a few in here are doing every day." There were a few grunts of agreement at what Robert said.

He stood up. "Unless you have anything else you want to ask me, I have a few things to do before lights out." As he was going out the cell, he turned back. "Just a thought. Whoever has passed the rumour around that I am Andrew Carnegie, in disguise, should be told that they have put my life in danger if the *Kempetai* get to hear of it. I expect you to do something about that."

It wasn't a Red Cross delivery but sacks of mail that arrived at the camp two days later. A Swiss national living in Singapore, Schweizer, turned up with his lorry carrying a dozen or so sacks of mail as well as other goods he had managed to procure for the camp. Robert had heard nothing more from the Camp Committee and had carried on with his duties.

"There are dozens more sacks in the Post Office but they only let me collect these for you," Schweizer said. Robert and the other internees, working in the Fatigues Office at the time, stood looking at the bags in the back of the lorry, astonished. "How the hell do we start sifting this lot?" one of them said.

Robert took command. "Get the bags in the office. That's the first priority just in case the Nips think they must do a second vetting. Eric, go and see if there's any spare labour in the yard. There are usually a few sods around who have decided not to work. They can help."

Eric nodded and shuffled off to do what Robert suggested. "Let's clear these two tables. Put the stuff on the shelves. We can empty a bag out at a time on the table and start making bundles. I've got the lists of names and locations somewhere…"

"Here we are." By the time Robert had finished speaking, the two tables had been cleared and stools were being put around them. Eric arrived with two helpers.

"Right, you lot, get started. We'll get more help. Any names you can't read or identify put in the bin over there;

we'll sort them out later. In the meantime, I need to find one of the camp committee and tell him what's turned up. I'll be as quick as possible."

Robert found one of the committee working in the kitchens and quickly told him the news. "There are bag loads. According to Schweizer, there are also lots more at the post office. I've got them started in sorting out the bags but it's going to take all day, maybe days." With that, Robert limped off but not before, he saw the camp representative racing off to tell some of his fellow workers. "So much for telling the committee first."

The next few days was like a dream with people walking around with little cards with just a few words on them. What the internees also found out was that by agreement with the Red Cross everybody could write a reply of up to twenty-five words although it was only to be about their personal situation and not about the war or about the Nips. So, aside from receiving thousands of cards, with most internees getting at least one card, everybody was also scribbling a note to loved ones. In most cases, a feeling of relief at hearing from family raised morale but Robert, one of the few who did not get a card, noticed that there were many who found it so painful that it made them become quiet and withdrawn.

Pat had a card from a sister he hadn't even seen, never mind corresponded with, for more than fifteen years. He enjoyed reading the card but told Robert later that it was like getting bad news from a stranger. "It said nothing, Bob. Only that life in England was terrible and hoped I was well. What does she think this is? A picnic." Seeing Robert's face, Pat apologized. "I'm sorry, lad. I'm a thoughtless sod at times. My Dora used to say that when she was alive." It was about then that it really crossed Robert's mind that maybe Joyce and some of his friends hadn't got away.

Chapter 35

Robert was walking back with a group of around thirty internees; it was late morning. Two Indian guards ambled behind them, smoking cigarettes with their *lathis* swinging at their sides. Swimming and washing in the sea was perhaps the one luxury afforded all internees, even those who were ill with one of the many ailments that swept the gaol regularly, made great efforts to be available when their turn to go to the beach came up.

Robert was talking to two of his fellow LDC comrades discussing the bombing down towards the City Centre that could be clearly heard two nights before and surmising what it could have been when they heard the prison alarm go off. The guards started shouting and waving their *lathis* and making the internees run back to the gaol, with some of the weaker men falling over and having to be helped. By the time they got to the gaol entrance, all the outside garden workers had been herded in and the Indian guards were hitting the swim contingent to hurry them up.

The yards were absolutely jammed packed with internees, trying to get to their correct floor positions. Geoffrey Blackmore was standing at the entrance to A yard and saw Robert.

"Get the camp list from the office, Robert. We will need it." Robert nodded and limped quickly across the few yards into the administration block only to come face to face with the Camp Commandant coming out with Colonel Sumida, the Commandant of Outram Road Gaol. Robert stepped aside and bowed. The Camp Commandant started shouting asking why he was not in the parade. Robert answered in Japanese that he had been instructed to fetch the Camp Registers. The Camp Commandant nodded and waved Robert to go into the Fatigues Office; Colonel Sumida said nothing just looked at Robert closely.

Robert came out a minute later with the Registers and looked for Geoffrey. He was still standing at the entrance and Robert went over and stood next to him. The Commandant stepped onto a dais that had been brought out for him by the yard cleaners.

"Where were you?" Robert whispered. Geoffrey guessed what Robert was asking.

"I was in the latrines when the bastards turned up. Then I couldn't find the list. Thank god you arrived or there would have been hell to pay." As Geoffrey whispered to Robert, they could see Colonel Sumida move to the side of the Camp Commandant.

As was always the case the Camp Commandant opened by giving a short prayer for the long life of the Emperor, and the internees all bowed low. The Camp Commandant then said that there was information that many internees were involved in trying to cause great disruption on the Island and that the *Kempetai* were proceeding to search the gaol and all internees must remain in the yard until the search had finished. With that, the Camp Commandant left with Colonel

Sumida.

For hours, the internees stood in the burning sun with occasionally one of the weaker men falling to the ground but no one was allowed to help him. The noise from the prison buildings was intense with those searching the buildings smashing stuff up. Suddenly, one of the *Kempetai* soldiers emerged and went running towards the administration block carrying a stool. A moment later, Colonel Sumida emerged from the administration block holding the stool with what looked like wires coming from one of the legs. He was smiling as he walked over to the dais and planted the broken stool on it.

"Shit." Robert heard Geoffrey say under his breath. Robert at the time was going through everything he had done in the last few days making sure that his back was covered and didn't hear Geoffrey say something to him. Robert suddenly realised that the Camp Commandant had also come out into Yard A and was shouting at Geoffrey wanting to know who was living in the cell where the stool had been found. Robert stepped forward and looking up the register, shouted out the names. He stepped back and Colonel Sumida took over. Very much in broken English, he shouted for these three men to step forward and Robert saw three men come forward, two of whom he knew reasonably well. The Colonel didn't even say anything; he just pointed at the entrance and the three men moved slowly to the entrance with a *Kempetai* soldier appearing and hitting them with his rifle and shouting at them to run to the waiting lorries.

All afternoon, this went on until finally more than forty men had been pulled out for having illicit radios or in a few cases having large amounts of money or drugs hidden in their cells. In one case, an illicit still had been found to Robert's amazement, as he couldn't for the life of him see how the cell was able to distil alcohol without half of the internees not knowing about it and the other half not demanding a drink.

At last, the *Kempetai* soldiers started to emerge from the various buildings and report to a senior NCO who went up to Colonel Sumida who had been standing beside the dais for some time; Robert was close enough to hear the NCO report that they had finished. Colonel Sumida wasn't finished, however. He spoke to the Camp Commandant and handed him a list of names. The Camp Commandant became irritated by another delay and waved for Geoffrey to approach him before handing him the list of names; Geoffrey bowed to the Commandant before going to one side and shouting out the names on the list ending with 'Edward Beverley, Rob Scott, Neal Forsyth and Robert Draper'. Geoffrey turned his head towards Robert, as he said the last name. Robert had just about thought he had escaped attention and his name being called brought a chill to him. He felt his legs go wobbly.

The three lorries were crowded with the *Kempetai* literally standing all over them. Some of the weaker men had fallen to the floor and it was impossible to help them up. Robert saw Rob Scott a few feet away and they both looked at each other with resignation. Someone behind Robert was groaning. It was to Outram Road they were sent.

They were all chased literally into the prison yard and shouted to stand in two rows; the current prisoners seemed to be in their cells. Two Eurasian men and a Chinese man were standing tied to posts at the far end of the yard. Colonel Sumida arrived at last in the prison yard and immediately shouted some orders and then marched up to the Eurasian prisoners. An order was again shouted and one of the Eurasian men was untied and taken over to a block and forced to kneel. Colonel Sumida purposely looked around at the new prisoners and then walked over to the prisoner, drew his sword and with one movement beheaded the man without any further ceremony. Two men standing near Robert fainted and others were sick; some cursed. Robert said nothing knowing that he would need all his strength for what lay ahead.

The Colonel turned and strutted towards the two rows of internees and in broken English shouted he would have their confessions or it would be worse for them. He yelled an order and the guards in turn started yelling and pushing the men into a small room at the far end of the yard which Robert knew was where the prison guards normally sat and watched the prisoners exercise. He guessed that the gaol was very full. The two remaining prisoners tied to the posts baked in the late sun; two men appeared from one of the ground floor cells and removed the body and then one came back for the head.

In the room despite the men being squeezed in, somehow there seemed to be space. Nobody wanted to be too close it seemed to another person. They needed space to think. After a while, Robert heard some men start to moan and even cry out, and one say, "What is this hell we're in? This can't be happening." They stood in the hot, airless room fearing every noise outside. Eventually, as time went on, Robert and Neal Forsyth organised everyone to have a drink from a tap that was in a little sink at the back of the room. Colonel Sumida had clearly forgotten about this luxury.

As the sun began to sink an NCO, Corporal Namura, whom Robert well remembered, arrived at the doorway and shouted something in a thick Japanese dialect. Robert said to those in the room, “He wants the ones who were in the cell with the radio to step forward.” Three men moved forward and Namura stepped aside and as they went out, he kicked one of them to the ground. He was helped up by his two fellow internees; Indian guards with *lathis* beat them as they hurried to the far end of the yard. Robert never spoke to them again.

Corporal Namura then shouted out four names and two men stepped forward, as they understood enough Japanese to understand that they were being called out even in the strong accent. They disappeared outside and Robert didn’t know until much later that they had been guilty of disseminating the information from radio broadcasts and that some of their written work had been found in their cells. Namura screamed again and Robert shouted, “He wants Woodcock and De Lacey to step forward.” Robert didn’t recognise De Lacey when he and Woodcock went out into the yard. He was yellow and emaciated and had trouble standing; Robert doubted he would last long under interrogation.

Then Namura went back to the administration block at the far end of the yard and was gone for perhaps an hour. It was now quite dark and from time to time there were screams and yells from the ground floor cells. It sounded like these men had been locked in their cells for most of the day and Robert thought for a moment that they had it worse without any water. He was standing with Neal Forsyth and Rob Scott talking quietly when Namura again arrived and started shouting out names. Most of the internees were able to understand when their name was called and the numbers quickly reduced until after perhaps another hour only Edward Beverley and Robert were left.

“Why us, Mr Draper?”

"I should think we are here for different reasons. Money, or should I say gold, is still foremost on their minds." Robert as an afterthought said, "I should think the financing of a Chinese upraising might be worrying them." Edward Beverley said nothing and instead moved away making Robert think that maybe that was a possibility.

Finally, Namura came in. Robert came to attention and bowed slightly. Beverley followed suit. Namura smiled directly at Robert and said in his thick accent, "Sergeant Sato looks forward to seeing you again." He turned to Beverley, "But he looks forward to you most." Robert saw him go white and he buckled a little with Robert moving sideways and helping him to stand up.

"Go. You know where to go," Namura shouted at Robert, "and take this fool with you." Robert helped Edward Beverley to the far end of the yard and through the administration block to the old workshops which he remembered were used as interrogations cells. As they had gone through the yard, he had heard the two men tied to the posts moaning softly.

Robert was handcuffed to a ring fastened to the wall in one cell and the door closed. Beverley was dragged by Namura and another *Kempetai* soldier into one of the workshops. Robert could hear nothing and eventually, even with fear coursing through him, he fell into a semi-sleep. It was the opening of the cell door that woke him. Without any discussion, the two guards who entered the cell uncuffed him and then pushed him out into the corridor and down it to the main workshop. Sergeant Sato was standing there with Colonel Sumida. Robert was dragged over to a chair in the centre of the cell; Robert looked around and could see tools still fitted on the walls.

"Your friend, Mr Beverley, was most unhelpful. He refused to help us. He says that he was told to arrange to give gold to men who were to stay behind and fight but he could only tell me that the gold was looked after by Mr Levy and he had arranged for it to be given out a little at a time. I know you will help us. Captain Ishuguru told me that Mr Levy was your friend." Colonel Sumida said all this in a quiet almost friendly voice.

Robert said nothing for a second or two and then said, "He is no friend of mine. I am a mere junior manager. He would not consult me on such important matters."

Colonel Sumida made no movement but Robert heard someone move behind him and suddenly, one of the soldiers had his arm around his neck and was forcing his neck back. "He will break your neck if you do not tell me the truth," Colonel Sumida said it a little more loudly this time. From the corner of his left eye, Robert saw Sergeant Sato move towards the wall where rows of pliers were displayed.

Robert answered in Japanese, almost shrieking, "I am telling the truth. I would not be trusted with so important a task. Mr Beverley is perhaps the most important businessman on the Island. He has many contacts. Why would he trust me, someone he didn't know, by telling me how the gold was to be distributed. I do not know anything about Mr Levy looking after the gold. I told Captain Ishiguru that I am only a junior manager. I was told nothing." He felt the arm around his neck relax a little and then it was gone and he took a breath and coughed.

Colonel Sumida then asked questions about various communists. "Do you know Li Bo? Do you know Sui Chen? Do you know Jai Sui Peng? How many times have you met

Chin Peng?" Each time Robert said he had heard of them, as their names were often in the newspapers, but he had never met any of them or dealt with them. This went on for what seemed hours, sometimes with Colonel Sumida speaking quietly and on other occasions, he would scream the words at Robert. On one occasion, Sato came within Robert's vision with a pair of large tongs.

Suddenly, Colonel Sumida said, "But you know Kenneth Chen." Robert felt his stomach churn. "He is a friend of yours, I believe."

Robert found his voice breaking as he said, "I know him. He was a senior clerk in the bank. The last I heard, he left the Island on 7th February last year. If he was a communist, he never said anything to indicate that; I heard him many times be critical of them. Mr Trehearne told everybody that communists would be dismissed immediately and I do not believe that Mr Chen would have been able to hide that fact in the bank."

Robert realised he was saying too much and stopped. Colonel Sumida smiled at Robert. "Chen is a senior member of the Kuomintang not the communists and is the Treasurer for Force 136."

"I know nothing about that. Kenneth Chen is a senior clerk in the bank. It is news to me that he is the Treasurer of Force 136."

Sato suddenly took hold of Robert's right foot as he was speaking and Robert's voice rose to almost a shriek as he finished and tried to squirm his foot out of Sato's grasp. "Please, I'm telling the truth."

The Colonel got up and came over and stood in front of Robert. "If you are lying to me, I will watch Sergeant Sato pull your heart out."

Robert even through all what was happening to him had been trying to work out what they knew. They knew nothing. It was obvious. He guessed that Edward Beverley was dead or perhaps very badly injured and no longer able to be interrogated. The involvement of Kenneth Chen was something new but he had no knowledge of where Kenneth could be hiding. He wasn't even sure where he had lived on the Island. It seemed that the Nips were not sure themselves who was behind the bombing a few nights earlier. Nor had they questioned him on where he had got the money from for his friends so it looked as though that information had been suppressed.

In as quiet a voice as he could muster, he said, "Ask Mr Beverley. If the Force 136 or the communists needed funds and if there was any collaboration on the bombing, then he is more likely to know. I am too junior and unimportant. It needs someone very important to be involved, maybe even someone who goes out regularly from Changi to organise any trouble in the City. I have never been out."

Colonel Sumida stepped forward, hitting the side of Robert's face with the palm of his hand, yelling with annoyance; he started shouting and waving his stick. "Where is Kenneth Chen? Where is he hiding?"

"I don't know. He was just a clerk at the bank. I didn't really know him. As far as I know, he had nothing to do with the gold. He had already left the Island."

Colonel Sumida picked up the pliers now lying on a table to Robert's left and threw them across the room. He screamed out, "I want that man." Just as suddenly, he then left the cell followed by Sergeant Sato and through the open cell doorway,

Robert heard the Colonel yelling at Sato about it being his fault that he could not question Edward Beverley anymore.

Moments later, two guards grabbed Robert's arms and dragged him through the cell door, and down the corridors before literally flinging him into a community cell where Robert saw some of the other internees sitting against the walls, some in a bloody state. There was no sign of De Lacey even though he had gone with that group for interrogation.

Chapter 36

Each day, the original group diminished in size with the fate of the others mostly unknown. Finally, after weeks of interrogation those that remained were moved into a ground floor cell at the far end of the yard. For a further ten days, they remained there, with each opening of the cell door bringing the dread of more interrogation or worse still immediate execution, and then one day, the few that remained were herded onto a lorry.

On the few occasions that Robert had been out in the exercise yard, he did not see any of the missing internees nor discover where they had gone. There had been executions but his cell had not been present at them and the names of the deceased were not always known. Through the small cell window, Robert had been unable to see any of the faces of the condemned. He had managed whispered conversations with other long-term prisoners but they knew nothing other than the Nips were giving no quarter to anyone who may have been involved in the insurrection.

Early in the morning, before they were herded onto the lorry one of the long-term prisoners brought in a bucket of water and two loaves of bread and Neal Forsyth and Robert doled out the rations as best they could. One of the Indian guards came in at some point and made two internees take the foul-smelling slop buckets out.

The previous night in the cell had been pitiful with some of the internees now in a very bad state. Robert looking around that morning decided that somehow, he was in better shape than many of the others.

Even after they were loaded onto the lorry, they had no idea where they were going. There was little or no talking as exhaustion had taken its toll and fear occupied their minds. Robert remembered that the ground floor cells were normally reserved for prisoners who were to be executed and being herded onto the lorry could only mean the worst. He kept his thoughts to himself. For some reason, none of those sharing his cell had been taken out and executed over the past ten days but he knew from his previous time in Outram Road Gaol that the *Kempetai* often took groups of prisoners out to somewhere on the Island and disposed of them.

The lorry stopped at the Justices Building and they were bundled out and hurried through the back entrance and up the prisoners' staircase into a court where a senior Japanese officer was waiting. Robert, with his now good understanding of Japanese quickly realised that it was not a trial merely a sentencing process. Two internees at a time were called forward, some details were read out and then they were sentenced to an indeterminate period of hard labour or imprisonment in one of the prisons on the Island that the Japs now used. Five times, the process was followed and sentences given out. Robert found the whole process incongruous. What was the point when in gaol the guards, with the *Kempetai* in overall charge, having the absolute right to decide your fate? Finally, it was his turn.

It had been nearly a month since he had been sent to Outram Road and after many interrogations in the first two weeks, he had been left largely alone. Apart from those who had been executed for being in possession of a radio, other internees he knew had died under torture and some others were literally hanging on by a thread. He was under no illusions that he lived on a knife-edge. His experience in Outram Road had held him in good stead; he knew the system and how to survive and he had managed to keep a low profile. Colonel Sumida, it seemed, had lost interest in him with the death of Edward Beverley.

So when his name was called out, he moved to the front of the internees to face the Japanese Officer who was conducting the proceedings, expecting the worst; the majority of his fellow internees had been standing there not understanding what had been decided about them. He at least could understand what was happening. A junior officer standing to his left said nothing for a few seconds and then to the judge, he said something about, "*Mr Asahi had sent a message that this man is a good internee, works hard and helps to make the camp work well.*" Robert said nothing. He barely knew the Camp Commandant other than when he made visits around the camp and presumed this was a report given to him by the camp committee. Again, he heard how he had been unhelpful to the *Kempetai* and then the senior officer announced that he was to be sent for hard labour for repeatedly obstructing the *Kempetai* in their work. The period of hard labour was not given.

Days afterwards, Robert thought about the decision and decided that the report from the camp committee had probably saved his life; it had made a difference. If the camp report had said that he was a difficult internee, then perhaps the sentence would have been worse.

After giving out the hard labour sentence, the senior officer rose from his chair and Robert and the other internees bowed and there was chaos as soldiers started beating them with their rifles butts as they made their way down to the cells. The internees were alike, in an awful state, clothes in rags, badly bitten by mosquitos, some with tropical boils, most showing the results of long hours of interrogation.

They were in the cells for perhaps thirty minutes before they were segregated, some to go for hard labour and others to be sent back to Outram Road or one of the other gaols on the Island. Robert and a couple of others who spoke Japanese, in the brief time they had, explained what had happened. There was a few 'but I've done nothing' and whispered explanations that the *Kempetai* couldn't afford to lose face.

Robert went with five other internees to a camp on the north of the Island on an old plantation at Pasir Ris where there were already a hundred or so other prisoners, of mixed races, only a few of them seemingly Europeans. They were put to work immediately cutting down jungle on the shoreline, facing the Johore shore about a mile away. That first night, barely able to walk in the heat, they followed the other prisoners back to a barbed wire compound where a couple of war damaged huts afforded shelter from the heavy rain that had been falling most of the day.

A meal of sticky rice with some green leaves was provided. There was little or no conversation and they learned quickly that there was insufficient space to lie down. There seemed to be a group of men in one corner who had space enough to lie down and the internees learned the hard way that these men held sway over the rest. The first night saw one internee die of exhaustion and there were continual noises as men moaned and moaned with pain or was it fear.

The guards didn't bother with them until the next morning when they yelled at them to get up and start another day. Each day was the same. They stood in line and collected a ball of rice and a mug of dirty rainwater. While they stood there, Robert, on the first day, watched one of the internees being dragged out of his hut unconscious.

The nightmare went on for weeks. The same routine every day. The same fear of guards and of falling foul of the prison gang who some nights searched the other prisoners in case they had hidden food. Two Europeans, not young men, had gone down with malaria and had been taken off somewhere. More internees had now joined them. Only Robert and a young scouser called Barry Graham, remained of the original group of five internees. As new prisoners arrived every day, Robert and Barry became long termers as even some of the prison gang succumbed to the brutality, heat and disease.

One day, after Robert had been in the Pasir Ris camp for four weeks, two of the prisoners, Chinese, seeing the sea only yards away suddenly ran forward and threw themselves into the water and tried to swim for Pulau Ubin, an island perhaps half a mile away, only to be gunned down by the guards. The prisoners scarcely stopped work to witness the incident.

Robert and Barry formed a barrier, working together, as the weeks rolled by, not letting anyone come in between them. Barry was a hard lad who had gone to sea when he was fifteen and had survived the trials and tribulations of sailing with hard men and with Robert's instincts for survival, they formed a strong team working their twelve hours every day and scrounging what they could to survive.

It was Barry, in fact, who finally succumbed. He came down with fever and eventually couldn't work and lay in the sick tent for two days with Robert taking him water and rice at the beginning of the day and at the end when he returned from work. On the third day when Robert returned from dragging trees out of the mud, coughing phlegm regularly, he found Barry gone. He had gone to the sick tent and found there a dozen men lying in filth with injuries and with fever, some clearly in the last stages of life, but no Barry. The old Chinaman, who was the orderly, said the authorities had come for him around noon and taken him away with two others but he didn't know where. When asked, he said 'yes, he thought Barry was still alive'. He never saw Barry again and try as he might in later years, he never found any trace.

At that point, Robert began to lose the will to live. Barry had been his rock. They had protected each other for weeks and they had learned to depend on each other, and now there was no one he could trust or talk to. As he worked, trying with other prisoners to dig ditches and move trees, he thought of the stories Barry had told him about Liverpool, of the strange places he had sailed to, of the girls he had known. It had got him through the days; he remembered that when they were allowed a brief stop for water they would talk of when they were free and what they wanted to do.

Robert lasted for some weeks after Barry had been taken away, working almost in a constant daze in the heat, eating what little food was doled out and becoming more and more isolated and in a dream. It was one day in this daze he heard shouting and looking up saw the other prisoners gesturing wildly at a nearby tree trunk. He didn't see it at first and then he saw the snake. It was green and black, perhaps two or three feet long, and rearing its head, only feet from him. He hit it with his shovel as it arched its head to strike and in doing so, he fell over hitting his head on a branch and knocking himself out.

He was dragged out of the undergrowth and left on the grass slope where other prisoners had been working. He had a cut on his leg where a thorn had ripped into the back of it. After a while, a guard came by and started yelling that he had to get up. He had lost one of his sandals in the mud and his leg had already come up like a balloon. He took a second thump to his shoulder from the rifle butt as he got up and promptly fell down with the guard now standing over him. The guard continued shouting at him and finally turned to two prisoners nearby and yelled at them and they ran over to help Robert to stand up.

Somehow, Robert dragged himself back to the camp at the end of the working day and got to the sick tent and lay down. He had tropical boils between his legs and his left leg was now dark and discoloured. His shorts were almost non-existent and his left shirtsleeve was torn away. The next day, he was unable to work with the pain and he was now suffering from a fever. It was sometime during the second day that he heard the men talking in the tent and felt himself being lifted roughly and almost dragged out. He did not know it but he went on a lorry journey for about half an hour and was placed in the sick bay in Changi gaol.

Chapter 37

Christmas 1943 and New Year 1944 passed without Robert knowing anything about it. Much of the time, he spent on the edge of death. Something kept him alive, an inner strength to beat the reaper. He did not miss much in the way of Christmas or New Year celebrations in Changi. True the gaol had had a special lunch although there was no extra food supplied by the Nips only food saved over from the rations issued each day so that on Christmas Day all internees could enjoy a few extra ounces of rice with a coconut biscuit and a little extra fruit jam. By all accounts, the woman and children got slightly more but only slightly.

Since October, the Nips still believing that one or more of the internees had been involved in the destruction of ships in the docks and in setting fire to godowns, had as a penalty cut the food rations of the internees and also cut many of the privileges they had been able to procure from other parts of the Island. No longer was there the luxury of a bathe in the sea and for a time the Nips even stopped the camp committee from purchasing extras such as tobacco and sweets for the camp shop.

For many, it was the low point in their incarceration despite the news that was constantly circulating of further victories for the Allies. What was long gone was the belief that within six months of the catastrophe in Singapore the internees would be sitting in Raffles again enjoying a g&t or *stengah.* The Nips kept adding to the problem of managing a mini city by producing more and more civilians whom they considered to be a risk to them if they remained at liberty, swelling the numbers of an already overcrowded gaol.

Of the fifty-seven men who had been taken away the previous October, following the explosions in Singapore City which the camp now knew to be not just communist work in setting fire to godowns but also the sinking of ships in Keppel Harbour by Allied commandos, only thirty-five ever returned to the camp. Many of them were in an awful state, some like Robert, and Rob Scott, having been given hard labour not for any known crime but to save face. Others like Neal Forsyth had been sent back to the camp after a period in Outram Gaol.

Over the months that followed until the internees moved, lock stock and barrel, to Sime Road, the thirty-five internees came back to the camp in ones and twos always leaving doubt as to how many might return. Twenty-two never returned, presumed executed for having a radio or for knowing of the existence of the radio or because the Nips believed that they had something to do with the insurrection in the City; some probably died during torture and others from exhaustion. What Robert learned later was that another radio existed but had not been found by the Nips and continued to disport news when they could get it to work, although he never entirely trusted the information as by the time he heard it, it had been enhanced to such a degree as to make it difficult to find out what was the actual situation.

Robert survived because he had the medical attention of

perhaps a hundred medics, all internees, many the leading experts in their field of medicine in South Asia. For weeks, he knew little. He was in a constant delirium and unbeknown to him, his friends had pooled the last of the money he had given them to buy drugs for him on the black market, through the contacts the Jews had.

It was well into March 1944, not long before the move to Sime Road, when Robert began to sit up and be a part of camp life again. The surgeons had even considered at one point removing his left leg below the knee but for some reason had stayed the execution and almost from that day, the drugs had started to work. He continued to cough and aggravate his chest but it was Michael Davison, the pharmacist and now leader of the Tanglin group, who managed to procure Chinese remedies when he was out on fatigues and these natural potions seemed to work. The doctors at the end of the war said that Robert was the one patient who should not have survived; if you asked Robert, all he would say was that he had no intention of dying as he had evidence he intended to give at any future war trials.

It was therefore in the fourth month of 1944, more than two years after the long march to Changi, that Robert took his first steps out of the sickbay and into the relative open air of Yard B where he walked for little periods each day. He had no idea whether he was now released from hard labour or whether at some point he had to return. All he did know was that although discipline in the camp remained very strict the contact with the Nips was now sporadic. As he got stronger, he helped more and more with the routines of the camp. He started by helping out in the kitchen, peeling fruit and vegetables, as he had done two years before, and on occasions, he sat with Neal Forsyth catching up on the news. It was in early May when Geoffrey Blackmore, a man now himself looking very thin and emaciated, came to see Robert. "Are you up for coming and doing a little work in the administration office again? Just a few hours, say a couple of times a week. You were always good at organizing the fatigues and we're shorthanded again. John Russell took over from you but he's gone down sick and shall be missing for a while and Hugh Bryson is taking over some of the camp administration but will be spending a good deal of his time dealing with the Nips about the tasks we need to complete. Paul Kennick has taken over the day-to-day running of the office and he needs more help with preparing the schedules. The Nips more or less leave it to us to keep a register of everyone with the Camp Commandant asking to see it every so often. Your Japanese will come in handy for those meetings and at *tenko.* We have also been told to expect another delivery of letters soon so your help there would be appreciated."

Robert was sitting at a wooden trestle table with two other internees, slowly chopping up sweet potato into cubes. "I think I'm ready for it, Geoffrey," was all he said smiling. Who knows the horrors of the hard-labour camp could be behind him?

"One other thing, the move to Sime Road is on and I have agreed to manage the task of organising it so your help with that would be much appreciated."

Robert looked quizzically at Geoffrey and then nodded. "I hope it isn't like Pasir Ris, all jungle and snakes. Hopefully, they give us the golf course and the old army camp and not the north end."

Geoffrey nodded. “We’re suggesting the camp as there are facilities already laid on but you know what the Nips are like. They treat all suggestions as suspicious. We shall just have to wait and see. Anyway, go see Paul tomorrow and I know he will welcome your help.”

As Geoffrey started to go, Robert asked, “Why are you stopping being Camp Administrator?”

“The docs are not happy with me. They think there’s something wrong with me so Bryson and Jarrett will take on my responsibilities and I will have more of a back seat once we’re up at Sime Road.”

Robert went back to working in the Fatigues Office and strange, as it may seem he found the routine a kind of security blanket enabling him to push away the horrors of Orchard Road, of Outram Road Gaol and of Pasir Ris. He commenced his language classes again, and Rob and Robert again used this as a cover for preparing a statement of what Robert had observed in Outram Road Gaol and of his own interrogations at the hands of Ishiguru, Sumida, Sato and Namura.

Chapter 38

The journey to Sime Road was a march many of the internees remembered for years afterwards. The Nips provided no transport other than the few lorries that were normally available, and as petrol was now desperately short, even on the black market, the number of trips that the lorries could make was severely limited. The result was that over three thousand men walked the six miles or so with all their personal belongings, in the heat, and with few of them with enough energy to survive a normal day let alone the march. Everything that could be carried was taken and, in the end, it took four days to complete the transfer of internees and all their kit to the new camp.

Even the men of Robert's age and those younger took some days to recover from the march yet knowing full well that they had a million and one jobs that needed doing to make the new camp serviceable. That no one died on the march was a credit to the camp committee who for weeks before had planned water stations, extra rations of bread and what to do with internees who collapsed on the way.

One thing many of the internees did notice on the march was that few of the local population took much interest in the stream of men as they walked on the roads towards Sime

Road, indeed even the guards took little notice such was their confidence in none of the internees trying to escape. What Robert observed walking with Michael Davison and the Revd. Cole was that the local Malays and Chinese looked as though they too were finding life very hard.

The location that had finally been designated as the new camp for the civilians was the old Sime Road barracks where the women would occupy the recreation buildings and some of the barracks with the men largely based in temporary huts that the Army had used before the surrender; most of the buildings were in a very dilapidated state. There was nothing like enough accommodation and for weeks before the transfer Geoffrey as the designated new camp coordinator worked with internees who had been architects in a former life and with experts in timber, spending hours planning the siting of new huts and the renovation of old army property.

Robert in company with fellow internees, when they finally arrived at their new home, found the camp overrun by rats and with many of the buildings without roofs; all their spare time over the first few months was spent in making the huts weather proof as possible and in erecting additional huts not just for the known internees but for the numbers of new civilians that seemed to still arrive from the Malay States.

What was now possible was for friends and comrades to be housed together and Robert spent much of his time organising the reallocation of accommodation to try and meet this demand. Whilst all this was happening, the normal routine of finding, growing and preparing food had to continue; fuel for the stoves for cooking had to be cut and dragged back to the camp, and the facilities in the separate camp for the women and children had to be prepared to the satisfaction of the Camp Commandant and the women's representative.

One thing that did become obvious from the start was that although there was plenty of timber nearby much of it was not suitable for use in the making of huts, and it would take too long to cut the wood to a size for use in erecting dozens of shelters. Robert was drawing up a revised list of internees for one of the huts when Geoffrey and the new camp committee chairman found him one late morning.

Robert was sitting in the shade behind one of the army concrete block buildings now used as the administrative offices, doing his best to wrestle with the problem of putting fifty men who wanted to be together into a hut made for much less numbers, along with the many other demands of nearly a hundred huts.

"We were told you were hiding," Geoffrey, looking very ill, said, as he squatted beside Robert in the shade.

Robert smiled back. "I needed quiet to work out the problems." He smiled again at the two men. "Talk about making life difficult. This lot…" Robert waved over towards a hut nearly one hundred yards away. "They want effectively the inner circle of the Singapore Club to be together. There's fifty-two of them and there's space for forty-six. They want us to build an extension; they can't seem to understand that we have other priorities. I've told them to draw lots for the forty-six berths. No, that's too simple. They have even said they will go to the camp committee and complain that I'm being difficult. Me! Hugh Bryson has told them that they can have an extension but only if they build it themselves. They're refusing to cooperate. And then, there's the Dutch. They want only Dutchmen in their hut and they're refusing to agree that there's some spare space; I've suggested we put in four planters who have always stuck together. But no…"

Robert continued outlining his problems with Geoffrey just grinning back at him, "I knew you would be good at it."

Robert stopped and looked suspiciously at both of them. "You two are after something?"

The Camp Committee chair, Major Collinge, had been listening and then smiled down from where he was leaning against the wall. "We understand that you know a Mr Hussain. At least he mentioned your name."

Robert jerked his head up at the mention of the name. "He has a timber yard just outside Bukit Timah village; he was one of our customers at the bank. Why, what's the problem."

Geoffrey said, "He's refusing to sell us timber unless we agree to support the Indian's claim for Independence and Sir Shenton repeatedly told us before he left for Japan that we can't condone such ideas without the approval of the British Government. Anyway, probably half the camp doesn't want them to have Independence."

"What the hell. We can say anything we like, surely. It can't be a commitment on Winnie?"

Geoffrey made a face at what Robert had just said. "Sorry but we really cannot make a commitment even if the individual members of the committee were so minded."

"So why do you need me? There must be other timber merchants on the Island?" Robert asked suspiciously, laying the work he had been doing on the ground.

Major Collinge answered tersely, "The Nips are using the timber business up at Tengah and the one over on Keppel Road, apparently, was more or less bombed out. They are also off limits so we need Hussain's timber or we will have men living outdoors for months."

Geoffrey came in. "We want you to chat to Hussain. He's come to see us at our request but he's refusing to do business with us. He says the only one he trusts, and who is honest, is you."

"He's just told us that Sir Shenton can take a hike and that Independence is what he wants for India. What we're supposed to do about it I really don't know," Major Collinge added, to what Geoffrey had just said.

"Of course, I told him that you are a complete reprobate but he says he doesn't trust any of us," Geoffrey remarked, trying to make light of the issue.

Robert got up, picking up his papers as he did so. "Well, what am I allowed to say?"

Geoffrey got up as well, saying, "Just don't say that we will support any independence move. Oh, and the Camp Commandant wants to see us this afternoon with the lists of names in the huts. After lunch, he said, before he has his sleep."

"Come on," Robert said, as he started to move out of the shade. "Oh, and if you're giving me this crap job, I want to see Mr Hussain on his own." As an afterthought, he added, "I presume we can pay for the wood?"

Geoffrey nodded as Robert folded up his papers and the three of them set off for the front of the administration block. "We've borrowed from Aldgate," was all Major Collinge said, as they walked down the road in the heat.

"Where do the Jews keep finding the money?" Robert said out loud to no one in particular.

When they arrived at the front of the building, Mr Hussain could be seen in a lorry that had so many dents in it that it was difficult to see a part of it that was not damaged. He was sitting in the cab and when he saw Robert approaching, he got out and was clearly pleased to see him.

"Mr Draper, Sahib, I am so pleased to sec you."

Robert took his hand and held it for a moment and then asked how he was and whether his family were well.

"My wife is fine. We manage in these difficult times. My sons are working for the Nipponese. They are building trenches. It is very hard work. We worry greatly for them." Hussain stopped what he was saying and looked more closely at Robert. "Sahib, you look unwell. You must look after yourself. I will get my wife to send you some fruit." Hussain said all this almost in one breath before looking around. "This camp is very big, Sahib. It is not well organised."

Robert nodded, "We've only just arrived, Mr Hussain. We need your help as we have many women and children to look after."

Mr Hussain raised his hands and showed his palms. "This is very bad place for women and children."

Robert didn't say any more about the organisation. Instead, he said, "My friend, let us go over there in the shade and sit under the mango tree. Let me borrow two stools and we can talk in private without all these prying ears." Robert looked pointedly at the administration block where Geoffrey, Major Collinge and half a dozen internees were watching them talk.

Robert walked across and took two of the stools on the veranda that were not in use, handing his papers, at the same time, over to Paul Kennick who had come out to see what the noise was about. "Come, Mr Hussain, let us go and talk about the good times."

Robert turned to those standing on the veranda of the block. “Perhaps one of you could bring Mr Hussain and myself some mugs of water.”

With that, Robert took Mr Hussain over to the shade of the mango tree, at that time defunct of any fruit, about thirty or so yards away, and placing the stools down, he offered one to Mr Hussain and sat on the other. They talked for perhaps half an hour, drinking the water that had been brought over to them, and the crowd in the administration block saw them on more than one occasion laugh at what might have been a joke and then Hussain wave his hands in the air as all Indians do when they get excited and Robert do the same to the evident amusement of Mr Hussain. Finally, they both stood up and shook hands and Mr Hussain then headed for his lorry, without a glance towards Geoffrey or Major Collinge who by this time were sitting on stools on the veranda watching the proceedings.

After much coaxing, the lorry finally started, and with clouds of smoke belching out of its exhaust, it set off down Sime Road. It didn’t stop at the entrance to the camp, and there was no security check by the two Indian guards. Not that there was much of a security perimeter for them to guard as in most parts of the camp there was only a single strand of barbed wire which internees knew to be the limit of their haven.

Robert picked up the two stools and meandered back to the administration block with Geoffrey and Major Collinge waiting on the veranda. Other internees had made themselves scarce but Robert knew that every word he said would be heard. Information was priceless in the camp. It was Paul who had just come out again and who stood behind Geoffrey and

Major Collinge who spoke first, to the evident exasperation of the Major. "Well, put us out of our misery. You seemed to have a lot to say to each other."

"He's got two young daughters and he is arranging their marriages and I was asking whether I could be invited to the weddings; I rather fancy a few good curries."

"Robert Draper if you want to remain a friend of mine you will cut out the jokes," Geoffrey said before Paul could say any more. "Do we have the timber, or not?"

"Oh, you can have the timber. I agreed a surcharge because he will have to send it up by buffalo carts, and he will have to hire a few carts; he has almost no fuel. He thinks he can deliver half a dozen lots of timber every day. If we can get permission and send our lorries down to the top end of Adam Road, he will drop some timber off there as well, starting tomorrow. I presume you know there are two internment camps on Adam Road and down at River Valley Road. Apparently, he supplied both with timber."

Robert walked down the veranda towards the Fatigues Office, before turning around, "I told him we had no influence with any independence talks and it was far more likely that him helping us now could be used one day to influence the British Government in believing in the cause for Independence. I reminded him that as far as I knew, he had never actually lived in India but that, if he wished for India to be independent, I would respect his wishes and give him my personal support."

The crowd at the far end of the veranda were still working out the significance of what Robert had told them when he added, "By the way, the Allies landed in France a few days ago." Robert disappeared into the Fatigues Office as there was a yell and a crowd of men came running after him.

The whole camp knew by lunch time and although the guards gathered something was up and came around suspiciously on extra patrols they could not get at the source of the great uplift in spirits. From Robert's perspective, it was, for once, a rumour that was accurate.

Mr Hussain was true to his word and delivered the timber cut to the lengths required, all on tick. In addition, he presented the women's camp with a nanny goat, with kids, and Geoffrey learned later that Robert had mentioned that he knew the women were desperate for milk for the children.

Dr Williams, the women's camp representative, sent a personal note of thanks to Robert along with a note from Kay, whom Robert had not heard from for nearly two years, saying she had put a plaque up in the pen the goats were kept in, saying the milk was donated by Mr Draper. As Robert with his Tanglin crowd, now all housed in the South Region of the camp, in a hut with a sign outside saying *Tanglin,* sat one evening gorging themselves on a slice of mango each, kindly donated by Mrs Hussain, Robert took the time to write a pencilled note to Kay to say that he would prefer it if the plaque could be amended to say 'kindly gifted by Mr & Mrs Hussain'.

It was in those months in 1944 when an inkling of hope began to emerge from the dark days of the already long incarceration. For Robert, the memory of his time being interrogated and in hard labour never went away entirely, particularly when he saw the *Kempetai* turn up at the camp but as their visits became less frequent and Sime Road became more of a backwater for the Nips, he began to relax.

Imprisonment on a diet less than half he had enjoyed when he had been free to choose could never be satisfactory but at least it provided some energy for struggling on.

That was not true of other internees however with many finding the endless tedium of working to try and grow food, prepare concoctions that could be edible, and just generally survive was tiring to the extreme. The numbers in Broadmoor were growing as more and more men grew depressed with the thought of imprisonment never ending.

The heat sapped the energy of everyone; the humidity always kept everything damp, and it rotted clothes quickly, to the extent that many men wore almost nothing worth mentioning. Many men no longer had shoes and what hats that were around were made of straw or banana leaves with many a man sporting a nifty outfit of loin cloth, wooden open toed sandals and a piece of rag around his neck. Most men now had tropical boils and suffered badly in the heat from rashes between their legs and between their toes. It was quite commonplace for some of the men to say that they had lost another tooth; some of the older men were practically toothless and suffered in trying to eat what food they did get. In the Tanglin hut, there were forty-two souls, each given about twenty square feet and if there were any arguments between them it was about this precious space. More than twenty of them had served in the LDC and they had almost become joined at the hip. They were not necessarily of the same age or for that matter of the same religion, or beliefs in politics but they became friends wanting to make sure that neighbours survived because the chances were if they survived then you did to.

Some of the men in Tanglin, as elsewhere, had

womenfolk, some had children, in the women's camp and the fear was always that they would get news of illness of a wife or child. The helplessness of the husband was always unbearable. One daily ceremony was therefore of huge importance and became a ceremony that all the men would always remember.

Each day, half a dozen or more women came out of their camp with the rubbish, two at a time carrying the dustbins, and as far as possible the Fatigues Office, with warning, made sure that fathers and sons were on duty to remove rubbish from the men's kitchens at the same time, on the days when their wives or mothers would be carrying bins out to the camp gate.

Robert often watched those scenes when a husband or son for a few seconds was able to smile at his wife or mother, although not allowed by the Nips to speak. All the internees at one time or another had watched the scene. As always, there would be a few seconds of silence before the parties turned back into their part of the camp. More than one hard-boiled old sod was seen to turn away on those occasions unable to watch.

Chapter 39

Robert had been working on the roster changes for the next day when the Indian guard brought the boy into the office. He was ten years old and he had celebrated his birthday only the day before. He could hear the boy's mother screaming and crying on the other side of the wire fence and when he looked out of the window, he could see her being helped away by two other women. The Indian guard pushed the little boy towards Robert and shouted that he was ten years old so he had to live in the men's camp. Paul came through from where he was working to see what was going on.

"What's your name, lad?" The boy had started to cry and at first didn't answer him. Robert got up and brought the little one around to sit on one of the stools beside the table he had been working at. "Here lad, sit on the stool. Take your time." Paul left Robert to it and the guard disappeared off someplace. The boy had a canvas sack with him and he was clutching it with all his might.

Robert asked again, quietly. "What's your name, please?"

"Steven."

"And your second name?"

"Tracey."

"Is your daddy in the camp?"

The little boy shook his head. "My daddy's in the army."

"Have you got an uncle or a friend in the men's camp?"

The little boy shook his head.

"Where did you live when you lived with your daddy?"

"In Serangoon camp."

Robert had nothing to give the little boy to wipe away his tears. The little boy had a clean but worn shirt. "Here, wipe your tears on your shirt. Your mum won't mind, this once."

Robert thought for a moment and then got up. "Come on, son. I know somebody who's really good with little boys and he knows all about trains." Robert took his hand and they wandered off down the corridor.

Robert stopped in the next office where two or three fellow internees were working on lists and asked quietly. "Do you know where Henry Preston is working this morning?"

The answer came back, "He's over on the new fields where we're tilling."

Robert nodded and turned to Steven, "Let's go and find Uncle Henry. You'll like him. He's got two big boys and both of them like trains."

With that, Robert took Steven out and through the camp to the fields and eventually, he saw Henry's pointed straw hat bobbing away as the men in that section toiled away at the heavy task of breaking the ground. Robert shouted to Henry who looked up and came across.

"We have a new member of the men's camp, Henry. This is Steven Tracey; he was ten yesterday. He has no family in the camp and I was wondering if you as a person who knows all about boys and trains could look after him. We have space in Tanglin so I can register him there, at least for the next few days."

Henry just nodded and wiped his hands on the back of his shorts. "Hello, son. As it's your first day, why don't we go and see if the kitchens can find you a rice biscuit? I'm sure they have something for new people." All this time, Steven said nothing, just kept looking around and clutching his bag. Robert walked back with them and left them at the kitchen doors where one of the cooks went off to find a biscuit.

When Robert came in from his language lessons that evening, he found that Henry had moved his position in the hut so that Steven could be beside him. Steven had fallen asleep and Henry was lying next to him talking quietly to Michael who had the adjoining space; he saw Robert and waved him over.

"Is he okay?" Robert asked, sitting down on the floor.

"A bit shell-shocked. He's eaten though. I think he's exhausted with what's happened."

Robert nodded. "I got a message across to his mum to say that he was staying with the Tanglin crowd and that you would look after him."

Henry nodded at that. "I just wish the lads were around. They would take him on. He didn't talk for most of the morning and then he asked me dozens of questions about trains." Henry was smiling as he was telling Robert. "Monty over there has even started making one out of an old piece of wood he found."

Michael had been sitting quietly and then spoke, his voice angry with Henry shushing him. "Bloody ridiculous rule. Even the Nips must see that lads of ten years are not men. This new General Saito should be told by the committee that it only causes disruptions. It's totally unnecessary."

Henry made a face at Robert in the gloom and then

Michael said, "I've got things to do," and he got up and disappeared off to the far end of the room.

Henry whispered, "Mary is unwell again and in the sick bay. Michael asked to see her but the Nips refused. Saito has told Collinge and the committee that there is too much slackness." Robert just nodded, knowing about the new Commandant wanting to have more discipline in the camp, and getting up he made for his space and putting his stuff away in his box he went out to the bucket for a mug of water. He felt the humidity hit him in the face as he went outside and realised that heavy rain was on the way.

'I hope to God the roof is mended. I don't want another night of drips,' he thought, as he drank from the mug and passed the mug to another internee who was waiting.

Michael was at the doorway as he came back. "Sorry to hear about Mary." Michael just nodded his head up and down looking fussed about something.

"I need to talk to you about the committee putting four more men in our hut."

"It's only temporary, Michael, until we get the huts finished in North area."

"It's not on Robert. I know you have a say on it. We are crowded enough."

"Let's talk it through in the morning, Michael. We've both had a long day and we may be up half the night if the wind gets up and takes the roof off like the last time."

Michael just grunted and marched off and Robert slid into his space, with Monty on one side already asleep and Alan, his bedfellow on the other side, reciting in whispered tones some speech he was learning for the camp play.

"Night, Alan," Robert just said, feeling the heat envelop him, as he squeezed into his space with the wind starting to whip up. At least it might blow the mosquitos away.

Chapter 40

Christmas 1944 was a sorry affair. True it was the first Robert had spent in the camp, but it was still a sorry affair. General Saito, the new Camp Commandant, could see no reason for frivolities and the internees celebrating their third Christmas incarcerated with no end in sight, found little to be happy about. The amazing thing considering that much of the male population were in their fifties, many much older, was that they were remarkably resilient and just kept going. There were a few deaths mostly through sheer exhaustion but in the sum of it they were remarkably small in numbers considering that Saito had again cut the daily ration of rice, placing ever greater pressure on the growing of food. More than thirty acres of market garden now extended out from the camp, some over what had been playing fields and some over the golf course.

The camp had procured some pigs from a Chinese family and there was some meat but the fish ration that had been plentiful at the beginning when they were in Changi was now only an occasional treat. General Saito became more strict as time went on refusing to allow the camp committee to negotiate deals with local fishermen and Chinese merchants and from what Robert could find out it was to do with the food supply for the Island now being seriously disrupted by the Allies. The Nips never admitted it but the occasional conversation with Schweizer, who as a Swiss resident was able to go around the Island, or Hussain who still supplied timber, allowed Robert to work out that the Nips themselves were now on reduced rations.

Monty had made young Steven a train for his Christmas and his mother had spirited across the wire a small gift of two coconut biscuits and a new shirt. Robert found him some card and with the help of the teacher of the class Steven attended two mornings a week he produced a Christmas Card and years afterwards Robert heard it was in a frame adorning the lounge wall of the house Steven moved into when he got married.

Mrs Hussain produced a dozen mangoes for Robert with a note in cryptic English in case the Indian guards found it. Robert spent some time reading it and finally decided that it was saying that the Allies were on the border of Germany. He reported his interpretation to Geoffrey who presumably passed it on to the camp committee and certainly, days later, he heard stories being passed around when he was queuing for his food of the Allies being near to Berlin and Hitler close to surrender. The rumour mill as usual added to the real story as each person passed it on.

What was exciting, just after Christmas, was the sound of a large plane in the sky. No planes had been heard over the Island for some weeks, for that matter no ships of any size had been seen going through the Straits, by any of the fatigue parties, for quite some time. Those who saw the plane said it was very high up in the sky and seemed very large, much bigger than any bomber they knew of; the Nips had reacted to the plane only after it had disappeared going north by sending up some ack-ack flak from guns somewhere over beyond Bukit Timah. The discussion for the next few days was whether this was the start of a campaign against the Nips and there was suddenly the worry that the Nips might take retaliatory action against the civilians if the Allies did attack.

Chapter 41

There were times in early 1945 when the days seemed never ending; they dragged. Every day was an effort. Internees were getting news, albeit in drips, showing that the Allies were getting on top of the Nips, and that the Germans had been beaten in late April. Tempers became frayed, internees wanted to know why they had been forgotten. To make it worse, Allied planes had been over the Island on several occasions with Japanese ack-ack guns fruitlessly blasting away. On one occasion, the internees had counted dozens of bombers flying over and Japanese fighters going up to intercept them. Bombs had certainly fallen on the northwest side of the Island.

Seeing the planes raised people's spirits for perhaps half a day and then there was a definite outpouring of despair, internees could be heard accusing the Allies of deliberately taking their time, some said that the Allies were letting them starve unnecessarily as there were hardly any Japanese left on the Island although how they knew this was questionable as few internees now left the area around Sime Road, and certainly none went further than a mile or so from the camp to collect wood.

It seemed the last straw was when for the third time in less than a year, the Nips had cut the daily allowance of food and no matter how hard the internees worked, they found it difficult to grow enough food for what was now well over four thousand people. That meant that few people went out on fatigue parties beyond the shoreline and golf course, the majority were hard at it growing crops on the now nearly fifty acres of land being used.

It was in this air of despondency that Robert was sitting on the veranda one day in late May working on the interminable task of ensuring enough internees were doing certain tasks when he saw the slow column of people coming up Sime Road. The Nips had just announced that there was to be yet another cut in the rice allowance and Schweizer was finding less and less food to bring in. The result was that the camp committee had at the insistence of the Nips ploughed up even more of the golf course to grow crops although much of it would not be ready for months and the Fatigues Office was having to put more and more people out on the fields and allow less time off. Robert like most people in the camp offices did this in addition to spending some hours every day, working on the land, tilling, harvesting and generally contributing to the task of trying to feed more and more people.

As he was sitting working on the lists, he saw the group of people coming up Sime Road and at first didn't fully understand what it was he was seeing and then Paul, who was returning from a visit to the women's' camp, shouted across to him.

"My God, Robert, there's hundreds of them." Robert, at the shout stood up and putting down his papers, came down from the veranda into the sun, feeling the heat instantly hit him. He hobbled over to where Paul was standing and along with the two other internees who had been working in the administration block, they watched the guards lift the barrier which for once had been down, to let the lead Japanese guard in. The group of civilians following on behind him were walking very slowly. They looked in a terrible state. There was little or no sound from them.

“We need help, Robert.”

“I’m on it, Paul,” said Robert who set off towards the camp kitchen. Then he saw a class of boys sitting in the shade under the mango tree and hurried across.

“Sorry, Mr Danvers. I need some of the boys.” With that, Robert instructed half a dozen boys to run to various parts of the camp and tell camp committee members of the large number of civilians arriving at the barrier; Robert then hobbled around the back of the administration block to tell the Japanese guards in their guard room. He knew that during the mid-morning, they no longer bothered patrolling but sat having tea. Robert was aware that the Camp Commandant was not on site so that saved any problem of the arrivals having to do *tenko.* Finally, he set off for the sick bay huts a few hundred yards away to tell the medics on duty that they were needed.

By the time Robert got back to the administration block, Paul had found some internees who had been on rat catching duties who immediately got involved in helping the civilians, taking over stretchers and holding up men and women who were in a pitiable state. Even after Robert got back, new internees were still arriving.

The Japanese guards took no part just standing at the gate and not interfering, allowing more and more of the internees to go beyond the barrier and help some of the civilians to shuffle the last few yards into Sime Road camp. Robert grabbed one of the boys who had just come back from finding committee members, and told him that he must run to the kitchens to tell them they needed to bring buckets of water.

As he was doing this, Robert could see Paul helping one man who had been using a crutch, to sit down against the wall, with a young man with his back to Robert also helping. Robert looked at the man on the ground. He was filthy, thin, emaciated, he had some sort of loin cloth on that was barely held up. He was moaning, and had his eyes closed and Robert could see that the left leg was badly swollen. The young man was now on his knees tending to him but even with his back to him, Robert knew who he was and the man on the ground. "Alex?" It was a question that seemed to take ages to come out of his mouth. Robert knew the answer but he wanted an answer from Alex. "Alex?"

Alex turned slowly when he heard his name. He looked at Robert and said, " Is that you Bob?"

Robert nodded and came across and put his hand on Alex's shoulder, now looking at David Masters who had opened his eyes. He barely said, "Hello, young man. You've changed a bit."

"You obviously haven't looked at yourself, David." David shifted slightly and moaned as he tried to smile back as Robert looked around and saw young Steven arrive with mugs and the older boys bringing buckets of water. Robert shouted Steven over and asked him to fetch two mugs of water. "Just sit there a while. I need to give a hand with the other arrivals. The medics have just arrived, so I'll get one of them to have a look at that foot." David just sighed and closed his eyes and

Alex sat down beside him.

Robert went and helped more arrivals to flop down on a grass verge as more and more internees kept turning up. Hugh Bryson, who had just arrived from working in the fields, took in what was happening and called Paul and Robert and a couple of the Fatigue Office workers over.

"We need to get them into the shade as soon as we can. The guards will insist on the women being taken to the women's camp first so once the medics have had a chance to check them over can you…" Hugh looked at George Hoskins who was the North camp representative and Mervyn Cooper, another North camp internee, "You two, can you get helpers to take the women over? It looks as though there are around thirty of them. Dr Williams is over there…" Geoffrey pointed to where Dr Williams was working with other medics fifty yards or so away. "Go see her. She will tell you what she needs."

"Paul go 'round and check how many there are and give Norman the numbers as he will have to draw what food we have in the stores to feed the poor sods. Oh, and you better warn the kitchens of the numbers although they probably have an inkling already."

As he was saying this, there was a lot of shouting just outside the camp with the Japanese guards getting involved and Robert could see Major Collinge trying to pacify them. It looked as though a final few stragglers were just arriving and were being harried by the guards. He saw some men hurry over to two women who were helping each other to move some fifty yards or so down the road and guards using rifle butts to prod the men, by now carrying the women, to get back in the camp.

"Now you, Robert. Never mind the job I gave you this morning, give that to one of the team on duty later. I need you to move the men out of Beach Road hut temporarily. Let's say a week." Robert started to say something.

"I know they will scream and shout but tell them that the medics need an extra hut for a few days for these poor souls. We have two new huts near completion so tell them that they can go back to their old hut or have a new one. The hut representative is a pain I know but don't give him any choice. Go find him and tell him we need the hut now."

Robert nodded, "He's working in the kitchens today so I'll go find him. I'll tell Carl as well, as the medics will probably want water for the showers." As Robert left, he saw Michael Davison. "Michael, David Masters and Alex are over there against the wall. Can you make sure the Tanglin crowd know?" Michael, who had been heading towards the medics, carrying some of the few medical supplies the camp possessed, nodded and shouted he would tell Dr Robertson as well.

For the rest of the day, it was chaos with one hundred and twenty-four male internees being registered, and housed in the Beach Road hut, and in another hut which had to be commandeered when it became apparent just how many had turned up, and in a part finished new hut, and with the really sick using every bit of space in an already full sick bay.

All the new arrivals were in a pitiful state and some remained in the sick bay for the duration of the war. Robert worked all afternoon rehousing the Beach Road group with the hut representative asking why the camp committee couldn't use another hut and demanding an emergency meeting of the camp committee. Robert then had the problem of a second hut having to be rehoused. Robert was patient explaining for the umpteenth time that the huts were nearest the sick bay and if there were any communicable diseases, they could be contained and it was for their protection.

Major Collinge passing by heard the heated discussions with the Beach Road representative and the raised voices and having heard what the representative had to say reiterated that it was on the advice of the medics that Robert needed to move the internees, and the hut representative finally agreed but arguing that it was like living in a fascist state.

Major Collinge and Robert made faces at each other and Robert mouthed a thanks to the major, as he disappeared off to another crisis. The huts were cleared by early evening with George Hoskins finding space for most of the displaced internees in North region and a few being housed in South region; most of them accepted the inconvenience when they saw the state of the men being moved into Beach Road hut and its neighbour.

It was a couple of days later when Robert had a chance after lunch to sit down with Henry, Michael and Pat, in the shade behind the Tanglin hut. Perhaps twenty or so other Tanglin internees were also taking the chance for an hour's break before the afternoon chores started. Young Steven had been helping Henry in the fields that morning and had sat down beside them and Robert saw him nodding off.

Henry smiled down at him, "He's made a friend at last. The Lassiter lad over in the Hill Street Hut. So, I think he may be over the worst." By this time, Steven was snoring and Henry took his straw hat off and put it gently over Steven's face.

There had been another postal delivery, making it the third

in as many months, and Schweizer had told Paul and Robert when he had turned up with the letters the day before that there were still large amounts of mail being sifted by the censors. Robert watched as many of the Tanglin crowd sat reading the cards they had received, and for the fifth or sixth time, trying to decide which one came first as many of the cards were not dated, and then trying to interpret the often-hidden messages. Occasionally, there was a sudden smile and then a wistful look and something whispered to a friend sitting close by.

Pat who seemed to spend much of his time unwell these days had had another card from his sister and it had caused much amusement when in a crabby voice he decided he had never liked his sister much anyway. "She seems to think that we are still living in our homes and have no rationing. All she said was that they still only get two ounces of butter each. Bloody woman." Robert had had a card from Peter Connaught to say he was in London and they were living in Wimbledon. He hoped that he was well and he would see him soon. Henry had received a similar card.

Michael had been a bit happier the last few weeks as his two daughters had been working in the fields with their mother and although they were not allowed to talk to each other, Michael was at least able to see them in the distance. He had apologised to all and sundry a few days ago for being crabby and the hut had cheered.

It was Henry who had the most cryptic cards, three in all with the censor having scratched out what looked like a whole sentence on one of them. He handed one of the cards to Robert.

"It says that Brian and Martin are now serving in the forces and Mona is staying with relations in Shimla. It doesn't say how she got to India. I put her on a ship to Australia."

Robert read the card and smiled at Henry's comment. "Are you asking me to be some sort of mind reader, Henry? I have trouble enough with Hugh." He had been watching Hugh come around the corner and head for them.

Hugh nodded at the men sat around him and then addressed Robert. "There you are. Hiding as usual." He said a few words to Henry and Michael and then said, "I'm sorry to interrupt your snooze time but I thought I should ask you. Did you register the women into the camp?"

Robert knew what he meant by 'Register the women into the camp' and shook his head. "George and Mervyn organised stretchers and took them into the women's camp and Dr Williams took over at that point. Mary Wilson would have registered them. I think, from what Mervyn said, they have put them in a wing of the old gymnasium whilst the medics sort them out."

Hugh nodded. "Didn't think you had done anything with them." He got out a piece of paper with a very scratchy scrawled note on it, "I've been to see Geoffrey in the hospital. It seems that there's two lots of new internees. One lot from Subang over in Sumatra and some poor sods, all women, from Muntok on Banka Island. Anyway, Dr Williams says they are mostly civil service women so I read the list out to Geoffrey to see if he knew any of them. He instantly said I should come over and tell you that Joyce, Joyce Connor, is one of them."

Robert's stomach instantly tightened up. Everyone in the immediate vicinity had gone quiet listening to the conversation. "Where is she?" Robert asked quietly.

"In the women's hospital. Apparently, they are in a hell of a mess."

It was Henry who said, "Come on, lad, she'll pull through."

"Can I see her, Hugh?"

"That my dear chap will as you know be very difficult. Alistair Cole has managed it by giving religious services in the women's camp so maybe you will have to take up orders."

Michael Davison sitting nearby smiled. "I never thought of that."

"Maybe David and Alex know more. They didn't mention anything mind you when I talked to them through the window of the sick bay last night."

Robert started to get up from the ground but Hugh put his hand out. "No use running around like a headless chicken, Robert. Just have some patience and I will think of something."

It was Pat, who had been listening quietly, who moaned, "Why must you talk about food?"

Hugh left them at that point with Robert in deep thought. Henry, Pat and Michael sat talking quietly about the card Robert had received from Peter Connaught to say that he was safe in London and looking forward to seeing them soon. Henry in his cards had not received any mention of the Thorsbys and there was a momentary discussion on where they could be.

Finally, Robert went outside and sat quietly treating his tropical boils with some salt he had managed to buy; he did this until the tannoy announced that all internees must return to their huts.

Chapter 42

Two days later, Robert was sent into the women's camp. He had been in once before, some months ago, when a sick person needed special food and the camp committee had managed to find some on the Island through Schweizer. Robert had taken it over to the women's hospital, a large bamboo and attap palm hut, built on a mound, at the far end of the women's compound.

This time, he was being sent in with new medical supplies that truthfully, any of the authorised medics could have taken in but Hugh and Dr Morton, the senior medic, advised the Nips on duty that it was urgently needed and nominated Robert to deliver the goods.

"You may not see her, Robert. If the guards go with you, then it's an in and out job."

Robert just nodded and said, "I can only try. And thank you."

Minutes later, he approached the gate to the women's camp and the Korean guard looked him up and down. He had timed the visit for mid-morning when he knew the guards had their tea and left a cursory guard on duty. Robert bowed and explained that he had been told to bring the medical supplies he had in his hand to the women's hospital immediately and he would only be a few minutes. The Korean guard, without a word, opened the wire gate and nodded him through.

Robert walked down the drive to the end where the women's hospital was, knowing that some women sitting in their huts were watching him. Children playing at the side of a hut stopped and watched him. By the time he reached the hospital, he had been seen and a nurse had emerged. It was Kay. "I hope you have a good excuse as to why you are here."

Robert climbed the steps but could go no further as Kay blocked him. "I've brought some medical supplies Dr Morton said you needed."

Kay took them off him.

"Can I see Joyce Connor for just a moment?"

Kay looked at him and frowned. "I didn't know you knew her, Bob. I'm sorry but I can't let you in without Dr Williams' say so. I'll go and ask. Anyway, she's not conscious."

Robert stood on the veranda for perhaps a minute or so and then Dr Williams came out. "I'm sorry, Robert, the ward is in isolation. It's too risky. I can tell you that she is very ill. They suffered very badly at Muntok and poor Joyce is one of the worst affected. We haven't been able to speak to her yet. It was her friend, Sally, who carried her from where the Nips left them on the road at the end of the camp."

Robert nodded. "Thank you. She's a special friend, Dr Williams. I wouldn't like anything to happen to her."

Dr Williams could only nod and put her arms out towards him. "I'll do my very best. Now you had better be off before those bloody Koreans come after you. You don't want to be in the punishment box."

Kay had come out and as Robert turned away, she added, "She's plucky, Bob. She'll do it."

The walk back to the gate was purgatory for Robert and he went through past the guard without bowing and getting away with it. It was perhaps as well that the Allied bombers decided to bomb the Island at that point and the alarm went off and over four thousand internees and guards hid in the newly built slit trenches and under huts with the shrapnel from the ack-ack guns over at Changi and Bukit Timah actually landing in the camp.

It was a few nights later that the camp committee called a meeting with region representatives and senior camp members. The meeting followed the evening meal, if it could be called that having been reduced to a piece of rice cake with a spoonful of jam or honey on it. Red Cross parcels had been delivered a few weeks before and many of the internees were seen eking out a few sardines or fish paste over many days to augment the rations. Men had started to succumb to the harsh rationing and more than one man died each day giving up on ever being freed.

There was an air of expectancy in the camp about the outcome of the meeting. When Robert saw them all together, he marvelled at the numbers that were needed to keep the camp functioning. Lieutenant Taguchi who had been nominally in charge of the camp for the past week or so was not present but Sergeant Major Tanaka attended, no longer looking like a man who could place a man’s life at risk.

In his broken English, he said that the Nipponese could no longer supply any food for the internees although he would do his best to get some supplies for the women and children. He said that the camp must rely on what they grew, as it was now not possible to get supplies from outside of the Malay States. After he said what he had to say, he stood up and bowing to Major Collinge, he left with the parting comment that all internees must be back in their huts by nine o'clock. Robert, as did everybody else, had noted that Tanaka was remarkably frank in his admission that the Island was effectively cut off.

Major Collinge waited until Tanaka had left and was out of ear shot and then said that the news, although not good, was only what everybody had been expecting, certainly the camp committee. He went on to say that there was no news of what was happening outside of the Island as the Nips had now been able to block the radio waves.

"If the Island is attacked, then we are very vulnerable. I have asked Norman Jarrett to have extra water butts placed in strategic places, as this may be the only water internees will be able to get for days during any fighting. Food will, I am afraid, have to be on hold and I suggest you tell everyone to start hoarding although quite what I am not sure." At someone's suggestion, it was agreed that Norman, the camp's resources officer, should find a way of making a large flag to be placed on a roof in the women's camp and he said he would find volunteers to take responsibility for having it erected when there was bombing or if there was any fighting around the camp so that the Allies would know to avoid that part of the camp.

The meeting broke up with Robert going back with John Russell who was now central region representative, deep in debate about how they could get people into slit trenches or to places of safety if there was fighting or worse still if the Nips decided to go on a rampage and massacre the internees. Everyone knew that they lived in a time when the war could go on for months or be over in days. Now it was just the waiting.

In early August, more cards were released from the post office and it became more and more obvious that the Nips had allowed the mail to become completely muddled with more than one internee getting mail from sometime in 1943 having already had mail from late 1944. It caused much amusement as well as consternation at times and only added to the frustration of waiting for the war to end.

About then, Robert started to go down with fever and he spent days on his mat unable to contribute to getting food or to organising the fatigues, at times in a complete delirium and with the tremors. The hospital had no room for him so in the end Michael had him placed outside the Tanglin hut, under a makeshift awning, with two other Tanglin internees both also suffering from fever. For the better part of a week, he was there with Pat and Henry in particular taking it in turns to feed and water him.

It was into the second week sitting up and feeling very weak, on his own, as Henry and Pat were on fatigues, and with the two other sick internees now in the hospital, that Robert saw in the distance something happening at the entrance to the camp. The barrier was down as usual but he had just noticed that the guards seemed to be missing when he saw what looked like Paul walking to the barrier and letting in Schweizer's lorry. Something was then said between them because Paul, working his spindly legs as fast as he could, had turned and run back to the administration block. He saw two or three people then emerge and there was great excitement. He saw some of them set off to various parts of the camp and he began to guess what the news was. When Mathew came running past a few moments later, he stopped when he saw Robert on the steps of his hut.

"The war, Bob. It's over. The Nips have surrendered. Schweizer has just told us. Some of the guards they've done a bunk." Martin continued up the road towards the fields to tell all and sundry as Robert slowly got to his feet.

"At last it's over," was all he said, as other internees emerged from huts around him and there was great excitement. "Maybe they can now get help for Joyce."

Robert didn't attend the camp meeting that evening but afterwards John Russell saw him on his way back to his hut, and said that until the Allies turned up the camp committee had ordered that everything must continue as normal and there should be no baiting of any of the remaining guards who it seemed had shut themselves in their little compound. Robert said nothing about that and later in the *Tanglin* hut, he was the same as everybody arguing that the Allies needed to come urgently or more internees were going to die.

Robert went back to work a couple of days later, just working slowly. No one had any energy left and there had been more deaths in the camp. Alex had finally come out of hospital and space had been found for him in *Tanglin* although that was only because Pat was ill again and had to be moved to the hospital.

Alex and David had still not told Robert much about their experiences in Subang only that the camp had been beside a river, with around three hundred internees, mostly Dutch, and that from the very beginning some of the internees had started dying under the harsh regime of the Nips and the jungle conditions. David was struck down more and more with malaria, especially over the last twelve months before the

Nips closed the camp. He had been lucky however as typhoid had been the biggest scourge, which Robert knew Sime Road had largely avoided although it had broken out maybe six months ago and had claimed a dozen or so internees.

"The worst was really at the beginning, Bob. We had a Nip, Major Senuchi, who enjoyed making us stand in the sun all day. Wouldn't let us help anyone who collapsed or who needed water. We lost five on one day alone. Then he would watch as the guards beat us if our huts were not to their liking. May he rot in hell."

"He wasn't there at the end?"

"No, he upped and went one day and then a Nip civilian took over and then finally, when our numbers were down to around eighty, they said they were bringing us over here. Because Dad spoke some Japanese, he had to do most of the negotiating but he wasn't really well enough."

"Anyway, one day this old tug turned up and we just about managed to get everybody on board and it took two days to get us to Kings' Dock where they dumped us in one of the warehouses. You remember Laz. Well, he was there; with I suppose about eight other lads. They helped to get us food and water or we would have died. As it is, two did die on the way and poor Jimmy Haughton is not likely to make it."

"So, when did the women join you?"

"A Japanese destroyer dumped them at the docks the day we were to walk to Sime Road. We had been told we had to walk the twelve miles to here. I don't know more than that. The women were in a terrible state. The Nips had abused them pretty badly from what I'm told. One woman said that some of the girls at some point just walked out into the sea rather than live in their camp. It took us two days to get here and the

Nips were bloody difficult telling us we were too slow all the time. One of the women died the second night and they just left her body up near Changi Road."

"How did you end up there and yet the Preston's got away?"

Alex drank some of the water had Robert handed him and then continued. "We were bombed at the docks and got separated. Dad and I ended up on the *SS Vyner Brooke* and all I know is that the others had already boarded on another ship, we think the SS *Sing Wo*. When we were going through the Banka Strait, we could see other ships were on fire and people in the water. The captain wasn't willing to stop but I think the *Relau* behind us took on some. We could just about see that."

Alex guessed by Robert's look that he didn't know what the *Relau* was. "It was like a tanker, Robert. The *Relau's* Captain took a bit of a chance before the next bombing raid. Anyway, further down the strait we got bombed and ended up having to swim for it. We managed to swim ashore on Banka Island near the lighthouse and were picked up next day along with maybe a hundred other men. The Nips took us over to Sumatra where they made us march for two days down to Subang. Some women joined with us for a while and then they were separated, and I don't know what happened to them. I don't know what happened to the *Relau* but there was a lot more bombing and big explosions behind us."

Chapter 43

It was on the 30th of August 1945 that camp life finally ended. Up to then, although the Korean guards were conspicuous by their absence and the Indians guards had disappeared altogether, the camp continued to function as normal as there was nowhere anybody could go. The strip of perimeter barbed wire was almost a security line keeping out the unknown. A few brave souls said they were going to go down to the city but as far as Robert knew, nobody did go down. They just didn't have the strength.

It was on that day that Allied troops arrived at the camp. Robert had been up to the hospital to see David who was still mostly in a fever and not always aware of his presence and he was on his way back from the short visit. From his brief discussion with a seemingly very old Dr Robertson he was told that men would die in the next twenty-four hours unless food and medical supplies could be procured. Robert could only nod and say, as everybody kept saying '*help is on its way, it must be*'.

He had stopped at hut 129B, as it was affectionately called, to tell them that they had permission from the camp committee to have a drink of the spirits they had somehow got on the black market but normal discipline applied. He then wandered slowly down the back lanes of the camp to reach the road near the gate for the women's camp. Four men were pulling a small cart with a makeshift coffin on it through the gates of that camp which were wide open and unguarded. The Revd. Cole was leading the cortege and nodded briefly to Robert as they made their way past him to the small hut near the administration block that now served as a mortuary. To Robert's knowledge, there were four more coffins in there already.

Women were following behind the coffin and Kay, one of them, came alongside Robert and took his arm. It felt so strange to feel a woman touch him again. "She's still not good, Bob," she whispered.

"We need to get them all out of here," he whispered back. They walked to the mortuary and stood there for a few minutes talking whilst two large Norwegian sailors acting as morticians took the coffin and placed it beside the other coffins. Robert suggested that Kay come over and have a drink at the main office near the barrier. Some of the other women were doing the same; something they could not have done only a few days before.

It was as they walked the few yards to the main offices that a car arrived with four British soldiers. The barrier was already up and they drove straight in. There was a momentary silence as the parties looked at each other and then the internees, men and women, ran the few yards to the jeep screaming and shouting. It was mayhem and it was the senior officer who, after a few moments, stood on the running board of the car and shouted for silence. He looked down on an array of smiling, filthy, thin faces. "Ladies and gentlemen. I need some calm. I need to speak to the camp authorities and get things organised and get you help."

Paul who was now standing by Robert said out aloud, "It will take ages. They're all over the place."

"Leave it to me, Paul. I've wanted to do this for nearly four years." With that, Robert ran, well, more limped around to the back of the administration block and pressed the alarm for an air raid and then over the tannoy, he said, "British soldiers have arrived at the gates."

No one was capable of work from then on in. Literally thousands converged on the entrance with the four Allied soldiers swamped by the numbers and trying to answer the million and one questions being asked. Robert eventually went and sat on his stool on the veranda of the administration block; he hadn't the strength to rush around. He had not a clue what had happened to Kay.

It was an hour later that Paul turned up, looking for him. By this time, things had calmed down and people had gone back to their huts or gone off with friends to sit and talk. The camp committee had disappeared off with three of the soldiers for a meeting.

"They want you and your registers in Saito's old office now. The medics are there with their lists already." Robert picked up his precious lists which he always seemed to be working on, and with Paul, he went over to Saito's office which even with the windows open was very hot with so many bodies in it.

"Give us the breakdown of numbers of internees, please, Bob," Major Collinge asked him as soon as he was in the room. Robert looked around and then read from the register: 3747 men as of last night, 682 women and 79 children, according to Mary Wilson. Robert looked across at Mary Wilson standing beside Dr Williams and saw her nod. "Of the 3747 male internees, 2764 are on normal duties, 667 are on light duties and the rest, 316 that is, are in the hospital or Broadmoor. Mary will be able to give you the latest breakdown of the women in hospital, it was 82 as of yesterday," Robert looked across at Dr Morton, as he said the figures.

"Take two off, Robert, Chalmers and McCaffrey, both died in the night," was all Dr Morton said.

Robert nodded as one of the officers said, "Good God, I know who you are. You're Robert Draper." Robert turned to look into the smiling face of an old bank colleague, Bodger, who he had last seen at Christmas 1940.

"Well, you turned out okay, Bodger."

The senior officer grinned at the name. "Well, that name suits you, Eric."

The meeting went on for perhaps another half an hour with each section saying what help they desperately needed and the medics outlining the need for urgent cases to be got to the first hospital ship available. Finally, the meeting broke up and Bodger came over to Robert and they shook hands. He looked at the scar on Robert's face and then the blue scar on his upper arm. "You've been in the wars, old boy."

Robert grinned like a Cheshire cat; he just couldn't help it. He had survived and then he came to his senses. "We have very sick people in the camp, Bodger. We need help urgently."

"You were at the meeting. It's all in hand, old boy. Colonel Neal is going back to Changi now and they will have a report on the radio in an hour or so. You watch, sometime tomorrow, there will be planes dropping essential stuff until we can get the hospital ships into the docks. They've already started dropping stuff over Changi." Robert just wanted to hug him.

Bodger went over with him to the veranda of the administration block and they sat on stools. Paul and another of the office helpers joined them, and slowly others did as well whilst Bodger told them about what had been happening in the world and especially on Singapore Island.

"Things are still a bit fraught here, as you can imagine. There are more than five thousand Japs over at Tanglin Barracks who are quite capable of having a fight and there are also quite a few others knocking around the Island."

"Don't let any of the *Kempetai* get off the Island, Bodger. Some of us have a score to settle."

Bodger looked hard at Robert. "Our first task is to disarm them and at the moment there are only twenty or so of us, so we're a bit outnumbered, you might say. As Colonel Neal said at the meeting, try and make sure that everyone keeps a low profile for the next few days, at least until we have got them to throw down their guns. Hopefully, the 5th Indian Division should start landing tomorrow and I think we have some more ships with troops coming down the Sumatra Strait. We had a bit of a problem with mines but it should be sorted out pretty quick."

Someone asked about how the Japs had surrendered and Bodger spent time explaining the events of the past three weeks since the Americans had dropped nuclear bombs on Japan.

As he was telling them about the events of the past few weeks, a lorry turned up with some supplies that Colonel Neal had found at the aerodrome and Bodger also got up to go.

"I need to get back. My Colonel is coming in shortly with a company of my lot to protect the perimeter of the aerodrome." He shook Robert's hand again. "Hopefully, we will get more time tomorrow to catch up on the news." As he was speaking to Robert, Major Collinge and Norman Jarrett arrived. "Right, gentlemen. I need to take you over to Changi for more meetings."

Norman Jarrett had, during the afternoon broken into the camp storehouse, which the Nips always kept under lock and key, and found lots of Red Cross half opened boxes which some of his assistants spent hours distributing to the hundred and forty plus huts and to the women's camp.

True to Bodger's word, the next day, late in the afternoon, a dozen planes came over and dropped case after case of food and medicines on a spot on the golf course where Norman Jarrett had arranged for giant crosses to be placed. About that time, Robert was at the barrier with Paul watching the Japanese and Korean guards march off without weapons with a single British paratrooper marching in front of them with a tommy gun.

That same night, there was little noise, no music or shouting, just the sound of thousands of internees munching their way through cans of bully beef, sardines, a type of ring doughnut and smoking copious amounts of cigarettes. There was one wag in the *Tanglin* hut who said that he had opened a crate expecting at least some brandy to go with the cigarettes, but for most, it was paradise. They would leave it until tomorrow to wonder what lay in store for them.

In the night, two more men died and did not see out the first day of freedom.

Chapter 44

The next few days went by as though they were one day. From nowhere, lorries started arriving with British soldiers and Army medics. The camp medics had agreed who was priority for removal from the camp and they were moved off down to the city for transfer to the hospital ships that had finally arrived. More food arrived, as did Lady Mountbatten, no less, with an entourage of nurses and officers to look around before they flew off later in the day to Sumatra and camps over there. The women and children were next moved out with great ceremony with husbands, sons and brothers going with them, leaving only the relatively fit to stay one more night. Steven, who had already been reunited with his mother purposely came to see Robert and Henry, with his mother, to thank them for looking after him.

Robert had been to see Joyce twice during the final day before she, with others, went off to a hospital ship. Throughout, she remained very weak and semi-comatose and Robert was not sure she even realised who he was. The medics had started her on a course of medicine and he heard them on one occasion speaking amongst themselves with great concern about her. He watched them take her off in the lorry to the hospital ship not sure whether he would ever see her again. He had no address for her only the knowledge that her father was a lecturer at the Victoria University in Manchester. A moaning, groaning David was transported off to a hospital ship saying he was getting better with Alex and Robert convinced that he wasn't and the doctors, in any case, not paying any attention to David's pleas. Geoffrey Blackmore now very sick was one of the first to be sent down to the hospital ship and Robert later learned that he had passed away. A friend and mentor whom Robert would think of in later years as someone who could have risen to the highest position in the service of the Island. Pat who had somehow survived the war was carted off and spent nearly two years in a hospital in Durban, South Africa before he came back to his beloved home in Tanglin.

Robert at the request of the camp committee agreed to stay to the end of the decamping to list who went where, as a record may be needed at some point. Alex went off with Henry to stay with him as Robert was not sure exactly when he would be home.

Finally, it was on the 5th September that Robert, along with Paul Kennick, and Hugh Bryson, walked around the camp for the last time, meeting Norman Jarrett and two of his colleagues doing the same. Little was said, more observations really. First one would say, "Do you remember?" And after they had remembered, another would say, "Was it here that…?" and there would be a debate about when and whether an incident had happened on a particular spot.

An army lorry was waiting to collect them at the barrier, along with three or four others who found it difficult to leave the camp. They were taken to the Municipal Building where they watched Major Collinge and Lady Lucy Thomas raise the Union Jack and a platoon of paratroopers stand to attention as the flag ceremony was performed and a bugler played. Many hundreds of people were there and Robert recognised men and women who had been reunited after nearly four years of separation.

Afterwards, Robert set up his files in one of the main offices in the Municipal Building and agreed a work schedule with Paul, for the recording of all the civilians who were being shipped over from Borneo, Sumatra and from the Malay States. Half a dozen volunteers including two women had agreed to assist and Paul went off to make sure that the powers that be knew where to bring internees, over the next few weeks, or where to report information on internees.

Robert came out of the Municipal Building later, standing on the steps with a glorious sunset and a few fruit bats heading off towards the north. He stood for a moment his mind going through the events of the momentous few days he had just lived through. He watched the bats and wondered where they had been roosting but immediately forgot about them as he looked across the Padang towards the sea. It was a wonderful sight. Slowly, almost reluctantly, he came back to the present. He looked down and saw a rickshaw driver at the bottom of the steps also looking out onto the Padang. “Are you good to take me up to Tanglin Road?” he shouted down. The driver nodded. “Could you take me through Fullerton Square?” The driver again just nodded.

The driveway to Mrs Lin Yuen’s house was completely overgrown. Shells had landed fairly close to the entrance by the looks of it but the house had been spared. It was quite dark by now and Robert asked the driver to stay for a moment whilst he went and got some money. The front door was locked. It looked as though it had been forced at some point and then repaired. Robert went around the back of the house. There was a light, a storm lamp or a fire possibly, behind the little hut at the bottom of the garden. Robert didn't shout but just hobbled towards the light, hearing the rustle of night animals in the undergrowth. Coming around the side of the hut, he saw Chunggy squatting beside a small fire turning the spit on some morsel of meat.

"Chunggy," was all he said in a very quiet voice.

Chunggy spun around as though he had been shot and let out a cry, more like the scream of pain an animal might make. "Mr Drapa, you come home." He had started to cry, as he scrambled across the space on his knees and was now holding onto Robert's legs. "I pray you come home one day. I pray every day. You have come." Robert couldn't say anything. He just stood and looked down as he felt the torment come gushing out of the old man.

It was some time before Robert said, "I have to pay the rickshaw driver. Do you still have some of that money I gave you?" Chunggy crawled over to his hut and rummaged under it in the gloom and pulled out a small bag. He handed it up to Robert who accepted it and went off and paid the driver, giving him a good tip. By the time he had returned, Chunggy had gone to the back veranda and opened the door to the house.

The house smelt musty and needing fresh air. He touched the light switch and, wonders of wonders, the light came on.

"I have no ice, Mr Drapa but there is whisky hidden in the garden."

"That sounds just wonderful. Do you think the water is working?"

Chunggy shook his head. “Maybe tomorrow, Mr Drapa.”

Robert nodded and said, “Maybe tomorrow. Now where’s that whisky.”